RDED

SPEAK EASY
SPEAK LOVE

McKELLE GEORGE

SPEAK EASY
SPEAK LOVE

GREENWILLOW BOOKS
An Imprint of HarperCollins*Publishers*

Speak Easy, Speak Love
Copyright © 2017 by McKelle George

The text of this book is set in Garamond.
Book design by Sylvie Le Floc'h

Library of Congress Cataloging-in-Publication Data is available.

ISBN 978-0-06-256092-6 (trade ed.)

17 18 19 20 21 PC/LSCH 10 9 8 7 6 5 4 3 2 1

First Edition

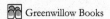 Greenwillow Books

To my sister Lauren, first reader and best friend

SPEAK EASY
SPEAK LOVE

CHAPTER 1
FALLEN INTO A PIT OF INK

Benedick Scott was on his way to freedom or profound failure or, if the usual order of things held up, both. Two chests, strapped closed and marked for delivery to an apartment in Manhattan, sat at the end of his bed. On his person he needed only his typewriter, slung over his shoulder in a battered case. He'd stuffed the case with socks to cushion any dinging, along with his shaving kit, a worn copy of *Middlemarch*, and thirty-four pages of typed future.

In the other bed his roommate snored like a cavalry crossing a bridge. Last year Benedick had heard his ungodly slumber three doors down, which was why he'd asked for him personally as a roommate this year and had been hailed as a martyr by the other boys. For a final time Benedick lifted his mattress and procured the old sheet rope. He tied it snugly to the bedpost and let it drop out his open window.

Luckily Chapman Hall was at the back of school property, and his room on the third floor faced the poorly tended outer wall, far from the reach of professorial eyes. Under the shadow of a sycamore tree, the orange glow of a cigarette flickered in and out of darkness, catching the edge of a jaw, then a gloved fingertip as someone tucked it, still smoking, behind his ear. Benedick gripped the windowsill.

Last chance, a faraway voice said; a voice that sounded an awful lot like his father. *Last chance to stick with the gilded lot life has seen fit to hand you.*

Benedick checked his pocket watch. Half past three. *Not for all the bourbon in all the bathtubs in all of Brooklyn.* He slipped out of his window with the ease of a ritual many times repeated and descended hand over hand, toes digging into the grooves of worn brick. He passed the second-floor window and nearly fell the rest of the way down when he heard a voice: "Why am I not surprised?"

Claude Blaine leaned out his window, arms crossed over the sill. His eyes gleamed in the darkness.

"Go back to bed, Blaine," Benedick muttered, adjusting the shoulder strap of his typewriter case.

"I figured when you weren't celebrating with the rest of us, you'd be passing through later." Claude inhaled a quick breath, gazing past Benedick to the sycamore tree. "Is that"—he lowered his voice, meeting Benedick's eyes again with comic gravity—"a bootlegger?"

Benedick sighed. Claude Blaine was one of Stony Creek Academy's finest, the sort of student who glowed. Admired by the boys and all the girls crazy over him. His family lived in London, and his ancestors were half royal or something, the type that had only ever been rich, whose wealth sank back so many generations their bones were practically diamonds. The type Benedick found utterly uninteresting and possibly contagious.

He continued down the makeshift rope without answering. Claude wasn't a snitch at least; in the many times he'd caught Benedick passing by his window, he'd never uttered a word to get him in trouble.

The rope grew taut with extra weight, and Benedick's head snapped up. Claude, already dressed, was climbing down after him. "What," Benedick whispered, "do you think you're doing?"

The grin Claude shot down at him sparkled.

The sheet started to tear. Benedick swore and hurried down, clearing the last window, but not fast enough. With a doomed ripping sound, the fabric rent apart. He swung his typewriter up to his chest to hug protectively as he fell and slipped on the dewy grass. His back hit the ground with a lung-flattening thud.

Claude landed on his feet with barely a stumble, the bastard, the sheet rope dropping around his shoulders like a fashionable scarf. With a breathless laugh he whispered, "Lucky we weren't at the top, eh?"

Benedick seethed in silence. And he was pretty sure he'd heard a smothered laugh from the direction of the tree. When he'd got his breath, he pushed to his feet, ignoring Claude's offered hand.

Claude leaned in. "So, we're going to a speakeasy, is that—"

Benedick clamped a hand over Claude's mouth. His eyes went meaningfully to the window at the far corner, and he mouthed *Winston*. The head boy of Chapman Hall, a bluenose as dry as the noonday desert, had been placed there precisely because it was the easiest dorm to slip out of. Benedick released Claude and pointed to the sycamore tree. Claude nodded.

They arrived under rustling leaves, and Prince detached from the darkness. A weight rolled off Benedick at the sight of him. His face was shadowed, but Benedick recognized his expression nonetheless: *What fresh nonsense is this?*

"Hello," Prince said, taking the cigarette from behind his ear with the polite poise of a king. "Who are you?"

Claude absorbed Prince with wonder. "Claude Blaine. Classmate of Ben's." He held out a hand.

Prince glanced briefly at Benedick, with only a trace of amusement at Claude's posh accent. Benedick cleared his throat. They had to lose the fancy-pants, and in the dark Prince cut a dangerous silhouette. Depending on what Prince had been doing before he picked Benedick up, he might even have a knife or firearm hidden under his jacket.

But Prince winked at Benedick and shook Claude's hand. "You can call me Prince."

Benedick glared.

"Prince?" Claude asked. "What an odd name."

"Nickname." Prince corrected him, with a wry smile. "Pedro Morello, more formally."

"I confess I've wondered where Scott sneaks off to every other week." Sometimes Stony Creek's more daring students took the train from Brooklyn to underground gin mills in Manhattan: for cocktails, rebellion, and girls with white arms and an astonishing capacity for cigarettes.

Benedick, who had more than once climbed back into his room smelling of gunpowder and moonshine, with some bruise or other purpling his skin and a sneer for propriety on his face, apparently suggested a different sort of adventure. Claude would be disappointed.

Claude continued. "No one else would dare the night before the regents exam—"

"I'm not coming back," said Benedick.

Claude looked at him suspiciously.

"They'll send the rest of my things to my father, I suppose, but I don't care about any of it."

"What about your exam? And graduation? You'll miss it, and they won't let you make it up, not with your record—"

"That's the idea." Benedick's voice was like winter.

He'd judged the necessity of this course of action weeks ago, during breakfast with his father. No sooner had Benedick buttered his toast when his father said, unprompted, "You're not really going to waste more time trying to write those silly novels, are you?"

"Yes," Benedick replied, "I really am."

To which his father made a few points clear: First, that was not a man's work; second, Benedick had two options his father would continue to support and fund, university or a job his father approved of (in the same stock company where he worked); and finally: "You're not a sap, son—I'll give you that—but you're vain as a dollar. Sure, I like it when people like me, but your emotions go on the inside, not in some flimflam story, begging for approval. What about the papers? The *Post*, that's different." At least journalism had a ladder to climb, which was more than anyone could say for some ink-stained penny novelist. Oh, and might he also find a nice deb girl in the meantime? Their money, though by no means insubstantial, lacked pedigree and history—and was further stained by his mother's sudden exodus to Hollywood.

"Don't look so scandalized, Blaine," Benedick said. "In fact I don't mind if you tell them you saw me running off—"

A light swung toward the trees. Prince grabbed Benedick and Claude by their jackets and yanked them behind the trunk of the sycamore.

"Who's out there?" a voice called.

"Winston," Benedick muttered under his breath; at the same time Claude whispered, "Now we're in it."

Benedick's fingers dug into grooves of sticky spring sap. The corner of his typewriter case pressed into his hip where Claude leaned against him. A second beam of light flickered through the leaves.

Prince adjusted his newsboy cap snugly on his head. His eyes danced with a giddy thrill Benedick hadn't seen in months. "Better run now," he whispered, "before he's close enough to catch us." Then off he went, silent as a deer.

Benedick patted Claude's shoulder. "Good luck," he said, and ran.

He was unsurprised, but still annoyed, to hear Claude's steps pounding after him. "Stuff your good luck," Claude hissed.

Up ahead Prince reached the top of the back wall and disappeared from view. Benedick scrambled up the old ladder. "Stop! Stop at once or I'll have you expelled!" Winston's shouts chased over the grounds, coming closer. Benedick swung over the pocked stone wall, held on a beat, and dropped the nine feet. Claude vaulted over a moment later like an Olympic athlete and landed easily with a few loping steps.

The Tin Lizzie waited on the side of a weedy dirt road. Prince hunched in front of the engine cranking. He glanced up at Benedick. "Get the ignition, would you?"

Benedick hurried to the driver's seat. He reached in and pulled down the spark retard until the pistons growled into a deep rumble.

"Hurry up, Blaine," Prince drawled, as if it were nothing, and Claude, grinning like a fool, clambered into the backseat.

Benedick slid over to the passenger's side. Prince got in and put the car into gear. They lurched forward, and the engine popped like a gunshot. Prince kept the headlights off, and Benedick loosed a breath.

"Should I take you around to the front?" Prince asked, glancing back at Claude. "Not too late not to get expelled."

"Oh, they won't," Claude said, with such breezy confidence that Prince shook his head in his what-will-the-rich-say-next? expression. Claude leaned forward, forearms crossed over the seat. "Say, are we going to a speakeasy, then?"

"Only the finest on Long Island," Prince said. He coughed. In a lower voice he added, "After a quick stop."

"What kind of stop?" Benedick asked flatly.

"Like maybe don't wear your best shoes, but no need to say your prayers either."

Benedick stared at him.

"What?" Prince asked. "The Masquerade's this Saturday. He's your interloper. That's not my fault."

"I won't be a problem," Claude interjected. "I swear it. Only tell me one thing: Will there be gangsters involved?"

Prince showed his teeth in a sharp smile. "How do you know *I'm* not a gangster?"

Claude's eyes grew round. "Are you?"

"No," Benedick said. "He's not. And wherever we're going, you're going to stay in this scrap heap of a vehicle and guard my typewriter like your golden little life depends on it. By the way, where the hell is the car, Prince? Why'd you pick me up in this hayburner?"

"I like the Tin Lizzie better. Anyway, Hero said she and Leo need it to pick up her cousin in the morning. If something happens, they'll have a good car."

If something happened on their *quick stop*. Sure. "Hero has a cousin?" asked Benedick.

"Who's Hero?" asked Claude.

Claude truly did not seem perturbed to be rattling along in a dark car to god knew where. Perhaps Benedick wasn't the only one to feel suffocated inside Stony Creek's walls.

They reached the main road, and only then did Prince flip on the headlights and shift to a faster gear. Stony Creek Academy was nothing more than a series of dark lumps behind them. "Hero Stahr," Prince said to Claude, "is the hostess and darling of Hey Nonny Nonny. You'll like her."

Benedick said, "She'll like him, too, I bet. She goes nuts over accents." She went nuts over fat pockets, rather, but that was just a slight tweak in semantics.

Prince raised an eyebrow at him.

Yes? Benedick returned the look. Claude ought to compensate for being such a pain in the ass by way of lovesick donation. "Look, the fourth-year exam isn't until the afternoon. How about Leo drops him back at Stony Creek on their way? Where's the cousin?"

"North Manhattan, near Inwood, I think."

"Swell. There you go, Blaine; you won't even have to bribe anyone." Not to mention, it was a little more incentive for Prince to stay out of trouble tonight.

Claude sniffed. "I wasn't worried. But if you don't mind, *where* precisely are we going *tonight*?"

"First," Prince said, "the coast."

Rum Row looked like a floating city, a line of rusted freighters, steamers, and rebuilt submarines shrouded in fog. Prince squatted on Breezy Point's rocky shore, his arms resting on his knees, the tips of his ears turned the color of apples.

Benedick, quiet and hunched in the chill of predawn, remained a few feet back. Beside him, Claude leaned in and whispered: "What exactly are we waiting for?"

"Shh." Benedick quieted him, but in truth he'd been wondering the same thing. Side trips when Prince picked him up were not uncommon, but usually they were a bit livelier. Not nearly so much time to stare at the mist-drenched horizon and doubt one's recent life-changing decision.

Prince glanced back over his shoulder, one side of his mouth hitched up in that smile of his. Benedick could not fathom the source of his good mood. Prince stood and from his jacket passed Benedick a tin flask, which, after a careful sniff, was determined to be one-third full of a liquid that was likely to be one-third brandy. Two-thirds guts and glory. Benedick sipped and grimaced.

He handed the flask to Claude, who knocked back a rousing mouthful, managing it with a fist thumped on his chest. "Bloody coffin varnish," he said hoarsely.

Prince regarded him; after deciding something to himself, he pointed. "That's the maritime line," he said. "Ten or so miles out. Past it, liquor is legal again. So. What you're looking at is basically floating warehouses of booze."

"And no one stops them?" Claude asked.

Prince said, "They're not doing anything wrong yet. They send rumrunners at night to get their cargo to shore, but plenty of it goes missing. Sometimes because of storms, but also because the runners will stuff canvas hams with rock salt, which they can throw overboard to be sunk if the coast guard catches them. After the salt dissolves, the sack will float back to the surface and get picked up by the runners, if they can find them again. Or sometimes they mark the current and send out crates to float to shore under the fog."

Claude had the unfortunate look of an adventurous puppy: devil minded and bored for the past half hour. "I see. And this—rather, are we some sort of rumrunners then?"

"*You're* definitely not." Prince grinned. "But for that matter, neither am I, since I keep to shore, but I've got a lookout who wires me the good spots for strays and—see there; they're starting in."

Half hidden among boulders made black by decaying moss, wooden crates appeared on the crests of incoming waves. Probably four that Benedick could count, spread widely among one another, along with the brownish heads of floating hams, all carried by the same tide.

"Are those ours?" asked Benedick.

"Catch that one before it hits!" Prince bent and dragged a crate through the sand.

Benedick went after the other crate and heaved it up before it smacked against a boulder a second time. A wave crashed into his shins, and ice-cold water seeped through his pants, stinging his ankles and leaking into his shoes. He skittered out of the water. "*Cold*—son of a—"

Prince kept laughing. "I told you not to wear nice shoes."

"These *aren't* my nice shoes." They were not Prince's worn boots either, but Benedick didn't own a pair of work shoes that matched Prince's definition. Work, in his family, meant looking polished and ready for business.

Had meant, rather.

He was free. He didn't care about shoes; he didn't care about any of it.

Claude was in the surf nearly waist deep, a hefty sack slung on his shoulder, his other hand out for lost liquor or whatever else the ocean felt keen to throw at him.

Benedick hefted the crate a good yard away from the water's edge. The soggy rattling was a familiar sound, even if the method of attainment was not. He strained to see through the mist, expecting the roar of a runner boat any moment, a shouted warning, the click of a gun cocking. The usual.

Weeks ago, when Benedick had asked Prince how their supply looked for the Masquerade, Prince had answered, "I'm sorting out some negotiations that will keep us flush once it pans out."

Was this part of those negotiations? Scavenging like buzzards?

More troubling was the insignia amid the FRESH VEGETABLES and ROUTE TRANSPORT on the crates—an insignificant-looking black stencil mark. One of the first things Leo had taught Benedick when he started helping Prince was that symbol: "If you ever see any shipment with this mark on it, you leave it be. No matter if you're sure it was supposed to be yours. You walk away. That's the Genovese family mark, and I don't want Hey Nonny Nonny caught up in that kind of business."

Claude set two sacks heavily into the gritty sand by Benedick's crate. "Do you think they mind?" he asked, as if he'd heard Benedick's musings. "Whoever these belong to?"

"They won't know the difference." Prince hauled over a third crate; he knocked his boot against it to get a stray piece of kelp off. "Far as they know, they're lost to sea."

There was no chance that Benedick had noticed the Genovese family mark while Prince hadn't. Instead of asking outright if Prince had targeted this particular shipment, Benedick came at the question sideways: "Who's your lookout anyhow?"

Prince's glance was sharp as a thorn. Then he was all shrugs and another lit cigarette was quickly stuffed in the corner of his mouth. "You wouldn't know him. I'll grab that last one; then let's hit the road. Any more ain't going to fit."

Benedick said nothing. When it came to Prince's very long-lost relatives, the best course of action was to wait, instead of poking inside and losing a finger.

They dragged a total of four crates and three canvas sacks up to the Model T and crammed them all in the backseat. Prince sang under his breath as they loaded, "You back-firin', spark plug foulin' Hunka Tin," the same war tune Leo always serenaded to the Tin Lizzie, and it warmed the bad whiskey in Benedick's gut with a feeling like home. Benedick gently maneuvered his typewriter under the dash so Claude could fit up front with them.

"Suppose we run into any police?" Claude asked as they pulled away from the coast onto a thin road.

"We'll keep on the back paths," said Benedick. "Anyway, there's hardly any patrol on Long Island."

Which made the sudden appearance of a car behind them all the more jarring.

"Prince—"

Prince chucked his cigarette out the window. "I see them."

"See who?" Claude asked.

The engine whined as Prince pressed harder on the gas pedal. The lack of surprise on his face was not comforting. They gained a little distance, only to veer around a corner and find a pickup truck shooting out of a skinny back road right in front of them. Prince slammed on the brakes, and the Model T skid to a swerving halt, leaving scant inches between them and the bed of the truck. The crates of alcohol behind them rattled and cracked. Benedick let out a breath, hands braced on the dash.

The truck's driver door opened, and a thickset man walked out. His mouth was full of the kind of grimy teeth that would make even a sincere smile look bad. And his smile was not sincere. In the passenger's seat a younger man glowered. "I think you know why we've stopped you this fine morning and why, when our shipments have been a few counts low of what we ordered this past month, we've been inclined to let it slide." He spread his hands, as if to demonstrate the generosity he'd offered.

Prince had gone still; he was scarcely breathing.

The man took a step closer to their car. He snapped gloved fingers, and the young man in the passenger's seat opened the door, an automatic rifle in both hands. "So here's the deal, kid," the man said. "You hand over what belongs to us and stay the hell away from our coast routes, and we'll say no more. That's the smart choice. Otherwise we teach you how to make smart choices."

"The crates," Claude whispered. "Right? We can give them back."

Benedick glanced at Prince, whose eyes narrowed.

Sorry, Claude.

Prince muttered, "Goddamned Italians," under his breath. He made a vulgar gesture over the steering wheel, then jerked the reverse stick into place. Benedick muttered a thank you to whatever god was listening that the engine hadn't quit in their unplanned stop. Prince pounded the gas pedal, and they lurched back.

Another set of headlights appeared behind them, the direction they were hurtling toward. In his newfound freedom Benedick had thought he didn't give a damn what became of him. It seemed he cared after all. He at least wanted to live.

Looking over his shoulder, Prince said, "Get the gun out from under the seat."

Benedick crouched down and found Leo's rifle. The weapon felt awkward in his hands. "Give that here," Claude said. With the rifle in one hand, he angled himself out the side window, his foot braced on the seat. One well-aimed shot took out the left headlight of the car behind them. "Ha! That's what three seasons fox hunting gets you—"

An answering bullet blasted apart one of the crates in the back. Benedick's first panicked thought was for his typewriter.

Prince yanked the steering wheel around, and they slammed over the edge of the road into the weeds, hard enough that the car bucked and Benedick had to grab Claude around the legs to keep him from falling out.

The Tin Lizzie swerved several yards off the road, tires squealing as Prince braked and changed gears. "Take over the wheel," he said.

Before Benedick could ask what in God's almighty name Prince was doing, his friend had flown out the door.

"I dropped the gun," Claude gasped as he collapsed back into his seat.

Benedick craned his neck and watched, in the grayness of dawn, as Prince grabbed the rifle out of the dirt, bent down on one knee, and cocked the gun against his shoulder. The car chasing them blazed past, blowing off Prince's cap. He fired a shot that took out the back tire. The car skidded and careened, both passengers cursing in Italian. The truck, roaring in the other direction, braked, kicking up dirt to avoid hitting them.

"My God," Claude said, "he's terrifying."

That jerked Benedick out of his reverie. He fumbled into the driver's spot. The gears ground with his clumsy shifting, but by the time Prince jumped in through the opposite door, Claude frantically scooting to make room, they were moving—away from the road.

Another shot blasted through their backseat, and Benedick

instinctively ducked, foot pressing the pedal down, as if that would help.

"Watch where you're going!" Prince barked as Benedick pitched them around a cluster of trees, branches clawing the car's side. The wheels took the bumps and ruts hard, further pummeling their precious load.

They crested a hill and hurtled toward nothing but rocky coastline and what appeared to be a small cliff. Prince released a string of poetic curses though Benedick paid attention only to the "damned brakes!" part of it.

He braked hard just before they hit the edge, but they tipped forward anyway. "Oh, God, oh, God," Claude muttered. Instead of tumbling into the ocean, they rolled down a relatively unimposing slope. Prince lurched over and grabbed the steering wheel. Throwing his whole weight into it, he wrenched them under the lip of a ridge, narrowly missing a craggy boulder. The engine died.

For several seconds they sat in silence, the only sound their quieting breaths. The sun peeked over the ocean horizon, mockingly picturesque. Benedick sneaked a glance first at Claude, then at Prince. Claude's cheeks were high with color, but other than that, he was still among the living and functional. Prince, cool as jazz, touched his hair. "Damn. I liked that hat."

"It was a very fine hat," Claude managed to say, voice thin.

Benedick laughed; he couldn't help it.

"Prince," he said once his mirth had faded, rubbing the

side of his nose. Most of the bottles had broken, running their contents all over the floor of the Model T. "Be a sport—won't you?—and reach under to see if Isabella is broken or drowning in whiskey."

Prince twisted and felt under the seat. "She's fine."

"On the bright side," said Claude, "we won't be easy to find here."

"Won't be easy to haul the car up either," said Prince. "Ben?" He waited until Benedick looked across and met his eyes; Prince's gaze was apologetic, searching. "You're all right?"

"Just jake. Blaine?"

"Been worse, all things considered."

"In that case." Prince turned on one knee, hunting around the ruin in the backseat. A minute later Benedick held the one-inch remains of a broken bottle of whiskey; Claude, a bottle of gin, which leaked into his lap through a long crack up the side.

"Boys," said Prince, holding up his replenished flask, "may we live to be shot at another day. *Salute.*"

"Cheers," said Benedick.

They drank, and Claude made a low sound in his throat. "Jesus." He coughed. "No wonder they were upset."

CHAPTER 2
LADY DISDAIN ARE YOU YET LIVING?

Beatrice Clark sat on her trunk, her chin in hand. The sun was hot already, even in May, but she refused to wait on the porch of the picturesque little lodge at the entrance gate. She stayed on the very side of the road, as far from the property as she was allowed to be. St. Mary's Society for Wayward Girls and Fallen Young Women occupied a lonely edge of Inwood Hill Park, with a winding drive leading up to it, and it was surrounded by a stucco stone wall. Difficult to scale, but a few girls had managed it before the trees had been chopped down. The ridge overlooked the Hudson River, and kept irreparable girls like Beatrice out of sight of the respectable people of Manhattan.

Tiredness hovered within reach like a crouched fox waiting

for a chicken, but she didn't give in to it. You couldn't get too comfortable; that was the trick. The comfortable way was usually wherever the current was going, and Beatrice rarely found herself wanting to go in that direction.

When the headmistress at Miss Nightingale's School had told her there was no money left for the last semester's tuition, Beatrice had been stunned; that was all. "We sent several notices to your father," Miss Nightingale said. "We received no reply."

Stepfather. Beatrice had mentally corrected her. "No, I don't suppose you would have." She'd guessed this might happen. She knew how much her mother's inheritance was and how much Miss Nightingale's School cost. Math was one of her best subjects, and she'd been aware from the start that she was just a little short.

But she'd worked so hard on *his* farm, every summer, and paid for a train ticket whenever he wrote and demanded her help, even when he got that bad attack of gout right before midterms. When he said they'd make up the difference in the end, as long as she did her share, well, she'd assumed that was the truth.

She'd believed in a lie, because the alternative was too hard.

"We will of course arrange for your safe return to Virginia. And perhaps," Miss Nightingale had suggested gently, in the face of Beatrice's steely expression, "you may complete your schooling in the fall, should the remainder of your tuition be paid?"

Beatrice had nodded; there'd been nothing else to do, so it felt, but pack her things, allowing herself to be helped into a winter coat and her trunk and suitcase hauled in a taxi to Grand Central Station. And so the current pulled. She stepped onto the sidewalk. Exhaust fumes, spiked by the scent of grilled sausages, weaved through the January air. She stared at the one-way ticket between her gloved fingertips. If she left the city now, she would never return.

A porter's furious curse brought her attention back. "Jesus Mary," the young man muttered, then glanced at her with a blush. "Begging your pardon, miss, it's just, what you got in this thing? A dead body?" He hauled her trunk out of the taxi's backseat.

"Parts of one," said Beatrice.

The porter snorted and dragged the trunk the rest of the way onto a luggage cart, though Beatrice had not been joking. He secured her suitcase on top and asked, "Where to, miss?"

Beatrice said nothing.

"Miss? Which terminal? If you'll let me see your ticket, we can find it, no trouble."

In reply, Beatrice let the ticket go. The rush of a passing car caught it and swirled it away from them. It landed several yards away in the gutter and was soaked instantly in oily slush.

The porter cursed. "Goddamn! That wasn't your ticket, was it?"

"Excuse me, may I see this for a moment?" Beatrice tried to push the porter's hands off the luggage cart.

His grip tightened around the iron handlebar, and he frowned. "What for? Look, we'll go to the ticket office and get you sorted— Ow! What the hell?"

Beatrice snaked her boot around the back of his heel as she gave him a hard shove in the chest, which sent him wheeling back and then toppling over the curb.

"Thanks for your help!" she called over her shoulder, and threw her weight into pushing the cart forward. It took a few seconds to gain momentum, but at a rattling jog she hit the intersection, where a milk truck nearly plowed her over. The driver swerved and called her a "dumb broad!" out his window, fist shaking.

"Sorry!" Beatrice gasped, hand out, but she kept going, pushing against the current of her life, running block after exhausting block, her breath clouding in the January afternoon. She was quite firm with herself whenever she felt like stopping. When she finally did stop, angry that her trembling body couldn't manage one step farther, she half wilted onto an apartment building's stoop but made herself stand. Out loud, she said, "Hold it right here, Beatrice Clark," and after a few minutes, satisfied she had control of her fear again, she sat on the lowest step.

Of course the sun went down, and it didn't take long for the landlord to call the police about a girl shivering on his stoop. When asked for her name, she refused to give it, and she ended up at St. Mary's, which she supposed was nicer than a jail cell, but not by much.

Still, better than the streets in winter.

Once her wits were about her, and she'd maintained a farce of docility long enough to be allowed letter privileges, she'd written to Miss Mayple, the only teacher at Miss Nightingale's School for Young Ladies to care more for a girl's understanding of advanced mathematics than how well she kept her legs crossed while balancing a book on her head. The first most important matter of business was whether or not Beatrice could take her exams later, if she could find the money, and still graduate. Secondly, Beatrice had an uncle. His name was Leonard Stahr. He lived with his wife and daughter on Long Island somewhere, but that was as far as her childhood memory stretched. Beatrice's birth father had died in the war before she turned eight, and her stepfather had wanted absolutely nothing to do with his wife's former in-laws—a radical, unseemly bunch, as he put it.

Beatrice didn't let herself hope too much, especially without a penny to her name, but two weeks ago the head matron had received a letter from one Leonard Stahr, requesting care of his niece as soon as possible.

"Mr. Stahr," the matron had replied, "while we at the society always appreciate the compassion of extended family members, we feel it wise to inform you that removing Miss Clark from the home at this point in time may not be in her best interest. As I understand, you have not seen her in nearly a decade, and it pains me to inform you that she is going to ruin as quickly as a girl can. We have reasonable cause to believe she was the instigator of a riot among a group of young girls last month. She threw a clock out a window."

Yes, well, Beatrice would pay for the clock. That was fair. She'd been very angry, and the doctor had refused to listen to her. A lot of girls at St. Mary's had worked the bars, brothels, and alleyways of lower Manhattan before being "rescued" by the society. They carried any number of sicknesses with them, which meant frequent visits from a physician. The *learned gentleman* had been administering douche and mercury treatments for venereal diseases—hypodermic doses twice a week until twenty (*twenty!*) doses were swimming like collected poison inside already sick girls.

One, in particular, had looked halfway to her grave.

Clock throwing was to be expected with that sort of idiocy; that was what Beatrice thought, but even so, she did try, she did say: "She's clearly suffering from bichloride mercury poisoning; she needs a hospital." (Though Beatrice might not have listened to herself, either, since she had also prefaced it with "you incompetent fool.")

Leonard Stahr had replied: "I first met my late wife marching at the head of a women's suffragette parade. So I must say, with respect to your position, that I have a deep fondness for rioting women, and you could not have made my niece more appealing to me if she came adorned with a cash prize. We will arrive to pick her up Friday morning, the thirteenth of May."

Beatrice knew this because the matron had given the letter back, along with the rest of her belongings, and refused to let Beatrice use any of the society's supplies as she was no longer "its responsibility." That meant no soap for three days and sleeping without sheets, but the other girls shared, and Beatrice wouldn't have minded even if they hadn't.

Late wife.

Her aunt had died. Beatrice's first thought, the cold reasoning of a survivor, was thank God that it wasn't her uncle who'd gone, that she was still blood related to the remaining members of the Stahr family. She winced at her own callousness. Her memories of Aunt Anna were warm and filled with high bell-like laughter.

A motor engine growled near the base of the hill, growing louder until a blue Lambda, covered in dust and smelling of petrol, crawled up to the gate. Beatrice went to her feet. The driver was alone—and a girl. She stood up in the roofless car and waved.

This had to be Beatrice's cousin, Hero, though she was nearly a woman now, stepping out of the car in a pair of heels and a skirt barely past her knees. She propped a pair of darkened driving glasses on her forehead and lit a cigarette. "Beatrice? My word, you're tall as a beanstalk! I won't reach your shoulder even in these shoes! Of course I'm not that tall anyway."

She wasn't—a compact package of curves—but what she lacked in inches from the ground, she more than made up in sheer sparkling gusto. She strode over to Beatrice, not wobbling once. The ends of her curled bob rested on the high points of her cheeks and looked dyed: a stark shade of red that matched her painted lips, which were curved with the patient smile of someone used to dazzling people.

Beatrice was indeed dazzled in spite of herself. Her cousin was more than beautiful; she was alchemical. It seemed impossible nature alone was responsible for so many assets in a single girl.

Hero held her cigarette to her lips between two leather-gloved fingers, then whistled the smoke out in a pinpoint stream. Her eyes drifted to the lodge house. "There's a rather birdish woman who keeps pulling back the curtain to watch us."

"That's the gatekeeper. She lives there with her husband. You came by yourself?"

Hero flashed a grin, revealing a gap tooth, and winked. "Sure did. Papa wanted to come, but he was feeling under the weather, so it was up to me." She glanced at Beatrice's trunk and the weathered suitcase on top. "Please tell me that monstrosity is stuffed with your collection of dancing dresses."

All of Beatrice's clothes, dresses included, were in the suitcase. The only fabric in the trunk was padding for her human skull replica and a glass-encased dead frog. "It will be heavy," she said grimly.

"Well, we're what we've got, so we'll make do. Toss your suitcase in, and we'll haul this sucker into the back."

Beatrice put her suitcase in the front seat. Hero removed her mauve jacket, pulled her driving gloves tighter on her hands, and waited until Beatrice came around the other side. Beatrice unbuttoned her dress shirt at the wrists and pushed her sleeves up. She eyed her cousin's cream skin and tried not to doubt if Hero had lifted anything in her life.

"On the count of three?" Hero asked.

"One," Beatrice said, "two, *three* . . ."

They heaved the trunk up together and shuffled to the car. "What in God's name," Hero gasped, "is in here?"

They got the trunk onto the backseat with some finagling and unladylike grunting, and Beatrice wiped her forearm over her temple. "A lot of books," she said, "and a chemistry set, tools, a medical kit that's nearly forty years old, but it was the only one they'd sell to me—"

"Are you going to be a doctor?" Hero asked it casually, dusting off her hands and walking back to the driver's door.

Beatrice tensed but didn't pause. "Yes."

"Well! How do you like that? Lord knows that's a handy set of skills to have in our neck of the woods." Hero bounced into the driver's seat; Beatrice followed suit, climbing into the passenger seat next to her suitcase the way an ordinary person would. "Do you need anything else?"

Beatrice looked up toward the main estate. "No."

"Then let's blouse." A second later the engine rumbled to life, and Hero adjusted her glasses over her nose. "We're going to have a grand time!" she said loudly over the screech of gears as she shifted. "And I'm pleased as punch you're going to be here for my birthday in a few weeks!"

With that, Hero spun them around, tires spitting out gravel, and roared down the road. Beatrice lost her hat when Hero accelerated into a curve and Beatrice let go to grip the side of the door. Hero watched the hat spiral away (her eyes off the road for a solid four seconds; Beatrice counted) and shouted over the wind, "Good riddance, right? Feels good!"

If Beatrice had Hero's hair, maybe; there seemed to be a certain standard of glamour that no strand dared disobey. Beatrice's curls followed no such master and in a few more miles would look like an electrocuted tumbleweed.

However . . .

It did feel good. Not the wind specifically, but rather not caring how messy her hair turned. After a while she shifted in her seat and came up on her knees to reach the trunk in the back. Hero obligingly slowed down until Beatrice found a pair of goggles. Hardly the fashionable driving glasses Hero wore (they were in fact the sort of bulky affair meant to guard against acidic chemicals), but they did the job. Hero grinned at her and shouted, "That kind of gear calls for more speed!" and Beatrice grinned back.

The Stahr estate was on Long Island, her uncle had written, in a quaint district called Flower Hill. Beatrice's memories of it were vague, but colorful and light. "What's it called?" Beatrice asked. "The house, I mean. Doesn't it have a funny name?"

"Hey Nonny Nonny!" Hero replied. "Mama always said it sounded like somebody saying hello—something you have to shout or sing!"

They sailed over the Brooklyn Bridge, through the motley streets of Brooklyn, and orderly rows and yards of Queens; then the road thinned, and they passed clusters of blossoming cherry trees and entered rural estates and fields. Beatrice took a gulp of the much fresher air, ignoring the uncertainty of it all, the way her entire life seemed to rattle behind the car as it traveled, like an empty can on a string.

They turned onto a drive, and Hero said, "Almost there!"

Beatrice straightened in her seat, surprised. The road winding in front of them was narrow and unkempt—barely a ribbon, choked with weeds, the gravel gone.

Then it appeared: white siding and charcoal gray roof, mullioned windows reflecting the patchy lawns and terrace. Even signs of neglect couldn't ruin the perfect symmetry. The garden had gone the way of the untended road. Long strands of ivy crept across the lawn and encroached upon the wraparound porch. Flowers, of course, but they looked vicious.

Beatrice wondered if the state of the place had anything to do with her aunt's recent death. There was no life behind the windows, the curtains limp on the inside of the dirty panes. *No one is here.*

But then a portly man rose from a porch chair and waved tipsily at them. Bald as an egg, he'd compensated for the lack of hair on his head by growing a mustache thick enough to sweep the floor of a tavern.

Hero parked the car by the porch and called, "Hi, Papa!".

Beatrice stumbled out of the car pushing her goggles up. They proved necessary as a headband, since the wind had indeed torn her hair to utter lack of respectability. Her wrist buttons were still undone, one sleeve bunched past her elbow, the other dangling loose. She looked like a mess, and outside of Hero's orbit she was suddenly embarrassed by it again; but she had no time to try to fix herself before her uncle was sweeping her up in a bone-crushing hug, lifting her a foot off the ground. "My girl, my dear girl!"

Her eyes watered. The sharp scent of alcohol emanated off the damp pores of his skin like an exhaled breath. This must have been what Hero meant when she said "under the weather."

He set her down. "Thank you for taking me in, Mr. Stahr," Beatrice said. "You can't imagine how grateful—"

"Horsefeathers!" he interrupted. "I'll be Uncle Leo, nothing less. I was dreadfully sorry to hear about your mother. Such a tragedy." Her uncle cupped her face in his hands. His eyes were blurred with drink, yet there was a spark of devilish charm in them that unlocked a memory, clear and preserved. Those same eyes and a voice (much less slurred) saying: "Even tricky girls can't get the jump on me—I'm wily as a ferret; ask your old man." He'd let her win three rounds of checkers, acting astounded each time.

"You look just like your father," Uncle Leo said after a moment. "I see him sure as day. Anthony was tall, too, grew up lanky and tough like a weed. Except those freckles, ha! I'm glad you didn't grow out of them. You were cute as a chipmunk back then."

"Oh, leave her alone, Papa." Hero patted his arm, her nose wrinkling at the smell. She held Beatrice's suitcase in one hand. "Come on, Beatrice. I'll show you your room."

They reached the porch; a hand-carved wooden sign hung by the door: HEY NONNY NONNY. Below it, someone had nailed in a more homemade post: VACANCIES.

"Vacancies?" Beatrice asked.

"What?" Hero tracked the direction of Beatrice's stare. She moved ahead. "Oh. We have a few boarders, is all."

Beatrice followed her through the door. She remembered the unassuming scale of the place. Only once inside did it become a mansion: the generous dimensions of hallway and stairway, the drawing room to the right, the dining hall stretching around to the left. The foyer was familiar—round, with a high ceiling, but the wood floor was dull, turned gray in the windowless lighting. Hero sighed and walked over to the light switch; she flicked it up and down several times but produced nothing more than an irate clicking sound.

"Applesauce," she muttered, then went to the end of the stairs and called up, "Hey, Mags?"

A pretty black girl appeared over the railing above them, her long arms folded up in angles, and a nest of wild hair. "Well, look who it is. You get the stray?" Her eyes found Beatrice in the dimness and widened in amusement. "She looks this side of crazy."

Hero ignored her. "We need two dollars to pay the power bill, and I'm broke as the Ten Commandments," she said. "Got any?"

"Hold on." The girl disappeared and returned a minute later. "One-sixty."

"Chuck it down, please. Are the boys back?"

"Not yet."

A shout came from outside. Hero's mouth pursed, and she set Beatrice's suitcase on the floor. "I better help him—no, don't even think about it. You're the guest."

She huffed out the door, and Beatrice caught sight of a photograph hanging on the nearby wall. The scene looked to be a bar: half a dozen people dressed in finery, pale ribbons twirling from the ceiling, sloshing cocktails in most hands. The faces were caught mid laughter, and all were looking at a woman standing on top of a piano. She was dressed in sequins and positively glowed, even in monochrome, as if there were a spotlight shining from inside her. Her hip was cocked, her hands were out and extended. Her face manifested joy, a happy freedom that stirred Beatrice right to her center. Someone had scrawled in the white border: "Hello, suckers! Anna Stahr and Hey Nonny Nonny, 1925."

Two years ago. Beatrice's eyes narrowed at the title. Either the owner of the bar had really liked Aunt Anna and Uncle Leo enough to name it after their house, or else . . . Aunt Anna and Uncle Leo were the owners.

Already the idea fit Uncle Leo like a glove. Some of the girls from Miss Nightingale's used to sneak into speakeasies in the city, and there'd been rumors of one of her stepfather's farmhands running a still in an underused shed; but until now Prohibition had felt largely distant and irrelevant to her life.

Something told her it had just gotten close enough to ask for a dance.

CHAPTER 3
WHEN THE AGE IS IN,
THE WIT IS OUT

Maggie stood beside Hero while she buttoned her father's collar, as if she were sending a boy off to school. Hero tucked an envelope into his vest pocket. "There's the extra money we need for the electricity this weekend. Don't leave until you know it will be turned on before tomorrow. Papa?" Say what you like, but it was always the girls who rallied first.

"Yes, dear." Leo tried to tug her ear, but she moved out of reach.

"Don't forget, either," Maggie said, holding up a piece of stationery. "You have to pick up Tommy and Jez from the station at five twenty. I wrote down the time for you." That was more than five hours away, and dealing with the electricity shouldn't take half that time; but there was no guarantee Leo wouldn't take a few detours on his way there or back. He still had friends among Flower Hill's estates, and most of them kept decanters of unaltered whiskey, imported straight from the Caribbean, behind locked cabinets. Leo had kept some himself, before Anna died. Maggie's first real drink had been a finger he poured after her solo debut downstairs. "God forbid we toast your career with brackwater moonshine," he'd said.

Maggie put the paper in his other pocket. *Sorry*, she mouthed.

This weekend was the first Masquerade without Anna. That truth hung around like a too-tight necktie. Early this morning they'd discovered Leo singing Anna's favorite ragtime tunes on the porch, slurring the words. He'd used the last of his personal hoard, and there wasn't a drop of extra booze in the house. On the outside he looked like hell's dirty laundry, skin sagging, but soon, the lack of juice would begin to crack and splinter him inside, too. Edges that cut. Hero had stashed all the rest earlier. If he'd tried to wheedle some out of her, he hadn't been successful. Hero loved her papa, but she loved her mama's speakeasy, too.

"Thanks, Mr. Stahr," Maggie added.

"Leo." He corrected her with a sigh. "Don't 'mister' me now. I'll get your boys picked up on time. Girls," he said to both of them, "you've done a lot of work getting this weekend ready, and I'm grateful." He put his hat on and touched the brim, a diluted wink to his old charm and energy. "You can count on me."

"I know, Papa. Drive carefully." Hero kissed his cheek.

Only after the Lambda was puttering down the road did Hero turn to Maggie. "Only Tommy and Jez? Where's your string instrument?"

Geez, that girl. Hero was as sharp as a tack and, like Anna, knew the temperature of the speakeasy at any minute with her eyes closed and standing on her head.

Maggie held up her hands. "Couldn't find one. Everybody knows the pay is lousy. Tommy and Jez only come out of loyalty."

And even that was wearing thin.

Maggie had been Hey Nonny Nonny's headline entertainment for a year and a half, she and her three-man band—Tommy on piano, Jez on drums, and the third, whoever had given into her begging for that particular night. Sometimes a sax, sometimes a trumpet, but most often a guitar. Tommy and Jez did far more gigs in Harlem and were always on her to do the same. In their eyes, you could make a speakeasy's stage hot, but sitting down to breakfast with the white owners of the joint the next morning was not part of the deal. Never mind if they'd become family the past few years.

Hero put a finger to the center of her valentine mouth. "Mmm. What about that girl we saw last month in Harlem? You even said how good she was."

"The girl with the cello?" Hero had spent the evening with some Princeton boy, whom she'd eventually suckered into footing the bill for their May Day shindig. Maggie remembered because she'd been irritated at their presence. There wasn't a finer girl in New York to hit the clubs with than Hero, but sometimes Maggie needed those nights to herself, with Tommy and Jez and the other musicians, without having to excuse the white couple as "cool" and "with her." One of the best numbers of the night had been a girl who'd whipped out a jazz solo on an instrument nearly the same size as she was. "I never met her. I definitely don't remember her name."

"I'd say there's a good chance she doesn't have a gig tomorrow night."

Maggie frowned. "Or maybe she's in high demand."

Hero waved a hand; she knew she was right. Maggie only wished Hero was wrong. Most female instrumentalists had to join an all-girl band if they wanted their due, and a cellist would have it worse, since it took a lot of muscle to twirl one of those suckers through an improvised jam number.

"I don't suppose that cousin of yours has any useful speakeasy skills?" Maggie asked.

"She's studying to be a doctor, which will be useful if any of us get shot."

"Great. Now God knows we're prepared." Maggie knocked on one of the wooden columns of the porch. "Did you tell her yet?"

"No." Hero sighed, dragged a hand down her face. She was still dressed in smart clothes from picking Beatrice up, as though she were about to trot off to a typing job. "I told her she should unpack and take a nap, maybe a nice bath. That'll give me some time to get everything settled and give her a proper, unalarming introduction."

"Proper and unalarming, sure. That describes Hey Nonny Nonny perfectly."

Hero turned on her heel and sauntered back into the house. "None of your sass, Margaret Hughes," she said. "Not until you get me a third member for your three-man band."

Maggie rolled her eyes but nonetheless went to the drawing room, where the ivory-handled phone was kept. She asked for the number to Tommy's apartment building and waited for what seemed like thirty rounds of hollering back and forth before he was located.

"Hello, sugar." His rich voice came over the phone. "Couldn't wait until tonight to talk to me?"

"Do you remember that cello player last month at Goldgraben's?" she asked.

"I guess." He was annoyed, wounded she'd ignored his question.

"Think you could find her before you and Jez catch the train in?"

"What for?"

"What do you think what for? So she can play with us."

There was a long silence. "You want me to play with a girl?"

"I want a cellist, who happens to be a girl."

Another silence, longer than before. "Mags—"

"Just try for me, Tommy. Please. We could really use a third. There's gonna be a big crowd tomorrow, Hero says."

"Hero says lots of things. But fine. I'll ask around."

"Thanks, Tommy. I'll see you tonight." Maggie hung up before he could weasel a kiss out of the deal.

She walked out of the drawing room just in time to see Hero's cousin hauling a stack of books in from the porch. A set of scales was balanced on top, and the tip of her tongue stuck out from the corner of her mouth in concentration.

"Oh," Beatrice said when she noticed Maggie. "Don't mind me. I figured instead of waiting on the mythical boys Hero keeps mentioning, I could haul in some of my things piece by piece; then when it's light enough, I'll take the trunk up myself."

Maggie's head tilted. "Not really the napping sort, are you?"

Beatrice blew a curl out of her eyes. "No, I suppose not."

"Well," said Maggie, moving past her. She'd help if she didn't now have to round up a comprehensive set number for a cellist who'd never played with them. "Don't mind us either, and you'll fit right in."

CHAPTER 4
MEN OF SOME OTHER METAL

By the time Benedick, Prince, and Claude made it back to Hey Nonny Nonny, the Model T limping along, it was nearly lunch. They were a miserable assembly, covered in grease, dirt, and booze, their clothes sweated through twice over. At this rate they'd be serving their tears at the Masquerade tomorrow.

Claude had grown quiet, a little less cavalier about missing his exam that afternoon, while Benedick's mood only improved the closer they got to Flower Hill. The days on Long Island seemed to have twice as many hours as in the city; a decent drink was two miles away, and an evening paper was six. That was what made Hey Nonny Nonny such a prime spot. A hidden pearl of nightlife and excitement without traveling to Manhattan.

In the daytime it was the opposite of the life he knew: very merry and very poor. Supperless one night and feasting the next; borrowing one another's last dollars for the sake of laundered tablecloths or a fixed microphone, knowing a good night could win them back the butter or milk they'd sacrificed for the next day's breakfast.

When they pulled into the drive, he was so caught up in how right it all felt that he almost didn't notice the girl on the shabby porch.

She was sitting cross-legged on a wicker chair, her skirt bunched around her knees so it looked as if she were wearing bulky trousers. She didn't seem like one of Hero's friends, her plain travel clothes a decade out of fashion and her untidy hair of no fashion at all. Not to mention the three books on her lap; Hero could barely be bothered to crack a gossip rag.

"Who is that?" asked Benedick.

"Must be the cousin?" Prince answered.

The girl lifted her head as they passed, and alarm spread over her features as she took in the bullet holes and the shattered window. Benedick checked behind them, just to be sure none of their semi-destroyed wares were visible.

The mysterious girl disappeared from sight as they went around the side of the house.

"I didn't see the Lambda," said Prince. "Did you?"

"No," Benedick said with dismay. "Maybe that wasn't the cousin, and they're still in Manhattan?"

Before anyone could suggest they unload the Lizzie and send it back on the road, it sputtered and sank several inches into the weedy ground, smoke trailing from the engine.

"I beg your pardon."

Benedick's heart issued an unwelcome thump at the sudden voice at his side. The girl from the porch was right by the door, and she was peering in at them.

She continued. "There's not a band of outlaws behind you to finish the job, is there? Your axle is bent, I don't know if you noticed. That's why the back wheel was rotating so poorly. Do you board here? I bet I could fix your axle, and possibly the leak, too, as a courtesy—if my uncle has any tools lying around, which, well, let's not hold our breaths, but—"

Benedick held up a hand. If he angled it right, he could block her mouth from his line of vision.

She blinked at his hand, then looked back at him. Her voice cooled and slowed to a more human pace. "What? Do you want me to stop talking, is that what that is?"

Perhaps she didn't know she was the sort of presence that required slow digestion at first. Her stare was direct—channeled through absurdly big eyes, the kind a more inclined man might trip and drown in, if he weren't watching his step—but she was not exceptionally pretty. She was just aggressively *there*.

"Yes, all right." Her gaze swept through the car, over them. Benedick's skin itched. "There's a chance you've been through some trauma. I'll speak slowly. My name's Beatrice Clark. I'm the landlord's niece."

Prince recovered first. He leaned over the wheel and offered one of his comfortable smiles. "Hello, Miss Clark. You're Hero's cousin? I'm Prince, and this is my friend, Benedick Scott, and his schoolmate, Claude Blaine. I guess we look pretty bad, but we had a somewhat unplanned morning. The situation is not as unscrupulous as it appears. Or smells."

The side of her mouth lifted. "I was warned about you, yes. Would you like me to get Hero?"

"Don't trouble yourself. Ben, why don't you take Blaine in so he can get cleaned up, and then perhaps you can show Miss Clark here where we keep the tools?"

Benedick cut his eyes to Prince, and received, for his trouble, a subtle throat clearing. He sighed, understanding that he was to keep the cousin occupied and away from the car.

"Pardon me," he drawled, making a show of opening the door so she was forced to step back. He unearthed his typewriter from under the seat; a quick peek inside showed Isabella had weathered the trip all right. "Come with me, Blaine. We'll get you a spare shirt to borrow for the ride back. And Miss Clark? If you'd do me the great honor of following us in, I'll point you to the special automotive toolbox once he's settled."

"I appreciate that, Mr. Scott." There was a dryness to her voice that suggested she knew there might not be a special automotive toolbox, but she trailed behind them nonetheless.

"I like this house," Claude said, stepping onto the wraparound porch, not a hint of irony to his tone. "Don't you think there's something deliciously untidy about it? Like a tree house in the woods."

"If your tree houses run the size of mansions," said Beatrice.

"Oh, this is much smaller than our estate in England."

"Of course it is."

Benedick opened the back service door and stepped inside a dusty hallway. Even with the two babbling accessories behind him, he felt his equilibrium realign, become right.

He'd have lost his nerve or his balance years ago if he hadn't had Hey Nonny Nonny to come and breathe in. There were things inside him that he lost outside its walls, that he could only seem to find again once he was back.

"How is it you're a boarder, again? You seem young." Beatrice's voice reasserted itself in his consciousness in a matter of seconds. It was a voice made for that sort of thing: precise, like an aimed arrow. Already he wished he could hear less of it if only because it was so difficult to ignore.

"I'm not," Claude answered. "This is my first time here. Scott and I go to prep school in Brooklyn. Or we did, rather."

Benedick interrupted. "The main stairs are this way."

He led them down a second hall, a threadbare rug beneath

their feet, passing a wall lamp that, when tugged, would open up a foot-wide passage to the kitchen. He heard Beatrice draw a breath behind him, signaling that her arrow voice was about to let fly again, so he spoke before she could. "Hey Nonny Nonny was owned by the Ottoman family—Anna Stahr's parents—before the turn of the century, then known simply as the Ottoman Cottage."

"You see?" Claude said. "Cottage."

"Anna"—Benedick continued—"was disowned by her parents, for both her unseemly brand of politics and her choice of husband, but she was the apple of her father's eye, so instead of cutting her off entirely, they gave her the deed for this property and told her never to contact them again. She rechristened it Hey Nonny Nonny."

They reached the staircase in the foyer, and he bounded up the steps two at a time.

Beatrice asked, "I thought you *weren't* a boarder? How do you know that story?"

He had only himself to blame for giving her the opening. Luckily they'd reached Prince's room. "Ah, here we are. Don't move an inch," he told Beatrice sweetly, then gestured at Claude to follow him inside. "I'll just be a few moments getting Mr. Blaine here settled."

He shut the door and grabbed a fresh shirt from a dresser drawer, along with a half-used bar of soap from Prince's washbasin. "Washroom's down the hall if you need it."

"You don't honestly think they'd expel me?" Claude asked, taking the soap and shirt. "By now they'll know I'm gone."

"Your family funds the fencing team and at least two-thirds of the library. You'll be fine."

Claude's expression drooped in relief; it always helped to have one's privilege confirmed. "Still, this car situation is a bit rummy."

"We ought to be able to patch up the Model T enough to get to Manhasset; then you can take the train back. That's what I do most of the time. Even if the car's truly done for, it's not quite two miles. We can walk. Give us half an hour. Maybe I can get some coffee and food in the meantime."

"Sure you won't come back with me?"

Halfway out the door Benedick glanced back over his shoulder. "Not on your life, Blaine."

The hallway was empty.

Not two minutes, and Beatrice Clark was gone. Dread swept over him.

He hurried down the steps, tentatively calling, "Miss Clark?" He searched downstairs, but found her nowhere. Finally, with resignation, he went outside. The Model T was in the same place, off-kilter, much less smoky, but Beatrice wasn't there either. Benedick checked the backseat. Prince had already unloaded the survivors of their trip.

As he shut the door again, a swinging branch nearly took his feet out from under him. With a strangled shout, he jerked back and tumbled to the ground.

"Oops—excuse me. I didn't realize you were there."

None other than Beatrice Clark finished crawling out from under the car, twirling a misshapen tree branch in one hand. "Turns out, your axle is fine, but *this* was lodged up in the frame. Can you imagine?"

Her question was not entirely rhetorical. He could hear the underlying accusation, but for once in his life words failed him. She was wearing a pair of men's coveralls, threadbare and stained, the sleeves rolled up past her elbows. Boots, the kind Prince would approve of, were tied to her calves.

"Would you like help, Mr. Scott?" She extended a hand down to him.

"Certainly not." He stood on his own, brushing himself off—not that it made much difference at this point. "Where did you find tools?"

"In the car. Most good drivers keep the basics with them, especially with the old Fords." She lifted the hood and propped it open with the branch. "Your other problem, at least what I could see from the bottom up, is that one of the . . . *holes* you acquired caught a valve, and it's leaking. The quickest fix, without a mechanic's shop, is to get some plain cloth and dip it in heated rosin—sap essentially—then lay a bit of rubber scrap over that and tie it tight. If you like—"

"I told you to wait inside," Benedick, frustrated, cut her off.

She turned and nailed him with a look. You wouldn't think such a skinny, odd, plainish thing could deliver such a blistering stare, but she managed.

"The first thing you ought to know about me, Mr. Scott, is I don't like being told what to do. Secondly, we both know 'special automotive toolbox' was your name for whatever distraction you were going to cook up to keep me away from the car, and of course now we see why."

Benedick stiffened defensively. He strode forward and snatched the branch in one hand. The hood slammed closed.

"Here's a riddle for you, Miss Clark, since you're so clever. If you figured out we were trying to keep you away from the car, why venture out to do precisely that?"

"Obviously you were hiding—"

"If you ask me, it speaks of a naturally rebellious nature; you yourself claimed the character flaw with pride. Now, as I recall, you were retrieved early this morning from Inwood, near northern Manhattan, which anyone can tell you is the location of a home for wayward and criminal girls. The conclusion practically draws itself." He turned the branch in his hand, faux-casually examining the knots and lines in the wood. "Seems to me you are at the charity of your relatives. With a reputation for trouble. I consider it a kindness to tell you that it might behoove you to mind your own business."

Color flooded into Beatrice's cheeks; however, it looked less like the flush of embarrassment than like a building rage. Her chin lifted. She inhaled through her nose, and Benedick felt a little as if he were at the end of a gun being cocked to fire.

"Fair point," Beatrice said. "Though it begs the question, Mr. Scott, of how a city prep boy knows a countryside house and its occupants so well. You are clearly rich, clearly educated, and as an actual rebel I consider it a kindness to tell you that you are but an amateur. For all your astute observation, it seems to me you and I are in the same spot, subject to the same mercies."

She stepped closer. Benedick resisted the urge to put back the distance between them.

"If we are destined to be enemies," she said, "remember this: I belong to Hey Nonny Nonny by blood, and you belong only by what appears to be arrogant whimsy. Sir."

Benedick stared at this frizzy-haired blight on his sanctuary and had the uncanny feeling of resuming an eternal battle. Destiny indeed. "Who says we must be enemies?" he said, switching tracks. He tossed the branch aside and offered a smile. Beatrice did not return it. "If you care so much, then go ahead and finish your good deed of the day. Sap's that way, if you need it." He pointed at the woods beyond Hey Nonny Nonny and took two steps toward the house but, unable to help himself, turned back. He held out his hands, every bit of his oily, dirty, sweaty, ruined clothes on display. "What about me is clearly rich?"

Beatrice laughed. Her laugh was as uninhibited and untidy as the rest of her. "Mr. Scott, even if a little ground ends up on your clothes, it doesn't stop you from walking on it as if you owned it."

His father walked like that. Benedick didn't. Did he?

Having no other reply (again), he went inside, this time to the kitchen. The pantry kitchen was barely bigger than his own bedroom: a stove, an icebox, one rickety cupboard, and ladles and spoons hanging from bent iron nails. Mostly it served as the secret entrance for the speakeasy.

Maggie was at the deep sink up to her elbows in a bucket of water, on her tiptoes so she could reach all the way in. He recognized the growling set of her mouth and knew she was pondering the value of one good scream.

"Hello, Mags," he said.

She straightened. "Ben! How you—whoa." She held up a hand and took a step back. "You smell like a drunk man buried alive and dug up again."

"Exactly!"

She gave him a funny look.

"I don't smell like a prep school graduate, now do I?"

"Dunno. Only rich white boys get away with being strange as you are." Her eyes crinkled at his frown. She flicked filmy water at him. "I'm joking."

"What're you doing?"

"Washing dishes, what's it look like? Never mind I've got five sets to practice for the Masquerade and the band will be here tonight; but the stack was taller than Prince, and all anybody can say is 'We'll get to it, we'll get to it.' When? When we're eating off the floor, that's when." Her cheeks puffed as she caught her breath. "I am *not* the maid, Ben. I'm not. Hey Nonny Nonny was supposed to save me from this kind of work."

Hey Nonny Nonny used to have a maid, back in its heyday. Two, and a housekeeper and a cook and a butler who'd managed the valets and waiters. After Anna's death they left one by one. Not out of disloyalty, but because they still had families to feed, and Leo stopped being able to pay them.

"I'll finish the dishes." He shoved up his sleeves, ignoring the urge to shout out the back porch: *See? Look!*

Maggie, doubtful, put a hand on her hip.

Benedick nudged her gently aside and grabbed a plate from the dirty stack. "You're not the maid," he said, "and I'm not rich and useless."

Maggie's face softened. "You are strange, though," she said, coming to his other side. He scrubbed and rinsed; she dried and put away.

"You meet the new cousin?" asked Maggie.

"Did I have the misfortune?" Benedick grumbled. "Yes."

"What? Don't like her?"

"Do you?" He didn't bother hiding his incredulity.

"Why wouldn't I? Don't know her much yet, but she was nice, I guess. You're just mad 'cause she's smarter than you."

"How do you know she's smarter than me?"

"'Cause she's the kind who's smarter than everybody."

"You cannot possibly know that already."

"Can so. Eyes never lie, and she's got brainy eyes."

"What kind of eyes do I have?"

"Dreamer eyes."

"Mags!"

"What? Ain't a bad thing." She turned at a muted thumping inside the open pantry. Benedick handed her the last glass just as the back wall shifted, got stuck a moment, then popped open.

Hero stepped through. "And whatever happened to Corney?"

"The Minskys bought him out," said Prince, coming up behind her. He had to duck through the entrance to avoid hitting his head. "They've bought out everyone from the rum line."

"We can't keep watering down our already watered-down supply— Ben!" Hero's eyes lit up. "You're home! Come here immediately, so I can kiss you." He walked dutifully over and leaned down to let her buss him on the cheek. "Are you finished with that dreadful school of yours yet? I hate seeing you only a few days at a time."

"Done as a Christmas ham."

"I guess that's about the only piece of good news I've heard all day. Did you meet my cousin yet?"

"Yes," said Prince. "If that's the right word."

"Were pounced upon," Benedick suggested dryly.

"*Obviously* you'll both be nice to her," said Hero. "She'll be here at least the summer, maybe longer. She doesn't have much other family. Hardly sees her stepfather—he owns some farm in Virginia, I think—and her mother died several years ago. I wondered if I ought to invite her to the Masquerade, after everything else she's been through, but I think she'll be just fine now that I've met her. That is, if there's even a party to attend. I hid our leftover stock from Papa, but—"

"Father Francis ordered extra wine bricks for Easter," said Maggie, putting away the last dish. She tucked the drying towel into her skirt and wiped her hands. "He'll donate some, I bet."

"That's a wonderful idea, Maggie."

Maggie crossed her arms. "Best get there quick, though. He locks up by two on Fridays."

"Where's the Lambda?" Prince asked.

Hero glanced at him, and they shared one of their silent conversations. "Papa took it to pay for the electricity and pick up the band."

Prince massaged the back of his neck. "'S all right. Only the Lizzie's not in great shape either."

"Claude can take the train," said Benedick. "That way we'll only have to make it a few miles. We'll drop Prince off at the church on our way, and Francis can bring him and the wine back after he locks up. I'll drive home by myself." He flushed at three identical expressions of doubt. "What's the worst that happens? I break down and get a bit of exercise."

Maggie pressed her lips together.

"What?" Benedick asked.

"Just imagining it, that's all. You strolling back, head held high, the car in some ditch." She grinned. Hero laughed, then Prince laughed, and Benedick's irritation was replaced by a rush of affection so strong it nearly stole his breath.

Maggie pushed curls off her forehead. She swatted Benedick with the end of the towel and hung it neatly over the sink. "I've got a stage to prep, if nobody minds."

"I moved the biggest speaker for you just now, Mags," said Prince.

She dipped in a theatrical bow of thanks and sauntered over to the pantry.

"Holler if you need anything." Hero herded Prince and Benedick out of the kitchen with her. "I have faith in Ben's driving skills, so long as somebody tells me who this Claude person is."

"Ben's schoolmate," said Prince.

"Ooh." Hero's interest notched up a level. "Handsome?"

"As the devil," said Benedick. "The kind of face that belongs on a dollar bill. Or the hundred-dollar bill. Multiple hundreds."

"Now, Ben, you know money isn't the only thing I care about." She put a finger to her temple and winked. "I also like to tap their foreheads. If it rings hollow, that's how I know I've found a real winner." She rounded the corner into the foyer.

Claude Blaine was coming down the stairs, finishing the button on his left sleeve cuff. He'd cleaned up, his hair damp and pushed back. "Oh, good." His smile was sheepish as he saw them. "I wasn't sure whether— Hello."

Hero planted herself right in front of him on the bottom stair. "Hello to you, too. I'm Hero Stahr. You must be Ben's stowaway."

"I—yes. Guilty." Claude blinked a few times. But he was no slouch in the charm department himself, and it shone soon enough. "That's a lovely name, Miss Stahr."

"Thank you, had it my whole life. You may use it if you like."

"Sure—ah, Hero, then. Claude Blaine."

Her lips curved, small and secret and sweet, like she'd already figured out everything there was to know about him. "So I've been told." Her hand reached over to the banister, blocking any prayer of escape he might have had. "You're not leaving, are you?"

Claude's golden cheeks grew a shade warmer. He glanced up at Benedick almost in question.

Hold on to your hat, pal, Benedick thought.

"I'm afraid I must," said Claude.

"And I'm afraid you must return," said Hero. "Tomorrow night's my Masquerade party. Give a girl a hand?"

Claude took her hand, a gut reaction as she extended it, and she pulled herself up next to him. "Oops—ha-ha—still too short." She climbed up one more step so she could lean into his shoulder.

She reached for her brassiere strap, where she undid a hidden pin, a black three-petal flower rimmed in silver, then took her time securing it to Claude's collar. His neck flushed a deep pink color that rose gradually to his hairline.

"That's your ticket in," she said. She leaned close and whispered in his ear. With a tug on his earlobe, she winked. "And that's the password."

Benedick glanced at Prince, who mimed an airplane nose-diving to the earth. At close enough range Hero could turn any man's heart to mud; that was why, though Benedick adored her, he'd never let her within spitting distance of his own.

Hero continued. "You'll have to wear a mask tomorrow, so remember to come in nice and close so I recognize that delightful accent."

"Oh, well. That's . . . all right." Claude surrendered.

Hero beamed. "I was hoping you'd say that. I think Prince and Ben are going to take you to the train station soon?" She glanced back at them.

"How soon is soon, exactly?" Prince asked. "The car might need more than a quick—"

As if answering him, the distant sound of an engine roared up, faded, then grew stronger as it came closer to the front of the house. Hero frowned and skipped down the stairs. She opened the front door just as the Model T pulled into the main drive and stopped.

"Is that Beatrice?" asked Hero.

The four of them moved onto the porch. The Model T that

faced them was purring like a cat. The engine shut off a second later and Beatrice jumped out, coveralls and everything, a smear of grease on her jaw. "You really ought to take her to a shop," she said. "But she'll run okay for now. Might want to refill the fuel tank . . ."

"We've got some in the cellar," Prince said, mystified. He hopped off the porch, went to the car, and unlatched the hood. His head bent as he studied the engine. "Hold on, is that—"

"Just a rosin patch." Beatrice went to his side.

"Looks good," Prince admitted.

"You'll need a new valve eventually," said Beatrice.

Hero whispered to Benedick: "What in God's name is she wearing?"

"Well." Prince lowered the hood, then put his hands on his waist. Nonplussed, he shifted his jaw and glanced at Beatrice. "Honestly, that's a great patch job. Soon as I grab some fuel, we can hit the road. Where'd you learn to fix cars?"

"I've worked on my stepfather's farm the past few summers," she said. "He hasn't bought a new truck or tractor in about a decade, so they were always breaking down."

"No kidding. Can you drive, too?"

"Obviously."

"Say"—Prince turned to Benedick, Hero, and Claude— "why don't we have Beatrice ride back with Ben?"

"No," Ben said immediately, appalled.

Hero laughed. "Goodness. You look like we're asking you to ride with a tiger. She won't bite. Will you, Bea?"

Beatrice aimed a very tigerlike smirk at Benedick. "I'd be happy to drive myself, only I don't know the area very well." Not an explicitly challenging comment, but he felt challenged.

"Fine." He lifted a shoulder in an offhand shrug.

"Honestly," said Beatrice, "you won't even know I'm there."

Already, having been acquainted with her less than an hour, Benedick found that incredibly hard to believe. Hero's small hand gripped his elbow. She whispered, "Try to keep a lid on the illegal booze-running talk, okay? I want to ease her in, not smack her in the face with it. But be friendly. Tell her how nice she looks; girls like that. And for God's sake, don't talk about your book."

Exasperated, Benedick asked, "Should I compliment her on how economical it was for her to wear one piece of clothing for her entire person or how the grease stains match her eyes?"

Hero slugged him hard in the arm, in the same breath turning to smile at Claude and asking if he'd like any refreshment for the road.

Benedick meanwhile gave Beatrice a wholly unperturbed smile and stepped off the porch as though he weren't bracing for the short drive ahead.

CHAPTER 5
COURTESY IS A TURNCOAT

Benedick knew the Manhasset station well from all his rides back and forth between Hey Nonny Nonny and Stony Creek Academy. The station wasn't big; his first time blundering through, he and his zozzled friends had complained at being dropped in the middle of nowhere to be robbed or some other hapless travesty. *Follow the black flower.*

Benedick saw Claude off on the 2:17. Claude had turned downright chipper, glowing pink as a spring tulip in the wake of Hero's attention.

Benedick had no doubt they'd be seeing him again.

The train chugged off, gaining speed with a clattering groan. Beatrice had elected to stay in the car, thank the white whiskey gods. Benedick turned from the platform to go and froze.

Farther down, near the station building, a figure leaned one shoulder on a wood pillar; the smoke trailing from his hand was the only hint he wasn't frozen in an unseen picture frame.

John Morello.

He had a thin suitcase by his feet; he must have gotten off the last outbound train. Indecisiveness paralyzed Benedick. Any moment John might see Benedick and know he'd in turn been seen. John and Prince Morello's relationship was a slimy black barrel in which Benedick tried not to stick his hand if he could help it. John and Prince shared an immigrant Italian mother, but John's father was a mobster bred straight from Sicily. The kind of family blood that tended to show up on your hands sooner or later.

The first time Benedick met John, Prince had offered this by way of introduction: "Stay out of his way."

However, given the events of the morning, Benedick had a feeling he was already in John's way by virtue of proximity.

Benedick strode forward. "What ho, John."

John's gaze shifted. He gave Benedick the old head to toe, his expression flickering with some inscrutable emotion that might have been amusement. "Hello, Scott. Rough night?"

"Most of mine are," Benedick quipped. "As I like it. What brings you to Manhasset?"

"There's a Masquerade tomorrow in Flower Hill," said John,

blowing out a stream of smoke. "I have a standing invitation, you may *recall*."

Benedick did *recall*. "Of course! You're early, is all. Headed to Hey Nonny Nonny? You're welcome to a ride."

"Not tonight," John said. "My family manages a few of the warehouses on the coast. There's been some trouble the past few weeks. I'll be sorting that out first."

Benedick's stomach twisted as he remembered the black mark on the crates they'd picked up. Then Prince had drawn the attention of a multimillion-dollar Italian racket to Leo's humble enterprise. The real question was why Prince, usually so careful, had done something so careless?

Benedick would not have been at all surprised if John, only nineteen, had been put in charge of a rum-running operation and the trouble that came with it, but he suspected John's arrival was much more to do with who might be causing said trouble.

"Don't suppose you've heard anything?" John asked quietly. The cigarette hung near his face, smoke trailing up like a question mark.

A cool customer, that was what Maggie called him.

Benedick considered that generous.

"No," said Benedick. "No, I haven't. Prince and I haven't been tailing coast routes since last fall."

"I see." John eyed the Model T, then tossed his cigarette to the ground and crushed it with his heel. "I suppose I'll see you tomorrow night then." He bent and grabbed his suitcase and strode away from the station toward a Buick Battistini speedster, silver as the moon, that had pulled up nearby.

All the car's headlights were intact, yet Benedick was positive he recognized one of the two men waiting for John as the same one who'd flashed his grimy-toothed smile at them this morning.

Benedick hustled back to the Model T and found Beatrice had moved from the backseat to the front, her boots propped on the dash. "Well, that took long enough," she said.

He dropped into the driver's seat and glared at her. "Look here—"

"Hey, Mac."

Outside his window a man hovered, his hat pulled low over his eyes. Benedick pretended his stomach hadn't taken a colossal leap into his throat.

"You're one of the Nonny's runners, right?" the man asked.

"Yes," Benedick managed. Relatively speaking. He cleared his throat. "Yes, what do you want? What is it?"

The man kept his chin ducked. He held up a folded piece of paper. "Got a tip for you. Five bucks."

"I'll give you ten if you'll go away as quickly as possible." Benedick fished in his pocket for his wallet. Though he was no doubt soon to be cut off and begging for his pennies, he still had a decent stash from his former life among the well-to-do.

The ten-dollar bill disappeared in the man's coat almost

faster than Benedick had pulled it free. Benedick took the folded tip with a sigh, and the man nodded gruffly and left.

"Are you thick in the head?" Beatrice asked. "He might have blown his nose in that, and you just paid ten whole dollars for it. Then again, someone like you probably does blow their nose in dollar bills, so it doesn't make much difference—"

"Whatever compels you to think I care to hear your opinions on my actions, kindly locate that inner switch and turn it off."

Truth be told, his brain was beginning to crackle and spit, much the way an engine might, sucking up the last fumes of fuel before it gives out entirely. However, there was not a Popsicle's chance in hell Benedick would admit that to Beatrice.

He unfolded the paper and read: Mosquito Cove, sundown, white lightning."

It was a real tip. He congratulated himself. No snot in sight. On the other hand, something itched at his poor cracking lemon that made him think it wasn't a good one.

"And?" Beatrice asked a bit coldly. "Get your money's worth?"

"Absolutely." He lied. He chewed his bottom lip, then searched under the dash. After a minute his fingers located the secret latch and unhinged the bottom paneling to pull out a worn map.

He spread it over the steering wheel.

The layout of Long Island had been meticulously marked and colored by Leo and then by Prince. Benedick was only half literate in their code—but enough to get the gist.

"How fascinating!" Beatrice looked over his shoulder. "This is a bootlegger's map, isn't it?"

She was aggravatingly nosy and even more aggravatingly clever.

"Wouldn't you like to know?"

"I would, truly."

Benedick paused. Perhaps, he conceded grudgingly, she was less rude than she was appallingly direct and, if altogether too intense for polite society, then at least unintentionally.

Then she kept talking: "Not that I have any personal fondness for alcohol, but I don't believe in legislating morals either. If Uncle Leo is a bootlegger, it's a sin I'm willing to forgive—"

"Sit back and let me think," he said, rolling his eyes. Hero had said not to overwhelm her, right? (If Beatrice Clark could in fact be overwhelmed at all. At this point Benedick had his doubts.)

Beatrice sighed and shifted over to her side.

Mosquito Cove was circled in blue on the map, which, if Benedick remembered correctly, meant neutral territory, a stop for a handful of river hawks, but a black X near the shore meant a grounded seller. Usually a warehouse or still, but in this case . . . Benedick squinted at the tiny S written above the X and the little sketched leaf.

"Sage," he muttered.

"What's that?" asked Beatrice.

He pressed his lips against a deep sigh. So—not a good tip after all. On the scale of best to scald-your-soul poisonous,

Sage's moonshine was one of the least toxic but also the most disgusting. Everyone with a toe in the Long Island racket knew him; he was too pathetic to get taken out, too much of a snitch for anyone to trust for more than bottom-of-the-barrel bailouts.

Even so, there'd be no Italians involved, and sure, Sage's take was the utter worst, but Prince was a genius at disguising nasty panther piss off the river. The results of swallowing one of his cocktails were borderline unholy, and Benedick meant that in the best possible way. With Prince's help, even Sage's moonshine would pull its weight at the Masquerade.

Benedick folded up the map. "I know just where it is." He cranked the engine and set them down the road. The floor was hot under his still slightly damp shoes, the steering wheel vibrating under his palms. The noise was pleasantly loud and raucous, but not enough to drown out Beatrice's voice.

"Are we going after this tip then?" Beatrice asked, sitting up straight.

"*I* am. I'm dropping you off at the lane, where you can put that strapping footwear to use and walk back."

"I'll come along, if it's all the same to you."

"It is not the same to me. The difference provided by your absence is roughly the breadth of the Atlantic Ocean in fact."

"Why not? You might like to have me there, wherever you're going."

"Where I'm going," he said, "is to secure some branch water

off a reprobate on the shady side of the East River. Hardly suitable activity for a pretty young lady such as yourself." He gave her coveralls a pointed glance.

"Stand down, Lancelot."

"You'll only get in the way, and frankly no one's going to give me imported hooch with you next to me."

"Because I'm a girl? I'm wearing pants. I'm covered in whiskey, oil, and a bit of dirt. No one will know the difference. Watch this." She sat back in the seat, spreading her legs wide, and adopted a fierce scowl. She pitched her voice low and gruff with a southern slur. "Call me a nancy again, ya hick, and I'll give ya a piece of chin music to next Wednesday!" She swore as if it were nothing, fist curled, then turned to him with a bright smile. "How do you like that?"

Benedick blinked at her.

Crude or not, if she thought she didn't look feminine, she was wrong. Her face, for one thing: this overeager quip of a face, with a noticeable overbite and a tiny, ridiculous, freckle-spattered nose, not to mention the absurdly huge dimples. Her corkscrew curls, even stuffed mostly in a hat, were like a weedy nimbus around her head. She looked like a pretty little rodent.

She continued. "Also, if you'll permit me to be outspoken for a moment—"

"There is no one in a fifty-mile radius who could hope to outspeak you, Miss Clark."

"—you look rather tired." She finished as if he hadn't spoken. "Strung out. Suppose things go south. Suppose you'd like some backup assistance."

He was closing in on thirty-some-odd hours without proper sleep, with naught but the exhaust of coffee and brandy to carry him through the next few, but he'd manage. He always managed. "Why do you care so much to come?"

"I'm interested, that's all."

He snorted.

"Also *concerned*," she amended. "From one human being to the next."

"That's not what you ought to be concerned about. You hardly know me, and what kind of girl lets a stranger drive her off into the countryside alone?"

She considered this. She assessed him quite seriously, then said, "I'm not worried."

The last resort of course was to put his foot down and say, *Over my dead body*, but he needed to be in finer form to wage the battle it would take to refuse her. And there was the tiny hope that the venture would prove so distasteful it would cure her of her obnoxious curiosity once and for all. "Fine. If it means so very much to you."

"You'll be glad. I'm useful in nearly every situation, except dance parties."

CHAPTER 6

A JADE'S TRICK

Beatrice could bear just about anything as long as she could understand it. Getting kicked out of Miss Nightingale's and her consequent stay at St. Mary's were by no means pleasant, but they were endurable because they were a reasonable consequence to factors in her life that, while perhaps out of her control, were comprehensible. Fixable. Once you knew the problem, you could solve the problem.

Which was what made someone like Benedick Scott so infuriating.

Just when she thought she had him pinned, some new element of his character reared its head, soundly contradicting the last conclusion and forcing her to start all over again.

They sat side by side on a fallen log, just off the shore of Mosquito Cove. The lapping bay water was visible through low-swooping branches and reed canary grass. The earth was black and slick from a rainy spring; insects chorused in the thick woods around them.

Benedick sat slightly forward. His vest was plain but finely tailored, and although it now looked to be in near ruin, he still had it on, like it hadn't crossed his mind to simply wear a shirt without one, a juxtaposition that seemed to represent him well.

He was not handsome, nor was he ugly. He was slender like a whip. His eyebrows, a few shades darker than his hair, slashed sturdily above his eyes, furrowed then in a frown. Beatrice was tempted to compare him to a weasel, but then there was his hair: too long and the color of sunshine, rippling wheat, and Yankee pride.

She flicked an ant off her knee. "What are we waiting for now—"

"Shh." His hand darted up.

Beatrice's mouth pinched. His rudeness meandered back and forth as well, from dismissively blunt to saccharinely patronizing.

"Hidden scouts," he said in a low voice. "Mostly anyone who would tip off agents. That houseboat belongs to a moonshine dealer." He nodded down the shore toward a run-down houseboat anchored to an even more run-down dock, both looking as though they'd emerged from some godforsaken swamp, mossy and rotting. "The tip said sundown, but the only supplier scheduled to be here at that time on a Friday is Sage, and he's stationary, for the most part. So sundown either means there's a new shark in town, and that's why his lackeys are off selling tips, or it's some kind of setup."

Well, well. Perhaps Benedick Scott was not as dumb as his earlier nonchalance suggested. Yet another contradiction: astute and blasé. Beatrice said, "Either way is a risk then, but I assume we came all the way here for a reason."

"Correct. But we're not going to risk anything. We will buy some of Sage's stock at roughly three times what it's worth, to keep things easy, and we will do it now—before sunset. I wouldn't arrange anything with a new supplier without Prince."

Arrogant or humble?

Not to mention that he'd been perfectly demeaning in other ways, but when he did elect to answer her, he did so in a straightforward manner that did not condescend to suggest she wouldn't understand him.

He was beginning to give her a headache.

But she still worked to understand because that was what her brain did. "Why Prince? If it's my uncle's speakeasy, don't you need his approval as well?"

"If I have Prince's approval, then I have your uncle's. Leo trusts him."

"He's awfully young."

Benedick slid his eyes over to hers, the uninteresting color of mud and bruised with tiredness but, at their center, bright as lights.

"Not so young. Anyway, he's been helping Leo since he was twelve. It's only this year that he does most of the trips alone because—"

"Because Aunt Anna died." Beatrice finished his thought.

Benedick's expression shuttered, as if a light had gone out. "Yes."

For a long moment there was quiet in the sticky warmth of Mosquito Cove, and though Beatrice hadn't known Aunt Anna well enough to feel the loss the way her uncle or cousin surely did, a tiny part of that sadness belonged to her, too.

But what was Benedick's excuse for looking briefly gutted at the reminder of Anna's death?

"Prince lives at Hey Nonny Nonny," she said. "But you attend prep school in Brooklyn, don't you? With that other boy, Claude." Beatrice tried, honestly she did, to sound polite. The word *interrogative* had been known to describe her conversational skills. *Nosy* was another favorite. But how could she be expected to learn anything if she didn't ask?

Benedick stood. He squinted at the houseboat. "Attend*ed*, past tense. I live at Hey Nonny Nonny, too." Which explained exactly nothing, but then he was off again, picking his way along an almost invisible trail, and Beatrice had no choice but to follow. "It's been quiet for half an hour. We ought to be clear."

The dock had been built when the water level was higher, so the dilapidated vessel bobbed several feet below them. A wind chime swayed in front of the cabin door, level with Benedick's waist. Beatrice stayed back a few feet as he used a long stick that had been leaning on a post to knock against the door.

"Not home!" came a cranky voice.

"Come on, Sage."

Finally the door opened. Sage glowered, his yellow eyes crusted. His forehead was white and smooth in contrast with the leathery red of his neck. His pants were on, luckily, but up top he was only wearing a thin nightshirt with a stain across his wiry middle. He shoved a hat jingling with fishing gear on his head. "Benedick Scott, that you? Been awhile. Haven't seen Prince neither since, ah . . .'"

"Last Thanksgiving."

Sage's eyebrows arched as he caught sight of Beatrice. "And who's this? Ben, you know right well this ain't a lady's work."

Benedick's gaze, a talented combination of annoyed and smug, swung back at her. *I was right*, it said.

"I'm interested in the chemistry of distilleries," Beatrice said.

Sage still looked doubtful but nodded to Benedick. "Yer here for some lightning? I never heard nothin'."

"We're taking in some extra stock for the Masquerade tomorrow. Are you coming?"

"Shoot. Hey Nonny Nonny's too fancy and 'falutin for my tastes."

"You're the picture of class in my eyes. Do you have extra store we can buy off you?"

"Sorry. 'Fraid I'm fresh out."

Benedick's jaw tightened. "Sage, I can see the barrels on your deck."

Sage sighed. "I'm telling you this only 'cause I like ya, Ben. And I'm sorry about it. Truly. The short of it is, I was paid a lot of money not to sell to you two anymore, and I needed the cash. That's it. Prince is a nice kid, works hard as hell, but nice don't feed me in the morning, if you get my drift."

Benedick said nothing, then crouched on one knee so he was eye level with Sage. "How about you let us handle any rivals for your fine product and we compensate your cooperation?" He pulled from his pocket a fold of bills, held together by a silver clasp, and passed it in front of Sage's face like bait.

Sage eyed the cash. "All right then. Come on. I got three jugs right here you can have."

Benedick braced on the deck railing and hopped on board. Beatrice followed, jumping past the hand he'd turned to extend, and landed beside him without help.

Sage rooted around and set three jugs in front of them, each with a 2 stenciled onto the glass and filled with mostly clear liquid.

"I want a sample," said Benedick, experimentally lifting one of the two-gallon jugs, holding it up to the light. To Beatrice's surprise, he passed it to her. She tried to look intelligent about her examination but wrinkled her nose at the flecks of who knew what swimming inside it.

Sage shrugged. He took a tin mug and uncorked a nearby

barrel, letting a stream of clear liquid ring into the likely dirty container. Once it was half filled, he handed it to Benedick, then went ahead and filled a cup for himself.

"You're not actually going to drink that," Beatrice said.

"Only one way to know if it's good, sweetheart"—Benedick, all money-voice and glinting yellow hair, tilted his head at her— "and that's by drinking."

"Wait." Beatrice set down the jug. "At least test it first to see what chemicals you're ingesting. Do you have matches?"

"What?"

"Matches. Hold still—" She reached into his vest pocket and, ignoring his recoil at her touch, retrieved a small book of matches. She struck a match over the bottom of her boot and lit the cup in his hand. "Different chemicals burn with different colors; yellow or red means lead or fusel oils."

The flame, dancing atop the moonshine, was mostly blue.

"However," she added, "blue won't hide the presence of methanol, which burns clear." Tugging her sleeve over her palm, she slapped her hand flat over the rim of the cup to smother the flame and gave the contents a few hearty shakes. After, she peered inside. "Large bubbles with a short duration indicate a higher alcohol content, while smaller bubbles that disappear slowly indicate the increasing presence of water . . . and other ingredients."

Sage scratched his cheek. "And that's what you call chemistry, is it?"

Benedick narrowed his eyes. "Well? Miss Clark?"

She wiped her palm on her pants leg. "It seems fine, in the loosest sense of the word."

"'Course it is!" Sage's shiny cheeks reddened. To prove it, he downed his cup in one large gulp.

"Cheers," Benedick told him. "Give me those," he muttered at her, snatching back his matches. He knocked back a mouthful from his own cup. "Jesus," he wheezed, pressing the back of his hand over his lips.

Beatrice pried the cup from his fingers and took a sip. Her tongue shriveled. "This will either loosen people up or kill them."

"And that's when we pick their pockets—" Benedick froze at the distant sound of a motorboat echoing down the bay toward their spot in the cove.

"Uh-oh," Sage muttered. "Here comes trouble."

A two-seat motorboat appeared and cut through the water straight for them. Benedick grasped Beatrice by the shoulder, hard enough that she winced with pain. "Ouch—" He pushed her down among Sage's crates and barrels and dragged one over to block her from view. "What's going on?"

"Be quiet," he said. The dark quality to his tone made her hold her tongue, for once. "In case it's the feds, there's a coffee can taped to the car's steering column with bribe money—or bail money, if they're straight."

He stepped back just as the boat pulled to the other side of the dock. The motor cut, blanketing them in stillness. Beatrice shifted so she could see through a gap between two barrels.

A lanky young man stepped onto the dock. He grinned when he saw Benedick. "My, my. Look who's back from Stony Creek." He turned to Sage. "I believe you were instructed not to sell to Hey Nonny Nonny." As if to emphasize his words, two hulking men followed him out of the boat.

One of them was the very same gentleman who had given Benedick his "tip." Beatrice's stomach made an unpleasant twist.

"Minsky, is that you?" Sage asked too loudly, squinting. "See, I knew you said don't sell to the Nonny's runners, and this fella here told me his name was Jimmy. Guess it's my own fault thinking everyone's as honest as me."

The same young man rolled his eyes.

Benedick stayed on Sage's front deck, hands in his pockets as if he hadn't a care in the world. Beatrice hoped he was smart enough to understand the trap he'd fallen into and keep his head down. "You must be in the doghouse, Connie, old boy, if they sent you to baby-sit a third-rate river port."

The young man—Connie or Minsky or whoever he was—soured. "It also means nobody's watching too closely." His musclemen smiled at the permission. They stepped closer.

Benedick took a step back, then stopped. His eyes darted almost imperceptibly to where Beatrice sat, and he deliberately moved away from her and thus toward his all-too-eager adversaries. This small act of unexpected chivalry made it all the harder to watch as the two men reached down, one grabbing him by the collar, the other gripping his arm. They hoisted him up, yanked his long sleeves past his wrists, crossed his arms around his middle, and tied the ends behind his back. The result was rather genius; Benedick was hunched, pinched; the fabric of his shirt was too expensive to rip easily despite the strain.

Beatrice crawled toward the cabin of the boat. No self-respecting bootlegger, even one as indolent as Sage, would hawk liquor on the East River without a gun. She just had to find it.

Benedick's eyes darted to where she crawled among the barrels and crates. She flapped her hand in a talking gesture. Put that mouth of his where it might be useful.

"I'm touched, really, at the level of ingenuity and commitment," Benedick managed, breathless. "Honestly, a good old-fashioned beating would not be remiss in my case—"

"Thank God for this," the second man muttered around a thick Eastern European accent. He shoved a soiled strip of burlap across Benedick's mouth, pulled back hard enough to make him gag, then secured a knot at the nape of his neck.

"I told the boys to keep an eye out for you," Minsky was saying. "Rather hard to get the runaround on Prince, but I knew once you showed your long-winded mug, we'd be able to deliver our message." Minsky tossed a hand toward the river. Benedick was dragged along wooden planks and held over the dock's end, his feet barely able to hang on. The man holding him winked. Minsky walked over, hands clasped behind his back.

There! Leaning on the cabin doorframe—

Beatrice elbowed past Sage and grabbed the sawed-off shotgun. The shot she fired over Minsky's head broke apart the quiet afternoon. Minsky jumped; Benedick was nearly dropped.

Beatrice leaped from the boat onto the dock. Minsky's imperious glower slackened; he blinked in surprise, then frowned. The stares were nothing Beatrice wasn't used to; if anything, she'd grown adept at using them to her advantage. She swung the still-warm gun up to her shoulder. "Hands off."

"Just so you know," Sage said loudly, "I did not, I repeat, I did *not* give her my gun. She took it *without* my permission."

Minsky turned to the man not holding Benedick. "You have a gun; use it, you idiot."

"But"—the man hesitated, even as he shrank from Minsky's glare—"even in pants, I cannot shoot at a girl."

"She's shooting at you!" Minsky snapped.

Without moving from her stance, Beatrice asked, "Are there scattershots in this gun?"

A pause; then Sage answered, "Why, no. Just re'g'lar slugs—"

Bang. Benedick's captor lost his hat and his grip. Benedick landed backfirst in the water. Beatrice hoped he knew how to swim.

"Get back in your boat," Beatrice commanded. "Or the next one I aim a little lower."

Under the dock, some sort of thrashing was happening, so Benedick was at least attempting to swim, if not succeeding.

Minsky and his men hesitated.

"I don't mind putting holes in you," she said, with another step forward, letting Virginia seep into her voice. "They'll send me back to St. Mary's, sure, but they warned my uncle, said I wasn't right in the head, said I threw a doctor out the window, and"—she pumped the fore end up and back: *click, click*—"I did." The used cartridge clattered by her feet. "Leave your guns on the dock. And then get out of here, or I'll shoot your motor right now and you'll stay all night."

Whether it was the gun or the maniacal glint in her eye, they listened. Each of Minsky's men set a pistol on the wood planks. Beatrice narrowed her eyes at Minsky himself. He half laughed, as though he couldn't quite believe any of this was happening. "I don't carry a gun."

One of his men yanked a cord, and the motor started. She kept the shotgun trained on the retreating boat. Minsky sat straight, watching her. Hard to say, as the distance between them grew, but he seemed somewhat less furious than he ought to have been.

Beatrice ran down the dock. "Mr. Scott? Benedick, are you—" She found him crawling up the marshy shore a few yards off, looking not unlike a rag at the end of a washboard, but alive.

Beatrice turned back to Sage. "Hurry. Get me two of those

jugs." She didn't think she could carry three; otherwise she would have.

Sage obeyed quickly, and Beatrice felt sorry to exchange such a useful companion as the shotgun for four gallons of half-poisonous hooch. "You owe us another jug," Beatrice told Sage. "Don't think I'll forget either." Gripping the handles, she hurried down the shore toward Benedick. He was on his hands and knees, coughing up brackish water. He'd managed to wrestle off his shirt and vest and wore only a soaked-through undershirt; he was also missing a shoe.

"Are you all right?" Beatrice set down one of the jugs and knelt next to him. "If you can stand up, the sooner we can get out of here, the better."

"I'm fine," he said hoarsely. The gag hung around his neck, but faint red marks indented his cheeks. She hauled him to his feet, then picked up the second jug. They entered the thick foliage, and she bent to avoid a low-swinging branch. Beech limbs leaned in and intermingled to make a choking vault over their heads. Even with four gallons of whiskey burning her shoulders, Beatrice occasionally had to wait for Benedick to catch up.

The Model T appeared at the end of the trail like an oasis. Beatrice put the jugs in the backseat, and Benedick went to the passenger's side without a word. The old Ford was cantankerous; all the engine fluids had pooled to one side with Benedick's wonky parking job. Beatrice cranked in front of the grille, and it took an inordinate amount of coaxing to get Benedick focused enough to operate the choke and ignition. When at last the engine was persuaded to start, she slid behind the wheel. Eyes closed, Benedick muttered, "You can drive," as if she weren't already driving.

She shot him a worried glance as they sputtered forward. Though she kept an eye on the side mirrors, just in case, she went slowly over the dirt road. Benedick's face had gone ashen, and it wasn't long before shivers began to jerk through him and spasm up his shoulders. He pressed his lips together, fists clenching.

Beatrice braked slowly and pulled to the side of the road.

"What—" he asked, or tried to before opening the door and vomiting up some of Mosquito Cove and that shot of Sage's moonshine. The shivering returned, worse than before.

She put a hand on his hunched, trembling shoulder. His skin was clammy and cold. "Take it easy. I think you're experiencing a mild form of shell shock, not to mention the repercussions of exhaustion. Possibly the beginnings of dehydration, too. I need you to take off all the clothes you're comfortable with."

With a small groan he shifted toward her. The glare he summoned was nothing to sneeze at, considering his condition. "N-no—"

She slapped away his hands as he tried to stop her from tugging up his undershirt. It went over his head and landed with a glop on the car floor. "There you go," she said. "Pants and socks, too, if you don't mind."

With a look to suggest she'd be more than happy to help if he didn't get going, she left him to manage on his own. Then she rummaged under the seat for anything that might serve as a makeshift blanket. She fished out a worn tarpaulin cloth probably used to cover the engine when the rain was bad and glanced up as Benedick fumbled out of the car and tripped free of his soaked pants.

She felt no embarrassment at the flash of his bare skin. The instant he'd begun exhibiting symptoms, he'd become a patient, not a boy.

She spread the cloth along the front seat of the car; it was rough and stank of mildew, but it was dry. "Lie down, please."

He grimaced and situated himself. Beatrice tucked the tarpaulin around him as if she were swaddling an infant. His head went near the open door on the passenger's side; his knees bent, and his feet propped easily on the driver's door. His eyes closed.

After laying out his wet clothes on the engine-hot hood, she came behind him, her stomach near the top of his head, and pressed her fingers gently to his neck. "Your skin is cool. No fever at least." She monitored his pulse against her own, kept watch on the twitch of his eyes under his lids. Her own breathing was clear; her mind, sharp. This was her element. The higher the stakes, the more her faculties calmed.

She hungered for these hiccups of mortality, could sense, almost, when a cough was just a cough and when it signaled an oncoming head cold. The farmhands had been good to let her treat them when they got heat stroke or felt ill; plus the estate vet had allowed her to assist with livestock births when he needed a hand.

But where she'd truly thrived was first at school, then at St. Mary's with embarrassed girls suffering menstrual cramps or even nongendered illnesses, wanting to avoid the touch of a middle-aged man and his judgmental eye.

Beatrice kneaded her fingertips into Benedick's temple and above the curve of his ear. Eastern medicine believed certain pressure points, when engaged, could relieve pain. His skin was fine and soft there; her hands, by comparison, were scratched from the woods, grease in the wrinkles and scars on her knuckles. Not a lady's hands.

After a few minutes Benedick's shivering subsided to an occasional tremor. His bright eyes blinked rapidly, then focused on her. A small line appeared between his brows. "Did you really throw a doctor out the window?"

"No, I threw a clock out the window, which was admittedly *near* the doctor's head, but I wasn't aiming for him. I was just trying to get his attention."

"Hmm." He wriggled inside the cloth. "I feel, ugh, *warm*."

"Slow down." She pressed on his shoulders. "I'll help you up. Not too fast, or you'll get dizzy again."

With her arm as leverage, he shifted upright, keeping the tarpaulin around him. "What time is it?"

"We've a good hour or two before the sun goes down."

With a vague grunt he slumped lower, the tarpaulin coming up to his ears. He stared out the windshield at nothing.

Beatrice said, "We can rest here a minute, but you need to drink something. Water, not Sage's moonshine."

"Do we have any of Sage's moonshine?"

"Four gallons."

He frowned. "You . . ."

"You're welcome. Given you've had a bit of a rough afternoon, I won't make you admit I was right."

"What?"

"About how glad you'd be to have me along." She smiled and shut the car door. She gathered his wet clothes off the hood—a tiny bit drier—and returned to the driver's seat. The car started much nicer this time. Half her day had been spent inside it, with Benedick. The air was close and ripe with alcohol, which had grown strangely familiar, of all the bizarre things to get attached to on her first day. "There's no need for us to be enemies at any rate. Saving your life must count for something."

"That's stretching things. They weren't going to kill me."

"I take it this wasn't your first time meeting them?"

Benedick sighed, shuffling a hand through his damp hair. Since he was no longer vomiting or shaking, Beatrice felt the need to avert her eyes from his bare chest. He roused himself quickly, to give him credit, like someone who'd been taught not to slouch.

That inner spring was the first thing about him she could relate to.

"I suppose Conrade Minsky could be called one of my ene-mies. Sometimes our schools played each other in sports and the like. But it's his mother who's got it out for Hey Nonny Nonny. Mary Louise Minsky. Their family owns a theater house in Great Neck. After the war her husband played racy films on the week-ends, then started serving beer and vodka. When he died, Mary Louise took over. She tried playing respectable films at first, but when that didn't work, they offered more . . . daring shows. Vaude-ville performers, burlesque dancers." Benedick shrugged. "I guess Anna and Mary Louise went to school together when they were girls, and they were rivals even then. Minsky's Ragland and Hey Nonny Nonny have always been the top joints in Nassau County, but it was never a deadly rivalry, just a constant one-upping."

Now Anna was dead, and the Minsky family was clearly still at it. "That's rotten of them to go after you like that."

"No honor code for bootleggers."

"I'm sure that's not true. Not for all of them. My uncle, for one, would be honest about it."

Benedick looked at her in that thoughtful, narrow-eyed way again. "How can you be sure? How long has it been since you've seen your uncle?"

Beatrice blushed. "Ten years, I think. I was eight when my father died, and we visited before then. . . . But it doesn't matter. I know he is because he took me in when he didn't have to, even after the society warned him he shouldn't because I was going to ruin—" She stopped, her throat tightening with agitation. "Anyway, I know what a good man is."

"Well, you're right." Benedick looked out the window. "He is a good man. And an honest bootlegger."

Beatrice turned on the blessedly paved road of Prospect Avenue. The coast of Hempstead Bay stayed on their right, its gray-green color flashing out at them occasionally through the trees. They'd driven by violet-studded farms and clusters of storefronts on the way here and now approached a village of huddled houses against the edge of the turnpike.

Here and there some sprawling estate, a glittering mansion rising up above the manicured hills, would catch Beatrice by surprise. All in all, it was not the sort of setting she'd come to expect for a speakeasy. Not that she'd spent much time in the underground gin mills of Manhattan either.

"Where is the speakeasy?" she asked. "I didn't see a storefront or an entrance or anything."

"Well, that's the point with a speakeasy. You have to know it's there."

Beatrice considered the idea that she had become, by association, a person who knew. "How is it—" she started to ask.

But Benedick spoke at the same time, with the exact same words: "How is it—"

"Sorry," they said again together. That annoyed Beatrice.

Benedick, too, if his pursed mouth was any indication.

"Miss Clark"—he tried once more—"how is it you knew what to do with the cloth?"

"Oh. The swaddling mostly treats the shock, which I believe was caused more from adrenaline, though I doubt that water was warm. The point was to keep your blood—"

"No, I mean, *why* do you know all of that? Why, for that matter, is your aim with a shotgun so good? I find your unlimited competence unsettling."

"My stepfather owned a farm. We shot cans sometimes. Or, you know, dinner."

"How barbaric."

She shot him a withering look. "Again, you're welcome."

"That only explains the gun savvy. Not the cloth or the fingers."

"I'm studying to be a doctor."

"A real doctor?"

"Of course a real doctor! I would have liked to attend the Woman's Medical College of the New York Infirmary this fall, only—only I didn't finish school. I had a semester left before I was sent to St. Mary's."

"What did you do to get sent to St. Mary's?"

"I ran out of money," she said, more viciously than she intended. She could always tell when her demeanor veered toward the dragonly because people tended to edge out of her way, as Benedick did now. "I'm sorry—no, I am not that sorry, come to think of it. I am still very angry about it. I didn't have enough money to pay my last semester's tuition, but I knew if I left the city, I'd never make it back, so my crime, my wayward-ness, if you will, was being homeless and alone."

"Then how did you pay for the first years of your school-ing?" he asked cautiously.

"When my mother died, she left me a small inheritance, and her will *specifically* said it was to be used for a school that would allow me to attend medical college, which always set my stepfather wrong. Partly because he wouldn't trust a woman as his doctor, he told me, but mostly because not a penny of my mother's money went to him." Grudgingly Beatrice added, "And I suppose he misses her. He's always seemed angry at her for dying, and I get to be punished for staying alive. I guess. I struggle with psychology. It's all too wishy-washy to be considered properly medical, in my mind. Gosh. I'm talking too much. Anyway, you probably get to go to any college you like, don't you?"

"If I like," he said, so quietly she wasn't sure she'd heard him properly.

"What's that?"

He didn't answer, but her brain had already been set on the track, fitting in the clues of the day like a jigsaw puzzle. "You sent Mr. Blaine back to Brooklyn to take his regents exam and attend his graduation, and you said you went to the same school. But you stayed here."

Oh, she had his number now.

And he knew it. His mouth had gone all thin, a battle-worn look to his eyes; she had a feeling she was about to press *his* dragon button.

Not that it stopped the wave of opinion from falling out of her mouth. "Do you mean to suggest that you won't be finishing school either, by *choice*?"

"I'm not suggesting anything that pertains to you."

"Isn't that typical? What's worse is once you've had your good time for the summer, someone will write a check or nudge a friend, and you'll still have your options laid out like a banquet."

His face darkened. "Have me all figured out, don't you?"

The suggestion punctured her cloud of irritation. She didn't have him figured at all, lest she forget. But it was galling to see him so flippantly disregard something she'd have given her left arm to achieve.

"Where are my clothes?"

"What?" she asked.

"My clothes. We're almost back."

Without her realizing it, the winding lane to Hey Nonny Nonny had appeared ahead of them. She handed him his undershirt and pants. He wriggled into them beneath the tarpaulin, cursing under his breath, bumping into her. At last his head poked out, and he blew his hair off his forehead. "Let me do the talking," he said.

They approached the house, which looked a bit sinister in

the fading light. Hero stood on the porch, Prince sitting on the steps in front of her. Uncle Leo was in the same chair he'd occupied this morning. All three perked up at their arrival.

Beatrice parked the Model T beside Uncle Leo's Lambda.

Hero was off the porch first, but Prince was right behind her like a tall echo. "Where have you been?" Hero asked. "Prince was back hours ago. We thought you'd broken down and we searched every road to the train station but couldn't find you."

Benedick opened his door and stood up, keeping one elbow on the doorframe, the other on the Ford's roof, shedding his exhaustion like a winter coat. His eyes brightened, and his pale, clammy skin managed to defy medicine and glow. "Have I got a story for you!"

And it was a story—in that it was not quite the truth.

But it wasn't a lie either.

Listening to him, Beatrice experienced the afternoon all over again, but this time there was no real danger. There was a boy who'd had a terrific idea that went a little off the rails and a girl who was a good sport and just the kind of sidekick you'd like to have along. Beatrice heard herself laugh when Benedick described her shooting off a man's hat, but it hadn't seemed that funny when it actually happened.

There was a sunniness in his words that somehow even disguised his appearance, erasing the boy shaking with exhaustion, flattening all his mercurial layers into one outfit of razzle-dazzle.

But the razzle-dazzle was also real. That was the most baffling part of all. He was this, too.

She let him do it, not only because she came out looking all right in his story, not a clock-throwing ruin of a girl, but also because Benedick's talking about her as if she were already one of them *made* her one of them.

Words.

What a tricky, tangled science.

Uncle Leo's booming laugh rang out. He slapped Benedick on the back so hard the latter nearly fell over. Only Beatrice saw his white-knuckled grip on the side of the car, the tremor through his arm.

Uncle Leo came to Beatrice's side. "Hullo, sweetheart. Welcome to Hey Nonny Nonny, eh? Ha."

Beatrice liked being called sweetheart. She liked it when Prince asked her how the car had run and if she'd had any problems with it. She even liked how Hero called Benedick a dickens' worth of trouble but kissed him as though she'd wanted trouble as an early birthday present.

Then Benedick glanced back at her and their eyes met and Beatrice realized the un-storied truth bound them in a private way she didn't care for at all.

CHAPTER 7
NOT TILL A HOT JANUARY

Crickets. Their loud chirping through Beatrice's cracked window made her think for a moment that she'd gone back to the farm. But this room was different; bigger, for one. She shook off the tremulous feeling she sometimes got when she relaxed.

Her more delicate tools now sat along the dresser top and window seat. She'd stripped off her coveralls and changed into a cotton nightgown. She sat in front of the vanity, which she intended to turn into a desk, timidly touching a brush to the ends of her hair. She'd pinned it earlier, but the coils had slid off her head and were now a big snarled knot hanging down her neck. Her arms were reddish tan but white at the shoulders. Her eyes

were big and round and green. "Like a fairy's," her mother used
to say, and her stepfather would correct her, in a mutter under
his breath: "Like a witch's."

Beatrice gritted her teeth and went after the first tangle.

"What a pity," her etiquette teacher had remarked, "that
you're so plain and not sweet." How unfortunate to be smart and
spirited and not handy with a teakettle. Otherwise she might have
made an acceptable wife.

There was a knock at the door. For an illogical instant, she
thought it was Benedick; even more mysteriously, her body
quantifiably reacted to the idea. Like an allergy. Increased heart
rate, a slight rise in skin temperature.

"It's me," called Hero.

Of course. Hero, not Benedick, was her relation in this
place. "Come in," Beatrice called, annoyed at herself.

"Oh, good." Hero slipped around the door, a silk robe tied
around her middle. "I was hoping you wouldn't be in bed yet."

Beatrice was used to sharing a room. At Miss Nightingale's she'd
boarded with a girl from Buffalo named Charlotte, who was fond of
saying things like "Don't you think it would be exciting to be poor
sometimes, Miss Clark? Poor and free, like the people in books!" Her
roommate at St. Mary's, an Irish girl, had been less imbecilic but often
passed the night chewing a kidskin glove slowly to shreds.

Having Hero in the space where she slept felt different,
perhaps because Beatrice wanted Hero to like her. Or maybe

because for the first time the added presence seemed to take up half the room. Either way, a foreign sensation of shyness overtook Beatrice.

"I just wanted to check on you," said Hero. She laced her hands together. "Make sure you were settling in all right. You had quite the day."

"I feel fine, thank you."

"I had hoped to ease you in to the idea a little more slowly." Hero's ice-blue eyes widened; she'd washed off the makeup she'd worn earlier in the day, but she was no less stunning. The kind of face to launch a thousand ships, that sort of thing. "But, surprise! Papa and I run a speakeasy." Her gaze turned wary. "What do you think?"

"I think I'm wondering where it is?"

"In the basement. The Masquerade tomorrow is always our first big bash of the summer. Of course I'd love for you to come, but if you're feeling a bit overwhelmed after today, I completely understand."

Beatrice was not overwhelmed; in fact a part of her was glad the day hadn't given her much chance to pause and think: *Now what now what now what?*

Hero watched her as if she were a hand grenade about to detonate.

"You're not just worried about my feelings, I guess," said Beatrice.

"Well, no." A zinger of a chagrined smile slipped through. "You've got to know Mama's speakeasy means the world to me. But you *are* family. I found this a few days before you came. Want to see?" She passed a feather-edged photograph over Beatrice's shoulder.

Beatrice brought it down to her lap. "Oh," she breathed.

There was Beatrice's mother, hands on her five-year-old daughter's shoulders, beside a laughing Aunt Anna, holding Hero on her hip. Their figures were slightly blurred, and Beatrice remembered that it was because they hadn't been able to hold properly still. The photographer had been annoyed at first, then charmed when Aunt Anna winked and thanked him for his patience. Coney Island, wasn't it? Yes, little Beatrice gripped a bag of kettle corn in her tiny fist. Hero's hair was pinned up with bows.

Beatrice's mother, Ursula Stahr at the time (she dutifully and legally changed both their names to Clark the same day of her quiet wedding), smiled in an almost bewildered way. An impossibly gentle woman, prone to sickness and nerves, who blossomed under the adoration of her first husband and shrank under the strictness of the second.

Next to Anna (who met her own husband by accidentally clocking him in the face with a women's rights poster), Ursula appeared like the dour face of reality. The sort of woman to be sorry she'd given birth to the daughter in front of her because it meant a life of humiliation and hardship.

Yet that same woman had left all her worldly possessions to her daughter's dream of becoming a doctor. Somewhere, not visible through a photograph, was a thread of steel under the pale skin.

Beatrice set the photograph down. Hero knelt, propped her elbow on the vanity top, and leaned one of her pillowy cheeks on her curled fist. "Funny, isn't it? I don't even remember that day."

Beatrice asked, "How did Aunt Anna die?"

"Influenza."

Beatrice knew that expression. The scarred look of someone who'd watched a life disappear from the confines of a bed. The helplessness of it. Wanting more time and wanting, in your exhaustion, for it to end.

The difference was that for Hero it was still fresh.

"The thing is, you're not at all what I was expecting." Hero traced a finger between the black-and-white faces of their five-year-old selves. "I was nervous. About how you'd like it here. About how you'd like me. I wanted—well, I know we don't know each other well. But I could do with a friend. That's all." She glanced up, the same shyness in her eyes that Beatrice felt.

"I could do with a friend, too," Beatrice whispered.

Hero broke out a smile that could melt glaciers.

"And I don't mind," said Beatrice. "About the speakeasy, I

mean. Your secret is safe with me." She picked up the brush again. "Mr. Scott explained it a little."

"Yes, that stinker. I told him not to overwhelm you, and what does he do?"

"He did try to go alone. I asked to come. To be fair."

"It worked out for him, I gather—here, let me." Hero stood, grabbed the brush from Beatrice's hand, and gathered a handful of messed curls.

"Oh, don't bother." Beatrice grimaced at the first pull of the brush. "It's no treat trying to get a brush through my hair, I assure you—"

Hero smacked Beatrice's reaching fingers with the brush's end. "Don't be silly. Anyway, it's always nicer to have someone else brush your hair. Don't you think?"

Beatrice rubbed her stinging knuckles, said nothing.

"Haven't you ever—" Hero shook her head. She brushed slowly, carefully, holding each section against her palm so it didn't yank on Beatrice's scalp. "Mama used to do it for me all the time. Just like this. Then we'd talk about boys. Like Ben Scott, for example . . ." Hero's reflection raised an eyebrow at Beatrice, too casually.

Beatrice's own brow flattened.

"It didn't even occur to me that you might end up liking each other," Hero said, undeterred. "Ben has notoriously refused every single girl I nudge in his direction. But it would be perfect.

If you and Ben got married, then he'd be actual family."

Before Beatrice could detail for Hero the multiple ways in which this would be disastrous, someone else knocked at her door. "Who is it?" Hero called gaily.

The girl from earlier, the one who said Beatrice was halfway to crazy, stuck her head into the room. "Hey there," she said to Hero. "Your room was empty. Look what Tommy brought me back." She held up a handful of cone-shaped, tinfoiled candies.

"Kisses! Get in here and share. Did you get properly introduced before? This is Margaret Hughes, Beatrice. She sings for us; one of our boarders, like Prince. What do you think of Beatrice and Ben as a couple, Mags?"

"I think Ben is a fine specimen of manhood, as judged by the expert eye of yours truly. But he's too in love with his typewriter." The words rolled around the chocolate sucked into Maggie's cheek. She dropped stomach first onto Beatrice's bed without a hint of self-consciousness. She stretched out her arm, and Hero grabbed a few of the chocolates and handed one to Beatrice.

"You've tried these, haven't you?"

Beatrice shook her head, unwrapped the tinfoil, and hesitantly set the chocolate on her tongue. It melted smoothly, sweetly.

"Tell Tommy thanks for us," said Hero. "When are you going to throw that poor boy a bone, Mags?"

"I never asked for the chocolates. He brings them of his

own doing." Maggie considered one of the Kisses, then sighed. "It would make things easier. But I think I already love someone else, so it doesn't matter."

Hero's eyes narrowed. "Who?"

"Wouldn't you like to know?"

Hero sniffed. "Nobody appreciates my expertise anymore."

"I'm sure Ben's a perfectly nice boy." Beatrice hedged. "And I can see he's a good friend of yours. But honestly, I find him a little . . . slippery?" Was that the word?

"He's got a silver tongue," Maggie agreed, nodding.

"But he's not dishonest," Hero insisted. "Maybe hard to explain? I say a little mystery in a person is like a nice dash of salt."

Beatrice said, "Only if I'm stranded in the desert and no other form of nutrition is available."

Hero sighed. "That's exactly the sort of thing he would say, too," which made Maggie laugh. Neither seemed too serious about pursuing the match, and Beatrice relaxed.

Relaxed, and this time didn't feel as if something bad might catch up to her.

"I heard you and he got into a tangle with the Minskys on the East River," Maggie said.

Hero paused in her brushing to shoot Maggie a look black enough to wither flowers. "Of all the nerve. Over Sage's moonshine. The next time I see Conrade I'm going to throttle him with that stupid striped necktie he's taken to wearing."

"If he shows his face again after Beatrice chased him off with a shotgun." Maggie grinned wildly.

Hero snorted. "Maybe I'll tell them we brought Beatrice on as the new muscle, and they'll all be too scared to try again." Hero had gotten through every tangle at last, and though Beatrice's hair was a poofed cloud, it was soft and allowed the long, continuous strokes of the brush without complaint.

They didn't care, Beatrice realized.

They didn't care that she fixed cars with sap or shot rifles or arrived weighed down with a trunk of medical supplies, science equipment, and a farfetched dream. In fact they seemed to like her for it. Surely, in the years since her mother had died, someone at some point had liked her for the same reasons, but as a sudden tremor started in her shoulders, she found she couldn't recall any.

In the quiet Hero started humming "My Blue Heaven."

Then Maggie sang, joining her smoky voice with Hero's sweet hum:

"You'll see a smiling face,

a fireplace,

a cozy room,

a little nest

that's nestled where

the roses bloom."

Perhaps it was Maggie's voice, husky and sure, perhaps the song, which lifted a lifetime of yearning and loneliness out of Beatrice to hang vulnerable in the air. Perhaps the comfort of having her hair brushed, with the taste of chocolate in her mouth, or the reminder of her mother, or just feeling safe and accepted for the first time in years, but—

"We're happy in my blue heaven . . ."

With no warning whatsoever, her eyes welled up, and she . . . Cried.

She ducked her head and cried as if she did it all the time, instead of almost never, which was the truth.

"Oh, honey." Hero kissed her cheek and handed her a handkerchief. "Maggie's singing does it to me, too."

CHAPTER 8

I WOULD MY HORSE HAD THE SPEED OF YOUR TONGUE

Benedick dreamed that Anna was alive.

He dreamed he'd gone back to Manhattan, but he was a writer, and Anna was married to his father, and they were all toasting the success of his first novel.

The sheer unlikelihood of this scenario, outside of the feverish quality of exhausted sleep, was enough to pull him awake breathless and disoriented. For a hazy second his room at Stony Creek and his room at his father's Park Avenue apartment swam together, and where he was or who he was remained a mystery, until he was hearing not snores nor the rumble of city taxis, but nothing.

Sweet nothing but the rustle of cherry blossoms and a room still dark, but not so dark that dawn wasn't far behind. The room was small and unheated and undecorated, with a slanted roof and piles of books and clothes and other assorted belongings he'd been depositing for years like a nesting bird. It felt like home.

He sat up. Searching for the cot he used as a bed had seemed too much trouble last night, so he'd dropped like a stone on the hideous fat sofa upholstered in red velvet, which he loved and everyone else hated.

He'd eaten something last night, he couldn't remember what, because Beatrice had made him do it, *staring* until he'd chewed and swallowed a portion she deemed commendable.

His nose wrinkled, and he slumped back. It was too early to be reminded about Beatrice Clark. With a deliberate mental turn away from her, he rose to wash and dress. A quick look at his pocket watch reminded him only that it had stopped working after a dunk in Mosquito Cove.

Never mind.

The sun hadn't even risen. He had several hours before anyone else would be up and preparations for the Masquerade would begin. Off in Brooklyn, dozens of Stony Creek Academy boys would graduate, and he wouldn't be among them.

He lit a lamp—the electric wiring didn't reach to the attic, another thing he loved—and lifted Isabella out of her case. The Remington typewriter fit just so on his desk, next to a beat-up dictionary and a globe worn through at the equator.

After a loving pat for Isabella, he went to the washroom,

taking his time, then boiled water in the kitchen for coffee, the quality of which had taken a serious downturn once business got slow, but yes, even that warranted Benedick's affection.

He was practically whistling until he set the thirty-four pages of his novel on the desk and rolled a fresh piece of paper into the typewriter. He'd written other stories, of course, but this was his first serious attempt. Now was the time, freedom at last, et cetera, et cetera. He ignored the panic creeping up his shoulders. He knew from experience that the moment he began typing, any ideas would somehow, in the journey from thought to fingertip, degenerate entirely.

He stood, practically *leaped*, to his feet and paced. Just to get the juices flowing. Maybe he'd jot down some ideas first. Anything that didn't have to sound smart and important and feed him for the rest of his life.

Naturally what came to mind was the madness of yesterday and, by ratio of presence, Beatrice Clark.

He was not sure he liked her, but it wasn't that he disliked her either. Rather, he considered himself lucky to have stepped in the path of a speeding train and gotten out unscathed. How was it that a girl could be so irritating that instead of saying, *My God, you were impressive back there*, which he did think—or had thought in the thick of things—he instead had to use all his gentleman's training not to strangle her?

She was like . . . weather maybe? Instead of a person?

Oh, that was good.

He dug out a paper and scribbled it down.

One could admire a bolt of lightning, after all, but from a distance. One didn't want to touch it.

All right, but she couldn't be both, a speeding train and a bolt of lightning. Using the metaphors together seemed a little heavy-handed. He'd come back to it. Something, something, about being a spectacle, but not, such as it were, beautiful in the traditional sense.

He was in the swing of his thoughts—literally, swift strides back and forth through the very short space of his room—when something banged on his floor. He stopped, looking down.

Thump, thump.

There it was again. Someone was definitely knocking on the ceiling under the attic, but nobody lived in that room. Nobody—

Oh, no.

He knelt and rapped his fist on his wood floor two times.

A long pause.

He'd nearly decided that was that before the knocks came again, this time with a pattern. Short taps and long taps. "Is that Morse code?" he wondered out loud, which settled the issue nicely. Who else would *happen to know* Morse code?

Well, he knew a bit, too, thank you very much.

Tap-tap-tap. Taaap-taaap-taaap. Tap-tap-tap.

No answer.

It occurred to him, too late, that he ought to have thought through the repercussions of the message he sent, but a heartbeat later there was a sound like a rushing wind, and in blew Beatrice at fifty miles an hour under her own steam.

Which, honestly, seemed only a mild exaggeration.

Her hair certainly looked as though it had just experienced high speeds.

"For Christ's sake," he said.

Her face went all exasperated, an expression he rather enjoyed. "Are you aware that SOS is a distress signal, you intolerable lunatic?"

"I am not a lunatic. You knocked on my floor. Uninvited, I'll add."

"Because you were pacing around! At four-thirty in the morning, I'll add."

"I don't suppose you possess among your character strengths the ability to ignore something that bothers you?"

"No," she said, without pausing to think about it. "While I'm up here, I may as well check your condition."

"Absolutely not. Put that hand back where it belongs, thank you— *Ow.*" He winced as she took hold of his ear and effectively turned his face around. He glared at her, for all the good it did him.

"The eyes and the mouth are the best judge for extended dehydration," she said, pulling at his lower eyelid, her other hand holding his chin. She smelled like cotton and some sort of metalish scent, like iron or oil. "To tell the truth, you look just fine, Mr. Scott. That's quite the rebound. I'm impressed."

She released him, and he rubbed where her fingers had been. He pushed himself to his feet. "Look, I'm sorry if I woke you, but you can—"

"Oh, you didn't." Her big eyes took in his room with rapt fascination. She was barefoot, he noticed, arching up on her toes to see over stacks of books and as unconcerned about her night-shirt and dressing gown as she'd been about his undergarments yesterday. "I was already awake. I don't sleep much. . . ."

"There's your trouble in a nutshell."

"Is this where you stay? I admit it's shabbier than I would have imagined, but also rather quaint— Oh! What a spiffy type-writer." She leaned over Isabella, finger extended to touch one of the keys. Benedick lurched forward and snatched her wrist.

"Don't touch," he said.

She blinked at him. Whatever was on his face, she unexpect-edly nodded and backed off. "All right. I won't. It's a nice one, though."

"Anna gave it to me as a Christmas present." Her last Christ-mas, before she'd died.

"Really? Say—" She squinted, like the know-it-all she was. "You're a writer, is that it?"

She made it sound cute. His voice grew a sharp end or two, but he answered, "I've been known to fence with the quill, yes."

"That explains a little. Though not how you ended up here in the first place." She raised an eyebrow, a suggestion.

He did not rise to the bait, letting his eyes flutter innocuously at her.

"I'll cut you a deal, Mr. Scott."

"I bet."

"If you tell me how you first came to Hey Nonny Nonny, I won't ask you a single other question the rest of the day."

Benedick's lips twitched. "Well. You know just the way to a fella's heart. All right, since the flame of curiosity burns so bright. It was my sixteenth birthday weekend. One of my school friends had heard about this great bash out in Flower Hill. We paid a wallop to get these pins and the passcode—significantly overpaid, as I learned later."

He braced his hands on his desk, crossed one ankle over the other, and leaned back. "I can't actually remember much of the night itself, since in my celebration I drank myself nearly into the grave, but I do remember thinking it was terrific. Friendly, I guess. Hey Nonny Nonny wasn't *for* anybody; it just was. Anyway, that was a Friday, and when I woke up Saturday morning, I was in one of the rooms with no clue how I'd got there, completely abandoned by my friends, and so sick I genuinely believed I'd done myself in."

"So sick you thought, *Gee, why don't I stay forever?*"

"I'm getting to that, and you are already violating your end of the bargain. Anna told me I was too young to be drinking that much. She lectured me." She'd mothered him, though it had taken him awhile to realize that was what was going on. "She told me I could come back if I promised to lay off the cocktails. Back then Hey Nonny Nonny was open nearly every weekend, slowing down only in the winter. They had another bash that night, and I stayed."

"Was Hero around?"

"Of course. Anna didn't let her drink much either, so Hero took it upon herself to take me under her wing, told me she knew a waiter who'd hook us up. The waiter was Prince."

"Did you fall in love with her?"

Benedick laughed, surprised. "No. Not at all."

"Then why did you come back?"

"Well, because . . . I liked it."

"You came every weekend?"

"Not every weekend, but a lot of them. I stayed for the summer, too."

"Your parents didn't mind?"

He shrugged. "Most of the boys I went to school with spent summers in Long Island or Connecticut, usually by the beach; it's not that uncommon, if your family doesn't own a house out here, to get invited to stay at someone else's."

Beatrice shook her head. "That's not how I spent *my* summers, I can tell you. Hey Nonny Nonny isn't really like a bar then. Not exactly."

"Hey Nonny Nonny was like the party for the people who couldn't stand the other Long Island society parties." Starving artists and their muses, the outcast rich and swank babies like Claude Blaine descending south in search of local flavor. He finished, "People were interesting and kind, not to mention the *music*. Anna used to dance on the tables."

Beatrice softened. Her face, with its dimples and freckles, was another animal entirely when it wasn't set to blazes. "I think you described it fine," she said. "And I see what you mean, why you'd stay."

"Why, Miss Clark, I didn't know you had it in you to see what I mean."

Her mouth thinned. He was beginning to categorize her expressions. This one was her *whatever-you've-said-is-idiotic* look. "Don't polish your gold medal just yet. I— Did you hear that?" She turned to his window and crawled up onto his sofa so she could peer through the glass.

He hadn't heard anything, but he was not entirely surprised to look for himself and see, out at the end of the lane, the outline of a car gleaming in the charcoal light of pre-dawn.

Beatrice's voice dropped to a whisper. "Look, Ben! He's getting out! What's he doing?"

"Who?" Benedick followed the point of her nose, now pressed directly to the glass, and saw a slight figure rooting around near the cellar doors. Doors that led, perhaps not coincidentally, into the speakeasy. On the basis of the dark hair, Benedick might have said it was John, but the jacket seemed ragged, the cap slightly askew. John Morello was neat as a glass of scotch.

"We have to go investigate," Beatrice said.

"What? No, we do not *have* to do anything of the sort."

"Of course we do. What if it's a burglar?"

"And what if it's not? Furthermore, what's this we? I was promised a vacation from your curiosity."

"That's true," she murmured, leaning back from the window. "And I am a girl of my word. You stay here."

Before he could ask if she meant to accost the poor intruder in her nightgown, she tightened the sash around her waist and strode out.

"*Wait*, you impossible maniac." Benedick hurried after her. "Are you incapable of minding your own business? We can wake up your uncle if you're so concerned."

"By that time whoever it is might be gone!"

"Perish the thought."

She ignored him. He nearly had to jog to keep up with her as she sailed out the back door, bare feet and all, and rounded the side of the house. The young man was right where they'd left him and straightened at their arrival. It was not John, though he had the same coloring. His fingers brushed the side of his jacket back; Benedick saw the distinct edge of a holstered gun and grabbed Beatrice's elbow.

He jerked her behind him, a position she opted to stay in for approximately half a second. She wiggled around to his side, but he maintained his hold on her arm.

"Good morning," she said pertly. She tried to pinch Benedick's hand, but he merely shifted his grip; it felt a bit like holding a touchy explosive.

The young man let his jacket fall back over the gun, hiding it. He slid off his cap, holding it to his chest. *"Buongiorno, signorina."* He grinned crookedly. "I very much like your dress."

"Thank you," said Beatrice, after an uncertain pause, glancing down as if to remember what in fact she was wearing.

"Are you looking for something?" asked Benedick. This time, when Beatrice pinched, he let his hand fall back to his side.

"Just making sure I know where to find the place. Maybe you know Pedro?" His accent was decidedly Italian, rugged and confident.

"Pedro?" Beatrice muttered.

"Prince," Benedick told her quietly. Louder, he added, "He's here actually. If you want us to get him?"

"No need." The same grin took up the young man's face. "We're half cousins, but he doesn't know the faces of his own blood, you know."

"We could pass along your name at least," Beatrice said.

"Borachio Morello." He bent and retrieved a bottle, nestled against the side of the cellar entrance. Tied around the neck was a piece of wood bearing the Genovese symbol. "You can tell him I got his message." He winked at her, flipped his cap back on, and, whistling, strolled toward the car waiting at the end of the lane.

"Satisfied?" Benedick asked as the car pulled away. He had the real urge to sit down in the weeds and take a nap.

"Not by half. Do you think it was only the bottle he wanted?"

"That's the way into the speakeasy."

"You're pulling my leg!"

"Nothing could induce me to touch any part of your leg," he said. "I'd guess our friend was perfectly aware there was a speakeasy here."

"Hmm. Well, we'd better tell Prince at any rate."

"Yes, I suppose so."

She turned to face him fully, just as the sun began to streak the sky, tiny smug smile in place, which sent the dimples marching to center stage. "Admit it."

"Never," he said automatically. "Admit what?"

"You're glad we came out. Admit it feels good to have acted, to have gained an answer even if we received more questions in exchange."

"I admit nothing except that you are a madwoman with a severe lack of respect for proper clothing choices." He straightened his shirt, though in truth he was not much better off than she was. "Now, if you'll excuse me, I'm off to enjoy my questionless day."

❖ ❖ ❖

Benedick was enjoying their bargain.

Today was the sort of day even a respectably polite person would have questions. For someone like Beatrice, it was a veritable parade of new things to learn, but Benedick made a point of sabotaging her attempts to field any inquiries to Prince or Hero instead.

When they gathered in the speakeasy to set up, he watched her find a barstool as far as possible from him. He waited until Hero climbed on top of her own stool, which frankly didn't put her too much taller than half the people in the room, and then sat directly beside Beatrice. Her eyes slid to acknowledge him as if he were a nasty breed of barnacle she was having trouble eradicating; he smiled back.

"Go away," she whispered.

"Never."

Hero cleared her throat. "I don't have to remind you tonight's a big night," she said; she wore a long skirt and sturdy Mary Janes, both of which she would shed by tonight.

Benedick had always liked Hey Nonny Nonny when it was empty—the promise of it. Each round table had a fresh tablecloth folded on top. The bar was crammed with foraged supplies: Prince's territory. The only piece of the party always in place was the chandelier hanging from the high basement ceiling.

"We had a rocky winter season," Hero continued. "But the November to March crowd always runs a bit thinner than summer's. There's no reason we can't recover."

Anna and Leo had been known to roll up their sleeves and pitch in, but it used to be that Anna also paid the busboys, waiters, and barkeeps to come early and set up. Now the Stahrs could only afford the hours of the actual party; that meant all prep work fell to their diminished five-person crew. Six if you counted Leo, and some days you could, some days you couldn't.

"Unfortunately," Hero said, "we're not set up for full weekends yet, but we can do every Saturday, and we have three big weeks ahead of us. Tonight is the Masquerade, our opening blowout." This was clearly for Beatrice's benefit. "Next Saturday is Decoration Day weekend, and then it's my eighteenth birthday. That kind of momentum will take us all the way through the summer, to Labor Day, so long as we don't trip over our own feet.

"Now where did I . . ." Hero turned. On her other side, Prince handed her a folded paper. "Thanks, sugar. Let's see . . . Prince will organize the bar, like usual, with Ben's help. Papa's going to pick up the extra hands. Francis will secure our outside entrance and make sure raid procedures are still in shape. Maggie of course is in charge of entertainment. I'll be handling the decorations; Beatrice, you'll be with me. Everything I ordered should be around this joint somewhere, so just ask. Everyone square?"

"As a city block, captain." Benedick saluted.

"Good," said Hero. "Maestro?"

Prince passed around the customary shot glasses. Beatrice eyed hers with more than a little trepidation. Benedick decided to give her this one. "Tradition," he told her.

Prince filled everyone's glass with half an inch of good whiskey, one of the last bottles they had.

"Maggie, if you don't mind," said Hero.

Maggie held her glass, waited a moment, then sang:

"Sing no more ditties, sing no more

Of dumps so dull and heavy;

The fraud of men was ever so,

Since summer first was leavy.

Then sigh not so,

But let them go,

And be you blithe and bonny,

Converting all your sounds of woe

Into . . ."

The last line was for everyone, and every time, no matter what, it was shouted as loud as everyone could go.

"Hey nonny, nonny!"

Maggie tucked down her whiskey. She twirled her empty glass and whooped a little. "Let's get to work, boys and girls!"

❖ ❖ ❖

Benedick set the last of their stock on the counter, two clear jugs of Sage's moonshine. "Technically he owes us a third." Benedick traced the number 2 with his finger, hearing Beatrice's voice: *And don't think I'll forget.*

Prince looked up from his list. He popped the cork on one and sniffed. "Good God."

"It's pretty awful," Benedick said.

"That just means we can stretch it further," Prince said after a moment. "We got a huge case of half-rotted strawberries. If I beat those up, and mix them with ice and mint, we'll only have to add a little of this stuff to prove it's wet."

"All right, well, it shouldn't be much trouble to swing by his boat this afternoon if it'll be useful. Think we have enough?"

"I'll make a half-ass sherry out of the wine bricks from Francis. Plus the old whiskey that's twice watered down. It was pure when we got it, so it'll hold."

"How much did we save from the coast?" Benedick asked it casually. He'd been waiting all morning for a chance to bring it up— or rather for Prince to admit on his own that he'd left a perfectly good bottle outside the cellar entrance, but Prince only shrugged.

"Four bottles total, but I'm going to use them to thicken the supply we have."

Maggie and the band were running through songs; the music cast a swingin' blanket over their conversation. Hero and Beatrice untangled garlands and baubles to hang around the stage.

Benedick leaned in. "What about the one you left for Bora-chio Morello?"

Prince's eyes snapped to him. "What did you say?"

"He was here before dawn. And I saw John at the train sta-tion yesterday afternoon."

Fight flew into Prince. When Benedick only arched his brows, Prince slumped a second later and muttered, "That was fast."

"Tell me," Benedick said.

Prince glanced toward Hero. Not the way he usually would, as if he were deciding if he should tell Benedick *their* secret, but more along the lines of I *don't want her to know.*

"Okay. Look." Prince rooted around the cabinets under the bar until he found a well-used map of Long Island. He spread it out on the floor between them, so Benedick had to crouch to see. Prince tapped his finger on Nassau County's southern beaches. "The Genovese family operates several rum-running drop-off points here."

"Sure. We've always known that."

"I did some digging and turns out the whole county is con-sidered Genovese territory. No other Italian family is allowed to do bootlegging business from the coast to the Sound. But I run tracks all over this area, and the only place you need to watch your step is on the coast. Why is that?"

Benedick leaned his cheek into his fist. He had no idea, truly. With all the rest of Hey Nonny Nonny's competition, it didn't seem as though they brushed up against Italians much at all. He'd assumed it was because they didn't care. "Because Nassau County is just a bunch of farms and wealthy estates?"

"That's part of it," Prince said. "But you know as well as I do that most of the parties out here are wet. Not to mention the clubhouses and gentlemen's lodges and joints like ours and Minsky's Ragland."

"So what?"

"Most of those places have a bootleg supplier, but none of them pull from the Genovese shipments."

"Maybe they don't like Italians. Leo never wanted to work with them either."

"Leo didn't care that they were Italian. He cared that people who double-crossed them ended up shot between the eyes."

"Funny. It's not like him to worry about such trivial matters."

Prince looked up, his forearms resting on his knees. "Guess who's the captain over the Nassau area?"

Benedick had an idea.

"*John*," Prince said. "John is the reason they haven't done business here the past few years. Almost exactly"—his tone turned bitter—"from the time he found out I was working here."

"Even you can't blame John for the turn Hey Nonny Nonny's taken."

"No," Prince admitted. "But after Leo started to . . . you know. I tried looking for other options."

Benedick grimaced. When Anna got sick, they'd shut down for a bit, of course, and everybody understood, but then Leo drank himself out of his best trade routes: botched meetings, people swindling him by wagging scotch under his nose. His broken heart sank them as swiftly as Anna's death.

"It took me four months to even find out John was the one in charge," Prince said. "No one would talk to me because they were too scared of him."

"Why would John care about Hey Nonny Nonny?"

"He doesn't. It's me he hates." At Benedick's skeptical expression, Prince scowled. "Don't give me that look. When we were kids, our mother despised him, and she adored me. It doesn't matter; the point is, eventually I got in contact with his cousin. *Our* cousin. He wants John's spot, and apparently not everyone is happy that he keeps a lid on all activity in this area. If I can find a way to turn an immediate profit, Borachio will partner with me. That's why—why I took those crates, why I left their whiskey for him. He wanted me to prove to him that I could."

Benedick nodded, considering all this in silence. He understood why Prince hadn't told Hero yet. Hey Nonny Nonny had to purchase booze to stay wet, but they were, as Leo often said, "honest lawbreakers." They never sold a drop except at their bar, and out of those profits not a cent went to organized crime, politicians, or law enforcement for protection.

What Prince was talking about, that was big money, and not in a good way. In a *send-you-to-jail-or-grave* kind of way. Was their humble speakeasy worth that kind of risk? When he looked at Prince, the answer was yes. This place was his heart, his home, his future. Benedick's, too.

"Don't tell Hero," said Prince. "I need more time."

Several hours later the decorations were set and the band had run through all their songs. Tommy played one-handed at the piano while Maggie leaned over to talk to him; the cellist laid down her instrument and stretched. Benedick, Prince, Hero, and Beatrice sat at one of the tables closest to the stage. Hey Nonny Nonny looked almost ready to go, the counters and floors scrubbed, white table-cloths in place, ashtrays and lilies, just in bloom, as centerpieces. Benedick cracked the bottom of a new pack of cigarettes against the table's edge. He offered one to Prince.

"If any of you get ash on my new tablecloths," Hero said from Prince's other side, her feet propped in his lap, "I'll pop you one." She braced a hand around Prince's neck and plucked the cigarette he'd stuck in his mouth free with her teeth. She turned it right way around, and Prince leaned in to strike a match between them, their faces close.

Kiss or get off the pot, Benedick thought.

Of all Hero's competing hopefuls, Prince had never thrown in his own number. Hero liked to test him, as if she couldn't believe any red-blooded man was truly that impervious to her charms.

Benedick gave Prince another cigarette, then turned to offer one to Beatrice. "No, thank you," she said. "I don't smoke."

"Of course not."

Beatrice said, "It can't be good for you."

"What do you know about it? My fencing instructor at Stony Creek smoked a pack a day, and he's healthy as a beast."

"First, I know something about nearly everything, and second, I'm only postulating, based on hypothetical theory. If you consider a chimney stack venting smoke, the buildup needs to be regularly cleaned, but there's no way to clean your lungs. Not to mention how nervous cigarettes make some people."

Benedick blew smoke right at her. Beatrice, bored, fanned it away. He was disappointed, of all things.

"Does it make you feel very clever to use words like *postulate* in normal conversation?" asked Benedick.

"Being clever makes me feel clever," said Beatrice. "But next time I educate you, I will be as monosyllabic as possible."

"*Goodness*, you two," Hero interrupted. Her tongue flicked the back of her two front teeth, against the gap. "It's bad enough I only have four hours to get ready, now my brain hurts from listening to you two bicker all morning."

"You need four hours to get ready?" asked Beatrice, amazed.

"Honey, I need *five*, but I'll make do with what I have." Hero examined her nails and, finding her manicure in a further state of disarray, frowned deeper. "Why? Doesn't it take you time?"

Pink blossomed on Beatrice's cheeks, darkening the freckles. "I only have one nice dress, and there's not much I can do with my hair, so I don't know what I'd do with extra time anyway."

Duly horrified, Hero sat up, feet falling from Prince's lap. "One nice dress? One? You know, I bet I've got something you can borrow. That artist fella from Paris sent me this frock as a gift, and it was too long and made me look like a lumpy dwarf. It might fit you. You have that waif look some girls can get away with." Hero pressed both hands to her own gifted chest, with a sigh that was both wistful and proud. "Lord knows I can't."

Beatrice stared at her cousin as if she were an equation missing a key variable.

Benedick leaned over to give her a few suggestions on how to become more ladylike, but the door in the far corner, the one leading to the outside entrance, cracked open. Tommy stopped playing.

And in walked none other than John Morello.

CHAPTER 9
A CHURCH BY DAYLIGHT

Hey Nonny Nonny was not what you'd call glamorous. And it hadn't been, even when Anna was around. It was just a little too rowdy for that, a little too come-as-you-are. The stage was a stage, but it was small, with no wings, no backstage, and no dressing rooms. Most of the time Maggie dressed in her room upstairs, but in a pinch she could shimmy down under the stage, behind a thin partition. If someone was dancing onstage, she got out of there fast, because if she didn't, plaster came down on her head.

Not glamorous, no.

But it was home.

"Honey, I'm just saying. If a ship is sinking, it's time to get off." Tommy looked up at her, even as one hand played the bass notes of "April Showers."

Maggie leaned over, plunking a few high keys to mess him up. It didn't. Nothing could knock Tommy off his beat once he'd found it. "You rather I go back to Philly?" she asked.

"Mags. You got friends in the city. Everyone who's been to Hey Nonny Nonny knows you have real pipes. You could stay with Jez and me."

Maggie said nothing. Her eyes drifted over the tiny stage she knew so well. Then past it, to the table of people smoking and laughing.

Tommy sighed, noting where her attention had gone. "What's so special about this joint anyhow?"

If Tommy didn't already know, she couldn't explain it to him. She straightened, about to dismiss the rest of the band until opening warm-up. And then John walked in.

Her heart went completely still, then picked up pace to make up for the pause.

She wasn't the only one. At the table Prince had turned into a breathing statue.

"Hey, Johnny baby!" Tommy called, laughing.

John's gaze ticked over to them briefly, but that was it.

John reminded Maggie, as always, of a gun. He was made of hard lines: lean, obstinate jaw, straight nose. Trouble, in other words. And like trouble, sometimes a girl found herself looking for it, wanting it, even when she knew it was a bad idea.

"Sorry to interrupt," he said in his quiet voice, but Hero had already sprung to her feet.

She looped her arms around his neck and kissed him hard on the cheek, an inch from his mouth. "John! You came! You stayed away so long I'd started to think our little establishment was too small potatoes for you."

He extracted himself from her hold, a little pink around the edges. Prince remained the only boy on this earth who could take Hero full throttle with no side effects.

Besides, John knew what she was about. "There's a dozen bottles of champagne in my car," he said. "Plus half a case of white rum for cocktails."

"Oh, you absolute gem."

He'd paid for his ticket, and Hero ushered him to the table as if she didn't see Prince's darkening expression. "Any special reason you're gracing us this year?"

He lowered himself into the chair, still without so much as a glance toward Maggie. "There's been a few business snags recently in this area. I came to get to the bottom of it." His posture took on a predatory angle toward Prince.

"I haven't heard of anything." Prince met the look. "Not anything that would concern you anyway."

Was Maggie the only one who saw the fledgling storm crackling between the pair? Thunder and lightning. Someone needed to break it up. She told herself that was why she spoke up next, not because she wanted John to look her way.

"Excuse me," Maggie said into her microphone. "But my band's hungry as lions, and we've still got one more song to finish."

She snapped her fingers at Tommy. After a bewildered pause Tommy sat down and tickled the keys of the piano. He knew every song, published and unpublished. Hey Nonny Nonny had warranted his time in its heyday, but now they were lucky he came back for such low pay—though it was true his salary sometimes came with a kiss or two.

He was an all right kisser. No firecracker, but Maggie had endured far worse on the sacred altar of jazz.

" 'Now listen, honey,' " she sang.

Finally John's eyes snapped up to hers: a combination of grieved and angry, as if to say, *How dare you?*

Her voice was pure as a bell; you could hear it five blocks away on a clear night. The first time she met John, the crowd had been bad, and he'd told her she sang too loud. Maybe she should have taken that as a warning from fate, but fate needn't have bothered. She had always known better than to fall in love, especially with someone like John. Letting her heart close to a white boy was problem enough, but for some people an Italian was worse. With olive Mediterranean skin and black hair that had a tendency to curl if it ever escaped his meticulous grooming,

John was as far from her world as he could be, and the breadth of their separation was on the outside where everyone could see it.

At the time, she'd had no idea who he was; no one had even known Prince had a brother, estranged or otherwise.

Come to find out, John had been looking for Prince for a while, and Hey Nonny Nonny was a big enough racket that word got around to his associates. Maggie had been fifteen at the time and green as hay, only a few solo performances under her belt. Hey Nonny Nonny had the kind of audience that did whatever it pleased: people running around, yelling at their friends.

Still, if they liked you, they weren't shy about it. They'd scream, stomp, and applaud until the whole building shook. Bawdy riffs were the most popular; they weren't right for Maggie's voice, but she sang them anyway because she was too afraid of displeasing anyone. If nobody wanted to listen to her, she'd never be a headliner.

That night she'd shout-sung the last notes, and it had made her pitchy, sharp at the end. Nobody noticed, though. Or she thought they hadn't, with all the whistling and clapping.

Usually when she left the stage, she'd hang out at the bar for a bit or maybe schmooze at a table if they invited her. She liked the compliments. She liked hearing that she was going places.

But this boy, this dark-haired boy not much older than she was, sitting alone at the bar, didn't care a lick when she took the seat beside him (it was the only one open; even back then he had a way of maintaining his sphere of personal space). He'd looked as if he hadn't smiled a day in his life, and she couldn't help taking it personally, her insecurities bubbling to the surface.

"What's the matter with you?" she asked. Whatever else she was, she was never timid. "Didn't like my song?"

Without turning, without so much as a blink actually—he was the stillest person she'd ever met, even then—he said, "The song was fine."

"Only fine, huh?"

He turned then. He was younger than she'd thought: a boy's skin, an old man's eyes. "You were sharp on the last notes."

Well! Someone *had* noticed.

Admitting it was another story. "Excuse me for missing the mark of perfection," she'd said sniffily.

He didn't apologize. "You're trying to sing like Bessie Smith and Ma Rainey, with the riffs and jams and shouting. Your voice is low, more suited to soft singing."

Just who was this kid, with his Bessie Smith and jams and know-how? He didn't know *nothing*. "Oh, yeah?" Her voice rose a notch.

"Yeah," he said, and he'd had the nerve to sound amused. "Try 'St. Louis Blues' next time, and sing it like a lullaby."

She'd marched away from the bar in a huff, cursing under her breath like a stevedore, annoyed that he knew "St. Louis Blues" at all. But she asked Anna if she could please have another spot for the next night, figuring he wouldn't be there anyway, and she could try it at least.

She'd sung "St. Louis Blues," and she'd sung it with a feather tongue.

And that boy, the stupid fathead, had been right. You could have heard a pin drop in Hey Nonny Nonny's rowdy crowd.

That was how she sang now, focused as a needle point, gentle as a thread of silk:

"Someday when you grow lonely
Your heart gon' break like mine"

Tommy and Jez knew the song, so they picked up her beat after the first stanza. She left her microphone to saunter down the steps of the stage. When the place was this empty, she didn't need it anyway.

The next lines picked up, jaunty and playful, enough for Jez to try some of his tricks and effects.

"I can't sleep at night
I can't eat a bite
'Cause the man I love
He don't treat me right"

There was no teasing John when he wouldn't be teased, but since she could get away with it without getting shot, she played this one for the team. She got closer to the table, tapping first Benedick, then Prince lightly on the head. When she got to where John sat, she sang a line right in his face. She knew how to play her voice to inspire tears, to put a dance into people's feet, to draw hands and mouths and hearts together, or in this case, to make someone smile.

He did try, she thought, to ignore her, but by the time she was close enough to touch him, he'd ceded a few inches to her approach, lips pressed tight as if resisting took physical effort.

Tommy peeled out the end of the song, and she popped up with a flourishing bow—and to applause! At least from the non-Italian side of the table.

"You're so talented, Margaret," said Beatrice. "I've never heard anything like it, and your voice is . . . is like . . . I don't know."

"Thanks, rookie." Maggie winked at her.

Tommy hopped down from the stage. "Hey, level with me, boss man. I got bad habits to pay for, and this gig don't pay shit. When are you going to get us in to play the Cotton Club?"

"Stop hustling, Tommy," said Maggie, annoyed.

"Oh, shut it. John don't mind."

Subdued, John ran a hand along the edge of the table. "I've told you before," he said. "We don't touch the Cotton Club. Owney Madden runs it, and that's not a fight anyone wants to start if we can help it."

"Well, at least you could set up a meeting. We're good, Mags and I."

"Perhaps. Miss Hughes is too young." John avoided Maggie's glare by turning to Hero. "I'd like to stay a few extra days if you don't mind."

"Sure," said Hero, surprised. "On the house, naturally."

"I insist on paying." He stood, adjusting his jacket. "Pedro? *Mi aiuti con lo* champagne?"

Prince's mouth pressed into a line, but he followed his brother all the same—not before grabbing Benedick's shoulder and leaning down to whisper something in his ear.

When they were gone, Beatrice asked, "Who was that?"

"John Morello," said Hero. "Prince's half brother. He looks like he'd slit your throat for a laugh, but he's a peach underneath all that."

"So, staying longer this time?"

Maggie hovered in the doorway of John's room. His suitcase was open on the bed. He took a folded shirt out and lifted his eyes to look at her.

"Business," he said, as if she might need reminding.

"It always is." She came into the room and plopped onto his bed.

"Please, come in," he said dryly.

"Don't mind if I do."

His visits were mostly about keeping an eye on Prince, but she liked to think he was around a little more often than was necessary to hear her sing.

"You know," she said, "I'm not too young for the Cotton Club."

"You're seventeen. And have been"—he hung the shirt and set it inside the closet—"since March."

"And here I'd thought you forgot."

"I didn't forget."

For someone who said he didn't care, he sure put a lot of effort into not caring. Sometimes she could trick him into admitting she was as charming as she thought she was, but most of the time, it was like dancing around a cinder block.

"I look twenty-one," she said. This time she wasn't here to coax out one of his slipups.

Maybe he heard it in her tone because at last he turned and met her eyes. He frowned. She liked his frown—which was good, since that was what she saw most. It suited him more than a smile, brought to mind his concentration, his refusal to be hurried, the dangerous edge of his judgment.

"And I'm plenty old enough," she said. "I wasn't a child even when I was one. Nobody'd ask anyway, and if they did, I'd get Leo to sign one of those papers. He'd do it." Lord knew her mother wouldn't.

"What are you saying?"

"Not the Cotton Club. I know that's not your beat. But your

family owns some of the clubs in the city. I thought maybe you could ask if one of the managers would audition me."

"Are you leaving Hey Nonny Nonny?" A faint line appeared between John's brows. "The speakeasy is down that bad?"

This was why she was here: She didn't have to explain jazz to him, and she didn't have to explain Hey Nonny Nonny either. Right before Christmas last year, John had taken her to see *Dance Mania* with Duke Ellington and Adelaide Hall at the Lafayette Theater. She sat side by side with him in an orchestra seat, not the balcony. He was good (if stoic) company. The boy wouldn't know a fun time if it kissed him in the kisser, but he had one of the most natural ears for music she'd ever encountered. When the song was so perfect he couldn't help himself, his usually barred eyes opened up like clear lakes. She could see the music in him. She aimed for that look every time she sang in front of him, because then she knew she'd struck gold.

Anna had passed away the beginning of October, and the show had not only soothed Maggie's grief, it had served as a reminder that she had dreams and talent, that she loved Hey Nonny Nonny, but her world didn't have to fall with it. John hadn't said a word, but he'd known what she needed. Maggie had felt it standing under the lit-up awning, flashy posters pasted to the door windows. *Don't forget, Margaret Hughes.*

Was she leaving Hey Nonny Nonny?

"Not if I don't have to," Maggie said. "Maybe it could turn

around. Hero's trying. And I'm gonna sing every Saturday to help her. But we barely kept ourselves fed last winter, let alone making a wage. If it goes under, I'll be starting over in Harlem with only my pianist to vouch for me."

John crossed his arms. "Margaret . . ." His stern-and-concerned expression reminded Maggie so much of her mother she instantly scowled.

Born and raised in Philadelphia, Maggie had grown up listening to her father play their beat-up piano alongside the radio, inventing riffs that always made the song better. And a mother who insisted he turn that "troublemaking" music down. All Maggie had ever wanted to do was sing, and all her mother had ever wanted was for her to find safe, respectable, decent work and keep away from boys. When her parents had discovered her plans to hitchhike her way to New York rather than help fold some white lady's laundry another day, her father had made a compromise and sent her to live with friends on Long Island. Good work, better pay, and far enough from Harlem that her mother allowed it. But close enough, her father said, to see the lights, to soak up those radio songs in the flesh, if she didn't mind taking the train.

A plan that lasted until the day she found a black flower pin under a church pew. Maggie had known a little about Hey Nonny Nonny because Father Francis was the pastor in the church in Nassau where servants of the rich white families came to worship. She'd seen him passing out those pins that morning and heard some of the adults whispering about a "masquerade."

He would have turned her away at the door if he'd recognized her, but she'd been wearing a mask and, at the cusp of fifteen, was tall enough to pass as older. She hadn't even been thinking about singing. She'd only wanted to dance and have a good time.

By dumb luck the girl who was supposed to open for the main performer hadn't shown up, and Anna had taken to the stage and asked: "Any of you suckers know how to sing a ditty or two?"

Margaret Hughes knew how to sing a ditty. And she was not timid.

The crowd liked her young voice, and she did three encores.

Afterward Anna, having guessed Maggie wasn't as old as she seemed, made her a deal: Maggie could sing some nights and learn the business, but she would stay with Hey Nonny Nonny and out of trouble. Then, when she was twenty-one, Anna would help her get a good contract at a bigger venue. She'd even written to Maggie's parents to ask if they thought Maggie's salary was fair, and assured them Hey Nonny Nonny was a respectable establishment. That last part maybe stretched the truth, but it was hard to resist Anna Stahr.

Maggie had answered her father's last letter—*How are you, my sweet girl?*—with a vague telegram. She still hadn't told them Anna had died, nor that she hadn't been paid to sing for eight months. If her mother knew, she'd make Maggie go home.

And if Maggie left now, she might never come back.

"I'm good," she whispered, half to herself. She blinked out of the past and focused on John again. "You think I'm good, don't you? I'm not asking you to lie—"

John held up a hand.

Wondering if he was about to tell her she'd gone and stretched their familiarity too far, she clenched her teeth.

"Of course I think you're good," he whispered. "Don't— It's fine. Let me ask around. Maybe you can sing a few nights as a special, to see how you like the clubs, then decide if you want a regular gig."

"Really? You mean it? On the level now." She leaped at him, straight off the bed like a pouncing cat, but there was no surprising that boy. He caught her waist and stepped back, and instead of hugging him, she ended up sort of gripping his shoulders.

Still not a bad position to be in, to her way of thinking, but tonight wasn't about that. She let go of him. "Thank you. I mean it. You won't regret it. I'll do my best songs, and everyone will think you're a whiz for finding them such a treasure."

His hands dropped from her waist. "Don't you have a show to get ready for?"

"You bet I do." She skipped to the door. "I'll be the one in the red dress. Don't be late."

CHAPTER 10

A STAR DANCED, AND UNDER THAT WAS I BORN

Hero didn't let go of Beatrice's hand, for which Beatrice was profoundly grateful. Her cousin looked stunning, all of her short, amply curved form poured into a beaded black gown. Her mask was angled and trimmed with gold glitter, her red hair hidden under a gleaming black wig; she was dressed as Cleopatra. The geometry involved, from her cheekbones to the dip below her ankle, needed its own theorem. Beatrice knew from firsthand observation there was nothing under the dress but stockings (no room for anything else, not even a chemise) and two black garters; the sequined clutch she held contained a tiny peashooter pistol.

Yesterday they'd gotten into the speakeasy through a secret stairwell that led to a door behind one of the bar shelves. This time Hero insisted they use the outside entrance for experience's sake. She pressed a kiss to her fingertips and touched Anna's face on the photo by the front door. "Wish me luck, Mama," she said.

The drive was lined with haphazardly parked cars. In the forgiving glow of dusk and a dozen porch lamps, the sordid state of the gravel didn't seem so bad, the unruly weeds had the feeling of an enchanted garden. Everything seemed better and luminous. John was waiting for them by the cellar doors, looking sharp enough to cut in a black suit, his jacket collar flipped up. A fedora sat at an angle on his head; no mask. Maggie and Prince were both inside already, working. Hero hadn't said when Benedick would arrive, and Beatrice had been too embarrassed with herself to ask.

"*Ciao,*" said Hero.

John inclined his head. *"Buona sera."*

She tugged one of his ears, and he brushed her hand off. Hero would have lost that hand, Beatrice thought, if she'd been anyone else.

The cement stairs were already lit, and at the bottom stood a burly man with dark skin and a scar through his eyebrow. Hero patted his massive shoulder. "Father Francis is the pastor at the church, but also one of our best bouncers. He and Papa served in the war together."

"Good evenin', Miss Clark." Father Francis had a faint brogue. He nodded at John. "Mr. Morello, good to see you at the Nonny." He began to open the door, but Hero slapped his arm.

"Francis! Is this how you do your job? Ask about our pins."

He cleared his throat. "Apologies. May I see your invitations, misses?"

Obligingly Beatrice showed him the black flower she had pinned to her dress sleeve. The Paris number had worked after all, once Hero stitched a few seams—in minutes, while Beatrice watched in amazement. Beatrice rather liked the finished product. It was loose, with no waistline, almost as comfortable as trousers. She'd examined herself in the mirror and concluded she either looked like a sap or quite pretty. One or the other.

"Very good." Father Francis's eyes creased with humor. "Password?"

Beatrice glanced at Hero. "Sigh no more?"

Father Francis held the door open. "Enjoy your evening."

Beatrice nearly stumbled when she walked in, hit all at once by the sudden shift in smell and sound; the spirit of the untrammeled. The wide, long room was draped in red and, in addition to the stage, the dance floor was large enough to fit more than fifty people, if they didn't mind bumping elbows. The sides were lined with rows of plush booths, decorated with colored lights. The crowd, all masked, wasn't too big, clearly a younger, poorer, odder sort. Like the jazz music that played.

"Hey, look, it's Hero!"

A girl appeared out of nowhere and grabbed Hero's arm and kissed her on the cheek. Her brown hair was bobbed severely;

the kohl lining her eyes under the mask. "Well, aren't you some-thing tonight, all trussed up? Hey, Dan! Hero's here!"

A rugged-looking boy sauntered over and gave Hero an appreciative look. "Why, if it isn't the infamous Hero Stahr. Who's your friend?"

"My cousin, Beatrice. She's the smartest gal in the city. Someday she'll be delivering your herd of blue-blooded babies, Marta."

"A lady doctor, what do you know?" Marta smirked.

John was already moving away from them, heading for the bar. He didn't even have to try for his foot-wide path through the crowd.

Beatrice glanced at Hero, whose personal orbit did the oppo-site: inviting people in. "I'll be back in two shakes," Hero told her, adjusting her mask. "Meet me at the bar. Prince should be there."

Beatrice was more than happy to take advantage of John's trail. He was already sitting and looked as festive as he had out-side. Which was to say, not at all.

"Already lose our hostess?" Prince appeared behind the counter, a rag slung over one shoulder. He wore a gray checked suit, but it was a touch too small for him, strained at the shoulders. As if some-one had tried to make a copy of John but forgotten to say *when*.

She shrugged. His eyes crinkled. "You look pretty," he said, in such a sincere way she actually believed him. He put a squat glass in front of her, two-thirds full with bubbling golden liquid.

"Oh, I'd better—"

"It's ginger ale." He winked and plopped in a cherry.

"Hello, troublemakers!"

Beatrice saw the tic in Prince's expression, his gaze glancing past her shoulder, before her cousin reappeared at her side. "Ain't it the cat's pajamas in here tonight?"

"Where'd you run off to?" Beatrice asked.

"I had to see if Ben's classmate decided to show." Hero flashed that ne'er-do-well gap at Prince. "Hey there, slim."

"Hey yourself."

"So can a girl get a drink?" Hero asked, propping her feathered mask on top of her forehead. A fine sheen of sweat covered the bridge of her nose. "Or at least a cig?"

"Did you find him then?" asked Beatrice.

"Not yet." Hero fanned her face with her hand, and Prince slid her a red-orange cocktail. "He'll break my heart if he doesn't show. I am done in for this one."

Prince glanced up to examine the ceiling. "You're done in twice a month."

"This time it's real," Hero said matter-of-factly; adding, at Prince's skeptical look, "Haven't you heard of love at first sight?"

"Maybe at first dollar. How much has he got?" Prince countered.

"Well, how should I know?"

"I bet you do. Down to the plugged nickel."

"For God's sake, don't be such a wet blanket, Prince. It's making me anxious." She downed her drink.

Beatrice glanced between her and Prince. "But . . . I assumed . . . you and Prince seemed so close."

"Oh! Oh, definitely not. My goodness, that would be like kissing my brother." Her head cocked in consideration. Prince raised an eyebrow at her. "If I had a brother."

"Is that him?" John interrupted. He lifted his cigarette, pointing toward the dance floor. "If it's not, then he's got some competition."

The wood floor was packed with frenetic dancers. Beatrice had been forced to learn to dance at Miss Nightingale's. Basic waltzes. The fox-trot. Not . . . this. The Charleston. She knew what it was; she didn't live *completely* in a glass vial. She just didn't know how to do it. It looked like walking, but in one place, and fast, feet kicking forward and backward, arms swinging with abandon. Frankly, the ten or so dancers on the floor looked foolish, as if they were caught in the middle of falling and falling and falling.

One boy, however, did not. Claude moved with grace, his rhythm lazy yet precisely on beat. He was comically good-looking, with wavy brown hair and the sort of face that begged to be bronzed and put in front of an academic hall. Hero couldn't keep her eyes off him.

Claude grinned at her, spun on his heel with deliberate slowness, and pointed to the floor space next to him.

"Is he one of yours?" Uncle Leo arrived, swaggering. He landed a wet, noisy kiss on Hero's head. To judge by his shining cheeks, he was already several drinks in. "Got a pin, all right, but I know I didn't give it to him."

"Hmm." Hero's hand fluttered by her throat.

"That's him," said Prince.

"Damn. I hate being summoned, but I can't stand it anymore. Bye, Papa. Stay out of trouble, you hear?" She kissed his cheek.

When she tried to wipe the residue lipstick off, he waved her away. "Leave it, sweetheart. This way it looks like the girls still like to kiss me."

Laughing, she leaned over to give Prince an affectionate chuck under his chin. "Save a dance for me, honey." She sauntered off, waving and blowing kisses at friends as she went.

"Wow," said Beatrice.

"Yes," Prince agreed, watching her retreat. He glanced back at Beatrice with a half smile. "Wouldn't it be awful to be in love with Hero Stahr?"

"How about a dance with an old man?" Uncle Leo asked, taking Beatrice's elbow.

"As long as you aren't worried about the state of your feet," she said.

"My dear, I'm as drunk as a glass of lemonade in July. I won't feel a thing."

Beatrice danced happily with her uncle and poorly with

another boy who stuttered and said, "Say, k-kid, you're a pretty girl and ain't got a dance p-partner, say, it's a shame!" When she returned to the bar, Prince was too busy making himself useful to talk with her—she'd begun to suspect this was what he did, and everyone relied on him to do it—so she found her own fun at the back booths, where people were playing euchre, poker, and bridge. Betting with pennies and candies, nobody took it seriously enough for it to be called proper gambling.

That didn't mean a girl couldn't play to win.

After several rounds the gentleman across from Beatrice set down his hand and laughed. "There's only so many times a man can suffer defeat. What do you say to a dance, Lily?"

The girl on Beatrice's right couldn't drop her cards fast enough. "Yes, please!"

"An excellent game," the man said as he pulled out Lily's chair. "You're a terrifying cardplayer."

Alone, Beatrice gathered up the cards, her mask on the table by her elbow.

"You look in need of an adversary." Just like that, the seat across from her became occupied again. Her new opponent wore a mask that covered the entire top of his head, fittingly equipped with horns, a garish masterpiece that looked like the product of hell's finest festival, leaving only a sharp chin available for inspection. His voice carried a manufactured country accent.

But beneath the mask were eyes the color of mud. The

color, more precisely, of being late for class when it was raining outside and slipping and seeing your best shoe coated in slick nasty brown and the obscenity that came out because the day was awful and everything was ruined.

However, if Benedick wanted to pretend he'd achieved anonymity with his mask, far be it from her to stop him from making a fool of himself. In fact, it might turn into the highlight of her evening.

"I'm afraid we need another two players," she said blankly.

He swept the cards into his hands with dexterity, shuffling a few times. "Cribbage? Gin? Svoyi Koziri?"

"I know gin."

He dealt, set the deck between them, and flipped the first card up. Beatrice examined her ten cards in silence, calculating her options and the percentage odds of reaching each option. She drew from the deck and discarded.

"What are we playing for?" he asked, and took his turn. It really was incredible. His voice was all but unrecognizable. Perhaps he should take to the stage if his writing never sold.

"A winner's bet?"

"If you please."

She shrugged at her humble earnings. "A nickel or two should suffice, unless you want more. I don't foresee you winning."

The smirk that appeared would have given him away if she hadn't already known who he was. "I'm penniless, alas. If I win, I want a dance. If you win, I'll give you a kiss."

"I don't suppose it occurred to you I might not want your kiss."

"If you don't want it, you can give it back."

She glared, flustered. Too late she drew without thinking. She could have used the seven of hearts, but she missed it. This was why sparring with him, and his prettily turned words, was so frustrating. Like using a bow and arrow against the wind. "If I win, you go away," she said.

"Done."

She concentrated on her hand, refusing to let herself get drawn in by conversation again. Not that he didn't try. Her dogged silence seemed to amuse him. He barely looked at his cards, and her confidence grew.

Until she laid down a king and he swiped it immediately. "Poor choice, Lady Disdain."

"What did you call me?"

He put his discard facedown. Her stomach fell. "I win," he said.

Beatrice stared at the set of jacks and royal run of diamonds he displayed. She cleared her throat. "Well. So you have."

He stood and held out a hand.

Very well.

Perhaps she could step on his toes five times and make it look like an accident. She placed her hand in his. A small shock went through her arm all the way to the bone. Revulsion no doubt. "Do you title all the strangers you meet with insulting characteristics?" she asked as he led them onto an unoccupied space of the floor.

"Only when it's very obvious."

Her hand tightened on his. As they sashayed through the first step, she landed pointedly on his foot. Except for a missed beat, he didn't react. He just twisted his ankle and set it back.

"Try to let the man lead, hmm?"

"I wasn't—"

But she must have been because his hold on her waist tightened, and then she was not leading and felt the difference.

"At first I thought you must have learned I was disdainful from someone else," she said. "Benedick Scott perhaps?"

"Who's that?" he asked, all innocence.

"You must know him."

"I don't, believe me."

"Lord Loquacious, they'd call him." They were dancing, she realized. As long as she let him lead, she actually did all right. He was irritatingly graceful, and this, even more irritatingly, didn't surprise her.

"Describe him, won't you? Maybe I've seen him."

She was tempted to say he was beyond description—the only truthful response that question warranted—but lurking within his request was the monster of opportunity. "He's Prince's little pet," she said after a pause. "The speakeasy's mascot. Quick on his feet, entertaining and whatnot, but not much substance underneath. He wants to write, I hear, but he's too much a snob for it. The upper class think some skill they acquired in an expensive class-room can pass as art, but they haven't got anything real to say. They don't understand the world outside their social circle."

By the time she finished, his grip was painful, but she pretended not to notice. Below the mask his mouth was a grim line.

"When I do meet this gentleman," he said at last, "I'll tell him what you said."

"Oh, please do. He'll have a few nasty things to say about me, too, I'm sure. But we really ought to be nice. Why would he be here at all if he weren't desperately lonely?"

He practically threw her away from him, taking a step back. Beatrice had always been plagued with a mouth that was a little too big and a little too full of salt and vinegar or, most offensive of all, too full of the truth. Still, she couldn't imagine Benedick gave a hill of beans about her opinion—even if he truly believed she thought she was talking to a stranger.

"Sir, perhaps you—"

"Excuse me," he muttered, the country accent gone, and stormed away. Beatrice watched him go, wondering if the slight twist in her stomach was, for the first time, guilt over speaking her mind.

CHAPTER 11

SHE SPEAKS PONIARDS, AND EVERY WORD STABS

Benedick knew the proverbial warning about girls who took the stuffing out of you, such as it were. Girls like Hero or his own mother, who had fled to Hollywood to star in films, whose effect paralyzed the tongue, turned the brain to potatoes. Benedick had always thought himself immune but had to consider if it wasn't happening to him now, with this unlikely candidate.

The bass sound of strings beat off the stone wall and tickled the back of his neck. His gigantic mask rested on his knee. This was his favorite spot in Hey Nonny Nonny—the area just to the side of the band, among their instrument cases and abandoned cocktails. Cast in the shadow of the staging lights, it was beyond the reach of most eyes. He sat, leaning his head against the wall, the lit end of his cigarette bright in the darkness. He watched it slowly burn up but didn't bring it to his lips. Every time he tried, Beatrice's voice prattled about clogged chimney stacks.

It wasn't as if he were one of those fellows who required girls to be sweet and adoring to him. Hero and Maggie, whom he considered on par with angels, weren't halfhearted about taking off their wings when the situation called for it. But Beatrice went horns first all the time.

"I thought I'd find you here." A figure materialized out of the gloom: Prince. He lowered himself next to Benedick and plucked the cigarette from his fingers. Without a word he blew it back to life and stuck it in the corner of his mouth. "Hello."

"I'm never going to amount to anything. I'm going to die in utter obscurity, with nothing to mark my grave but a few pages of meaningless drivel."

Prince didn't blink. "We agreed," he said, "no three-syllable words after midnight."

"*Syllable* is a three-syllable word."

Prince sighed, glanced over. "Look, I know your brain is large and perpetually at war with itself, but you will be published. You're talented."

"You've barely read my work."

"Yes, but I listen to you talk. More than enough to fill a book."

Benedick grinned and stole his cigarette back.

"I saw Beatrice," said Prince. Benedick sat up straighter, like a plucked harp string. "Curious girl."

"You understate it, Prince."

"Seems she danced with a rather obnoxious gentleman." Prince blew a smoke ring, followed by a sharp stream that knocked the top of the ring and made it a heart. "Why can't you be nice?"

"Me?" Benedick flared up so quickly Prince startled backward. "I'm obnoxious? The most long-suffering saint would lose patience with that girl. I am, in her eyes, little better than the speakeasy's mascot. She analyzes people like projects instead of actual human beings. I find her insufferable, and if it comes to sides, I expect you to take mine, Pedro Morello." He took a deep breath, hot as a fired gun. *Him*, be nice!

"Well, at least you might have left her alone," said Prince.

Indeed.

In his defense Benedick hadn't disliked her so thoroughly until after he'd spoken with her, but he had been the one to seek her out. With the intention of bothering her, no less. He just hadn't expected to lose the spat. Was that it? Or had he expected another outcome entirely?

"Rest assured," Benedick said coldly, refusing to peek down that hidey-hole, "I will certainly leave her alone in the future."

"Interesting," Prince said.

"What? That she shares the same gene pool as Hero? I agree."

"No." Prince looked amused. "You. I've never seen you this passionate about a girl."

Benedick reeled back. "You misuse the word *passionate*, Prince. And the word *girl*, for that matter, as she is more accurately a spawn of Satan." Suddenly aware of the heat in his voice, he sank back and waved a dismissive hand. "But I see your point. The next time she says something to me, I'm going to smile and say, 'That's nice.'"

"An excellent plan." Prince pushed himself up. "And now's a good time to put it into practice since she's coming over here."

In his haste to sit up, Benedick slipped and smacked his elbow into the wall. "*Shit*—damn."

"Yes, that's how we say, 'That's nice,' in Italian, too."

Benedick scrambled to his feet. "She'll see me if I try to leave and know I'm running away from her. Make yourself useful for once. Give me something to do."

Too late. She arrived, and at her side was none other than Claude Blaine. Well dressed, handsome, sure of himself. Claude beamed brilliantly. He looked too rich for this place, a bit as though he were pandering to the masses.

"Miss Clark said she saw you wander over here, and so she was right, as I suspect"—here, Claude turned his golden smile in Beatrice's direction—"she often is."

Benedick was gratified to see that not even Claude's charm could woo Beatrice. She smiled, but in a way that said she knew she'd been flattered and she saw right through it.

Better luck next time, old boy.

"I've brought you an admirer," she said, turning to Benedick.

"As I know how desperate you are for them. And for you, Signor Morello, a summons to return to the bar."

A call Prince rarely ignored. Benedick was about to lose his ally. He asked, "What was it again you needed me to do?"

Prince considered and said, "Favor Beatrice with your company?"

I hate you, Benedick thought.

Prince smiled as if he'd heard him.

"Never fear, Mr. Scott," said Beatrice. "You won't be so burdened. I delivered one package and am to escort the second." Naturally, Prince offered his arm, and away they went together, his nemesis and his best friend.

Claude watched them disappear into the crowd, then turned back to Benedick, the devil in his eye. "I saw your father at graduation this morning," he said, leaning in, his arms crossed over his chest.

"Oh?" Benedick feigned indifference.

"I covered for you, though I'm not sure he believed a word I said. I told him you had friends in Flower Hill who were in dire need of help this weekend, and naturally you, being the good-hearted gentleman that you are, went at once to assist them."

Naturally. No, Ambrose Scott wouldn't have believed a word; Benedick could guarantee it. Scott men were not known for their altruistic tendencies. But his father had listened, and he'd heard at least two important words: Flower Hill.

"You didn't mention Hey Nonny Nonny . . ." Benedick hedged.

"Well, not in such specifics. I didn't say it was a speakeasy, though if you don't mind my saying, I doubt your father gives a damn for Prohibition. I only said it was an enterprise. I was quite vague, to tell the truth."

Good God. His father knew precisely where to find him. Benedick dragged a hand down his face and was filled with the profound desire to either flee immediately or drink himself into a nonsensical stupor. Luckily, he was in prime position to engage in the latter.

Claude either couldn't see or didn't understand the abject horror that must have been all over Benedick's face. "Honestly, Ben, *is* that what you're doing here? Not that it's not an okay joint, for the countryside, but it's not our usual crowd."

Benedick bristled at the "our."

Even Claude, who really was the better end of their apparently hateful kind, could not shed the mark of a snob.

"Well," said Benedick, skirting an answer, "I'm sorry it's been disappointing to you in the end."

"On the contrary," Claude said, the words crisp and bouncy in his accent. "I brought half of Chapman with me, and everyone's having a fine time, so far as I know. The music is first-rate. And the *girl* . . ." His eyes drifted toward the bar, though it was too far, with too many people between them, to see properly. "Hero Stahr. She is the most wonderful creature I've ever met. That's all. I refuse to magnify. Except—she is perfect." His laughter, Benedick hoped, signified self-awareness over how ridiculous he sounded. "Only there's the niggle of a feeling she's too worldly for me."

"That feeling tells the truth. Let me know if it gives you any racing tips." A sudden craving for inebriation struck Benedick: tobacco or large quantities of alcohol. Preferably both.

"That tall fella, Prince? She's not his girl?"

Oh, she was. But not in the way Claude meant. Benedick said, "No, she's free as a bird." And Claude would fall for her song, and then he'd be looking at the sky, wondering where the hell he was, and she'd be gone as a dove that'd flown the coop.

"My mother arranged for me to spend most of the summer at Newport," said Claude. "The Vanderbilts stay at The Breakers every summer, and she wants to get on the dowager's good side. They're still dead set on finding me an American deb . . ." He trailed off.

Benedick's attention had glazed at "the Vanderbilts."

"I'm going to send a telegram tomorrow morning," Claude added. "Hero said there was an extra room here if I wanted to stay. It will be weeks before Mums gets wind of what's happened to lecture me about it."

"You're staying?"

"Yes!" Claude practically burst with the word. "I have to. That's honestly how it feels, Ben. I just have to get to know her."

Bless his heart.

"That's swell, Claude. Truly. Now what do you say we have a cocktail or three?"

CHAPTER 12

HE'S NOT IN YOUR GOOD BOOKS

Beatrice could not understand how she'd landed in her current predicament. No, that wasn't true. Logistically she was aware of the series of events that had led to this point: Hero, leaving on Claude's arm—"I've got to show him to his room"—and Prince helping a halfway-to-snoring Uncle Leo to his feet: "Beatrice, would you mind keeping an eye on Ben?"

It was just, in God's name, *why*?

She'd assumed one of them would be back, even as the party waned into its twilight hours and only John, the band, and Father Francis remained, smoking and drinking onstage.

Neither Hero nor Prince had returned, and both had made such a fuss about Beatrice's helping Benedick that she had the grudging suspicion they'd done it on purpose. If this was another you'd-make-a-swell-couple ruse, their plan had sorely backfired because Beatrice was even less inclined to him than before.

He stretched up from where he'd been draped like discarded laundry at a table. He swayed a little, then fumbled his way behind the bar, only to stare intently at the shelves filled with stacked glasses and a now sparse selection of bottles. The hidden door was the shelf case on the far left, but after pondering, Benedick went to the one on the right. He jiggled the wood, heaved against it with both hands, even kicked the bottom.

With a sigh, Beatrice slipped off her stool and went around to tap him on the shoulder. He turned, glaring. "I have no need of your assistance, Miss Clark. Kindly remove yourself from my presence at once." His voice carried a bit of slur but didn't slow, didn't simplify.

"I'd hoped inebriation might reduce your pompous rhetoric, but it appears sobriety was your last restraint. That's not the right shelf, Mr. Scott. Come here."

He followed her to the left. "Pompous rhetoric," he murmured. "I very much enjoy trying to guess what you'll say next, except you are"—he paused, then sighed—"so horrible."

They had a problem. Beatrice ran her hands along the lacquered shelves and lifted bottles to peer around the side and underneath, but she couldn't find a handle or anything that would open it. She'd watched Prince slip in and out at least three times but apparently should have paid closer attention. Benedick was no help; eyes closed, he leaned dolefully against the shelf.

She glanced at the stage. Father Francis would probably know, or Maggie. But interrupting them would take just as long as going to the main entrance. "Listen," she said, "we're just going to have to leave the other way."

"On second thought," he said, beginning to slump to the ground, "that seems terribly far. I've decided I'll sleep here tonight. Good evening, Miss Clark."

"*No*, don't you dare."

To her surprise, he straightened, blinking as if he were more astonished by his obedience than she was. Tugging at his jacket sleeve when necessary, she coaxed him to the main door. Maggie waved cheerily—almost smugly, Beatrice thought—from the stage as they left. They made it to the cellar stairs, but someone had turned off the light.

They fumbled up a few steps in the dark.

"Not to worry," said Benedick. A hiss, and his face swam into view behind a lit match. "I know where the light is. The string hangs down. By the door."

Beatrice spotted it just as Benedick yelped in shock that the match was burning him and dropped it. She tried to find the string again, hand raised and searching; Benedick was doing the same thing, and they knocked into each other, limbs tangling, just as her fingers brushed—*click*. A tiny hanging lamp flickered on.

Again his face appeared, cast in swaying shadow, unbearably close to her own. He leaned against her. Whatever he'd been drinking, she could smell it full force. Just then he looked very young. He blinked slowly, eyes drifting to her shoulder. And he frowned.

Beatrice glanced down and noticed the small spider crawling on her sleeve. She let go of the string and flicked it off with two fingers. "Stand up, Ben. I'm practically carrying you."

"Right, sorry."

He shifted but only ended up leaning on her more.

"I'm up," he said. "I think I'm standing."

In defeat, she drew an arm around his torso. "I guess you won't bite."

"Only if you ask me nicely."

She shoved against the cellar door, guided them both into the blessed fresh night air, and kicked the door closed with her foot.

"You're quite strong, you know," said Benedick, still on her shoulder, as they made their way into the house. "You shoot things and don't fear spiders and are about as sweet as a lemon. What would a man even do with you?"

"The better question, Mr. Scott, is what would I do with a man?"

"Nothing?" He said it like an uncertain child in a classroom.

"Precisely."

Why were there so many stairs in this house? Of course Benedick's room had to be at the very top, and he had to be so close she kept feeling his cheek on her temple: warm and frankly not unpleasant enough considering how drunk he was. In fact drunkenness only shot him down to common, if that, which didn't seem fair.

At long last they made it to his room. His bed—if he indeed owned one—would be even harder to find in the dark, so she deposited him on the ugly red couch. He was too big for it but curled like a content cat against the cushions and seemed to fall asleep instantly.

"*Ben*," Beatrice said, irritated, and forced him back up so she could get his jacket and tie off. She unbuttoned his cuffs, but let the shirt stay on. She tugged off his shoes, muttering that *this* was what she'd do with a husband, no doubt, and she'd much rather get paid to act as nurse, thank you very much.

She set his jacket over his shoulders as a blanket and straightened. There would be no sentimental watching of his slumber. Anyway, Benedick Scott was not the sort of creature that wanted for coddling, even like this.

Only when she was in her own room, removing her shoes, did it occur to her that she might never get another chance to use his typewriter.

The instant she'd seen it, she'd envisioned how good her admissions letter might look. Then he'd gone all dicey about it. . . .

Not that—

Obviously she was not in the habit of using someone else's possessions without permission, but on the other hand, she could have left him on the floor behind the bar. One might consider a measly page and an ounce or two of ink payment for services rendered.

Excellent reasoning, Clark.

So decided, she went through her things to retrieve the information pamphlet on the Woman's Medical College of the New York Infirmary. There were other colleges, but Beatrice wanted the one Elizabeth Blackwell had founded.

Armed with notes and the pamphlet, she edged open the door and peeked in, but Benedick hadn't moved from where she'd left him. She cracked his window open a few inches, letting the chirp of deep night waft in, and turned the knob of the flat wick lamp she'd brought from her room until a dim glow lit the room.

She sat and loosened the paper already set into the platen. He'd typed one paragraph:

Perish the thought, me in love with this magnificently hideous bluestocking! For surely she was ugly, and yet there was never a question of attraction, because she had such beauty of thought. A luminous intelligence that outshone her perceived flaws. Small-minded criticisms of her visage could not withstand such tenderness, such strange, endless mystery in her eyes, of which most mortals had no conception, that left behind a sense of having encountered something truly exquisite.

Beatrice read it twice, the second time involuntarily, her eyes driven back up, so she might experience the paragraph again. Not that it wasn't as wordy and tangled as what she'd expect Benedick to write. Maybe it wasn't good. She wasn't any proper critic of literature, but there was something . . .

A curious catch in her chest. A snag in her own self-perception, thinking someone might consider intelligence as attractive as a pretty face and figure. And she felt—

Unsettled? Was that the word?

Benedick had written it; this idea had come from his mind. She twisted in her chair, so she could see him. He released a soft snore and turned over, the jacket slipping to the floor, arm flopping over his head. A button near his collar was loose, the thread frayed. She had the sudden urge, against her finest principles, to mend it for him.

She turned pointedly away, rolling a fresh sheet through the feed. Her fingers sat big and clumsy on the keys. The letter went slowly. And perhaps not well. The harder she tried, the heavier each word felt, wrong and misshapen.

She kept at it for over an hour and was thinking of how to end it when Benedick muttered. She shot him a panicked glance.

His bloodshot eyes fluttered but ultimately closed again, one leg stretching over the couch's side.

She was out of time. She hastily typed the last line, "With best regards," then slid her letter out and hurried on tiptoe from his room. When she woke up the next morning, she realized she'd forgotten her pamphlet and notes. Meanwhile, she'd kept his paragraph. An accident, she would argue, if he noticed. Even if she'd folded it. Neatly. And put it in her slipper.

CHAPTER 13
WHAT HIS HEART THINKS
HIS TONGUE SPEAKS

Something was wrong.

Benedick sprang awake, sat up before he was fully conscious, and quickly concluded it was a hangover. That was the problem, ow, Jesus, Mary, and—

No.

Something else.

He tipped his head back, let his eyes sink closed, and massaged his scalp. The headache faded somewhat, but the feeling did not. He cracked one eye open and examined his room. His gaze landed on his desk and focused slowly, the other eye opening. An empty typewriter. A kerosene lamp that didn't belong to him. Gripping the back of the desk chair in one hand, he

SPEAK EASY SPEAK LOVE

eased to his feet. Notes with unfamiliar handwriting.

And yet not that either—

The distinct sound of an automobile door closing floated through his open window—he *never* opened his window—and he stumbled through the mess until he could see out to the driveway.

A blood-red Rolls-Royce Silver Ghost Piccadilly Roadster.

His father's car.

And beside it, adjusting his hat, his father.

Son of a bitchin' bastard.

Benedick nearly tripped shooting back from the window. He rubbed his eyes, which felt coated with sand. His water basin, filled with half an inch of murky used water, sat precariously on top of a stack of Shakespeare tomes, and behind it a cracked six-inch mirror. Was it the rarely cleaned mirror causing the yellowish pallor on his face or was that his actual flesh?

Not that it mattered how undead he looked; there was no time to do anything about it. It was unlikely anyone else in the house would be awake, not after the Masquerade. And his father was the type to stroll right in and help himself to the hospitality no one was providing.

Benedick threw off his booze-rank shirt and undershirt and was halfway through the buckle on his pants when the knob on his door turned. No knock or any sort of warning. He froze. Had his father moved so quickly, determining with nothing more than parental instinct where to find his son?

But the nose that appeared around the edge of the door was pert and freckled, and then holy God, there she was, summoned like some sort of bloodhound to witness this disastrous moment, and likely the next, and the next, until eternity. Beatrice glanced first at the empty couch, then found him, wincing.

"Get out, you wretched blight—" He threw himself at the door to close it, but she managed to get her foot, and one of those damned rugged boots, into its path.

"Hold on just a minute—" She grunted, pushing back (she was nearly as strong as he was; that was disheartening). "I left something in here that's very important to me; it will only take me two seconds to grab it—"

He flung the door open. She stumbled in and caught herself on his bare chest. She jolted back, shaking out her hand as if she'd sunk it into a vat of manure.

Benedick asked, "Why are any of *your* belongings in *my* room?"

She narrowed her eyes. "I practically carried you up here last night, when you were content to sleep on the bar floor, so I hardly think . . ." She continued, but he stopped listening. Her voice was doing nothing for his headache, right between the eyebrows and out the back of his head. She looked as if she'd been up for hours—

"You're awake," he interrupted.

"My God." She stared at him. "Is this fact only now occurring to you? Just how intoxicated were you, Mr. Scott?"

"Be quiet, you very-near-to-respectable-looking monkey. Go downstairs and make sure my father doesn't come up here."

"Wait, your father?"

He hopped out of his pants and kicked them to the side.

"Ben! I'm still in your room!" She cupped her hand to the side of her face, shielding her gaze, a healthy pink blossoming under her freckles.

"I'll be as exposed as I please within my own quarters, and if you don't like it, I suggest you leave. Downstairs, if you're going anyway."

She made an aggravated noise in the back of her throat, but she went, leaving him to stuff himself into the best clothes he could find. He scrubbed his face, shaved, and fingered leftover pomade through his hair.

He strode into the drawing room ten minutes later, in a buttoned vest and collared shirt, but no tie. Matching gray slacks and worn leather shoes, used but well maintained. In other words, sharp, but not as if he were trying to impress.

Ambrose Scott was six feet five, with broad shoulders, a lion's mane of hair on his head, and a trimmed golden beard. Without saying a word, he exuded a message: *I, unlike the rest of you sorry saps, am here to win, to dominate, to triumph.*

Benedick expected, in the best-case scenario, Beatrice to notice the moment he came in, relieved to be able to flee, or in the worst case, to find her close to tears after a round of his father's demands and entitled rudeness. To his surprise, neither even glanced up as he hovered in the entrance.

They were discussing economics.

He was fairly sure anyway.

His father didn't seem quite impressed—he never was—but he was giving Beatrice his full attention, which wasn't nothing. "An interesting point of view," he was saying, then pulled out his handkerchief to cough.

"Are you ill, Mr. Scott?" asked Beatrice. "You've been coughing." Too politely, a restraint of her usual brashness.

"Only a cold," his father said dismissively. "Saw a doctor for it two days ago."

"May I offer a secondary diagnosis?" she asked.

Mr. Scott gave her a slow, calculating look.

Without waiting for an answer, she stood and gestured at his collar. "May I?"

"May you what—"

She leaned down, placed a finger in his collar, and pulled it slightly off his neck. "As I thought. Your skin's inflamed where it touches your shirt. Have you switched dry cleaners recently?"

"As a matter of fact . . ." Mr. Scott raised an eyebrow.

"Common starch ingredients include formaldehyde, phenol, and pentachlorophenol, which can irritate the lungs. An allergy, in other words, which might not have manifested until an excess amount was used, or a different brand. Especially in someone who's suffered respiratory problems in the past."

"I had asthma as a boy," Mr. Scott said, then, as if he couldn't let even this minor weakness stand, added, "You know who else had asthma as a boy?"

"Theodore Roosevelt," said Beatrice.

Mr. Scott smiled. She'd done it. He was impressed. "Just so. I'll inquire about the brand of soap, and we'll see if you're right. A very clever discovery, for such a young girl."

"Well . . ." Beatrice brushed off her skirt, looked up, and saw Benedick. Quietly she finished: "I'm very smart."

Benedick came into the room, and Mr. Scott turned. "Evidently. Hello, son. Is Miss Clark here one of your acquaintances?"

Benedick caught himself about to say "unfortunately" and instead said, "A very recent one." He sat on the couch beside her and propped his foot on one knee, keeping his gaze level with his father's.

Mr. Scott smirked, then turned to Beatrice. "Tell me, Miss Clark, are chemical ingredients something they teach often in girls' schools these days?"

"I shouldn't think so," said Beatrice. "At least not at Miss Nightingale's. I taught myself the basics of algebra before ever attending school. There was only one teacher, Clarissa Mayple, who was able to privately teach me advanced mathematics and chemistry."

"Fascinating. And they allowed it?"

"No. Not as part of my regular curriculum. I studied with

Miss Mayple on my own time. She was very kind to tutor me."

"I admire that sort of work ethic and ambition in a person," said Mr. Scott. "Ben, on the other hand, could barely be bothered to attend the minimal amount of class at Stony Creek Academy. Your genes never manifest the way you think they will."

"Perhaps I'll marry Miss Clark," said Benedick, eager to cut this line of conversation short, "and then you'll have her as a daughter."

Mr. Scott grinned, approving, as ever, of his son's boldness. Part of the reason they always fought was that Mr. Scott loved to see fight in people. "I'm not sure she'd have you."

"I wouldn't," said Beatrice, "and, for the sake of all women, I must hope he remains a bachelor all his life." She said it in jest, and Mr. Scott laughed; but then she looked away with a sudden frown. "Can I make you coffee, Mr. Scott?"

"That would be lovely," Mr. Scott said as she stood.

Benedick looked at her: *How domestic; you know how to make coffee?*

She raised an eyebrow back: *Not well; drink it with caution when it comes.*

Benedick was so sure he'd read her correctly, so sure she'd read *him* correctly, he was at once stunned and disgusted. Her expression showed a similar sentiment; then she hurried out of the room.

When she was gone, Benedick turned again to his father. "I don't recall leaving this address with my things."

"Nor did you leave anything, compensation or otherwise,

with your things, and as such they remain at Stony Creek, where you are welcome to pick them up yourself. I'm not your valet."

Benedick's mouth pressed into a grim line. His most valued possessions were already with him; he didn't mind losing his school trunks, if it came to it.

His father continued. "That Blaine kid talked like this might be a speakeasy. Must be in the basement, by the look of the place. Is that what you're doing here? Rum-running for some bootlegging mogul?" The trace of curiosity in his voice further proved that anything, even something illegal, was better than his son's becoming a novelist, which was considered a bit above a trained circus animal but a bit below a trained circus clown. "Of course there's no business in being a lackey. You've got to run it yourself if you want to make anything of it."

"I help with the speakeasy," Benedick said. "If I'm needed. That's not really why I'm here."

"Then why are you?" Mr. Scott asked plainly, all pretense of politeness gone in one question. "To write? How is this setting preferable than anywhere else—your own home, for example?"

"My freedom, for one," Benedick snapped.

"Are you free?" his father asked, quiet as a snake's hiss. "Do you know why fine art is a product of the upper class, son? Because to create anything, you don't need only talent; you need comfort and peace of mind. How do you expect to indulge yourself with hours of payless work with the threat of unemployment hanging over your head? Do you think you'd be able to spend your morning writing a poem knowing you wouldn't be able to feed yourself or your family that day because of it?"

"I won't get married," Benedick said. "I'll support only myself."

"I see. And you're willing to starve for your art, is that it? My boy, you've had a silver spoon in your mouth since you were a babe."

Benedick said nothing. He couldn't; that was how these conversations went. Just when he needed it, the English language abandoned him, words crumbling unformed in his mouth.

"I suppose they're kind to you here?" his father asked, eyes roving the room. Benedick saw the furnishings through his eyes: once grand, around the turn of the century, but worn through with living. The dust on the shelves, the threads loosening on the drapes, a vase of flowers that hadn't been changed out, all the stems dried and drooped over. "The poor tend to be, because they have nothing to lose. The rich cannot afford it. I am the only one who is honest with you."

Benedick worked to unclench his jaw. "That's not—"

"I've paid for your schooling. I'll pay some more, and you'll be properly graduated. I'll pay your tuition at university, or I'll set you up with a job at my firm. You have until the end of the summer to choose one. After that, you won't see a penny from me, nor an offer for one later." Mr. Scott stood, placed his hat over his head. "I'll expect a telegram with your decision two weeks before fall term begins. Please give my apologies to Miss Clark."

Benedick stood after him. "You can take my name off your accounts today if it suits you."

Mr. Scott leveled his high-powered stare at his son, but in this, at least, Benedick could match him. "I've decided, and I won't change my mind," Benedick said. "Do what you like."

"My offer stands," Mr. Scott said slowly, "as I gave it." He walked out of the room. Only when Benedick heard the car motor start did he sink back onto the couch.

He was still sitting there, head back, unmoved and miserable, when Claude entered the room, dapper as the sun. "Hullo."

Benedick frowned at such insulting chipperness.

"Glad someone's up. I'm nearly dying for a cup of tea, but the kitchen is beastly hard to find." Claude went straight for one of the bay windows and pulled apart the drapes. "My God, it's beautiful out there. Don't you think? I swear, there's a kind of music in hearing the wind through the trees. Wouldn't you agree?"

Benedick ground his knuckles into his throbbing temples. "No, I would not, you blister. And if you're going to continue to sound so idiotic, go do it outside. With the musical trees and whatever."

Claude looked at him over his shoulder, seeming for a moment hurt and disappointed; then he brightened. "You'd say that. You always were a loveless worm without any soul, weren't you?"

"Well done. I'd compliment you if you hadn't sounded so nice about it."

Beatrice came in balancing a tray with a coffeepot and three mugs. "Did your father leave? Good morning, Mr. Blaine. You can have his cup." Beatrice set the tray on the table in front of Benedick and dropped a glass bottle of aspirin in his lap. "That's my contribution. It will do you more good than the coffee. How do you feel?"

"Splendid."

Claude sat beside Beatrice and leaned over to help himself to coffee. "He drank too much."

"Yes, I had a front row seat to that spectacle last night."

Only then did he remember her earlier statement—"I practically carried you up here last night"—the wrongness he'd sensed in his room, the extra lamp, the notes.

He thought of her reading his novel and felt immediately sick. Though perhaps that was the hangover. Or the unexpected encounter with his father. Either way, a pounding had developed between his brows; it matched the clenched thump of his heart. *You dum-dum.*

He'd expected it to feel better.

He'd made his choice, and just now he'd stuck with it!

Wasn't there meant to be some kind of reward for following one's heart? Something at least in the same building as happiness?

"Ben, you're starting to look worse."

He felt Beatrice's weight beside him and her cool hand on his forehead. He'd closed his eyes at some point. Strangely, he didn't recoil at her touch.

"Mr. Blaine, would you mind terribly fetching some sort of food? As plain as you can find, and dry. Something with salt maybe."

Claude said, "Oh! Yes, naturally I can; however, I'm not sure where the kitchen is."

"Take the left hall, and follow it all the way to the end; then turn right. The house is cottage-sized, remember. You can do it."

"I'm perfectly fine," Benedick muttered.

"I'm sorry, your idiocy muddled some of your words. Say again?"

"Don't get sassy."

"I'll get as sassy as I like. Do you think you can make it up to your room before you're lost to the living?"

I am the only one who is honest with you.

That wasn't strictly true, was it? Beatrice was honest. Gratingly so. *The upper class think some skill they acquired in an expensive classroom can pass as art, but they haven't got anything real to say.* And while Benedick's very presence here was proof his father's approval held little sway, some part of him, loath as he was to admit it, had gone up in arms over Beatrice's criticism.

If Hey Nonny Nonny closed, how long could he, in good conscience, sit in his room writing while the others were working to keep themselves fed? Had he ever even asked for his precious attic room? Or had he just assumed it would be there? *I belong to Hey Nonny Nonny by blood,* Beatrice had said. *You only belong by arrogant whimsy.*

"You would tell me, wouldn't you?" He opened his eyes.

"Tell you what?" She monitored his face in a detached way he recognized from the last time he'd felt on the wrong side of Prohibition.

"You would tell me if my writing was meaningless garbage."

Her expression shifted. "Oh. Last night, I didn't mean . . ."

He brushed a hand past her forced apology. He stood, too quickly. Beatrice gripped his upper arm, stopping his dangerous sway to the left. He rubbed the top of his brow. "I wonder if you would mind doing something for me."

"Give it a name, and we'll see."

"I'll trade you the papers you left in my room for a favor."

Beatrice arched a brow. "The papers for which you have no conceivable purpose and which have no value?"

"Except to you, and you're lucky I don't keep them as payment for whatever you were doing loitering around last night." He didn't wait for her answer and went back to his room, Beatrice following at a close distance in case he tottered over.

On his desk were the thirty-four pages of his in-progress novel. He picked them up, fingering the edges, then handed them over to her and her terrifying frankness. "Tell me what you think."

He was amazed how casually he did it.

Tell me what you think.

Not *tell me if this thing that defines my anxieties and desires is utter trash*; not t*ell me if I, as a human being, as a person on God's earth, am any good at all.*

He gave them to her as if they were paper and ink and nothing else, not as if he were giving an executioner her ax and stretching his neck on a slab with an invitation: *Whenever you're ready.* He wasn't sure he liked that her opinion was so weighty and sharp, but there it was. She was honest, yes, but more than that, he suspected she was a much better person than he was. He trusted her character, and he was not entirely sure he trusted his own.

"What's this?" Beatrice held the pages to her chest, looking up.

"My novel. It isn't finished."

"And you *want* to know what I think? Honestly?"

"Are you capable of being anything but?"

No one else would have the fortitude to crush his dreams so thoroughly, if it was indeed absolute rubbish; everyone else actually liked him.

She smiled. "I'm afraid not. You have a deal, Mr. Scott."

CHAPTER 14
SEEK NOT TO ALTER ME

Maggie's feet hurt. The Thursday after the Masquerade, a rainy spring was melting into summer, and it made the day muggy. Not quite wet but smelly. Like sour wool and cigarettes and how she felt right now on the inside, but that was New York for you. The smell was part of the whole angry package.

John had left Hey Nonny Nonny Tuesday afternoon and called her yesterday with the time and place for her first audition. He'd moved faster than Maggie had expected, and she'd walked herself to the train station without telling anyone where she was going. The Masquerade had gone off without a hitch, all things considered, so she felt guilty strolling onto a new stage when the old one wasn't dead and cooled. She was only getting a feel for the lay of things; that was what she told herself.

Not that it mattered.

She'd shown up in front of three white men, only the pianist looking fully sober, and left three minutes later without singing a note.

She strode down the streets of the Village prepared to clock the next sucker to look at her funny. She wore a maroon jacket, an attempt to look professional, but she wished she could throw it in the closest garbage bin. Her return ticket was bunched in her pocket, but with the way she felt, she could stomp her way back to Hey Nonny Nonny and have energy to spare. She heard her name—*Margaret*, not Maggie—and turned to see John jog across the street. She'd walked by him and not noticed, and normally she was aware of him like a moon to her tide.

Her shoulders loosened. "What're you doing here?" She kept walking, and he fell into stride beside her. He took off his hat and let it dangle from his fingers. His other hand he kept in his pocket.

"Your audition," he said. "I parked by the theater. I didn't think you'd be done so quickly."

"You didn't have to come."

John raised his eyebrows. "How did it go?"

"Rotten," said Maggie. "Didn't even get to sing."

"Why not?"

She spun toward him, pointing at her face. "'Cause this

beauty is half a shade darker than a brown paper bag, that's why."

John stopped. Anger flickered across his own face.

"Don't," she said, reading his expression. "Don't bother. Not like they're the only ones to do it. They didn't like my hair either." She snorted, then kicked at a passing fire hydrant for good measure.

"Your hair."

"Too big. Too curly. The girls keep their hair bobbed now, they said. Nice and smooth."

"If I had known . . ." John began.

"Who you were keeping wet? Whatever. The joint was seedy anyway. Hold this, I'm hotter than Hades." She wrestled her jacket off and thrust it at him so she could adjust her blouse.

His head tipped in the direction she'd come. "I'll give you a ride home."

"Fine." She followed him down the sidewalk, considered for a moment, then looped her arm through his. He stiffened but didn't try to get free. She wanted this boy for today, and anyone could just try and tell her otherwise. "Nothing better to do than drive a girl all the way back to Long Island?"

"You shouldn't travel alone."

Maggie laughed. She couldn't help it. Sometimes that was the only way to get where you needed to go, as he well knew. "I can handle myself."

"I know."

"Sounds like an excuse to get me alone with you."

Now he wriggled to get his arm loose. "I didn't say—"

"Buy me an ice cream"—she interrupted—"and we'll call it even."

When John pulled that shmancy silver car of his into Hey Nonny Nonny, he paused. He glanced over at the Lambda and the Model T, accounting for each; then he turned off the ignition.

"What's Prince into that you're so worried about?" Maggie asked.

"Who says he's into anything?"

"I don't know, but I overheard a phone conversation the other day . . ." John straightened, the interest in his eyes sharpening to deadly points. Maggie pointed at him. "A*ha*! See? There wasn't any phone conversation."

John sat back in the seat, rolling his eyes. "Let me take care of Pedro."

"Seems like *Pedro* can take care of himself."

"Seems like you should mind your own beeswax."

Hearing such schoolyard slang out of his mouth, Maggie laughed. Only at his lips softly curving did she realize he'd probably done it on purpose to distract her.

"What would you have sung?" he asked quietly, gaze drifting to the porch.

"Hmm?"

"If they'd given you a chance. What song?"

"'His Eye Is on the Sparrow.'"

His eyes closed. "Good choice."

She looked over at him and allowed one minute to feel sorry for herself. She'd done a great disservice to her heart by soaking up his company willy-nilly this past week. His collar was unbuttoned, his sleeves rolled just enough on his forearms to be out of the way as he rested his fingers on the steering wheel. The song he was silently hearing played out over his face.

Damn. She'd gone and let herself fall in love with him. Again. This was the third time, but she had a good head for common sense and could usually talk herself out of it by asking one question: So what? So what if some days he understood her better than anyone ever had? So what if they'd had whole conversations without saying a word, using only music? So what if his quiet strength and disregard for societal niceties was often exactly what she needed? So what if she found every part of him, from the harsh slant of his eyebrows when he frowned to the invisible darkness he carried under the surface, the most beautiful thing in the world? So what?

The facts were these:

He never ate sweets, and Maggie loved sweets.

They disagreed about Josephine Baker.

He could be obstinate, detached, and unapologetically ruthless.

And his skin was not the same color as her skin.

There you had it. Show's over, folks.

They walked inside together. John handed over her jacket but froze before he let go. His eyes darted to the drawing room. Ears like a bat, Maggie thought, hurrying after him as he crossed the foyer.

Prince sat on the floor in front of the coffee table, papers and maps spread out. The sight, in and of itself, was not unusual. Prince was always working. Maybe nothing would have happened, except that when Prince glanced up and saw John, he immediately slid two of the papers under the others, out of sight.

John ticked, like a car changing gears. He strode into the room.

Maggie hesitated, then followed. "John brought me home from the city," she said, apologetic. Prince had been obviously relieved when John finally left on Tuesday; now here she was hauling him back.

Prince dragged his gaze from John to her. "What were you doing in the city?"

"Oh. You know, just scoping horn talent . . ." She trailed off, the lie catching like a fish bone in her throat. John would tell her not to feel guilty for doing what she had to for her singing career, but even if Hey Nonny Nonny had one foot in the grave, the other was still in the land of the living. And here was Prince, burning the midnight oil to keep it there. The same boy who chased off handsy patrons after the raucous numbers and taught her the Italian lullabies his mother used to sing to him.

"Planning new trade routes?" John asked. He sat, the picture of unconcern, on the couch across from Prince. "Do you have the extra money to buy them back?"

Nobody said anything.

John didn't sound accusatory; he sounded politely interested in how someone else was faring in the business.

Maggie slowly lowered herself into an armchair.

After a long minute Prince apparently decided to treat the question as if it had been asked in sincerity. "No. We don't have that kind of money, and even if we did, we've compromised a foundation of trust. We'd always get the worst bargains from our old suppliers. Perhaps we could stay alive that way, but we won't profit."

John's eyes gleamed. *You're right*, Maggie translated the look. But was John upset that Prince was right—or glad?

"I think our best chance at making money is to change," Prince said softly. "Start a new enterprise, bigger than what we've been doing."

"How so?" John's voice went even quieter than his brother's.

Maggie was sure her heartbeat was audible. She didn't know Prince as well as Hero knew him, but she understood his ambition and decency often went to war with each other. Most often that amounted to a near inhuman work ethic, but sometimes she saw in him the same thing she recognized in herself, the *wanting*, the urge to do whatever was necessary for a chance at what you knew in your gut you already deserved. It made you cutthroat.

This time decency won out.

Prince shifted one of the bigger maps around so John could see it. He pulled a red pencil from behind his ear. The past seemed to settle in the room with them. However long ago, there'd been trust between them, and protection. Prince drew a curved arc just off Long Island's coast. "I think Nassau County is a missed opportunity. The most prominent rum-running ports—and, therefore, the most heavily watched—are in New York Harbor and Atlantic City. Shipments have to be in and out quick. But if you sent your shipments through the Bronx into Manhattan, nobody would look twice."

John's face tightened. "The land mileage is significantly higher. Not to mention you'd have to get it through the East River, which means another boat. You'd lose money."

"I thought of that."

John made a noise that was half frustration, half desperation.

"You only lose money if you have to reach Manhattan in a certain time frame, but if you had the option of storing large quantities with a low likelihood of being searched, you could make that difference up. Hey Nonny Nonny is a perfect hold-over; plus there are only two Coast Guard boats patrolling the entire North Shore, and the coves and terrain make it difficult to be detected. And—" He held up a hand to John's reddening face. "The families around here don't go to speakeasies; they host their own parties. Having booze brought right to their door, as long as it was good quality, would make a killing." He paused, met John's eyes. "I can make Hey Nonny Nonny an asset, but I need someone who already has a bootlegging racket in place. Don Vito could keep a share—"

"No." John's voice swung down like a hammer.

Prince fell silent.

"No," John repeated, nearly a whisper. He put both hands on the table and leaned toward Prince. "Anna and Leo Stahr were not bootleggers; they were club owners, who happened to have a comparatively tiny supply and demand for alcohol. The operation run by Don Vito is a bootlegging, extortion, loan-sharking, gambling business worth millions of dollars. This is laughable; you wouldn't cover the price of the bullets they'd use to plug you for asking in the first place, *bastardo*."

Prince's face shuttered. Even Maggie winced. With clear effort, Prince said quietly, "But you could ask. I'm half Italian, and if you vouched for me—"

"I wouldn't put my word on anything so sure to fail."

Prince's fist hit the table, rattling the coffee cups, but he composed himself a sharp breath later. He slid the map off and folded it with deliberate calmness. After he'd gathered the papers, he stood and stared down until John, slightly braced, as if Prince were going to strike him next, also rose. Prince was still a bit taller. "You can't punish me for her forever," he said.

John, hit after all, turned his head, and Prince stalked out of the room.

When he was gone, John slumped in his seat and pushed his hands into his slick black hair.

Maggie should leave him alone. Even if John wasn't John, the inner workings of the mob were none of her business. But Prince was. "Do you have to be so hard on him?" she asked softly.

John said nothing.

"I thought his idea sounded all right."

"It was all right. It was better than all right; it was smart."

Maggie frowned. "Then why'd you make out like he was some dummy for even suggesting it?"

John lifted his head from his hands, his hair disheveled. Maggie stood and came over to sit by his side. "He's too smart. Everyone knows not to touch Hey Nonny Nonny, but he made sure they couldn't ignore him. He doesn't need my approval if he wants to do this. Only the old bosses refuse to work with non-Italians. He's sharp, a good fighter; they'd take him and his ideas. They'd run him dry, and if things didn't work out, they could shoot him between the eyes and there'd be no score to settle, no vendetta. Because he's nobody."

Except to you, Maggie thought, and having John Morello on your tail didn't seem like any kind of picnic to her.

"So *help him*," Maggie said. "He doesn't need you, but he came to you. Just now. And you threw the offer back in his face."

"I don't want him involved at all, Margaret. Do you think it'd be any better for him working for me? He'd get half a dozen new enemies just by being my brother, and Hey Nonny Nonny with him. He's in over his head."

"Why not just tell him you're worried about him?"

"He thinks I'm lying to keep him from muscling into the family business."

"I can see why he might not think your concern was coming from a place of affection. I'd think you hated me, too."

John averted his eyes; he remained cold, like tightly coiled steel. You couldn't force him like this. You had to unwind him first, or he'd snap.

"Who's the *her* he mentioned? Your mother?"

She brushed a strand of his hair behind his ear. He said nothing, and she sighed. "You won't convince him to leave it alone by making your side look bad. What he wants is to stay at Hey Nonny Nonny; no convincing necessary. If you want Prince to mind his own business, help his business stay open."

"I can't just donate crates of booze every weekend, and I don't have time to stick around all summer. I came last weekend to make sure the *giamoke* didn't get himself shot before the main Canadian shipment was through."

So much for flattering herself into thinking he'd lingered for her sake.

"Although," John murmured, "I could make sure it goes under."

Maggie stiffened. "What?"

"He's hounding bootlegging rackets because he needs booze. You said yourself he won't leave Hey Nonny Nonny. If there wasn't a speakeasy to supply, there's no reason he wouldn't find honest work instead."

"Oh, John."

It wasn't that he was wrong.

On the contrary, he was very much right. Prince cared about bootlegging only insofar as it concerned Hey Nonny Nonny and Hero.

"I'll make sure you get a singing contract somewhere," he said. "A good one."

"Now, wait just a minute," she protested.

John's face boarded up immediately.

"I shouldn't have told you." *Any of it*, the ensuing silence added. The voice of someone who'd learned to trust nothing and no one. Maybe if she hadn't been so recently in love with him again, it would have felt less devastating to watch him pull away.

But as it was . . .

"Listen to me." She took hold of his chin and waited until he looked at her. Wary, he met her gaze. "Leave the speakeasy out of it, and I'll help you keep an eye on Prince, okay? I don't want him hurt any more than you do."

He remained uncertain, so she pulled out the best weapon in her arsenal. She hooked her hands over his shoulder and sang into his ear. "'When the things you've planned need a helping hand, I will understand,'" she sang. "'Always, always. Days may not be fair always. That's when I'll be there always.'"

"All *right*." He leaned away, with a breathless laugh. "Dirty play, Hughes," he grumbled under his breath, but he found a piece of paper and wrote his address and phone number down, the first time he'd ever given them to her.

CHAPTER 15
BAIT THE HOOK WELL;
THIS FISH WILL BITE

Tell me what you think.

What a brilliant phrase. Not that Beatrice had ever needed an invitation to tell anyone her thoughts, but it was nice to have one anyway.

Or it would be, if anyone actually wanted to hear her thoughts.

Behold, she thought, looking at the back of Benedick's blond head in front of her, *Exhibit A*. What the normal person felt after a few days in her company was that no further time was required, thank you. She was not surprised that she was once again trying to figure out how to be herself when herself was more than anyone wanted, but she was disappointed.

It was early Friday morning, the sky torn between raining again and allowing a bit of sun. Beatrice made her way—along with Claude, Hero, Prince, Maggie, and Benedick—toward Roosevelt Field. Claude and Hero led their little pack, latched together. Beatrice was impressed Hero didn't sink into the moist grass with her heels. Of course she had Claude's steady arm to bolster her. Benedick was a bit behind them. He glanced back, and Beatrice sent him an insult in her mind, which he received and whipped around again.

Obviously *friendly* was too high a word for what they'd been, but she'd enjoyed, well, not him exactly but the challenge of him. The pleasing clang of their minds butting together. Sure, he made his little remarks, but he'd also gotten a rather concentrated taste of her personality in a short period of time and taken it all without much fuss. He'd even thanked her for being honest about not liking his book.

"I didn't care for it," was the exact phrase she'd used, but what she'd meant was: *I couldn't find you in it.* She'd expected his novel to have the same essence as him: sharp, optimistic, infuriatingly full of itself and irritatingly admirable because of it. Instead, it was boring: a thirty-four-page mask. Attempting to explain this, while also making sure he didn't think she found the real him appealing in any way, had gotten messy. Frankly, he'd looked a little beaten up at the end of it, but he'd thanked her, so she'd thought . . .

Well. The next time they'd spoken, instead of taking his

dogged silence as the social cue it was, she'd filled it. Her tongue, still giddy with the idea of *tell me what you think*, had run away from her. Thinking it might help to hear about her own struggles, she'd told him how she'd worked long hours and long summers on her stepfather's farm, how every dollar she made went to books and science supplies, how she'd studied with Miss Mayple instead of going to social dances with the other girls.

Until finally he'd snapped at her. "Fine, yes! Thank you. Your life has been much harder than mine and you are clearly a more stalwart, enterprising person than I can ever hope to be."

"What an extraordinary imagination you have," she'd replied, "to make yourself the center of my life before I'd even met you. If only you could use it to write a novel that doesn't make me want to poke a fork in my eye so I can stop reading!"

And that had been the last words they'd spoken to each other for the past four days.

At the end of the narrow roadway a row of white hangars sparkled with the not-quite-risen sun, much larger than they appeared from a distance, bearing the logos of different aviation companies. "Roosevelt Field was named after President Theodore Roosevelt's son Quentin, who died in flight combat over France in the war," Claude told them. The flat, windy field was ideal for flying even if the dirt runway was muddy.

They passed a line of biplanes, propeller noses tilted to the sky, toward the last hangar, which was open and frenetic with excitement, the smell of cigar smoke and machine oil in the air. Farther ahead, rows of chairs were lined up beneath a large pavilion. Claude pointed to where a group of people stood, including the mayor and an official photographer. "See that chap in the bowler hat? That's Raymond Orteig. Born in France, but he owns hotels in Manhattan. He's offered a twenty-five-thousand-dollar prize to the first aviator to fly nonstop from New York to Paris." Claude smiled. "Since the money's in New York, all the best pilots come to Long Island. I'd say it's the cradle of modern aviation, and here you live not ten minutes away!"

Claude was beginning to grow on Beatrice, not unlike the way a fungus might. What sun had shone on his birth for him to gain that inimitable glow? He was sure of his place at the top of the world, and it made him not arrogant but generous and enthusiastic. He introduced Hero to the people under their tent as "the incomparable Hero Stahr" and, like any born gentleman, took off his hat when he kissed her cheek.

Once again Hero had put her clever needle to Beatrice's frock, and to tell the truth, Beatrice felt rather sharp—but something about these people made her think they could see the dirt and grease and scars under the lace gloves Hero had loaned her. Why else did they keep staring, heads slightly tilted as if they couldn't pinpoint the reason she didn't belong? Only by telling herself, *First transatlantic solo flight, history in the making,* did she resist the urge to claim illness and retreat to the car.

Beside her, Maggie tugged her hat down over her ears. Perhaps because it was the first time Beatrice had ever seen the jazz singer look as if she'd like a bed to hide under, Beatrice finally realized it wasn't her they were staring at. One look through the crowd and it was clear: there was not a single other black person here.

Beatrice felt she should say something, but she didn't know what to say. She turned to Maggie, who read Beatrice's expression in an instant. Shrugging off the discomfort as if it were a stuffy coat, Maggie tipped her chin up. "I like eyes on me," she said. "Why do you think me and the stage get along so well?"

Prince leaned in between them. "Want to check out the old hangars?"

"Yes," they said at the same time, in relief, and all three turned away from the pavilion and the pretty faces and clothes. Almost in unison their strides lengthened to a more relaxed pace, glad to get some distance from a crowd to which none of them quite belonged. They kept an easy silence as they approached the unused hangars. Small packs of people, mostly boys, hung around, smoking and laughing. There were all shades of skin here. At the open doors of the hangar, a group of mechanics had ventured out to watch the flight. The remains of a gutted plane sat behind them. The floor was beaten earth; the windows were streaked with rain-washed grime. One of the men nodded at Prince.

"Do you mind if we look at it?" Beatrice asked, pointing.

The man glanced at his crew. "This ain't a museum," he said.

"Say!" A second man, five feet tall, if that, pointed right at Maggie. "Say, that's the gal who sings at that joint in Flower Hill. Voice like an angel, swear to God. If you don't mind me saying so, miss."

The first man scoffed. "You ain't never been to Hey Nonny Nonny. They wouldn't let the likes of you through the door."

The second man's ruddy brown cheeks flushed. "Have so. I took my girl there on May Day."

"Thank you, sir, that's very kind." Maggie touched her hat and stepped forward. Unlike Beatrice, Maggie looked grown-up in her lavender dress suit and gloves. "If you let us take a peek at these airplanes, I can get you into our Decoration Day party this weekend." She winked. "I got sway with the owners."

The first man rolled his eyes. "Fine, *fine*. Don't break anything," he added in a grumble.

Maggie gave him a winning smile. "I'll be back later, so don't go anywhere, boys." Then she sauntered into the hangar, Beatrice and Prince trailing behind her.

"I had no idea," Beatrice whispered loudly to him, "we were with somebody so famous."

"Sway with the Hey Nonny Nonny owners," Prince said. "Can you imagine?"

"Let's ask for her autograph."

Maggie glared at them over her shoulder. "That's enough out

of you two smart mouths. *Thank you* would be just fine, considering I wouldn't be caught dead in one of these." She approached the first plane and poked its rounded metal side with a finger; her nose wrinkled with disinterest.

Beatrice ventured closer; she peeled off one of her gloves with her teeth and pressed a hand to the cold underbelly of the plane. "Hard to believe such a big heavy thing can stay up in the air."

"Hard to believe something can go across the whole ocean in a day," said Prince. For the second time since Beatrice had known him, he wore a jacket, but he was the kind of person who looked classier with his sleeves rolled up, so it didn't seem to fit any better than it had before.

"Prince, is your mother still alive?" Maggie came to the other side and ducked around the wheel frame to look at him.

Prince startled, knocking his head on the edge of one of the silver propellers. He rubbed the wounded spot, messing up his hair. "What? She— Yes. I don't see her much."

"Why not?" Maggie asked.

Prince gave her an assessing look, and Beatrice got the feeling there was a root to these questions she wasn't aware of. Finally Prince shrugged. "When I was ten, she moved back in with her family, but she didn't want me to come. She paid rent on the boardinghouse room we were in, like we were still living there together, but she was gone a lot. At first she came by every day, then every other day, then every week, and finally one day the landlord said we had to get out because we were so behind on rent. She wasn't around, and I wasn't sure where to go, so I just . . . left for good."

"That's terrible," said Beatrice. "I'm sorry."

"Don't be. Mama's *family* was all her old husband's family, and I was the result of her fooling around with someone else, so it's not like I would've been welcome. Anyway, then I found Hey Nonny Nonny." He smiled sideways at Beatrice. "Same as you."

Maggie, who'd looked increasingly thoughtful at Prince's story, blinked. "Same as us all. My family's still in Pennsylvania. My father sent me here to find steady work with my aunt, but I only agreed so I'd be closer to the city and the jazz clubs."

"My father died in the war, when I was eight," Beatrice said. "My mother was sick a lot, but what actually killed her was tuberculosis." Beatrice chewed absently at the edge of her glove. "Not quite a year after the vaccine came out. I was eleven. My stepfather is my guardian, I guess. Or at least until September, when I turn eighteen."

Maggie released a soft breath. "What are we going to do if—"

Outside, a cheer rose as the *Spirit of St. Louis* roared to life at the end of the airstrip.

"We're going to miss it!" Beatrice hissed.

"Not if we run," Maggie said, and flew toward the runway,

one hand on her head to keep her hat in place. Prince grinned at Beatrice and took off.

Beatrice followed, but Prince was fast, and Maggie was faster. She wished, as she often did, that she had been in her dungarees and boots. "These damn shoes," she muttered as the short heel slipped again in the slick grass. Prince came back and took her hand. She gripped tight, half laughing as they sprinted to the edge of the gathered crowd, making it just as the plane began to rumble down the strip. Lucky Lindy gained speed slowly—too slowly, Beatrice thought, for the amount of space he had—but he bounced along, faster and faster; then *up* he went, clearing a tractor by only fifteen feet. He veered to the right to avoid the high reach of trees on the opposite hill and was on his way, flying into the sun.

In those final seconds when the *Spirit of St. Louis* was no longer tethered to earth, Beatrice's cold little heart burst free from its ribs and climbed out of her mouth in a shout. She giggled like the young girl she was supposed to be. Something was coming, something marvelous, and it was somehow not a surprise to turn and find Benedick watching her from several yards away, across a whole line of politely clapping people. His thick golden hair was windswept, his brown eyes nearly hazel with the rising sun in them. For no reason whatsoever, an unsettling sensation blossomed in her chest: an accelerated heartbeat. The heart was an organ of instinct over reason. What was it doing?

She pressed a hand to her chest. *Excuse me, sixty-five beats per minute is quite sufficient.*

Hero found them a few moments later, pushing through the crowd. "Where did you three run off to?" she asked.

"Nowhere," said Prince.

Hero frowned. "Mmm, well, if you wouldn't mind making yourselves useful." She handed Beatrice a few black-flowered pins. "Don't forget the other reason we're here."

She approached Prince, who waved her off. "That's your job," he said. "Nobody in this crowd will look twice at what I give them."

"Those mechanics seemed thirsty," Maggie reminded him.

"For a straight shot in a bar, maybe, and *no* dancing."

Hero said, "That's nothing a kiss wouldn't change; they don't know what they're missing. Do as Beatrice says."

"There's a command I hope to never hear," Benedick drawled. He arrived with his hands in his pockets, Claude beside him.

Beatrice's mind hoisted on the balls of its feet. Her first reaction was not to be offended but hopeful he might be pulling out of his depressive mood to spar with her again.

Unfortunately she was robbed of the chance to retaliate when a tall woman interrupted their group: short blond hair and the eyes of a cocky hen. She looked to be in her late forties, her neck uncommonly long and bedecked with tasteful jewels.

Between her gloved fingers was a pearl-inlaid cigarette holder. Two young men flanked her, one in his early twenties, the second younger and, upon closer inspection, the very boy who'd accosted Beatrice and Benedick on the East River. He recognized her, too, if his widening eyes were any clue.

"Miss Stahr, it's been awhile since we've seen you out and about," the woman said. "And you, Mr. Scott. Why isn't your bachelor of a father here?" She had a fat voice, overinflated and conscious of itself. She spotted Prince and Maggie. "Oh, and you brought the help. How charitable."

"I don't believe I've had the pleasure." Claude stepped in seamlessly, smile and extended hand already up. "Claude Blaine."

"Mary Louise Minsky." She put her fingers limply in his before drawing back. "Who are you?" She glanced at Beatrice, not simpering, the way she'd been when addressing Benedick and Claude, but not as condescending as she'd been to Maggie and Prince.

"Beatrice Clark. Hero's cousin."

"How nice. This dreadful wind got to your hair, too, didn't it?" Mary Louise's swept chignon didn't seem tousled in the least. "These two strapping gentlemen are my sons, Brett and Conrade. It's your birthday soon, isn't it, Hero darling? Congratulations. Will there be a party?"

"Thank you," Hero said, in the same tone of voice other people might say, *Burn in a fire*. "We'll be celebrating at Hey

Nonny Nonny, of course. Claude's offered to host."

Mary Louise arched a fine eyebrow. "You are determined to drag this insufferable death rattle out as long as it will go, aren't you?"

Hero flushed, mouth pursing.

"Don't look so distressed, dear. I'm only here with your best interests in mind. I'm suggesting diplomatically that you step down."

"Diplomatically?" Hero glanced around, then stepped closer and lowered her voice. "Your *gentleman* of a son tossed one of my associates into the river for a few gallons of moonshine."

"I don't know what you mean," Mary Louise said bluntly. "Though the business does have its unseemly moments. All the more reason to spare yourself the unpleasantness."

Hero stuck her chin out. "I don't think it's stealing when we're only in a position to do so in the first place because you infringed on all our old trade routes."

"Your father and I have a clear understanding of which routes belong to whom. Perhaps I don't sound serious enough, Miss Stahr. You're still a child, as your quaint little party reminds us. You've limped along this far, but you'll be in over your head if you continue to draw attention to yourself in this climate."

Hero didn't answer, but her lip quivered. Mary Louise folded her hands in front of her. "Lovely chatting with you," she said. She glanced at Claude. "You're always welcome at the Ragland if present company doesn't suit you, Mr. Blaine. Boys, come along." Her sons trailed behind her. Conrade, frowning, spared a final glance over his shoulder at Beatrice.

"What a horror that woman is," Claude said. "I bet a vengeful fairy at her christening is to blame. What do you think?" He arched both brows at Hero until he got a halfhearted smile. He kissed her flushed cheek. "I can't stand seeing you look so sad, prima donna. Let's make sure every rich sucker here knows your birthday party is going to be the only shindig worth mentioning this summer."

She answered by looping her arms around his neck and kissing him with such enthusiasm they drew several offended coughs from lookers-on. When they pulled apart, Hero readjusted her scarf and helped wipe the lipstick off Claude's mouth. "I think that's a swell idea."

"Come on, Maggie," Prince said. "One of us has got to sweet-talk those flyboys, and only one of us has a voice like a swear-to-God angel."

"Just a moment, Prince," Hero said, like a grappling hook. Prince didn't move. Her eyes flitted over to him from where they'd been on Claude. "I'd like a quick word before you go." Then she aimed her gap-toothed smile right into Claude's eyes. She pressed her chest to his arm. "I'm dizzy as a mayfly. Would you mind terribly getting me something to drink, please?"

"Sure, I don't mind." Had she asked him to jump in front of

the el train, Claude would have gone with a smile.

As soon as he was far enough gone, Hero leveled Prince with a cool look. Both his brows lifted, but she didn't wait for him. She walked in the other direction without a backward glance, hips swishing.

"Fight it, Prince," said Benedick dryly.

Prince closed his eyes, pinching the bridge of his nose. He sighed and gave Maggie a handful of Hey Nonny Nonny pins, then tugged his cap hard over his head, and went after Hero.

"That girl," Maggie muttered. "She's only tugging 'cause she can. Somebody needs to rescue the poor boy; then we'll go back to the hangar." She said the last part to Beatrice and hurried off without waiting for an answer.

That left Beatrice alone with Benedick. She turned to him, and he averted his gaze and shook his head before she uttered one syllable.

A wave of disappointment swept through her.

Never mind, she thought, and turned back to the main crowd as she fiddled with one of the pins. She was terrible at doing nothing.

She'd forgotten, perhaps because he was so uninterested in it, that Benedick came from this shiny world. Here he was "Ambrose's boy," and he never failed to answer, with aplomb, when called upon, but he kept to himself when he had the choice, shoulders hunched with a misery that seemed to do with more than just gray weather. How carelessly he switched himself on and off; engrossed and uninterested at the same time. The kind of person to make friends easily and not even want them.

Soon enough he was chatting with an older gentleman and looked, for perhaps the first time since she'd met him, perfectly polite and deferential. The old man leaned on his cane and occasionally used it to rap Benedick's shoe.

"Miss Clark, you look quite different unarmed and in a dress."

She turned, and there was Conrade Minsky. He smiled; he had rosy cheeks, and for some reason she couldn't stop staring at them; they seemed absurd on his face.

Conrade nodded toward Benedick. "Leave it to Benedick Scott to chat up Payne Chutney like it's nothing. The old dodger looks about ready to croak where he stands. I heard the estate is positively infected with Chutneys all hoping to get a slice of his fortune. Maybe he'll give Ben a couple of thousand for sheer audacity."

Had he sauntered over here to gossip with her, of all things? Finally she said, "You're risking a lot on the assumption that I'm unarmed."

Conrade looked at her, his head tilted. "Are you hiding a shotgun under your skirt?"

"Not all weapons are long-barreled guns."

"I can't tell if that means you have a smaller gun or if you consider your tongue a weapon."

"If I were you, I wouldn't press me to find out."

His smile widened. "Miss Clark, would you like to come out to the theater sometime?"

"Your mother's theater? The vaudeville shows?"

"You've heard of us, I see."

"What's your angle, Mr. Minsky? If you're hoping to ferret some insider information by telling me I have pretty eyes, I'm afraid you won't have much luck."

"I never said you have pretty eyes."

"And I don't have much interest in vaudeville shows. Alas, an impasse."

"What would interest you? A shooting range? Trouser shopping?"

"How about a padlock over the door of your family business?" Beatrice asked. "Put that in your mother's ten-inch cigarette holder and smoke it."

Conrade laughed—which frankly caught Beatrice off guard. Even more so when he leaned in and said, "I think your eyes are stunning." He straightened before she could reply, the mirth dropping out of his face. "Hello, Ben," he said. "If you'll excuse me, Miss Clark. I'd hate to say anything untoward in front of a lady, and Mr. Scott tends to draw such indiscretion out of me. Maybe you'll save me a slow dance at Hero's birthday party?"

"You're not invited!" Benedick called at his retreating back.

Conrade turned, walked backward with his hands in his

pockets, and grinned. "Not by you anyway," he said, and spun around.

"Not by anyone," Benedick said, turning to Beatrice, "I should hope."

"What makes you think I would?" she asked.

"I don't. I'm just confirming."

"Maybe he actually likes me. Did you ever think of that?"

"Oh, yes, you and your stunning eyes."

"Maybe they *are* stunning."

"They're not."

Her teeth ground together. As calmly as she could manage, she said, "Even if he was flirting, I am not the kind of girl to be flattered into forgiveness, so you may take your concern and shove it elsewhere. I do have some suggestions if you'd like directional advice."

"Of course you are never that kind of girl. Maybe all the other silly, common girls, but never you, *brilliant* you."

She stepped close and jabbed him hard in the chest. "I've had just about enough of this. You're only acting so nasty because I didn't fawn all over your stupid novel!"

"That is not—" He stopped, lowering his voice to a hiss. "That is not why."

"Then you admit you are acting like a nasty little stink."

His face twitched with exasperation. "I wouldn't sic you on my worst enemy. So there, that's the real reason. I'm sparing

Conrade Minsky a scratched face, one man to another."

"How about I scratch *your* face? Can't make it worse."

"I—" He visibly stopped himself. His eyes closed, and his hand curled into a slow fist, which he pressed briefly to his mouth. After a careful breath he opened his eyes and said, "Good day, Miss Clark."

And then he walked away.

She stood there aghast. How dare he walk off in the middle of a sparring match? And then she strode after him. He picked up his pace, a tic appearing in his clenched jaw.

"Is that any way to treat a lady?" she asked.

There, she'd practically gift wrapped it for him. *If I happen to come across one, he'd say, I'll be sure to take that advice to heart.*

Nothing!

She grabbed his arm. He yanked it free but whirled around, so quickly they almost collided. "Do you want something, Miss Clark?" His swift stride had carried them far beyond the pavilion and the crowd. No shade to block the morning sun, which had turned away from rain to become obnoxiously bright. In this setting he had the advantage, his hair lit up like gold, his clothes tailored against any sort of rumpling.

Breathless, missing a glove, she said, "You spent three pages on a man ruminating over the coffee grounds in his cup!"

"That was metaphorical," he hissed. "It represented the shambles of his life. Haven't you ever read a modern novel?"

"What about the ten pages he spent wandering the streets, hating everything, and possibly lusting after cockroaches? I couldn't quite tell."

"That was stream of consciousness; it's *art*."

"And what about . . ." Beatrice trailed off. She didn't want to admit to stealing that other paragraph, the one she didn't want to give back because it was sort of lovely. He had a gift for storytelling: the way he described their encounter with Sage? Or first coming to Hey Nonny Nonny? "What I mean to say is, maybe you ought to write something happier."

That was not the right thing to say. Immediately his expression darkened, and it had been no ray of sunshine before. "Enough, Beatrice. I asked for your honest opinion, and I got it and I thanked you. I assure you there's no need to dump salt on it."

"If I had known you'd act like this, I would never have agreed to read it."

"Really? Do other people's feelings matter to you now?"

That one stung. "Would you have preferred that I lied?"

"I asked because I knew you wouldn't."

"Then stop condemning me for it! You avoid me, you won't speak to me—"

"Sharp as a marble, as ever, Miss Clark. I'm not avoiding you; I am *indifferent* to you, so far as I can be when you're not chasing me across a lawn."

"But why?"

It was a silly thing to say.

She felt it all the more when he gave a hard and pointed laugh. "The street cuts both ways, wonder girl," he said. "You can't dole out judgments and expect not to be judged."

"I don't!"

"Oh, no?" he asked quietly. "You don't assume if someone has money, they've automatically had an easier time than you? That their suffering is not quite as deep as yours? You don't think that if only you were in my shoes, all your problems would be solved? You don't resent my choosing not to use my advantages in the same way you would?"

Beatrice found she had nothing to say to that.

"Well, I apologize," he said. "I'm sorry I haven't buckled down and made something useful of myself. I'm sorry I couldn't accept my gilded lot like a proper heir, but you'll find a lot of humans behave in their own interests—"

"That's not fair! I am just as human—"

"Are you, though? You're more like a train, always moving forward, stopping for no one, and God help anyone who gets caught under your wheels. You don't care if anyone likes you because no relationship with any flesh-and-blood person matters so much as becoming a doctor. No one wants to be told all the ways they're falling short of your lofty standard of humanity. Kindly allow me the relief of not engaging with you."

Beatrice felt as winded as if she'd sprinted the hundred-yard dash. Her breath came short, her chest rising and falling; spots of heat erupted along her neck and collarbone. She wouldn't admit to him that he was right and it had made her so lonely at times, nobody saying a word to her, only trivial greetings in a cramped dorm room at the beginning and end of a day. Studying, studying.

So, this was what it felt like to get hit between the eyes with the truth?

She couldn't say she cared for it, but neither could she blame him. Some dazed part of her even wanted to compliment how poetically he'd eviscerated her; he *did* have a way with words.

"Yoo-hoo!"

Beatrice glanced up. Hero waved, pulling Claude along.

"Claude says everybody's headed to the Cherry Hill Club. Prince has utterly refused to join us, but I know you won't disappoint me."

"I'm afraid," Beatrice said carefully, "that I will. I'm not sure a country club will be good for my stomach just now."

"You know what?" Benedick said. "It would be terrific for mine; I'll come."

Hero's red mouth pursed as if they'd each said the exact opposite of what she'd wanted.

Beatrice had only herself to blame. She'd gotten too comfortable; wasn't that always the way? She'd been here a week. What did she think, that she could just arrive somewhere, out of the blue without any money, and have a home forever after?

Of course not.

She yanked her nightshirt on, washed up, and climbed into bed. *A* bed for now. Not her bed. She supposed she'd never have one until she'd saved up and bought one for herself. She bunched up the sheets around her chin, ignoring the way her heart caught every time she heard a footstep overhead.

She hadn't gotten any closer to sleep when her door opened and a pale blur slipped inside. Without a word Hero crawled into Beatrice's bed and, smelling of perfume and powder, snuggled against her. "Oh!" Hero hushed. "How cool you are." She dug her toes into Beatrice's calf and put her warm cheek on Beatrice's bare shoulder. "Mmm."

Beatrice didn't know what to say. Hero didn't seem sick or hurt. "Are you all right?" she asked finally.

"Isn't Claude a dreamboat?"

Beatrice twisted onto her back. "The boatiest. Objectively speaking."

"But truly, do you like him? I'm asking because you're so sensible. I can't tell my own head when I like them like this." Hero sat up on her elbow. Her skin glowed luminescent in the darkness. Oh, she had it all over, like a bad rash. "Of course the real matter at hand was that heated discussion I spied between you and Ben. Lover's spat?"

Even his name was like getting struck by a paralyzing needle; Beatrice's skin tightened and recoiled. "No. A regular spat. Between two people who don't like each other."

"The line between like and dislike is almost invisible when attraction's involved." Hero's tone turned sly.

"Which it isn't!" Beatrice made an Olympic effort to keep the dragon out of her voice. She only partially succeeded.

"If you'd give him a little something to hang on to, compliment him, take his arm—"

"*Hero.*" Beatrice sat fully upright. "I don't want to hear it! I don't like him, and I don't secretly hope he likes me, and here's something else: You're a real piece of work, do you know that? I bet you're only trying to push us together now because you saw me with Prince, and you're worried you might lose your most loyal manservant."

Hero's mouth opened.

The silence was awful. Hero drew back, as if she were gathering every invisible piece of herself like scattered clothes, then slid off the bed and was out the door before Beatrice remembered to breathe again.

Beatrice drew her knees up and rested her forehead on them. Well, there was a nice and tidy way to prove Benedick right. She knew she wasn't much for charm; it had always been her policy to be honest and to be kind, and then at least she had nothing to be ashamed over.

Of course kindness and honesty didn't always go hand in hand, did they? Occasionally one trumped the other, and that was where she got into hot water. Like with Benedick. Like with Hero.

Benedick could loop a brick around his neck and drown in a lake for all she cared, but as it turned out, she did care, very much, about Hero.

Just like the rest of them, Beatrice had fallen head over her heels for her charming cousin. Based on that first day meeting her, Beatrice hadn't been sure they'd get along as friends. Family was family, but you didn't always do more than politely stand each other when it came to things like fun and conversation.

But then Beatrice did like her. A reckoning here and there of true fondness that expanded outward. Until suddenly she looked around and wanted to punch out the lights of some middle-aged woman for hurting Hero's feelings.

Only now Beatrice was the one hurting her feelings.

She lifted her head so her chin rested on her knees and glared into the darkness. *Don't be such a piker, Clark.*

So decided, she marched from her room to Hero's. She knocked on the door and opened it without an answer, before she lost her nerve. Hero was brushing her hair at the end of her bed. Her eyes narrowed at Beatrice's entrance.

"I'm sorry," Beatrice burst out clumsily. "Please. I was only mad because Benedick said some things to me that were very . . .

well, true." She finished lamely. "But I'll kiss him on his stupid mouth if you'll be my friend again."

"Beatrice." Hero's eyes had gone from coolly regarding to surprised and then at last to tender. "Come here, you daft bird." She patted the space next to her, and Beatrice shuffled over like a cowed puppy. She sank next to Hero and folded her hands in her lap.

"Are you tired of me?" Beatrice asked.

"Maybe I am just at this moment, but aren't you a little tired of me, too?"

"I lost my temper."

"So? Everybody does some time or other. Sometimes I'll be sick to death of you and wish you'd jump out a window, but the way this works is that even when that happens, even if I actually tell you to jump out the window, you don't have to. You can stay. I'll expect you to stay even after I tell you to go away."

That was the single most baffling and perfect thing Beatrice had ever heard. "That's nuts."

Hero laughed. She tucked her arm into Beatrice's. "In normal protocol, I would take up not speaking to you for at least a day, except for an underhanded gibe at your hair over breakfast, but in this one particular case we'll skip that step and go straight back to loving each other."

"Do you?" Beatrice asked, surprised.

Hero turned to look at Beatrice over her shoulder and batted her eyelashes hard enough to start a windstorm. "Do you not?"

Beatrice laughed. "I guess I do."

Hero pulled her back, until they were nestled under the covers together. "Anyway," said Hero, "you were maybe a little right. I might have gotten just the teensiest bit jealous. Prince wouldn't take me to look at rusty old planes, I know that much, but I don't want to look at rusty old planes, so I guess that's not really fair."

"You've never been sweet on him?"

"Not like that. It's easy to be sweet before you like them. And a girl's got to have her spark. I depend on Prince like my own arm, but kissing your elbow doesn't make you dizzy, if you know what I mean."

"Claude makes you dizzy."

"As a merry-go-round. He kisses like a matador. At the airstrip today I kept imagining what it would be like to be Mrs. Claude Blaine. Going to luncheons and parties and charity banquets. Wearing pretty hats like those women. He's a real gentleman. Do you think he'd love me, even though I'm not cultured or upper class?"

Beatrice couldn't think of any boy who'd care how cultured Hero was. Forget how she looked in a dress and heels; she was witty and warmhearted. "He'd be a dope not to."

"I bet I could make him happy," said Hero. "We'd live in a big house, I guess. And the only thing I'd worry about was which fancy school to send our perfect children to and whether we should summer on Long Island or in Dorset."

So far Hero hadn't mentioned a single advantage that pertained to Claude personally. She seemed more infatuated with his ability to show her the world and all that was in it than the boy himself.

"He played halfback on the football team"—Hero continued—"and he was an honor student. His parents want him to stay in America and get into politics. He's got two older brothers and a sister who are practically running Britain by now, he says. He's going to law school."

"Oh, law school. Of course he could love you. You haven't known him long, that's all."

"I guess not. But I have a gut feeling. That's how Mama knew to marry Papa. He gave her a card after she clocked him. And that night she took it out and thought, *That's my husband.*' She knew it then. She always said if I ever found a man I loved, I shouldn't waste time. I should go right up to him and say, *The thing is, I love you. How about we get married?*'"

Beatrice had never put much stock in gut feelings. Most of the time it was a rotten piece of meat more than anything else, but it was also true that the same molecules that registered information in the brain also appeared in organs like the intestines, stomach, heart, liver, kidneys, and spine; these, too, could send and register information. So one could, she supposed, have a legitimate "gut" feeling.

"I don't know what will happen without the speakeasy," Hero whispered. "Papa just drinks all the time; how's he going to pay for everything without a job? I'll be the one handing out keys to a run-down boardinghouse, taking care of him until I'm an old maid."

Beatrice turned her head. "I thought Aunt Anna's family had money?"

"Oh, they do. But Mama was disowned on account of going to feminist rallies, running picket lines for factory workers, marrying Papa, selling illegal liquor in her home." Hero ticked off the reasons on her fingers.

"The speakeasy will do great tomorrow, you'll see. One weekend at a time."

"I wish you weren't going away."

Beatrice frowned. "Where am I going?"

"Why, to medical college, of course. You said it yourself."

Hero's bald confidence both warmed and terrified Beatrice. "So I did."

"If I marry Claude," Hero murmured, snuggling into Beatrice's shoulder, "I'll get him to pay for your schooling. Don't you worry."

CHAPTER 16

SHALL I NEVER SEE
A BACHELOR OF
THREE-SCORE AGAIN?

Benedick turned over on his cot, feeling more or less like the last tulip in spring. Last night they'd opened the joint up again, but unlike at the Masquerade, he'd stayed dry as a corn husk. He usually did. There were only so many mornings one could wake up having been chewed up and spit out by that great noble experiment of Prohibition.

All in all, it had been a success: enough people to fill the room and enough booze to fill the people. Of course Benedick thought they owed a sizable chunk of their attendance to a flock of gossipers who had come to see for themselves where Claude Blaine had ventured off when he didn't show up at the Vanderbilts as he was supposed to, and the rest didn't properly count because Leo and Father Francis let vets drink free because of Decoration Day. But there had been a party for the second weekend in a row, and that was a victory.

Besides, his lousy mood had nothing to do with the speakeasy. Fair or not, he was placing 100 percent of the blame on an opinionated little twerp named Beatrice Clark.

Ye gods, his room was boiling, and it was only morning.

And stuffy.

Just like my writing, he thought miserably, turning over, not bothered enough to get up to open the window.

Someone pounded on his door. So raucous and demanding it had to be Beatrice, but of course she wouldn't knock at all, would she?

"Ben!" The door opened and filled all the way a moment later with Leonard Stahr. "Good morning!" he bellowed.

Benedick sat up, stared at him, speechless. "Is it?" he asked eventually.

"You bet your ass. Get up; we're going into the city. It's ten already, and you're not even dressed."

Benedick did as he was told—not that there was much choice. Had he hesitated too long, Leo might have tugged his pants on for him. He hadn't seen Leo like this for months. This was the man he'd first met, eyes clear and hungry, the entrepreneur husband of Hey Nonny Nonny's hostess.

"What are we doing in the city?" Benedick asked, once he'd

exited the washroom. (Leo had serenaded the proceedings, which had not made Benedick go any faster but had given Leo a good laugh.)

"First, we've got to collect Prince," said Leo. "At this hour he's probably grinding away somewhere, but both the cars are here, so he can't have gotten too far."

Of course. Prince, the beast of burden; Benedick, the parasite. Benedick had once stupidly envisioned pitching in with the money he'd make selling his short stories, one by one, editors lapping them up as fast as he could type them. He muttered, "But what do you need *me* for?"

"Ben—" Leo set his hand on Benedick's shoulder; his palm, heavy and sure, nearly covered it. When he was fully upright, Leo was near to the same size as Benedick's lionlike father, only Leo was more a bumbling bear than a cat of prey. "You know I love you," Leo continued. "And it is with love that I say that sometimes what you need most in the world is a swift kick in the pants." With a hearty squeeze, Leo released him.

They discovered Prince (where else?) in the empty speakeasy, chewing the end of a pencil as he pored over several pages of shipment transactions: what had been used last night, where they were running low. By the look on Prince's quiet face, they were running low approximately everywhere.

He glanced up, a cup of coffee halfway to his lips, as Leo

steam-engined up to the bar. "What's this?" Prince glanced at Benedick, who shrugged.

"Looks like coffee!" Leo said. "But you know best, you're drinking it. Put it all away; we've got an errand to run."

"An errand?"

"Yes, yes. In the city." Leo waited until Prince had put away the papers and come out from behind the bar. "God's teeth, I forget how you shot up like a skyscraper this past year until you're right next to me. We're going downtown to get my baby a proper birthday present. I need you there because no one knows Hero better, and Benedick will make sure whatever we pick has taste and class. We can't let that new dandy of hers show us up, can we?"

"Well, all right." Prince surrendered softly. "But can we afford—"

"We can, we absolutely can." Leo crooked his finger at both of them and did not move until they had shuffled close enough for him to draw his arms around their shoulders in a conspiratorial huddle. "Several of that Blaine boy's sloshed friends stayed the night yesterday and I believe are planning some sort of beach picnic this afternoon. Don't ask me what I charged for the absolute most special rooms in the joint, but I will say each of the blighters could have sneezed out double what I asked and not batted an eye." Leo winked at Benedick. "Anna always gave me a talking-to for that little trick, but we did get Ben out of it, so she could never be too mad."

The argument could be made that a better birthday present

to Hero would be to use that money to buy more supplies for the speakeasy, but Leo was hard to resist when he was like this.

With a helpless shrug Prince asked, "When are we going?"

The day was sweltering; Leo kept the top down on the Lambda as they roared over the Brooklyn Bridge into Manhattan. His speed seemed especially brazen as they passed the multitude of cars going on to Long Island for the holiday weekend.

Certainly a good day for the beach.

Would Beatrice go with Hero and Claude and the pack of highbred vacationers? Hero would probably invite her, but picturing Beatrice lounging in the sand, getting a tan, smoking a cigarette between red lips, playing a round of lazy badminton—the way Benedick tended to think of Long Island beach trips—was nearly unfathomable. He stopped himself from going down the twisty brain trail of wondering if she even owned a bathing suit and what it looked like.

Ah, well.

His brain went there after all, without his permission.

Because the only logical answer was one of those old ridiculous Victorian jumpers, with blue-and-white stripes and puffy breeches and a sailor's collar. No lipstick, no sunglasses. A sunburned nose. She would not play badminton. First, she would swim a mile in the choppy water, and then, not winded at all, she would proceed to study jellyfish and lecture anyone who would listen about some sciency mumbo jumbo—

He stopped himself.

If he could think of scenes for his novel half so well as he could ruminate on how the unconventional Beatrice Clark might fit herself into the conventional world, he'd have an actual book in his hands.

Shadows fell across Benedick's face, jolting him out of his reverie as they crawled along the city streets. The building that had blocked the sun was the skyscraper on Wall Street where his father worked.

They parked near the shopping district, and Benedick shook off any feelings of his father. Leo's soberness brought back a lightness to Prince's step that Benedick hadn't seen in a while, as if Leo had reshouldered some of Hey Nonny Nonny's burden.

They didn't bother with clothes; they had little chance of surpassing Hero's finessed eye. But when they went by a tailor's shop, Prince paused. "There," he said, pointing at the display window, where a Damascus Vibrating Shuttle sewing machine sat on a velvet stand, with a price tag of $27.95—monthly installments optional with a $4 deposit!

"That's perfect," said Benedick, and it was, never mind that he wouldn't have thought of it until Prince pointed it out. Hero always looked top-shelf and far classier than the rest of them, but it was all by her own doing. She took gifted frocks and old pieces of her mother's and had no trouble looking as if she had the same salary as any other girl a boy like Claude Blaine would normally date.

"There it is," Leo agreed quietly. "Go haggle with the store-keep, Prince. Ben and I will pick out some fabric and thread to buy with it."

Inside the cool and dim store, Benedick perused the shelves with Leo while Prince talked with the owner in the back. He let a swath of blue silk slide over his fingers.

"So, Ben, any special girl for you? In my day a nice ribbon was an okay gift."

Ben snorted at the thought of Beatrice's wild nest bedecked with colorful bows. Then he colored because his mind had gone to Beatrice in the first place, and she was *not* his special girl. Or even special.

She was just a girl.

"Not me," said Benedick. "I'm a bachelor for life; you know that."

"You've told me so, but I've never believed it. I said the exact same thing at your age."

"Until you met Anna."

"Girl like Anna is hard to forget, but there's more of them than you'd think. You know who reminds me of her?"

"Hero?"

"Certainly! Hero's got the same sparkle, always has." Leo stroked his mustache. He glanced toward Prince. "Of course you've always been more brotherly toward her."

"I couldn't hope to keep up with her anyway."

"But I rather thought Beatrice had the same spunk as well."

Benedick worked very hard to remain fascinated with the fabric in his hands. He didn't glance up. "She doesn't seem like Anna or Hero at all to me."

"Not in personality, no. But that's not what I mean. They've got the same ferocity on the inside. The kind of girl where you can only hang on for the ride and hope your hat stays on. Break your heart three times in one week, and you're glad for the chance."

Benedick turned away. "I hadn't noticed."

Prince returned, looking cheeky. "He'll do three dollars and fifty cents a month over six months, but if we buy some yards of fabric today, he'll sell for twenty upfront."

"Good lad!" Leo slapped the back of Prince's shoulder and went with him to sign the agreement.

Benedick stayed back, his eyes drifting traitorously toward the ribbons, but even if he had felt inclined to give Beatrice a gift, a ribbon seemed all wrong. So did all the other usuals, as his mind went through them: flowers, chocolates, a pretty piece of jewelry, a poem about the luminescence of her eyes.

What on earth, he imagined her saying, holding up a gold-chain necklace, *am I supposed to do with this?*

Too bad he couldn't gift wrap something like, say, an education.

Even if he was in a position to pay the last of her tuition, as he no longer was, he had a feeling she wouldn't accept a donation of that kind. If only he knew a doctor . . .

An idea wormed its way in, right through his she's-not-my-girl-and-I-don't-give-a-damn mantra. He recalled his conversation with poor Payne Chutney, practically dying where he stood. When Benedick told him he was forging his own path, away from his father's financial assistance, Mr. Chutney had been impressed, lamenting his vulturelike relatives swarming over his fortune. Why not, Benedick had suggested, give some of it to no relatives? Give it to charities and libraries and hospitals. Mr. Chutney had rather liked the idea, though he admitted he was already giving to such organizations.

Words came fully formed to Benedick's mind. A patron after death. Mr. Chutney could be a benefactor to anonymous individuals who would truly need such a gift. And Benedick had the perfect girl, the perfect character, whose story would make the idea seem worthwhile.

She only needed the proper framing for other people to see what he saw. And then it was as if she'd bought her own way in because it was her own life he was using as a bartering tool.

They were a satisfied, jovial lot pulling into Hey Nonny Nonny that afternoon—a mood that dimmed slightly at the sight of a parked Oldsmobile the color of a stained undershirt. Two men emerged from it as Leo pulled to the side. The first man was shorter than

Beatrice but well over two hundred pounds, most of it in his stomach, which he carried in front of him like the breast of an overfed pigeon. His black beard didn't match the ashy hair visible beneath his fedora hat. At his shoulder, the second man was thin and several inches taller, his neck crooked and bobbing like a crane's. He looked like a sullen tourist, with a floppy fisherman's hat hanging low on his head and a tiny gap of hairy skin between where his pants ended and his wool socks began.

"Hullo!" Leo called as he stepped out of the car. "Can I help you gentlemen?"

"Happy afternoon to you," the first man said. "We're a coupla out-a-towners seeking accommodation." The smile he presented was charming, if devoid of actual warmth. "I'm Mr. Joe Hansen, and this here's my partner, Mr. Henry Smith. You're not the master of the house?"

"Indeed I am." Leo shook Mr. Joe Hansen's hand, then Mr. Henry Smith's. "I'm Leonard Stahr. And my boys, Pedro Morello and Benedick Scott."

Mr. Hansen's brow lifted a fraction at Benedick's name, as if he found it mighty interesting. "Your sons?"

"Not as such. This one I claim as my own." Leo put a hand on Prince's shoulder, who went a bit warm around the cheeks. "Ben's father is some sort of money what's-it on Wall Street. Ben spends his summers with us."

"Wonderful!" Mr. Hansen didn't probe further. In fact he

seemed deliberate in his effort not to give Benedick a second glance.

"You look familiar," Leo said. "I wouldn't know you from somewhere, would I?"

"Don't think so!" Mr. Hansen said. "We're from Connecticut. Just have one of those faces, I s'pose."

"Ah."

"So! Any rooms for a few weary travelers?"

"Washroom's shared, but I can give you two rooms on the second floor. How long are you staying?"

"Oh, we'd hoped a week or two, if it's all the same to you."

Leo considered a moment. He hadn't had a drink yet that day. "I'm afraid," he said slowly, still friendly, "that we're booked for the weekend. You'll have to check out Friday morning. But I can give you accommodation for the week, if you'd still like it."

They were not booked, of course, but neither Prince nor Benedick would question his decision, especially not when his old instincts were in fighting form.

Mr. Hansen glanced at Mr. Smith. The pause between them seemed unnecessarily weighty; then all at once Mr. Hansen's countenance became bright and blank as paper. "Of course!" he boomed. "Something is better than nothing, what?"

Leo said, "Very good. Come with me, and I'll see that you're registered."

"I can take your bags," Prince offered, stepping forward.

"Certainly not." Mr. Smith swung his bag up by his chest. "Precious equipment in here. Very fragile."

"We're pheasant hunters," Mr. Hansen said conversationally.

Mr. Smith scoffed. "Pheasant *scientists*, pheasant *observers*," he corrected.

Mr. Hansen said, "Who kill our studied quarries."

"Preserve!" Mr. Smith shrieked.

"Beg pardon?" Leo asked.

Mr. Hansen shook his head. "Most sincere apologies, Mr. Stahr. Smith is an old man, and his wits are not as blunt as I wish they were. But he's as honest as the skin between his brows, God bless him."

"Yes." Mr. Smith's lips puckered. "I thank God that I am as honest as all the other old men who are not honester than me."

"I don't know what the blasted hell you're talking about," Leo said, "but so long as you've got money to pay for your stay, you're welcome. Come with me."

Benedick arched a dubious brow at Prince. Prince lifted a shoulder, but he looked squirrelly, as if he, too, were trying to place where he might know the two men.

Once they'd gone inside with Leo, Prince got the sewing machine out from the back of the car. Benedick followed behind him but paused at a tinny sound coming from the drawing room.

He followed it in, and there was Beatrice, on her knees, fiddling with the dials on the radio box. She hadn't noticed him come in. He had not yet sunk so far in his silly obsession that he could read her mind, but he knew when it was chewing on a bone. Obviously there was the minor barrier of his eloquent declaration of their forever separation, but he was feeling a bit more confident with his letter idea still buzzing in his head.

"Whatever it is that's eating you," he said, sitting down, "it must be suffering horribly."

She glanced over, startled. Her eyes went immediately cold.

Oh, right.

He might also have called her a heartless automaton and declared her incapable of human interaction.

Well!

She'd only got back what she gave. Fair was fair, and what did he care if she was looking at him as if he were a hair discovered in her soup? She was a fingernail in his, and that was the way the world was.

"Yes, well," she finally replied. "Some of us are indeed burdened with thoughts of weight and substance."

The radio hummed in the background at low volume. He knelt beside it, careful to keep a hefty distance between them, and tapped the wired covering. Static. "Is your weighty brain blocking the radio's electric waves?"

"*Electromagnetic* waves," she corrected him. "And I suppose it's possible."

He gave her an incredulous glance. Her face was entirely serious. Pressing her temples with her fingers, she closed her eyes.

"What are you doing?" he asked.

"Drat." She sighed. "I was hoping it would work on you, too." She cracked open one eye, like a backward wink. The skin around her mouth twitched.

God in heaven. He'd *missed* her, and no one was more surprised about it than he was.

The radio crackled with renewed life.

"In case you missed it yesterday, folks—"

Benedick cranked the volume dial.

The brisk, efficient voice of the radio announcer: "He made it. Charles A. Lindbergh—Lucky Lindy, as they call him—landed at Le Bourget Airport, Paris, at five twenty-four yesterday afternoon, safe and sound."

They listened to the rest of the announcement in silence. He turned down the volume as an ad started.

"Isn't it . . ." She began to speak, barely audible. "Isn't it just—"

"Yes," he said. A little guarded, she met his eyes, and he smiled. "You'll find a way, Miss Clark. You're that sort of person, you and this Lindy fellow. Nothing's impossible for you." He stood to leave. No need to ruin it by staying. They didn't have a great track record for conversations lasting over a few minutes, and he could give her this small one.

CHAPTER 17

SOME CUPID KILLS WITH ARROWS, SOME WITH TRAPS

Like the good double agent she was turning out to be, Maggie kept tabs on Prince's comings and goings. Not that there was much to report, except to say it was exhausting watching him do in one day what might take an ordinary person three.

Still, now that she was looking for it, she could see the tripped wire in Prince. As if someone had lit a fuse on a faraway stick of dynamite. That was what was in his eyes now, a burn building up to an explosion. Used to be he'd had what Maggie thought of as *good* eyes.

Maybe that was why he couldn't catch a break in this business. Immorality paid better.

With the weather getting warmer, she took to leaving her window open so she could hear every time one of their cars left, and so far Prince hadn't gone anywhere without Benedick or Leo or their whole unruly gang in tow.

Until the Tuesday after Decoration Day.

Maggie only realized he was gone—both the Lambda and the Ford had stayed silent and parked all night—when the sound of knocking woke her up. On the other end of the hall, Hero's voice asked: "Prince, are you in there? I've got some plans I want to talk to you about." More knocking, the creak of an opened door, then Hero's soft curse. "Where the hell is he?" Followed by the soft stomp of her retreat.

Maggie sat up straight in her bed. *Could be nothing*, she thought, but it didn't stop her from scrambling into a skirt and blouse as quickly as she could, not even glancing at what her hair might be doing before scouring Hey Nonny Nonny from its secret halls and staircases to the woods close to the house.

Even if someone had picked him up, Maggie would have heard any car, she was sure. That meant he'd walked, and why, why would he walk unless he didn't want anyone to know that he'd gone?

Benedick didn't know anything; neither did Leo. Maggie even called Father Francis and had barely set the receiver in place before it rang again under her fingertips. She picked it up. "Hey Nonny Nonny residence."

"Margaret?"

John's voice. There was a small echo, but he sounded different, unattached from the rest of him. And tired. Lord, he sounded so tired.

She nearly keeled over where she stood. How? How had he found out so quickly? Even for him, it was supernatural.

"I got a good tip about King Oliver over at the Cotton Club," he said.

Oh.

Gravity knocked Maggie back into her limbs. She blinked, processing his words in real time. He wasn't calling about Prince at all. "Cotton Club?" she managed to say; her voice was thin.

"He turned down his regular booking contract, so they offered the gig to Duke Ellington."

"Duke Ellington?" Her responses weren't exactly blinding anyone with the glitter of intelligence, but those words were magic: *Cotton Club, Duke Ellington.* They didn't sound real. They were the dreams of a little girl singing along to her father's out-of-tune piano.

"Right, but Ellington only has a six-man group, and to play the Cotton Club, he needs eleven." John paused, but when Maggie didn't say anything, he added, "He's auditioning for some new chorus girls."

"Chorus girls. Okay."

"I know it's not a spotlight role," John added, never mind that Maggie's heart was thumping out of her chest, "but it's a good gig, and you'd meet a lot of the right people. I set up a meeting for you on Saturday."

At last Maggie found her voice. "This Saturday?"

"Seven, at the Jack Mills studio."

Studio.

Did John remember, Maggie wondered, that Saturday was Hero's birthday? Without Maggie, Tommy wouldn't show. Hero would have less than a week to replace her, if she could find someone at all. If Hero could afford anyone else even if she could find someone.

"Margaret?" John asked.

He had to know, didn't he? John Morello was no fool. Just as he knew she'd waited what felt like her whole life to sing in the Cotton Club. Her heart would not allow her to say no, and what was worse, Hero would understand. They all would. Might even congratulate her.

And John *knew.*

He'd be hurting Hey Nonny Nonny, and nobody could blame Maggie.

Well, nice try, but it still felt rotten. Silently she tucked Prince's absence away like a secret. "Yeah, yeah, I'll be there," she said softly. "Of course I'll be there."

"Congratulations," he said, so quietly she almost missed it, and a few seconds later she was talking to the operator asking if she'd like to reconnect or place another call.

Maggie replaced the receiver.

It was another hour or so before Maggie spied Prince returning. Walking, as she'd suspected. The jacket he'd likely donned in the dark hours of morning was slung over his shoulder in the late-morning sun. His gait was unhurried, the set of his shoulders comfortable, not hunched under the weight of secrets.

Maggie ran out the back door and hopped off the porch to meet him. "Where have you been?"

Prince slowed to a stop, frowning. "Nowhere."

"Getting more booze? Why didn't you take the car?"

"Who's asking?"

"*I* am, hotshot. Hero's party is in four days."

"So let me worry about it. I don't tell you how to sing, do I?"

Maggie drew back, stung. Prince moved to walk past her, but a window snapped open, and Maggie's first question got an echo: "Just where have you been all morning?" Prince glanced up and Maggie turned. Hero, all cleavage and furious blue eyes, stuck her upper body out of her window.

"Did something happen?" Prince asked eventually.

"We were worried," Maggie muttered.

"My whole day is hours behind," Hero said. "Get up here, and bring Maggie with you."

❖ ❖ ❖

Prince brushed off any inquiries on his whereabouts by saying he'd gone on a summer stroll, as if he were the kind of person who had time for that (as if he hadn't left sometime before four o'clock in the morning). *Phonus balonus*, Maggie thought, and surely Hero, who knew him better than anybody, would call a jury on such a fib; but in her own flip of character, she accepted his explanation with this little gem: "It is a lovely day to be outside." As if she were some darling country estate lady.

Maggie stared at them as though they'd both swallowed too much gin, but Hero herded them into her room and shut the door. She paced around, stroking her chin like a film villain, occasionally popping up on her tiptoes in a flex of energy.

"I think it's time for the first farm skim of the year," Hero said.

"In June?" Maggie asked. "It's too early."

Every year the farms in Nassau County had more produce than anybody knew what to do with (or so Anna had claimed), and sometimes they'd hike along the edges of the vast orchards and strawberry fields to fill a bag or two with extras. They made all sorts of hard cider and fruit-tinged beer with their loot.

"Never mind," said Hero. "This isn't about the fruit. This is about Beatrice and Benedick."

Maggie glanced at Prince to check if she was the only one confused.

Prince leaned against Hero's wall, his usual spot, arms crossed over his chest. He raised an eyebrow at Maggie. He didn't know either then.

"More specifically"—Hero continued—"it's about making sure Beatrice and Benedick fall madly in love."

"What?" Maggie laughed. "Those two have been sniping at each other since Beatrice got here."

"*Exactly*," Hero said, pointing at her. "They can't seem to leave each other alone."

Maggie looked again at Prince, who in turn looked thoughtful.

Objectively, *there* was a good match for Beatrice. Same work ethic, same unadorned goodness. The ability to take care of each other. Such an obvious match, in fact, it was not so hard to imagine Hero sliding Benedick between the pair as a buffer so they wouldn't elope and abandon her to some sturdy cottage in the country.

"I like it," Prince said, to Maggie's surprise.

"Really?" Maggie asked.

Prince lifted a shoulder. "I think Beatrice impresses Ben, and he challenges her."

"Like all great romances," said Maggie dryly.

"Why not?" asked Hero. "Besides, romance is the easy part. The surest way to get people to take a second look at a person they thought they didn't like is to tell them that person likes *them*. Loves them even. Dreams of having their super-brained babies."

Maggie bet Beatrice didn't dream of having anyone's babies, but she shrugged. "You got it, boss."

"Thank you all for coming today."

Hero said it as if she'd given any of them a choice. She leveled them with a haughty look like a princess of the old regime. The day was almost offensively nice. Warm but not overwhelmingly hot, especially under the shade of apple, pear, and peach trees.

Beatrice muttered, "I don't see why Claude gets out of this."

"Mr. Blaine went to the Hamptons for a few days," Hero said, "and will be culling those fields for fresh blood to attend my birthday party. Meanwhile, we shall cull these fields for our spirits. And I do mean that figuratively and literally." She was wearing an old pair of grass-stained slacks, too big on her; her hair was held back by a scarf. She stood at the edge of one of Flower Hill's illustrious farms, under the shade of a wayward peach tree in bloom. A burlap sack hung off her hip. The slope of the ground allowed her to look down on her subjects, even with each of them technically taller than she was.

Beatrice rolled her eyes. She'd put herself as far as humanly possible from Benedick, and Benedick had been only too happy to accommodate her. Maggie tried to see what Prince and Hero saw and had to admit that if nothing else, the pair ignored the other to such a complete degree that each had to in fact be astonishingly aware of the other.

Maggie couldn't help but think of John and how he went out of his way to ignore her after doing something thoughtful for her. It was a battle, making sure they stayed apart. Maybe Hero was on to something, and Benedick and Beatrice were halfway to falling in love.

"Never mind that this is illegal," Beatrice added.

"You ought to never mind," Benedick muttered. "That moonshine didn't walk itself off Sage's boat, now did it?"

"That we paid for. I'm following the spirit of the law, not its letter. Theft is still theft."

"How noble. I expect they can see the sparkle of your halo all the way in New Jersey."

"A shame there's no law against inane speech, so you could ignore that, too, and spare us your dull wit." She smiled.

Then again, Maggie thought. *Maybe not.*

"A-hem." Hero interrupted. "If I may continue?"

"One other thing," Beatrice said.

Hero scowled. "Yes, cousin dear?"

"Nothing is in season yet. Not until the *end* of June at least."

"First of all, there are always some early birds. We're not looking to cull the entire orchard, just enough to fill a bag or two each. Secondly, I've tasted brew boiled out of tree bark, so if we have to make do with a little under-ripe fruit, that won't be the end of the world." Hero examined her nails. "I can do this all day, Beatrice."

Beatrice's lips twitched with a suppressed smile.

Hero glanced up and winked. Then she turned on her heel and shimmied herself expertly through the wire fence. "Onward, comrades."

The branches were thick with blossoms and the plump bobs of early peaches. The more or less plan was to pick a tree with no low-hanging branches—hard to climb down, in other words—and hoist Beatrice and Benedick up, separately, to get the best fruit someone "saw" at the top. Then Maggie, Hero, and Prince would conveniently forget about their quarries, trapped high and hidden from view, and wander back only to let slip a little gossip.

"Won't they assume we're smart enough to know they might hear us?" Maggie had asked. "Isn't that suspicious?" Beatrice and Benedick were no dummies.

"They won't be thinking about that," Hero had replied, "when they're rewriting every conversation they've had into one of suppressed passion."

Maggie adjusted her sack on her hip and glanced over at Benedick. He squatted roughly fifteen feet away and was picking up a decidedly rotten peach out of the grass, turning it in his fingers. He was, bless him, absolutely the sort of boy who could sit pondering a worm and wondering what on earth it was up to for hours at a stretch.

He didn't deserve to be a buffer. Maggie hoped Hero was right.

Turning the rotted peach over in his fingers, Benedick sauntered closer to Prince. Then, casual as anything, he lobbed the
piece of fruit at Hero. It smacked her in the shoulder, and she
whirled around. "What's the big idea?"

Benedick met her glare with comically wide eyes and pointed
at Prince, who straightened from his bag. Prince looked between
them. "What? Hey, I didn't—" A peach caught him in the chest.
"Ow! That was hard as a rock!"

"Maggie did it."

Hero pointed at her. Maggie fisted her hands on her hips.
"Say again, now?"

"Miss Hughes." Prince shook his head solemnly. He bent
in search of his own ammunition, but Maggie had already sent
a bloated peach at his head that broke apart in clumps of gloop
through his hair and knocked his hat to the ground.

Maggie burst out laughing.

"Woo-hoo! Votes for women!" Hero pumped her fist.
"Come on, Beatrice! Ha, I forgot we outnumber them now."

She squealed as Prince pushed up his sleeves and muttered,
"That's it." To Benedick, Prince said, "Don't stand there like an
idiot; get in formation!"

Honestly they couldn't have planned it better. Prince hoisted
Benedick up a nearby tree so he could strike from "an aerial
position," and then it was too easy to suggest they have Beatrice
do the same, to even the playing field. Even easier to get caught

up chasing one another, abandoning their tree-stuck warriors to their fate.

"Beatrice first," Hero whispered breathlessly, once they were out of earshot. "Prince, keep an eye on Ben." She motioned to Maggie, and they strolled in Beatrice's direction. Hero jabbed a finger at a tree several yards ahead of them. The leaves rustled, and through the bouquets of leaf and blossom, the outline of Beatrice's skirt was visible.

"Shoot," Hero said loudly, "I think we're turned around, Mags. Do you see the boys?"

"They're back that way. Didn't you hear Ben telling Prince not to throw anything too hard at Beatrice in her tree?"

"Oh, right. We should have put Bea on the front line. I forget that he loves her."

Well, that was as good a segue as any. A branch snapped. A handful of half-grown peaches tumbled to the grassy floor.

Hero arched both brows at Maggie. They edged a bit closer.

"Poor Ben, though," Maggie said. "The only time he ever falls in love, and the girl can't stand him."

"You can't blame Beatrice either," said Hero. "The way that boy acts around her. He's nervous, of course, but even so, sometimes he needs a good smack in the head."

"Ah, that's a lousy excuse. She'd get the message if he just walked up to her and said it: *Beatrice, I love you. I think we should marry and breed.*"

Hero barely suppressed her snort. "Can you blame him? He thinks she hates him. I don't know if I'd have the nerve either."

"At least it's not another fella stopping her. She just loves her doctoring too much."

"Well, that's what we'll tell him. He's not to blame. He's brilliant, good-looking, tenderhearted, and any girl would be lucky to catch his eye. If I were Beatrice, I'd be flattered I was the only one who had. How's my hair? Did I get the last of the peach out?"

"Sure did," said Maggie. "Where *is* Beatrice, anyhow?"

"I'm sure it was that back row of trees there . . ." Hero trailed off, tugging Maggie along. *Perfecto*, she mouthed. They found Prince and swapped. Maggie kept an eye on Beatrice's direction to make sure she didn't march in unannounced, and Prince and Hero went to deliver a similar speech near Benedick's tree.

Poor Beatrice, in love with a scoundrel who only ever mocked her! If she ever confessed her feelings, he'd only mock her more. Love! What a tragedy. Et cetera, et cetera. Maggie heard bits of their conversation through the trees; Prince was pretty convincing extolling Beatrice's virtues, lamenting the fact that she hadn't chosen *him* instead.

They returned, Hero pink in the cheeks and grinning like an imp. "And they say Cupid only uses arrows."

CHAPTER 18
THERE'S A DOUBLE MEANING IN THAT

To think, just this morning Beatrice had been annoyed at Benedick for his fickle nature, laying out her flaws in such sharp dissection, and then two days later telling her nothing was impossible for her. Was it so difficult for him to manage to behave in a straightforward manner?

Now she scrambled out of the tree so fast she nearly fell and broke her ankle. As it was, she did lose half her peaches and was obliged to scoop them up again before she jogged through the orchard in search of Hero and Maggie.

She found them with Prince once the fruit on the trees had turned to apples, the scent growing sharper. *I demand an explanation* was on her tongue, but she had to pause and catch her breath, and in that pause Hero spoke.

"There you are! Thank goodness. I thought maybe we'd lost you. We better get a move on soon. Here, hand me your bag."

Beatrice ducked under the strap as Hero slid the bag free.

"Hero—" she began.

"We'll add these together," Hero said. "Would you mind terribly finding Benedick and telling him we're ready to leave?"

Beatrice did mind. She minded very much.

Her heart made a sudden lurch that nearly launched the traitorous thing up her throat.

Nonsense, she thought firmly. After all, what better way to get answers than from the source of the question at hand?

"*Fine,*" Beatrice said. "*Where is he?*"

"Oh, that way somewhere." Hero pointed vaguely to the left, her attention on the peaches.

Beatrice went quite far, farther than she expected, calling his name, and was at last rewarded with a muffled shout. She turned and braced a hand on her forehead to block the sun. "Ben?"

"Above you, ow, damn—" A grunt of surprise, and then— crash!—he landed among fluttering leaves and snapped twigs at her feet. She startled away as he groaned, holding his wrist, and shifted onto his back. He swore softly, eyes closed.

Pressing a hand to her chest, Beatrice let out a breath. "Didn't you grow up on Park Avenue? You have no business climbing trees without a ladder." She stepped forward and nudged his inert form with the toe of her shoe. "Are you hurt? Why are you holding your wrist? Here—" She went down on one knee next to him. "Let me see it. I think I'll be able to tell if you've knocked one of your bones out of place."

He let her have his hand with surprising willingness. She held it up and felt over the ridge by his thumb.

"Did you come looking for me?" he asked.

She glanced down. Even having fallen out of a tree, he looked as if he had done it on purpose; any disarray had been suffered with style. "Yes. Does this hurt?" She squeezed and twisted, and he flinched a little but didn't show the kind of pain a break would cause.

Uncertain, he met her eyes. The left side of his face was striped red from a nasty run-in with bark. *Do you love me?*

"No," he said, answering her earlier question. "Not much."

It was rather harder than she expected to ask him out loud. His eyes, which had always been brown, were now not *just* brown, but a salty caramel forest, a home for woodland creatures; she wanted to climb in them and make a nest. As if some membrane had dissolved in her sensible brain, unleashing a foreign girlish miasma.

She cleared her throat. "I'm sorry, Ben."

His eyebrows arched. "Pardon?"

"I don't think you're here because you're lazy or because you're desperate for love. I didn't mean it when I said it like that. And I don't think you're a bad writer. I stand by what I said about your novel, but I've read, um, other things that you've written. Also, when you tell a story out loud— You have a very nice—it's a way you have, I guess, to make a person feel like she's got something in common with the rest of the world, when before, she just felt alone."

Oh, dear.

He actually seemed quite frightened, as if she were not apologizing but rather peeling off her skin to reveal green scales underneath.

"Anyway," she hurried to say, "that's it. We've had a rough time of it before, and I wanted to do the decent thing and apologize."

He narrowed his eyes. "Did Hero put you up to this?"

Beatrice blushed. She dropped his hand. "No, she didn't. In spite of what you think, I *am* a human being, with normal human feelings, and I just—"

"I'm sorry, too."

Wincing, he pushed himself upright with his other hand. She swallowed when it put him next to her, his arm close enough to press against her own, but facing the opposite way. His head turned to hers, his hair brushed with dappled, leafy sunlight, and she could see, a little, at this particular angle, how a girl might consider him handsome were she so inclined.

"I've only been such an ass because you're so damned right most of the time." His lips twisted in a wry smile. "And so damned better than me at everything."

He didn't seem *un*-in-love with her, at that.

All at once she had a rattling feeling, as if a trolley were coming and she was still half a block away. If she ran, she could catch it. Or she could stay where she was, and no one would ever know the difference. Carefully she sat back, away from him.

"Miss Clark," he said, "have we just made the hard turn from enemies into friends?"

"I'd like that," she said. "If you don't mind being wrong and inferior most of the time because that's not something I can help."

His small, wry smile split into a grin. And she decided not to ask him if it was true that he loved her. She was very sure it changed nothing on her end, and there was something nice and indulgent imagining the marks of love in his gaze.

CHAPTER 19
LOVE THEE AGAINST MY WILL

So, *so*.

Beatrice Clark loved him.

Ha-ha.

There was no accounting for taste, was there?

Never mind. Just because a person loved you didn't mean you loved her back out of sympathy. Though it was the sort of detail to derail a person's attempt to stay on task.

He had *practical* matters to attend to, objects that begged his attention. He required a certain customary mental sharpness in his day that he now found elusive.

However, the quantity of his writing had fairly exploded.

It was shameful how fast it poured out of him with this

frisson of anticipation. Obviously he'd have to be totally heartless not to care a little. Obviously he would have been gentler with the poor creature if he'd known about her affections. Obviously he might have paid more attention to the numerous occasions in which they'd been in close, unseemly, and provocative quarters.

Oh, God.

This stuff—what he was writing—was pretty good.

What if he had become one of those dappers who could only write sappy love stories for the women's magazines for a penny a page?

If he *had*, he'd just made himself a pretty dime in under an hour, which was not bad at all.

And just to mention, not that it mattered at all, but it did make a fella feel good about himself—didn't it?—to warrant the attention of a girl like Beatrice because she wasn't the sort to like just anyone. She was so aggravatingly righteous surely you had to have at least one or three redeeming qualities to merit her esteem.

On the other hand, there was no guarantee the whole thing wasn't a big fat lie. He released his fresh chapter from the typewriter and blew lightly on the still-wet ink before setting it aside.

The only safe course of action was *absolutely nothing.*

He would not treat her any differently; he would deal with her love if and when it was declared publicly, and then he would . . . um.

Not . . . reciprocate.

Clearly.

But even mentally rejecting her was quite a workout; it would be more difficult in actuality, one assumed, which frankly baffled him because two days ago he hadn't cared two figs about hurting her feelings.

A precise series of taps made their way through his window. Benedick jolted as if the soft *putt-putt* had been a clap of thunder; he'd been at it since dawn. He stood up and looked out. The Lambda and Tin Lizzie were accounted for, as well as Mr. Hansen's hideous Oldsmobile.

Mr. Hansen and Mr. Smith were setting up hunting equipment, scouring the fields with their binoculars, and then, apropos of nothing, rapping on wood panes outside the house. Feeling between the grooves; checking, it seemed, for hollowness.

Benedick frowned. He hurried outside and came upon the pair of pheasant hunters just as they squatted near the cellar doors. "Hello, there," Benedick called.

Mr. Hansen straightened up. "Mr. Scott!"

"Came out for a walk. Looking for buried treasure?" Benedick laughed, *no suspicion here, none whatsoever*, and tossed a chunk of hair out of his eyes, putting on his very best privileged voice. "Actually I couldn't bother either of you for a smoke, could I? I'm short on just about everything at the moment."

"Sure, don't sweat it." Mr. Hansen passed him a cigarette

and lit it himself with an engraved silver lighter. The initial in the design was a *D*, not *J* or *H* for Joe Hansen.

"God bless you," said Benedick, feigning relief, because he still thought of chimneys, thanks for nothing, Beatrice Clark. (Who loved him, so it was all right.)

"Listen, kid, we didn't want to say nothing before"—Mr. Hansen leaned in—"but Smith and I wouldn't mind finding a decent blind around these parts. We actually heard this bed and breakfast was more than it looks, and it don't look like much, frankly."

Benedick kept his face placid. He blinked as dumbly as possible. "Hey Nonny Nonny?" He acted surprised. "If there's something here, no one told me about it. What's your scene?"

"Nothing fancy, mind. We try to stay away from the younger, partying crowd; we just want a nice beer at the end of the day."

As Benedick himself was fancy and young, he got the feeling they were trying to avoid running into him. "There's an easy joint not far from here, if you don't mind Queens. Not for me, of course, but I'm willing to help a neighbor out if you're interested."

Mr. Hansen and Mr. Smith exchanged a look. "Sure, son," Mr. Hansen said. "What do you got?"

Benedick gave him the address of Rack 20, a rough bar so padded by bribes it could afford to take a hit. He was just finishing up the password when a popping gutted engine came up the drive; it was a telegraph boy on a motorbike.

"S'cuse me a minute," Benedick said, and jogged over to the front porch.

The telegraph boy tipped his cap. "Mornin'. Got one for a Miss Clark? And, uh"—the boy squinted, turning the envelope around—"looks like P. Morello."

Benedick handed him a dollar, a fat tip he couldn't afford, but what the hell, and took the telegrams. The messenger nodded his thanks, and hopped off the porch to turn his bike around. The window envelope on the first only revealed the name P. MORELLO, and Hey Nonny Nonny's address. With one finger, Benedick slid it open and peered inside. "THE BOOKS ARE OPEN. Stop. 54 HEWLETT HARBOR. Stop. SUNDOWN."

Whatever that meant.

"Who're they for?"

Maggie appeared at his shoulder. She must have heard the motorbike. "Not you," Benedick said. "Why? Waiting on something?"

"Maybe, maybe not." She glanced sideways at him.

Before he could answer, a hand snatched the second telegram away, a miniature planet of bony elbows and curls suddenly at his side.

The girl who loved him.

"That's mine." Beatrice plucked up the one meant for her. She shimmied the card loose and read its contents quickly. She let loose a raucous laugh. "Oh! Oh, it's perfect!"

"What?"

"Miss Mayple says that even without an official high school diploma, I can take the regents' examination. If I pass, I'll be allowed to enroll in college regardless of high school credits!"

With no warning whatsoever, she flung herself at him, arms clamped around his neck like a bow tie, knees bumping his. As though she were trying to get an indelible impression, for scientific research, to take with her forever. She sealed it off with a kiss on his cheek. It happened so fast she released him before he fully recovered, and he stumbled back into the porch column, the back of his head bumping against the wood.

"Ouch." He rubbed the sore spot.

"Sorry!" Her eyes widened, looking up from her treasured telegram. If she realized what her lips had been up to, she didn't take it back or at the very least pair the kiss with an insult. Which was altogether disarming. "I'm so excited. Are you okay?"

He felt like climbing a mountain, not for any heroic reason but for something stupid, like picking her a flower; he felt subservient to her whims, desperate for her not to command anyone but him; he felt terrified for feeling all those things after a tiny kiss, a nothing kiss, a fraction, a weed, a sneeze, compared with a dozen other tokens of affection he'd received in his life.

"Fine," is what he said. "You know, you have to pass the exams first before they mean anything."

On her way back inside she shot him a grin over her shoulder. "Ha! I could have passed the regents' exams when I was fourteen."

He smiled, pinched, thinking of the useless letter he'd written for her. If only she ever took a wrong step. If only she wasn't so brilliant and sure and steady on her planned path. If only she needed him. "When is it?"

She checked the card. "Early June. So, next week? Soon, at any rate." She turned back.

"I can take you into the city when it's the day?"

Her smile widened. His heart hurt. "Thank you," she said. She fairly bounced back into the house; Benedick sagged slightly in her absence.

"My, my."

He turned to Maggie, who tried (not very hard, if Benedick was any judge) to keep her grin in check. She arched her brows and tapped her cheek. "My," she repeated slowly, clucking her tongue, "my."

Benedick flushed. "She would have kissed a lamppost if there'd been one nearby."

"And yet it was no lamppost standing in her way. Why don't you take her out tonight?"

"Take her out how?"

"Don't be thick. Put your glad rags on, show her a ripping time or two." Her lip curved. "Jazz conquers virtue, don't ya know?"

"You are acting positively wily, Margaret Hughes. I demand to know your angle."

"My angle is someone's got to step in and help you dum-dums out, how's that?"

"Mags," Benedick said, a bit plaintively, "I can't actually do that. What would she think, me asking her out on the town out of the glory blue?"

"Say you're celebrating. She gets to take a test, which I guess is happy news for some folks." Maggie held out a hand. "I'll take that telegram to Prince; you go polish that silver tongue of yours and get to it."

Chewing the inside of his cheek, he gave her the telegram. Mr. Hansen and Mr. Smith came back around. Mr. Hansen hopped onto the porch and opened the front door. "Thanks for the tip, boy," he said, nodding before he went inside.

There was also *that*.

It wouldn't be a bad idea to check out Rack 20 tonight himself, just to see if the pheasant hunters showed up or not. Not that Rack 20 was the place to bring a nice girl, but at least then the evening would have a slightly less obvious date overture.

He pulled his shirt straight, feigning self-importance. "Very well," he told Maggie. He pointed at her. "But not because you told me to."

CHAPTER 20
THE PRINCE WOOS
FOR HIMSELF

*T*he books are open.

Maybe, Maggie reasoned, the telegram meant the books of
a real buyer. Maybe 54 Hewlett Harbor was a regular old rum-
running drop point. This was Prince's job, as he'd reminded her,
and it might be no more suspicious than Tommy's buzzing her a
line about a new trumpet player ripe for the picking.

Still.

Maggie tapped the envelope nervously in her palm as she
climbed the stairs to Prince's room, but she wasn't halfway
up when Hero, still dressed for bed, hurried past the landing,
clutching her robe to her chest. Maggie paused, then followed.
Hero adjusted her slip in the dusty wall mirror, pushed a flower

arrangement out of her way, then opened Prince's door without knocking.

Maggie got a bit closer until she was able to just see into the room. Prince stood at his window in slacks and an undershirt, the smoke of the cigarette between his fingers drifting out through the open crack. He turned as Hero came in, *swish-swish-swish*, straight to the washbasin in the corner of the room. He frowned.

Hero said, "The bathroom is all steamed up. It's ruining my hair." She pulled a lipstick out of her brassiere and began to paint the child out of her face. Maggie wished she didn't know where this was headed, but boy, did she.

"Don't get your makeup in my sink again," said Prince.

"Someone's in a mood."

"Where the hell are you going anyway? It's ten o'clock in the morning."

"Wouldn't you like to know? Claude hobnobs with more genteel society, the brunch-eating kind." She capped the lipstick. Her lidded eyes belied her sharp interest in his reaction. "Do you love my new lipstick? Claude got it for me from Saks. I think he likes to see me wearing it."

Prince snorted. He picked up the shirt hanging on his bedpost and slid it on. "You like it because he wants you to like it."

Hero scowled. "I *like* it, too. And you sound like quite the snob, given that that's my father's shirt you're putting on."

Prince froze, hands on the buttons by his chest. He met

Hero's eyes in the mirror, his darkening with what could have been anger, but what Maggie recognized as hurt.

Hero didn't give an inch. If anything, her voice dropped cooler. "Claude seems tacky to you. But you don't know how sweet he is. He's got a good heart, unlike some people."

Oh, Hero. That's not the way.

Prince yanked his belt off his dresser so hard it snapped. "So what, you going to marry him? You're pretending same as you do with everyone else. And you know what? He is a good person, you're right. So let's hope he isn't too heartbroken when you get bored of him in a month."

"That's what you think of me, isn't it? That I'm not even capable of real love. Well, I am! I really love him, Pedro Morello. I hope he does ask me to marry him because I'd say yes!"

Maggie took her cue, before the pair of them started throwing things. She knocked on the door. "Heyo," she called casually, as if she hadn't heard a thing. "Can I come in? Messenger boy stopped by . . ."

Hero stormed past Maggie two points of bright color on her cheeks. "Good luck," she snarled. "He's acting completely impossible."

Prince sat on the edge of his bed, lacing up his shoes. He didn't look up as Maggie came in.

"Telegram," she said, and handed it over.

"Thanks." Prince read it. Maggie watched him expectantly—

but was disappointed when Prince said nothing. A forbidding gleam entered his eyes.

"You okay?" Maggie asked. "You know that's just Hero checking in, making sure you're still with her. She's anxious about her party, even if she won't say it."

"I haven't gone anywhere, have I?" Prince finished with the laces, and his foot hit the ground with a hard thud. He stood and tucked the telegram into his back pocket. "I'm glad for you, Mags. About the Cotton Club, I mean. That's big-time."

Maggie had told them to give them time to find a replacement. As she'd predicted, nobody was anything but happy for her.

Then Prince was gone, and maybe it was nothing, but the feeling in her deepest gut said different. After that fight with Hero, he was walking reckless.

Finally she shook her head and marched downstairs to the drawing room. She gave the operator John's number and waited what seemed like half a century before a breathy voice came on the other line. *"Pronto?"*

A woman's voice.

"Hello?" Maggie said.

"Hello?" the voice answered.

"Um, Mrs. Morello?" Maggie guessed.

"I am not Morello!" the woman shrieked. "Who are you? How did you find me?"

"I'm sorry, please, I need to speak to John. Is he there?"

"John has that bastard's blood in him. *He's* the bastard, not my Pedro, not my prince—"

"Give the phone to John, please. It's very important."

"John is not here." Abruptly the voice sounded calm and lucid, and then the line disconnected. Slowly Maggie replaced the receiver in the cradle. Now what?

You know damn well what, Margaret.

She just didn't like it.

She ran back up the stairs to get her good shoes. She was hoofing it to town. From there she could get a telegram to John and then maybe catch Father Francis at the church. He'd give her a ride to Hewlett Harbor without asking too many questions. She hoped.

Once she was ready, she jogged back downstairs—just in time to watch Hero fling open the front door and launch herself into a waiting Claude's arms with an embrace that might turn a weaker mortal to a diamond.

"Hello," he said, laughing.

"I missed you!" she said into his shoulder.

"Well! It was only a long weekend, and now I'm yours again forever." Despite his la-di-da tone, he was clearly pleased as pie at her reaction, his ears bright pink. "Miss Hughes! How are you?" He pulled away from Hero as Maggie stepped behind them.

"Just dandy. Say, I don't suppose it'd be any trouble for you to drop me near the station before you go? Only a few minutes out of your way."

"Why, sure," Claude said. He turned and waved at a car in the drive, which held three of his friends, all of whom stared at Hey Nonny Nonny and Maggie with fascination and delight. They waved back with gloved hands and the conviction that they were engaging in something scandalous.

"I'll be," said Maggie.

She climbed in the back with Hero and Claude and a pretty redhead. "Boys, you've met Hero," Claude said. "This is Margaret Hughes. She sings at the speakeasy. Miss Hughes, this is Trent Douglas, Skipper Mellon, and Lucille York."

"How do you do, Miss Hughes?" Lucille leaned over. "Do you know, I attended a charity banquet with my parents last year, and William Du Bois gave a speech." Lucille nodded, and Maggie got the impression she expected to be congratulated on her forward thinking. When Maggie said nothing, Lucille added, nervously, "Do you—have you met Mr. Du Bois, Miss Hughes?"

"I'm sorry," Maggie said. "I can't say that I have."

Lucille stared at her. "Oh," she said after a long, uncomfortable beat. "Of course."

Skipper, the boy in the passenger seat, was pretending Maggie wasn't there. Hero wasn't paying the slightest attention, her hand on Claude's arm. "Which way to the station?" the driver,

Trent Douglas, asked, with bright waspish charm. As they pulled out, he launched into a conversation about football with Skipper, while Lucille pretended to care.

Maggie slumped back in her seat. Some days, you couldn't make it off Hey Nonny Nonny's porch without being reminded about the world outside its doors. How much longer could she stay sheltered? How long could any of them?

Maggie glanced over at Hero and Claude and tried to picture them married, and truth be told, Hero Stahr, who could pretend with the best of them when it came to boys, didn't seem to be pretending this time. "How were the Hamptons?" Hero murmured, stroking his flawless golden jaw. "You seem worried."

"Do I? Oh, well, there's just a fuss about college in the fall and how I ought to be out meeting the right people—as if that matters, next to you."

"Claude, sweetheart, of course it matters. I'm just some dame you met at a swanky bar, and you have a nice, golden, shining future. The kind that requires a college education."

"I don't want any kind of future that doesn't have you in it, Hero. That's the kind of shining future for me."

Brother, Maggie thought, but there was no Prince, no Ben to share a knowing look with. Only Lucille, who was still leaning over the seat determined to be interested in football.

Hero poked Claude. "I'm going to find a crack in your perfect knight's armor, buddy boy—you wait. No one is this wonderful."

He laughed and turned his face, his nose in her hair. His lips brushed her skin. "Tell it to my mother."

"Who's that? The queen of England?"

He laughed.

They dropped Maggie off right in front of the telegraph office, and she wondered if all of them at Hey Nonny Nonny weren't one step away from the next thing, with the past already dying under their feet.

CHAPTER 21
ALL HEARTS IN LOVE USE THEIR OWN TONGUES

Beatrice knelt on her floor and set aside her chemistry book. That was her best subject by far. Actually biology was, but how many sciences did the regents' exam cover?

Her grammar was all right, but her spelling occasionally drifted toward phonetic rather than correct. Oh, and Latin! How could she forget Latin? That book was moving to the top of the pile.

Beatrice straightened, hands on her hips, surveying the wide arc of books and papers she'd laid out, the remains of her school days, both official and otherwise. She stiffened. Where was her history textbook?

Would she have to know her capitals? Recite the Preamble

to the Constitution? " 'We the people of the United States,' " she murmured, " 'in order to form a more perfect Union . . .' "

There was a knock at the door, followed by an amused "Miss Clark?"

"Yes?"

The door opened, and Benedick poked his head in. "Were you reciting the Preamble to the Constitution?"

"You've heard of it?" She smiled. She was happy to see him. (There, she admitted it.)

He stepped inside. He wore a suit. Not the nicest one he'd ever put on in his life, she was sure, but it was tailored to his whip-like frame so exactly that he looked sort of . . . dashing.

He glanced over her books. "I thought you said you could pass this exam unconscious? What are you doing studying already?"

"It relaxes me."

"Well, if you think the medical world at large can spare you, I could use that big brain of yours tonight." He clasped his hands behind his back and examined the knickknacks in her room. He picked up the skull replica off her dresser and turned it over in his hand with fascinated horror. "It's like the lair of a mad scientist in here. . . ."

"What do you need my brain for?" She climbed to her feet, dusting her skirt off.

He turned and set the skull down. "You know those pheasant hunters staying in the second-floor rooms?"

"Mr. Hansen and Mr. Smith, yes."

"I caught them snooping around outside this morning, almost like they were looking for something. I told them about a bar down in Queens, and I thought about heading there tonight, just to see if they show up or if they were only fishing."

"Not a bad idea."

He waited, watching her. After an extended beat of silence, his eyes crinkled. "So you'll come?"

"Oh! Well, yes. I can come if you like, though I don't think the evening will require any great mental exertion."

"Wonderful," he deadpanned, again seeming amused. He stepped closer. "There is a minor stipulation, if you don't mind."

"All right?"

"It's just I'd rather they not notice me, and I'm afraid I'll draw attention to myself, young buck out on the lam, no pals with him, so I was hoping we might act as if we were out together, you know, boy and girl."

He didn't have to look so intense about it. Or get so close to make his point, did he? She leaned ever so slightly back. She didn't want him to know his proximity unnerved her, but really. "Oh, well, just pretend?"

"Only pretend, but still convincing, if you get my drift."

"Okay." She agreed cautiously.

"Good! Get dressed, why don't you? It'll take about an hour to drive, and I want to get there early."

"You mean, dressed in something else?" She glanced down at herself dismayed. Hero had left for that brunch whatever and had not yet returned to help her navigate her apparel.

When she looked back at Benedick, he was pensive, and she, an open target. In this, she wouldn't even blame him. *Go on*, she thought with a sigh, *let's have it.*

She even had a good comeback.

I only offered my brain for the evening, sir; the package in which it comes is nonnegotiable.

Ha.

But he didn't take the opportunity. "You look fine, obviously as *you*," he said. "Not a thing wrong with it except that you look too much like Beatrice Clark, and we are meant to be incognito."

Confused, she frowned. That was a rather generous way to address the issue, considering.

"Come on, Hero won't mind if we pick through a few of her things. Nothing flashy, just a bit of a disguise, what do you say?"

Why was he being so nice?

He—

Oh, yes. He *loved* her, was *in love* with her.

Or was he?

She sent him a sidelong look as he ushered her toward Hero's bedroom. Only a pretend date, was it? It was the worst moment to recall this key detail about their dynamic, right before he was holding skirts up to her waist and setting this and that on her shoulder, his fingers on her hair before deciding, "A hat, I'm afraid, is the only surefire way to disguise that," in his dashing little suit and smelling faintly of sandalwood cologne when he got close.

Her whole body was prickly and warm by the time the affair was over. Scientifically speaking, she was unclear whether the sensation was pleasant or unpleasant.

She'd never even held hands with a boy, and this had never bothered her. Her mind, she'd reasoned, was so occupied with complex theories and thoughts that it left little room for that titillating nervousness that seemed to overcome other girls when a pair of broad shoulders sauntered too close to the senses.

Thank goodness, she had congratulated herself, *you will never have to deal with that distraction.*

She found a peach cotton skirt that worked well enough and dressed it up with one of Hero's brooches pinned to her own blouse. Benedick led her outside and opened the driver's side of the Lambda for her. "You're the better driver," he said.

The evening wind swept over her flushed skin and cleared out her head nicely.

Also—hot damn!

She'd driven only beat-up trucks before. Now she understood Hero's hell-for-leather driving approach. She accelerated into a curve and was pleased by the responding roar of the engine.

There were eleven miles of curved pavement between

Hey Nonny Nonny and where they were going. Benedick only slid closer as they got into Queens. He put an arm around the back of her seat, and directed her to a lit-up street in the busier part of town. If this was a pretend date, he was awfully close considering there wasn't a soul around to see them yet.

They parked, and after Benedick helped readjust and pin her hat in place, he held out his arm. "I'm not worried about you," he said, "but for appearances' sake?"

She slid her hand into the crook of his elbow. He led her to a shabby tenement building, with a stairway that led to a discreet well. A vertical neon sign above this dip read: Bernie's Watches.

The shop was tiny and square on the inside, framed by waist-high cases of pocket watches and ticking clocks. An old man behind the cash register pushed grimy glasses up his nose. "What can I do for you kids? Looking for anything specific?"

Benedick surveyed the glass cases, examining the array of choices one by one. He stretched a hand down and lifted a silver pocket watch. The chain was rusty red, and the back was engraved with a rose design. "I'd like this one, but with a new chain," he said. "Put it in a pine case. Velvet lining."

A hard smile creased the old man's face. He coughed and punched three keys on his register. Behind him the wall caught and slid open. The strains of a piano and disorderly laughter filtered back.

"Much obliged," Benedick said, setting the watch down.

Beatrice held on to him a bit tighter as they entered a hallway that might have belonged to any tenement building on just about any street in New York. Somebody showed them down a flight of stairs, which showcased a variety of displeasing smells, and opened an unpromising door at the end.

Then they were there, right inside a wallop of music and smoke and gin. Rack 20 was not like Hey Nonny Nonny. The ceiling was low, and the space minimal, the whole room warm and humid with bodies. Summer-worn men with skinny girls on their laps sat at the bar, nursing tumblers of bronze-colored liquids and chewing the ends of cigars. There was only a piano in the corner; a small audience urged a girl on top of it to take off her stockings, and she did, after some halfhearted protest, and played with her toes.

Benedick tugged Beatrice into a far corner booth, blocked off in shadow except for a dim hanging lamp. She sat down, and he leaned over her. "Don't get handsy," he said. "This booth has a reputation."

All that cooling wind in the car, for nothing. Her blood was back up to scorching in an instant, making her skin pink.

"Be right back," he said.

She touched her hat, surveying the room. Now she understood why he hadn't worn his best suit and why they'd decided on a simple cotton skirt and sheer black stockings for her. This wasn't a fancy crowd.

Benedick returned with two lowball glasses. She drew hers

close after he set it down, with both hands, to prove she wasn't afraid of it. The wood of the table was tacky, as if someone had spilled a few drinks. She tipped the amber liquid toward what light she could find, sniffing. On the basis of the smell, it could very well be embalming fluid.

Unbuttoning his jacket, Benedick slid in next to her. "I asked for the nonbiting variety, not to worry."

"I wasn't. How is it you know about this place?" she asked.

He shrugged. "Oh, we serious thinkers are wont to gather in dank little holes such as this, brooding over claret and brandishing our old copies of the *Liberator* at each other." He swallowed half his drink in one go with nary a flinch.

She lifted her own glass and sipped. Her tongue recoiled in shock, then tingled, as if it might be going numb. "There." She set the glass down. "Not so bad, if you remember not to breathe—" And then she promptly erupted in a fit of coughing.

He grinned. "Look at you, our little teetotaler all grown up."

"I'm not a teetotaler." She tried not to wheeze. Another cough, and she had it all out. She wiped the corners of her eyes. "Do you know, when I was in school, there was a nationwide competition run by the *Boston Herald* to invent a word for someone who drinks illegally. The winning student got a cash prize, and guess who it was?" She tapped her chest.

Benedick's face slackened. "No, you didn't."

"Yes, I did! I thought you'd be impressed, Mr. Writer."

"You can't have."

"I'm telling you I did. One hundred dollars. The prize was supposed to be two hundred, but there was a boy who came up with the exact same word, separately, so we split the money."

He leaned his cheek onto his fist, and then she understood.

"Oh," she said.

"Scofflaw," he said. "I thought I was so clever. Someone who *scoffs* at the *law*."

"It *is* clever, I think."

He smiled. "I always thought it was nuts that two different people, on their own, could think of the exact same . . ." He trailed off, straightening suddenly. "There they are."

Mr. Hansen and Mr. Smith. Dressed in suits. And no beard on Mr. Hansen. There was, however, a jar of pickles at his hip.

Benedick pressed closer to her. He turned his face into her ear, as if he were whispering a sweet nothing, but what he actually said was "What's with the pickles?"

Mr. Hansen approached the bar. "How about a drink?" he called jovially, putting the jar of pickles on the stool next to him like his best lady friend. He was trying to look silly; that was Beatrice's guess. Not unlike his ruse at Hey Nonny Nonny.

"The bartender's tough," Benedick whispered. "He doesn't sell to anybody he doesn't know. That's why I chose this joint." Behind the counter half a dozen framed photos

and newspaper clippings hung on the wall beneath a sign: DO
NOT SERVE!

"No can do, Mac," the bartender said, with a Scottish brogue.
"Never seen you. Try the gin mill down the road."

"Why, I'm Izzy Pupferry," Mr. Hansen said, laughing, "the
famous Prohibition agent!"

Benedick stiffened at the word *agent*.

"Get the name right," the bartender growled. "The bum's
name is Dogberry."

"Pupferry," said Mr. Hansen. "Don't I know my own name?"

"Maybe you do. But the lowlife you're trying to impersonate
is Dogberry. D-O-G-B-E-R-R-Y."

"Brother," said Mr. Hansen, "I ain't never wrong about a
name. It's Pupferry."

"Dogberry!" roared the bartender.

"Pupferry!" Mr. Hansen shouted back.

"You're loony," said the bartender, neck red. "I'll bet you
anything it's Dogberry."

"I'll bet you a drink."

"Don't do it, Louie," Benedick murmured.

Louie called his other customers. "These are my regulars,"
he said. "They know their way around the speaks."

They nodded, some of them swaying a bit.

"There aren't many of you regulars," Dogberry remarked
kindly.

"Now, listen," the bartender said, "that nosy Prohibition agent"—he pointed behind the bar at a newspaper photo that was far too small and grainy for anyone sober, let alone drunk, to see properly—"that's Dogberry, isn't it?"

"Yeah, sure," the swaying one said.

Someone spit.

"Not Pupferry?" Mr. Hansen suggested innocently.

"Let's take a vote. Who says Dogberry?"

Every hand raised.

"What's happening?" Beatrice whispered.

Benedick pushed her gently out of the booth. "He's an agent. I can't believe this trick is going to work. . . ."

"All right." Mr. Hansen sighed. "All—eight, are you?— drinks on me." He laid out his (or rather, if Benedick was right, the United States government's) money on the worn wood. Triumphant, the bartender served the drinks—

—and promptly paled as Mr. Hansen, aka Dogberry, leaned over the counter and passed him a summons just as Beatrice and Benedick made it to the door. "There's sad news here. You're under arrest."

Benedick took her hand and tugged her up the stairs and out of the watch shop. "A fed just capped the joint," Benedick warned the storekeep but didn't say anything else until they were sitting in the car.

Beatrice drove them away from Rack 20 but kept her speed

slow, puttering aimlessly down the streets, watching hapless partyers go in and out of the cast light of streetlamps.

"I thought maybe the Minskys had hired them," Benedick murmured. "You know, as spies. Two guys we don't recognize, get the password and pin, make a report of how much we're selling, how many patrons we get, that kind of thing. Prohibition agents, that's different."

"They'll be gone before Saturday."

"But why are they there at all?" Benedick asked. "Why us, specifically? Calling the feds is low even for the Minskys, not to mention stupid because it brings agents into their territory as well."

"Maybe the Minskys didn't tip them off."

"But who else would have? We're nobody's competition at this point." The difference in Benedick was marked. His lighthearted nature had fled the coop, and with it their pretend tête-à-tête, but this was better. She adored—was that too rosy a word?—being with him when there was a problem. Not that she was celebrating this new sinkhole they'd stepped into, but there was the most exhilarating sense of equality in working in tandem.

His brows knitted together into a troubled point. "What do you think, Beatrice?"

"Mr. Dogberry clearly has a reputation. Somebody will know something about him, and we can find out who might have paid him off."

Benedick's brow remained knotted.

"What is it?" she asked.

"I'm worried the agents might be on the mob's money order. They always have some on their payroll, and it's possible Prince has aggravated them to the point of retaliation."

"So they sent an agent to take care of the speakeasy to . . . teach him a lesson?"

"Maybe." He didn't seem satisfied by that answer.

"Well, look, why don't we ask Prince when we get home tonight? Get right to the bottom of the thing."

He sighed. His hair—his stupid, lovely hair—had flopped onto his forehead a little disordered. The expression on his face wrecked her heart. "Yes," he said at last, looking over. "That sounds like you." At his half smile, she nearly thought she could love him back.

CHAPTER 22
TURN ALL BEAUTY INTO THOUGHTS OF HARM

There was still time.

It had taken a little cajoling on Maggie's part, but she'd managed to beg a ride out of Father Francis by agreeing to sing in church the following Sunday. That is, if they let her sinner soul through the door with all the lying she'd done in the past few days. The gritty air of Hewlett Harbor got caught in her lungs as she shuffled through the six o'clock herd of docked sailors, down the slope of a harbor street.

There had to be a million pier warehouses and ports, and none of them seemed marked with numbers. A block or two away, boats ran silently in from Long Island's South Shore, hauling in booze in an unstoppable swarm, like fruit flies on a fallen peach, too numerous and quick and young to swat them all.

Finally she found a dark-skinned dockworker to take pity and point her in the right direction, but he shook his head in warning as soon as he did. "Won't be nothing but trouble that way, girl. Best mind your way."

"Thank you, sir." Not that she listened. She hurried down the street and found 54, which turned out to be more of a tene-ment than a warehouse, with sallow brick walls and the windows all boarded up.

No sign of Prince, and sundown was getting close. The door didn't budge an inch when she tried, so she walked around to the alley. Strings of laundry flapped over her head, and her foot-steps scattered a cluster of pigeons or seagulls or some other screeching bird into the air. A stack of crates in the corner made a shadowy monster.

She'd hauled one of the crates over so she could see, if she got on her tiptoes, into a high cracked window not boarded up, when she heard her name:

"Maggie?"

She turned.

There was Prince in his shabby brown jacket and newsboy cap, looking bewildered as a saint, but whole and unharmed. He helped her down from the crate. "What are you doing here?"

"Looking for you."

"Why?" His expression shifted from worried to suspicious.

"Because"—she began, then faltered—"because you shouldn't be down here."

Prince's eyes narrowed. "You read the telegram."

"I had to—"

"Because John told you to?" His voice simmered now, like boiling water. "You were spying on me for him."

"It's not like that. He's only worried about you. He doesn't want to see you hurt."

"Oh, I bet he said so, and you just believed him. You took his side instead of mine. But I guess I'm not the one who can buy you a chance at the Cotton Club, am I?"

"Hey." Maggie jabbed his chest with her finger. "That's not why, and you know it."

Prince huffed. He looked away guiltily. But he didn't apologize. "I would have made this deal with him," he said. "You were there. I tried, and he didn't even—"

"I said you ought to come alone." A young man, cigarette in hand, filled the opening of the alley. Early twenties, hat cocked low on his head; chin shadowed with a crooked cleft. His jacket was heavy and dark, despite the warm weather. Two other men, thick enough around the neck, flanked his sides. Maggie could guess what purpose they served.

Prince shifted and put himself slightly between the three men and Maggie. "She's no trouble," he said. "Go wait on the pier," he told her in a low voice. "I'll be there quick enough."

Waiting on the pier sounded excellent, but Maggie pressed her lips together and shook her head. "No, I'm not leaving."

"Say," the young man in the middle said. He pointed his smoking cigarette at Maggie. "You are the one who's going to sing for Duke Ellington, *sì*? John asked many favors for it." His eyes tracked over Maggie in a way that ground her teeth together. "So what makes you so special?"

One of the bulky men muttered something in Italian.

Maggie shifted uncomfortably as the young man barked a laugh. "True. If you lullabied John, maybe you're a witch. Sing something."

A beat of silence passed, and it seemed he truly expected her to sing right there in the alley. Finally she shook her head.

"No? Maybe you change your mind once we're better acquainted. Let's go."

"Borachio—" Prince started to protest.

"She comes." Borachio cut him off. "She knows we're here now, and she comes."

He led them around the side of the building onto a crumbling sidewalk. An old saloon occupied the ground floor. Ironic; perhaps that was why they had chosen it. Maggie crossed her arms tightly around her middle and huddled closer to Prince.

Borachio jimmied the boarded-up door until he unearthed a padlock. He unlocked it quick as a snap and heaved the door open. Inside there was nothing but a yeasty mold smell, shadows, and another locked door, which led upstairs to crates upon crates of burlap-covered booze, swelled barrels, and boxes of ammunition. There was barely room to walk.

Gray light crept in through the grimy windows, but even that was fading with the sinking sun over the harbor. Maggie heard a whimper and startled at a man crumpled against the side of the wall. His wrists and ankles were bound, a gag tight on his mouth. One side of his face was streaked with blood, and his eyes bulged with fear.

Maggie's fingers reached to grasp Prince's jacket.

"That is Henry," Borachio said, nodding at him. "Our dockmaster. Or used to be until tonight. This—all of this—is our latest shipment from the *Caraibi*. At midnight John's men come to haul it in trucks to the city. Marco?"

One of his men heaved a sledgehammer—from where? Had he had it the whole time?—into one of the barrels with an earsplitting crack. The scent of booze stung Maggie's nose as it spilled over the floor, seeping sticky and warm into the bottoms of her shoes. Prince shifted.

Borachio tossed a book of matches to Prince, which he barely caught. "Burn it," he said. "Wait until dark. My boys and I, we go down the pier to a nice Italian bar where lots of men see us and know we're not near the building. Don Vito will be very upset to lose such a valuable shipment, and John will have to answer for it."

Prince's inhaled breath was audible. His eyes darted to the dockmaster, still bound against the wall. "What about him?"

Borachio smirked. "He is part of the shipment."

Henry groaned, but whatever they'd done to him, he didn't manage more than an inch or two of pained movement. The poor idiot was a witness, was what Borachio meant—and probably working for John besides.

"Prince, no," Maggie murmured quietly. "Let's go."

Click. A pistol was cocked, just like that, and pointed at Prince and Maggie. The entire room went still. Borachio smiled. "And you, *bella*, you come with me."

Maggie's grip on Prince's sleeve tightened.

"What for?" Prince demanded.

"To sing," Borachio said in a precise, quiet voice. "The entertainment in that bar is shit."

That was not the reason, but Maggie couldn't imagine the alternative, her brain sputtering like a scratched record. Maybe he'd take her outside and shoot her. Except Prince would know, and if they killed Prince, too, they'd sign their own death warrants.

When had she started thinking of death as a bargaining chip?

Prince moved so quickly Maggie didn't even realize he had until his body, sliding fast over the spilled booze, feetfirst like a baseball player into home, barreled into Borachio's legs and pitched him into his sledgehammering associate.

Prince twisted onto his feet without looking back. He

grabbed Maggie by the arm and hauled her down the stairs. Maggie scrambled not to fall. A bullet splintered the plaster wall of the stairwell over their heads.

They sprinted across the dusty, abandoned saloon and had nearly made it to the door when a second gunshot cracked the air. Maggie felt the heat of it, even before Prince crumpled. She tripped over his fallen body and went down with him.

Panic gripped Maggie from the inside out. She fisted his shirt in her hands, his jacket, and pulled herself upright.

He groaned, eyes fluttering.

Not dead, n*ot dead.*

Footsteps cleared her head. She looked up, at Borachio approaching. His hat had flown off, and his dark hair was askew. He panted, pistol aimed at her head. The other two men pounded down the stairs behind him.

"A shame," he said. Then *bang,* a third shot. Maggie winced, and Borachio cried out, his hand a blossom of blood, his gun on the ground. She saw a black boot pass her, then looked up at John, gun raised, like some sort of avenging angel—or rather, as if hell had cracked open and a harried Satan had kicked him out.

The sledgehammer man swore and stumbled back into his companion.

John was on Borachio in a moment. His gun was tucked away, but Maggie caught the glint of a blade in his hand. John had his cousin twisted around, the side of his face streaked and spurting blood before Maggie knew what had happened. John slammed Borachio into the nearby wall and pressed his wrist into Borachio's throat hard enough that he gagged and wheezed; his skin mottled crimson. Maggie heard something pop or break in his neck. "John, stop!" she blurted. "You're going to kill him."

Tension rolled up John's back. His shoulders bunched; then he stepped away. Borachio slumped, hacking, rubbing his throat. The gash on his temple left a shining splatter along the dust-covered floorboards. The two men had not budged from their positions near the bottom of the stairs. Only when John turned to them, snapping something in Italian, did they flinch and move to carry Borachio out.

When they were gone, John hurried to crouch at Prince's side. Maggie shifted back to give him room. "You idiot," he growled through his teeth. He was shaking. Prince tried to say something. John tore Prince's coat away, revealing the stain of red on his shirt.

John made an awful noise, like a dog whimpering. He cut through the shirt with the same blade that had just cut a man's face, and it was quiet for a moment, the sort of silence that grows in intensity and covers half the world. Then John choked out an exhale.

"It only grazed you," he said hoarsely. "Possibly nicked a rib, but that's the worst of it. You'll be fine." The mask of ice John usually wore, the one that Maggie could pick and pick at but never unearth a hint of soul, was cracked all over, leaking with emotion.

His eyes shot up full of wrath. "What the hell is wrong with you?"

Prince sucked in air. "They're not going to . . . come after you? Later?" Saying that, he was himself again—decent, reasonable, soft—despite the blood, his crazed hair, and hollow eyes.

John snorted. "Those *vigliacchi?* Unlikely."

"I'm sorry," Prince whispered. "I thought . . ."

"You're an idiot," John said. "But so am I. I didn't think Borachio would dare go after you so directly. I should have killed him." His eyes flashed to Maggie, as if in accusation for stopping him.

"Our cousin." Prince winced, sitting up. Maggie came to his side and let him lean on her shoulder. His entire body trembled.

"My cousin. You don't have any direct relation to him."

"I would," Prince muttered, "if you'd claim me as your brother for once in your life."

"That's what you want?" John glowered; he tossed a hand to the dark spot of bloodied floor just a few yards away. "Being my brother nearly cost you your life."

"If I were actually your brother," Prince said in a low voice, "your enemies would be my enemies. My business your business. If I were actually your brother, we wouldn't be here like this at all."

John's lip curled. "Well, is it any wonder after a mess like this," he said coldly, "why I wouldn't want to go into business with you?"

Prince laughed quietly, a damaged laugh. "I suppose not."

John averted his eyes. Borachio had hit him where it hurt, with Prince. He was too shaken, not that he showed it, to keep up his facade of hatred. "I should have told you," John muttered. "Told you not to trust him."

"You could still open up Nassau County," Prince said. He swallowed, hiding another tremor of pain. "With me."

"We discussed this," John said quietly.

"No. *Just* me. Leave Hey Nonny Nonny out of it."

Well. If ever there was a phrase Maggie never expected to come out of Pedro Morello's mouth, it was that. Even John was shocked. "What?" he asked.

"I know Long Island like the back of my hand," Prince said. "If you turn a new profit, there goes the last of Borachio's argument, and there'll be no sideways deals. I'll just work under you."

John's reaction had the appearance of fury, but Maggie saw the flash of panic buried in his eyes.

"Aw, but Prince," Maggie said softly, "if you do that, you have to leave us."

To her continuing surprise, Prince said, "I know."

"You don't know," John snapped. "You're in it or you're not. You have no other loyalties, *finito*. No Leo, no Hey Nonny Nonny. No Hero."

"I'm ready," Prince said.

John said nothing. Maggie finally realized the dark flecks on his cheek and neck were blood.

"It's not about the money," Prince whispered.

"Pedro," John said, tired, "you're in love with her."

Prince didn't say anything. He didn't have to. The truth was there, a solid thing in the alley with them. "Nonetheless," he said, "I will give her up. She's happy with him. Leo barely knows I'm there anymore. I don't want to be just the kid they took off the streets."

John held up a hand. "You don't know what you want. And you don't know me; otherwise you wouldn't be so quick to put yourself under my heel." His voice refrosted in record speed, back to its old icy self without so much as a hat tip. "We'll discuss this later, perhaps when you're no longer bleeding."

Beaten, Prince released a breath, slumping. Maggie was now the only thing keeping him upright.

John grabbed his other arm. Hard to believe the same hands that had sliced a man's face just minutes earlier could now be applied with such gentleness. "Come on. Up. We'll get you to the car."

Prince leaned heavily on his brother, fist pressed to his wound. His face clenched with pain, but he didn't utter a word of complaint as they walked slowly out of the saloon.

"Where do we take him?" Maggie asked. "The hospital?"

"Can't afford that," Prince muttered, grimacing. "Beatrice can patch me up. I drove the Ford here anyway; we can't leave it lying around."

"I can't drive," said Maggie. "And you're in no kind of shape to do it either."

"I will," said John. They found the ol' flivver waiting a few streets down. John helped Prince lie on the backseat, then turned to Maggie. "Stay with him. I need to take care of a few things before we leave."

Probably it wasn't more than fifteen minutes, but it seemed to grow dark as sin in that time. Maggie felt as if she'd waited for John to come back from war when he finally materialized, matched in every way to the night around him.

He nodded at her, then checked on Prince in the backseat and pulled a bottle of vodka out of one pocket. The good stuff, straight as a demon's tears. Liquid gold, and John didn't care a whit pouring it onto the gash across Prince's ribs. By the time John finished, Prince was panting, uttering a series of fast Italian words. John smiled, a bonafide Morello gem.

"I thought you said your Italian was rusty. Here." John put the rest of the bottle in Prince's hand. "I'd drink it. The drive won't be smooth, not in this tin can."

Prince snorted, his expression that of a man who needs a drink for more reasons than physical pain, and took a long impressive pull off the top.

"*Salute*," John muttered.

He shut the back door and moved to the driver's seat. Maggie sat at his side, and it was a full minute before he looked at her, the first time he'd done so directly since shooting Borachio in the hand. "Are you all right?" he asked softly.

Maggie nodded.

John started the car and pulled onto the street.

You'd think the harbor would be less busy at night, but it was exactly the same, just more delivery trucks. Noisy and arrhythmic. Maggie twisted around to check on Prince; his lips disappeared into a thin line, his eyes squeezed shut against the pain. "Keep drinking," Maggie suggested, and then she sang to him, one of the Italian lullabies he'd taught her.

"You're killing me," John murmured.

She shifted across the small divide. John moved the throttle, and the Ford surged ahead. Her cheek pressed his carved shoulder. Safe and solid. He didn't shrug her off. By the time they got to Manhasset, Prince had finished most of the vodka and promptly left the land of the conscious, his face the shade of a bruise.

She wasn't long after him and woke the entire car ride later, at the stretch of silence after the engine turned off. She was still nestled against John, she realized, as a knuckle brushed her cheek, a soft entreaty for her to wake up, and then she was awake, and his hands were to himself.

She sat up, glanced in the back. Prince was still asleep.

"You were right about Hey Nonny Nonny," John said quietly, but she could hear him, so close. "Better if it was thriving."

"No. I was wrong, too; otherwise Prince wouldn't be so

ready to drop it like a hot potato. Never was about the speakeasy at all; it was about Hero."

"I didn't realize she and that English kid were that serious."

"She said she'd marry him if he asked. Who knows if she meant it?" Maggie yawned. "Just get rid of Claude."

John froze, glancing at her sharply.

"Geez! I don't mean kill him, you nut." She laughed at his stricken expression. "I just mean, you know, split them up. Slingshot her back into Prince's waiting arms."

"Split them up how?"

"That's your line of expertise, isn't it? Intimidation?"

"He's connected to the Vanderbilts. I'm not sure it's wise to point a gun at his face and threaten him."

"Fine. Maybe we can find a way to make it look like Claude's some kind of cad, spreading his wild oats."

John snorted.

"Okay, how about this? We let Claude think he might get arrested because of his involvement with Hero. Something that would tarnish his reputation nice and good so he runs for the hills."

"I'll think about it," said John.

Prince groaned, turning over.

Maggie sighed. "I'll go wake up Beatrice."

CHAPTER 23
A KIND OF MERRY WAR

Somewhere Benedick owned a clock. Beatrice could hear its onerous ticking in the room, buried who knew where. Occasionally she glanced at Benedick, wondering if he'd dig it out, calculate how long he'd spent in her company, and declare the evening over.

Certainly it was late. The world outside his window had been dark for a while. But they shared a lack of interest in sleep. Neither had suggested they part ways when they returned from Queens. Benedick had dug out a folder that Leo and Prince kept of agents and rum suppliers and other who's who records, and now here they were, Beatrice on his bedroom floor and he on the ugly sofa, sorting through her uncle's handwriting and glued to newspaper strips.

She could imagine him years from now in the exact same position, his ankle propped on his knees, sheets of wrinkled paper in his lap, his fingers turning the edges. "Look here," he said. "I knew it." He passed her a rather sizable stack of papers, held together by paper clips. "There's practically an encyclopedia about them. They love the press."

Beatrice read the first page.

New York Times, March 17, 1925. DOGBERRY AND VERGES SEIZE SACRAMENTAL WINE, the headline read. The blurred picture was of a squat man with a striped hat and his lanky, hook-nosed partner.

"New York's finest hooch hounds are at it again! Izzy Dogberry and Moe Verges, posing as cigar salesmen, seized thirty cases of wine that were supposed to be sacramental wines for religious use at home in a cigar store on the Lower East Side. Dogberry offered this comment, marveling at the 'remarkable increase in the thirst for religion.'"

Beatrice flipped through the rest, eyebrow raising.

The agents had arrested over four thousand people and boasted a conviction rate of 95 percent. They were notorious for never taking bribes (alas) and using a wide range of disguises instead of guns. Dogberry had been at one time or another a German potato packer, a Polish count, a Hungarian violinist, a Jewish gravedigger, a French maître d', an Italian fruit vendor, a Russian fisherman, and a delegate from Kentucky to the

Democratic National Convention. And now, at Hey Nonny Nonny, a pheasant hunter from Connecticut.

"Quite the résumé," said Beatrice.

"To put it nicely."

"Dogberry speaks six languages. He's rather clever."

"Et cetera, et cetera, *ne plus ultra, jus in bello*—"

"Is that Latin?" Beatrice asked flatly. "Are you showing off?"

Benedick lifted his gaze and grinned.

She regarded him for a moment. "Ben, what kinds of marks did you get in school?"

"What?"

"I was just thinking about how your father drove all the way out to Long Island."

Benedick's brows arched high. Not angry yet, but he transformed at the change of subject, the opposite of relaxed.

"I don't mean anything by it," she added, "but I can't imagine he doesn't see how smart you are, in your special aggravating way. I'd be sad to lose you, too, is all."

Benedick's gaze turned quizzical. "I can tell you—" He stopped at the sound of knocking. But the knock wasn't at his door; it came from below. At Beatrice's door.

She stood, frowning, then hurried down the narrow curve of attic stairs. There in the hall, in front of her room, John and Maggie held a bloodied Prince between them.

"Sorry to bother you," Maggie said.

"You're not," said Beatrice. Of course they weren't. Already Beatrice was taking in Prince's pallor, his glassy eyes, trying to ascertain where all the blood had come from. "What happened?"

Benedick came behind her; she heard his clumsy halt, the stuttered noise of surprise.

"I'm fiiiiiiine," Prince insisted in a loud whisper. Never mind the crimson stain on the left side of his shirt.

"The bullet only grazed him," said John.

Bullet, right.

Someone *had* shot at him.

Never mind. Blood first, cause of blood later. Beatrice opened her door and motioned for John to set a gasping Prince on her bed. "Oh, your pillow smells nice, like flowers," Prince said.

"He's drunk," Maggie explained dryly. "We put some vodka in him to help with the pain."

Beatrice rolled her sleeves up to her forearms. "Shut the door and turn on the light, please. Watch your eyes, Prince." She set her hand gently across his fluttering lids to shield him as the room lit up. She peeled back his shirt to locate the wound: a shallow, diagonal slash across his ribs. "Ben, hand me that bag over there. The leather one. There should be a bottle of rubbing alcohol. . . ."

Benedick brought the bag over, holding the small glass bottle of disinfectant between his fingers. His voice was high and quick. "Miss Clark, you're not a licensed physician yet. Technically you were a bootlegger even before you came to Hey Nonny Nonny."

"Ben, I know you're worried, but stop talking. This will sting a bit," she told Prince, dabbing the disinfectant on some gauze. "Not that you'll feel it in your state." She cleaned and bandaged the wound. "Stop flinching. You can take a bullet, but not medicine for it? The shot burned the edges of your skin. I can make some salve for it. Is your pain external or internal?"

"Well." Prince's face bunched as he tried to decide.

She pressed her fingers lightly around the cut. A hiss slid past his teeth, as she expected. "Now sit up straight—slowly. Breathe deep."

He couldn't manage it all the way before crumpling back down in pain. "There's your problem," she said. "The bullet bruised his rib. That will keep him sore for a week or so, but he'll be fine as long as he takes it easy."

"Hear that, Your Highness? *Easy.*" Maggie crossed her arms. "He'll be okay," she added, softer, to John.

That was apparently all John needed to excuse himself from the room. Maggie made an apologetic grimace, then followed him out.

"Do you think we ought to wake Hero?" Beatrice asked Benedick.

"No," Prince said, so abruptly she drew back. "No," he said again, softer. "Please. Don't tell her. Later, later . . ." He trailed off, got up a contorted smile. "When I've got it straight, I'm goin' to show her. They'll come crawlin' to me on their bellies. I've got a kind of feel for the big money."

"Okay." Beatrice stroked his curling hair and smoothed his cheek. She glanced up at Benedick, who had the edge of his thumb between his teeth, his brow bunched up in a frown. "Do you love her, Prince? Is that it?"

"Sure, I love her," he whispered. "But not to keep. Not to—to touch. You can love someone who's a stranger, who's a friend."

Beatrice motioned for Benedick to help her get Prince's shoes off. "He can sleep here for tonight," she said quietly. "Probably best, until morning."

Benedick grabbed the spare blanket from the foot of her bed. He lay back on the floor at Prince's other side, with the blanket bundled up under his head as a makeshift pillow. He didn't appear the least interested in sleeping. "I'll keep an eye on him," he said. "You take my room."

Beatrice nodded and packed up her medical bag, but after she closed the door behind her, she didn't retreat to Benedick's room. She marched downstairs. Maggie and John were in the foyer near the door, speaking in low voices.

John glanced up as Beatrice approached.

"Who shot him?" she demanded.

John's face remained placid. "That's none of your business."

"Like hell it isn't." Beatrice stuck her chin out at an angle those St. Mary's nuns used to hate. John wasn't overly tall. They were nearly eye to eye.

"Beatrice," Maggie said, "just let it be."

"No." She jabbed John in the chest. His eyes flashed, like those of a massive black bear poked out of slumber. Beatrice nearly backed away. Nearly, but didn't. "What about the Prohibition agents?"

"I don't know what you're talking about," he said.

"You didn't send any agents to Hey Nonny Nonny? Not to put Prince in his place?"

"No," he said flatly.

Beatrice's eyes narrowed. If nothing else, he didn't seem worried about her enough to lie. "I want you to know that if anything bad happens to Prince because of you, I won't let it go. You'll have to answer for it."

He didn't bother with a response. At least not of the verbal variety. He turned, just shy of rolling his eyes, and nodded at Maggie before letting himself out the door.

"I know I'm not . . . ," Beatrice said into the silence. "I just wanted him to know."

"I get it." Maggie put a hand on her hip, staring at the wood grain of the closed door as if she could see John's retreating back through it. "You're not the only one he'll be answering to."

CHAPTER 24
ARE YOU GOOD MEN AND TRUE?

Benedick did not sleep for more than a few minutes at a time, it felt, and he was awake when Prince first groaned into consciousness the next morning. Benedick sat up, bone tired but mind still crisp as a cold apple. Prince's face was pale, half buried in Beatrice's pillow. He muttered something about cursing the Lord, the devil, and all other deities that might be working with them, his fingers fluttering clumsily against Beatrice's bandages.

"Good morning," Benedick said, chipper and loud.

Prince winced, then cracked open an eye to look at him.

Benedick smiled. "You look like hell."

"I feel like hell."

"Good." Silence stretched between them. Finally, unloosing his clenched jaw, Benedick asked, "Are you going to tell me what happened?" More silence. "I deserve to know."

Prince curled in on himself. His heavily lidded eyes stared at nothing. "I made a mistake," he whispered.

Benedick wanted to shout until he was hoarse; he wanted Prince to swear by blood and on his mother's grave he'd leave any business with the Genovese family alone, but seeing Prince like this gave the urge the same flavor as booting a puppy.

"What was I supposed to do, with Hero going to the beach, and Leo shopping the first day he's sober in months?" Prince's voice dragged gravelly. "I had to make up the difference." Doing extra work didn't bother him, Benedick knew. He'd wager to say Prince even liked the opportunity to offer Hero and Leo some leisure when he could, but the world always took on a different shade after you'd failed.

"Look," Benedick suggested, "luck's got you by the oysters this week, but it might not be such a bad thing."

Prince lifted his gaze, eyes disparaging.

"The pheasant hunters, Mr. Hansen and Mr. Smith? They were Prohibition agents. Beatrice and I discovered it when we followed them to Rack 20 last night. They're packing up this morning, but just in case, we'd better keep tomorrow an actual birthday party."

"Don't sell the drinks," Prince muttered, rubbing his eyes.

"Correct." Just a swinging, friendly get-together. Not a business with profits made from selling liquor. So close to the truth, it was hardly a disguise.

This piece of news was the last domino over Prince's soul. He appeared crumpled on the inside, like an old newspaper. "If we don't make any money . . ."

Then they might not be able to pay for the resources to open again the next weekend. Benedick had a vision, for the first time in his life, not of cashing in his book royalties but of a steady paycheck from a Wall Street firm, the ease with which he'd be able to make up the difference when they had bum weeks like this one. And for the first time he saw the appeal.

"Never mind," said Benedick. "One weekend can't sink us. We might not make a profit, but we cleared our debts; everything's paid for."

"That's true."

The cushion from the past two weeks would at least keep the house fed and lit, and they also had Claude, who'd footed a lot of the expense for the party, his own swanky gift, aside from the illegal expenditures.

Prince pushed himself upright. He settled back on the headboard and rubbed his shoulder. "Why'd they bother with us?" he asked, almost to himself. "Especially . . ."

"Now? I know. You'd think they'd have bigger fish. And they're straight, according to the papers. They don't take bribes."

"Just because they tell the papers they're straight doesn't mean they are," Prince said.

"John wouldn't send them, would he?"

"John?" Prince's surprise was genuine. "No. I don't think so. If he wanted us closed that badly, he'd do the dirty work himself, and if he did send someone, it wouldn't be from the right side of the law."

A brisk knock interrupted their conversation, followed by Beatrice. Benedick's morning righted itself in time to her stride. "Hello, patient," she said. "How do you feel?"

"Like a train ran me over," said Prince.

"Sounds about right. The vodka you fell asleep to certainly didn't help." Beatrice, efficient and competent and mesmerizing to watch, checked Prince's bandage. Prince's skin was bruised, the slash of skin where the bullet had nicked him enflamed, but Beatrice declared it uninfected. "No heavy lifting or cartwheels, and you'll be just fine. Take these." She set a few aspirin and a glass of water on the bedside table.

"Thanks," said Prince. He held the glass of water but didn't drink it. Finally he asked, "Hero doesn't know?"

"As per your orders, she does not. Last I saw, she was downstairs making calls about her party."

Prince nodded and knocked back all the aspirin at once.

Benedick yawned. He tried not to, and tried harder still to hide it when it became inevitable, but Beatrice sighed, not looking at him, book in her lap. "You shouldn't have slept on the floor."

They sat side by side on the porch, nestled into a wicker love seat, and the afternoon sun warmed their shaded spot. Her shoulder pressed lightly to his. Her presence next to him felt like the quiet hum of an engine. "I didn't sleep on the floor," Benedick murmured. Beatrice flicked her eyes sideways at him. "I was awake most of the time."

"Semantics, Scott," she said, just before the front door opened.

"Well! Mr. Scott, Miss Clark. You two have a lovely weekend, you hear?" Mr. Hansen, also known as the Prohibition agent Dogberry, tipped his hat at them on his way down the porch. He and Verges had loaded their bags into the Oldsmobile. Benedick and Beatrice were stationed in their current spot to make good and sure they left.

"Thank you," said Beatrice. "And yours as well."

"Got any humdinger plans?" Dogberry grinned. He set his foot on the porch step and rested his hands on the considerable swell of his belly.

"I wouldn't call them humdinger," said Beatrice. "I'll be studying."

"Oho! No parties for you?"

"Jazz gives me a headache. To say nothing of the demon liquor." Her voice was prim as a widow's collar; her lips were a thin line. Benedick nearly believed her.

"Just so." Dogberry nodded solemnly. He glanced at the book in her lap. "You in school then, Miss Clark? Last I checked, it was summer."

"I'm soon to medical college, I hope."

"Nurse?"

"Doctor," Beatrice corrected him, her tone that of a cumulonimbus on the horizon.

"You kids!" Dogberry huffed. "Full of spit and fire. Isn't that right, Mr. Scott? Out here to save the world with a novel!"

Benedick stiffened. He had not, to his recollection, told the disguised agents he was a writer. "Why not?" he asked. "A person ought to accomplish something in his life."

"There are worse things, you know. Don't put so much weight in a *job*." Dogberry suddenly looked a lot more like *Dogberry* than like Mr. Hansen. His gaze was penetrating, and for the first time Benedick wondered if it wasn't strictly the speakeasy he was after. "You could fail as a human being. Want to know what I think is the greatest thing a person can be? *Kind.* I put kindness before anything else!" He puffed out his chest, waiting, and at last Beatrice succumbed to the twinkle in his eye.

She smiled back. Benedick did not feel the same urge.

"More than a good wit, I'm guessing?" asked Benedick.

"Oh, gosh, no, smarts is one of the worst! You can be a tiptop person without brains, absolutely top-shelf. Isn't that right, Smith?"

"What ho!" Verges called from the car.

"You see." Dogberry touched the brim of his hat a final time. "Take care, Miss Clark. Mr. Scott. And remember, a place is just a place. A job is a job. Any can go at any time. Better to be a good person."

"Thank you," said Benedick. "I'll remember that when I'm homeless with a clean conscience."

CHAPTER 25
OUR OWN HANDS AGAINST
OUR HEARTS

The same Christmas Anna had given Benedick his typewriter, she had gifted Maggie her own electric Victrola. Her father would have swooned, which was partly why Maggie had never told him. Anna had meant it with love, but it was still a reminder of the advantages of living with an affluent white couple. Before money had gotten tight, Maggie had spent any extra she earned on new records. She put on "Creole Love Call," performed by Adelaide Hall and the Duke Ellington band, recorded just this year. John had given it to her, making out like he'd picked it up in a haymarket instead of its being one of the hottest jazz standards this year.

Maggie sang along in her room, at half voice, swaying and searching for the bass chords, practicing for her audition tomorrow night. Just when she thought she'd found her rhythm, nerves would catch her, and she'd lose it.

After half a dozen failed run-throughs, Maggie lifted the needle, rubbing her brow in defeat. It was past dark; she ought to call it a night and get some sleep.

But if she was honest, the nerves weren't only over the audition. The Cotton Club wasn't the only thing on her mind.

John had let Borachio live, and his cousin hadn't seemed the type to forgive a grudge easily. What if John got plugged up with bullet holes in some alley? She shook out her hands, chasing away the thought. She moved to set the needle back onto the record, but a scream came from the hallway.

Maggie opened her door, just in time to watch Hero, yanking her dressing gown around her middle, hop out of her bedroom.

"Somebody die?" Maggie asked.

"There's a dead mouse in my bed." Hero wriggled, as if she could still see it. Her mouth puckered into the beginnings of a pout. "Where is Prince?"

Maggie didn't think they'd spoken hardly a word to each other since their fight yesterday morning. Hero still didn't know he was sporting a bullet wound along his ribs.

Down the hall Beatrice opened her door in her nightgown and frowned. "What's wrong? Who's screaming?"

"Dead . . . mouse." Hero pressed her hands together, wincing. *Here come the eyelashes*, Maggie thought as Hero began to flutter them. "If one of you wouldn't mind just tossing it out the window and maybe taking my sheets off to be cleaned . . ."

Beatrice gave her a flat look. "I'm studying, Hero. My regents' exam is on Monday."

"Well, *I'm* practicing," Maggie argued, "and my audition is tomorrow night."

"I guess neither of us can help you then," Beatrice said matter-of-factly. "Hero, you are perfectly capable of taking care of that mouse yourself. Maggie"—she raised an eyebrow in Maggie's direction—"don't give in to her." Then she shut her door, as if it were nothing.

Maggie looked sidelong at Hero, whose full mouth immediately puffed. She came over and tugged on Maggie's arm. "Mags, pleeeeease. I hate mice more than anything in the world."

"More than a party without gin?"

"What I really hate is a party without jazz. And guess what I've got tomorrow? On my birthday no less."

"Aw, that's not fair—"

Hero poked her in the ribs. "You owe me."

Maggie sighed, lifting her eyes to the ceiling. "Fine. But after this, I don't want to hear about it."

Hero beamed with victory. "You go get that gig, and I won't say a word." She winked and hurried down the hall.

"Where you going?"

Hero glanced back over her shoulder. "Well, I can't sleep in *my* bed tonight with contaminated sheets. So I guess I'll have to sleep with Beatrice. That'll teach her." She swept into Beatrice's room without knocking.

Shaking her head, Maggie went to locate the mouse. The little thing was buried at the bottom of the sheets, where it had probably gotten twisted up and panicked. These days Hey Nonny Nonny was crawling with all sorts of creatures, with the weather turning warm. They ought to patch up the holes and cracks that made it easy for them, but that was a ways down the long list of things Hey Nonny Nonny needed.

Using a handkerchief, Maggie plucked the mouse up by the tail and tossed it out of Hero's window into the dark. She stripped the sheets off and dumped them in a pile on the floor. As usual, Hero's room was strung with dresses and jewelry and stockings, all of it fine. Her Masquerade costume was still draped across her vanity chair, and Maggie picked up the Cleopatra wig. No person's hair would be so perfectly cut, not a strand out of place. It belonged under a spotlight, where the unreal sparkled.

Maggie draped one of Hero's silk scarves across her shoulders and pretended she was wearing a long gown. "Hello. I'll be singing 'Downhearted Blues.'" Of course the wig wouldn't stay even half on over her curls.

After plopping in front of Hero's vanity mirror, Maggie attempted to wrestle her hair flat. Pins in her mouth, she sang through her teeth: " 'Gee, but it's hard to love someone when that someone don't love you. . . .' "

She nearly fell out of her chair when the door opened. There was John, as if her singing had conjured him. They stared at each other a moment; then Maggie spit out a pin. "What are you doing here?"

"I was looking for Hero," John said. "But I heard you singing."

"I was barely singing."

"I can feel when you sing," he replied, which might have been the most romantic thing he'd ever said to her. As if realizing this, he averted his eyes and shut the door behind him. "What's wrong with your hair?"

"It's Hero's Cleopatra wig. I was just trying it on."

"Because of those club owners? They don't know what they're talking about."

Maggie lifted a shoulder. "I know. I just thought I'd try a more . . . sophisticated approach." She stood, tossing the scarf back and tilting her chin. "*Ladies and gentlemen,*" she said softly, "*for the first time ever in Carnegie Hall, Miss Margaret Hughes.* The audience gently applauds." She demonstrated. "What do you think?"

John pressed his lips together, his face unreadable. "Not your style."

Maggie tossed the scarf off. "Oh, you mean something like . . . 'Shake it like a bowl of jelly on a plate,' " she whisper-sang. She shimmied and pointed at him with a wink. His lips twitched. So close to a smile. She sashayed in, poked his unmoving bulk. " 'I may be late, but

I'll be up to date, when I can shimmy like my sister Kate.'"

He snatched her hand, and she fell silent. His eyes were warm, like a fire lit beneath the ice. "It's crooked," he murmured, reaching up to her hair. "Come here." He pulled her closer to the window, where Hero's lamp was. He tilted her face to the light. After plucking a few pins free, he righted the wig and secured it in place.

"You're pretty handy with those."

"Sometimes I help my mother with her hair." John's hands fell away. He wasn't wearing a jacket, she realized, just sleeve garters and an open collar. Strangely casual, for him.

"Hero's in Beatrice's room," Maggie said. "What were you going to talk to her about? You're not armed, I hope."

He hesitated. "I'm not *now.*"

Maggie glared at him.

"I may have talked to Claude first."

"You said it wasn't a good idea to threaten him."

"I didn't, exactly. I merely suggested a few things, and I was only going to suggest a few things to Hero."

Maggie studied him. The breeze from the window lifted the gauze curtain, where it brushed her arm. "Prince would be furious if you told Hero he loved her."

"Even better," he said quietly. Maggie waited, searching his face. In his eyes, a hint of guilt, grief, and a rainy desire that made her toes curl a bit. She laid her palm on the lapels of his vest, the rhythm of his heart answering beneath it. How *slow* the beat was, as if he were taking ponderous leaps between living and dead. "We didn't grow up together, you know. I knew about him, but we didn't meet until I was nine, when I was sent to live with my mother, who hated me, but we agreed about Pedro, so that kept us from killing each other." His head tipped up. "I am not a good person, Margaret, but if I can let Prince stay one, the world is a better place."

Then he sucked out the rest of the space between them. His mouth pressed over hers.

He shuddered when her fingers found the nape of his neck, as if he were afraid. He transformed entirely in her arms, into a creature she barely recognized: slow and gentle and warm as the sun. It made her wonder if he'd ever done it before.

He broke away first, panting a little, his eyes two wells of deep and dark, and it was wonderful, in that moment, just to stare at him with this new ribbon of you-and-me between them, like a song.

"Encore," Maggie murmured.

He frowned, as if confused—and then Hero's bedroom door opened, and John sprang away from Maggie with those unearthly reflexes of his.

Hero stared at them. Rather, at Maggie, then John, then back to Maggie, because John had launched a whole yard between them, his back against the wall, his skin flushed.

"I forgot my brush," she said, but what Maggie heard was: *Just what is going on here?*

Maggie had forgotten entirely—poof, presto—that they were in Hero's room. She'd lost the fact of them in any room at all, the whole universe compressed to the small, intimate space. Maybe there was no space small enough that would allow them to be together.

"I . . . got the mouse," Maggie finally managed to say. Apparently she was going to do all the talking. His regret perfumed the air like a red cloud. "And I used your hairpins. Sorry."

Hero's expression said she couldn't give a damn about mice or hairpins.

When no one else spoke, Hero asked, "Is it a secret?" Looked between them again. "We'd support you no matter what. There's no reason to be ashamed—"

"I am not ashamed." John's head snapped up.

Maggie blinked. The passion of his declaration struck through the room like lightning.

But then he straightened his lapels, adjusted the collar Maggie's fingers had worked slightly askew, and said, "I'm not ashamed because there's nothing between us to be ashamed over."

He walked out, just like that, and Maggie opened her mouth wordlessly, too stunned to refute his dismissal. Hero met Maggie's eyes and a split second later went after John. Maggie briefly closed her eyes, exhaled, and then one by one removed the pins to take the wig off.

CHAPTER 26

HOW LIKE A MAID
SHE BLUSHES

Benedick and Prince spent the better part of the evening agent-proofing the speakeasy, taking care to lock up any purchase records, sealing all compartments with imported alcohol. Benedick offered to do it alone—neither of them had told Leo—but Prince insisted, even as the exertion dampened his skin, drained his cheeks of color. At least tomorrow they weren't expected to do any serious labor, not with Claude's hired entourage.

Sometime after dark Prince straightened with a wince. "Let's go out the main entrance, lock up behind us."

They climbed the cellar stairs, their feet finding the path easily without a light.

"One weekend won't give us a reputation," Prince said, "do you think?"

"Nah. Besides, the crowd will be different tomorrow, I imagine. More blue blood." Benedick shoved open the cellar doors. Prince made his labored way behind him. While he caught his breath, Benedick looped the chain in place and secured the padlock.

They walked around the house, toward the main door. Almost to himself, Prince muttered, "I guess I ought to talk to Hero about all this. You didn't tell her?"

"No, actually. But maybe Beatrice . . ." Benedick trailed off. Claude was waiting on the porch, his arms crossed.

"Excuse me. Mr. Morello," he said as they approached. His voice came out blade sharp, his face pinched with an unflattering combination of hurt and fury. The rigid line of his shoulders was backlit from the light in the house. "I'd like a word with you about your brother."

Prince stopped, ankle deep in nettles, before he reached the porch. "My brother?"

"Exactly what line of business is he in?" Claude pressed. Benedick had never seen Claude's temper in true form, but now the full breadth of his wealth and influence glittered behind his eyes like an army.

Prince, scrappy and used to fighting on an empty stomach, settled back into his own upbringing; he cocked his chin up and asked, "What's it to you?"

"The conversation was not exactly conducted in clear terms," Claude said. "But I'm sure I was being threatened."

"Threatened?" Prince asked, not bothering to hide his incredulity.

"From what I gathered, as a benefactor to the speakeasy," Claude said, "which is absurd. I may have lent my participation to certain activities, but I haven't done anything, with proof, that could be held against me in a court of law."

There it is, Benedick thought. Bootlegging was fun so long as you weren't the one paying for it. "Of course not, Claude. Don't be a moron."

"He seemed rather serious to me," Claude said. The volume of his voice maintained its gentleman's decibel, but underneath it was a real note of fear.

"At first I thought it was simply a misunderstanding, that he thought I was trying to cut into his business," Claude continued darkly. "But then I realized what it was truly about."

Benedick could not hope to guess where this would be arriving. Prince's expression was just as blank.

"Hero," Claude snapped. "Why else would he come at me with such ridiculous accusations?"

Silence. Then Prince asked, "You think John was threatening you because he was jealous of you and Hero?"

"That's precisely what I think."

Prince laughed, making Claude flush. "That's— No."

"No?" Claude asked, red faced.

"Come on, Claude," said Benedick. "You can't think so little of Hero."

"What I think is that even if she's terribly fond of me, she's not fond of anything so much as her mother's speakeasy."

Well. Claude was rather more astute than he let on.

Claude laughed tightly. "If I were her, I'd certainly consider that some dago mobster with a rum business was more useful than a prep graduate from Lancaster," he said. "Though I'm useful, too, I guess, when she wants to go to luncheons and beach parties. We're all useful, little tools in her box that she can call upon at will. You know that, don't you, Prince?"

"That's enough," said Prince, voice flatter than flat.

"Look here." Claude strode off the porch, passing between Benedick and Prince. "I watched him go into her room with my own eyes."

He disappeared around the corner. After a beat of grudging hesitation, Benedick went, too. Prince, taut as a rope, came up by his shoulder. The window to Hero's room was lit, and to Claude's credit, two shadows moved just past the gauzy curtain. One with John's slick hair and one with Hero's bob.

"I told you," said Claude. "I said it, and there he is."

"Get off your high horse," said Benedick. "Even if that is John up there with Hero, they could be talking about anything. She could be setting him straight after threatening you, for all you know." He froze as the pair of shadows moved together. Before he could gather the brains to suggest they go inside, the vague silhouettes had pressed together in something that very much resembled kissing.

Damn, *damn* . . .

"Prince, come on," Benedick said desperately, anything to stop him from watching this. Too late. Prince's eyes were unblinking, absorbing the devastation like a sponge.

And then a moan slid out the still-open window and slithered over the grass toward them like a poisonous snake to bite Prince in the heart.

Claude choked on a breath, then clenched his teeth.

Benedick grabbed him by the shirt and pulled at Prince, who stumbled easily, following as Benedick dragged them both around the house and into the foyer.

"All right, let's not think anything rash," Benedick said. "Let's all . . ."

He wasn't sure what to say.

For a moment no one said anything, no one even appeared to be breathing, and then Prince was up the stairs, moving quickly, considering his injury.

"Wait, Prince." Benedick chased after him, Claude following close behind. "Just let it be."

But as they approached, John burst out the door, looking recently kissed, from his slightly swollen mouth to his rumpled collar. Hero followed seconds after, trying to grab his sleeve. "John, please wait, don't just—"

They both froze. John turned positively scarlet at the sight of Prince in front of him. Hero tugged on her nightgown. "Oh. Boys. Hello, fancy meeting you here."

The tension in the hallway grew solid and flexed its muscles. Benedick's hands opened, as if he might need to catch something.

"What . . ." Prince spoke first.

Hero huffed a little breath. Whatever she was going to say, John stopped her with a warning look. "Don't," he said.

A spark of outrage lit in her eyes but cooled a second later, as if she'd overturned a rock and found a snake. "How could you?" she said quietly. "How can you just leave?"

John's expression remained like granite. He jerked his jacket in place and moved away from her. Benedick braced himself, but Prince, who'd looked keen to slug his brother in the face, now bore an uncanny resemblance to glass recently in contact with a hammer. He stepped back, out of John's path.

Claude was less acquiescent. Perhaps because John glanced at him, his expression so blatantly *knowing* and unapologetic, Claude made the mistake of grabbing him by the arm. "Now, see here, you bastard—" The voice of an imperious king.

John's arm was free, and Claude was knocked back first into the wall before he could finish his sentence. Benedick darted forward at the same time as Prince. Benedick braced Claude upright as his eyes fluttered dizzily. Prince barricaded himself in front of his brother.

"Enough!" Hero snapped. "For God's sake, what has gotten into all of you?" She hurried toward Claude first. "Oh, you big dumb darling. We've got ice downstairs. John, if you please, you're no longer welcome."

Benedick inwardly cringed to hear her voice change. She addressed Claude as a beloved pet and John as an adult with adult problems like hers.

Claude shook himself off. "I don't need any ice," he said thickly, and stalked off to his room.

Hero didn't go after him. She rubbed one temple, glanced back at her room. "Can you take care of this?" she asked Prince, fluttering a distracted hand, then disappeared through her door.

For those living in a speakeasy, rough mornings were par for the course. Yet out of a very impressive roster, this one claimed the championship without breaking a sweat. The mood around the breakfast table was dreary the way swimming pools were wet. A tide of fresh misery swept over the table when Hero, all bedroom eyes and bedroom hair, a pale pink dressing gown barely hanging on her shoulders, shuffled in and plopped into her seat with a yawn..

Last night Benedick had brought Claude the ice he'd refused and tried to cheer the poor sap up. The gist of his heartache: He'd hoped, after such declarations on his part, after such kisses and so on and so forth . . . But that wild girl had kept her heart to herself, while taking all of his. Claude had decided to take his broken heart and return to the Vanderbilts, who would welcome him with open arms and crustless sandwiches and suntans, and he wished Hero every future happiness. As any true gentleman would.

Prince, on the other hand, when Benedick had gone looking for him, had pretended to be asleep with such stubbornness Benedick had let him be.

Beatrice noticed the change in the room after Hero sat down; of course she did. Benedick had almost knocked on her door last night for no reason except a strange certainty that any problem would feel less heavy with her around. She lifted an eyebrow at him in question. He shook his head at her: *I'll tell you later.*

Only Uncle Leo, enthusiastically going after his biscuits and gravy, seemed unaffected. He swallowed a large bite and eyed each of them. "We're a quiet bunch this morning! Isn't anyone excited for the party tonight? Maggie, you look half ready to cry into your coffee."

"Oh, I—" She straightened, made a valiant attempt to smile. "I'm nervous, is all. My audition is tonight."

"Audition? Tonight?" Leo set down his fork. "Maggie Hughes, you won't be singing?"

Maggie became intensely interested in her breakfast. "Not this time, no."

Leo frowned. "You'll stick around for the toast before you leave at least?"

"I can't." Maggie was practically whispering. "I'll miss my train—"

Claude stood up so quickly, the rest of her sentence stuttered to silence. "I'm leaving as well," he said, kicking his chair out. "I already called for a cab."

"But—" Hero struggled to speak. "What about—"

"Something rather important has come up." Claude adjusted his vest. "Everything is paid for. I hope you enjoy the party, at my expense, and have a wonderful birthday, Miss Stahr." He walked out of the room.

Hero blinked, then glanced at Prince, her usual habit in moments of confusion or distress. Prince remained quiet, his expression so callous Benedick winced. He couldn't recall the last time Prince had so much as frowned at Hero.

Hero flinched and pressed a hand to her chest as if someone had torn out her heart and kicked it viciously across the room.

Prince stood. "I had a bad night," he said, barely audible. "I think I need a walk before enduring the coming festivities."

"Prince," Hero said, rising to follow. He not only didn't acknowledge her but moved deliberately faster to get out of the room.

Don't do it, Benedick thought, but of course Hero went after him. Benedick sighed and set down his fork. He caught up just as Hero grabbed Prince's shoulder and spun him toward her. He turned, hiding the pain of the movement, only to press back against the wall as if standing too close to her would burn him.

Beatrice came to stand beside Benedick. "What's going on?" she whispered. Benedick reached for her arm, a request to wait, a promise to tell.

Hero crossed her arms. "What's the matter with you?"

"I said I was tired."

"But you . . ." Hero trailed off, blushing, rather than admit she expected him to come to her defense.

"I'm allowed not to bend over for you for one morning without the world collapsing," Prince said. He wouldn't look at her.

She took a deep breath. "But it's more than that—"

"I don't know, Hero. I really don't," Prince said. "If you can't figure it out on your own, I can't help you."

"Would you at least—"

"No!" His hands flew up in disgust. He sighed, turning away. "Stop treating me like—like a *tool* you can whip out whenever you need a problem fixed."

"Prince?" The gentleness of her voice was worse than her frustration. His eyes widened; then his whole expression shadowed and grew teeth.

Benedick jumped in before he could bite. "Prince, I know Maggie would appreciate a ride to the train station, and I'm a garbage driver." He tugged Prince toward the door. "Let me talk to Claude. I'm sure he's only tired. Or his parents caught up to him."

"Fine." Hero grabbed Beatrice's arm and pulled her in the same fashion toward the stairs. "I've got my own list of things to do. None of them involve boys. Maybe we'll see you at the party; maybe we won't. Come on, Beatrice."

Beatrice looked back at Benedick over her shoulder, getting farther away by the second. She lifted her shoulder apologetically. Benedick waved. Stupidly. It was just that knowing she existed somehow gave him a curious sense of center in this otherwise crumbling ruin of a day.

CHAPTER 27
LOVE ME! WHY?

If Hero minded Claude's absence, she hid it behind the important goal of looking, as she put it, as murderously devastating as possible. "It's my birthday, isn't it? Mama'd go to the damn party, and so will I." They bathed and powdered, then helped Maggie dress up for her audition and waved her off at the train station.

At least, since Claude was hosting the party (or had been?), there were actual caterers to set up the food on pristine white tablecloths, decorators to arrange the massive bundles of gardenias, Hero's favorite flower.

There was a harpist, along with a string quartet, Claude's solution to Maggie's absence. They had to lug Hey Nonny Nonny's beat-up piano out of the way to make room for the harp, and Beatrice was surprised to discover a bit of resentment toward the collared gentleman who sat behind it, where Tommy had once pounded out jazz. Maggie deserved the biggest stage with the biggest spotlight, and that wasn't Hey Nonny Nonny; but Beatrice missed her.

By the time she and Hero went down to the party together, the drive was filled with cars. Hero looked the way she always did, which was to say, no working candles for a mile around. Her red hair, faded to a rich auburn, had been coiffed so perfectly the curved ends on her pale cheeks appeared sculpted. A jewel-studded band sat behind her ears, an intricate brooch on one side. The pearls on her neck and wrist were incandescent with her ivory dress. Beatrice was amazed at how quickly Hero seemed to refind that inner zest.

"Are you ready?" asked Hero at the door.

"As I'll ever be."

"I can hardly take my eyes off you."

"Soon as we find a mirror, that will change."

Beatrice's dress was her own for once: a simple Sunday gown that had been her mother's. It was barely recognizable after Hero got done chopping off most of the top and all of the sleeves and shearing an open line up the seam. The hem hit Beatrice's calves except for a slit up the right side that went past her knee. Beatrice brought her hands up to her bare shoulders and wished for a shawl. Hero said it would ruin the effect, though Beatrice wasn't sure what effect she was meant to be giving off. Her hair remained the same stubborn curly length, but Hero had parted it on the side and arranged it in ripples over Beatrice's ears, in a way that almost looked bobbed.

Hey Nonny Nonny had been polished to a shine, draped in white sheaths of fabric and flowers. The basement was full of people. Beatrice heard, "My word, Beatrice!" and turned to see Uncle Leo and the boys waiting not far off from the entrance, waiting for them probably. She tried not to be too offended at his surprise.

Behind him, both boys were dressed in shiny tuxes. Prince looked a little rumpled, but grand, his cravat shifted to the left, while Benedick looked as if he'd come out of the womb in a tux. Only after Uncle Leo said her name did Benedick even react, as if he hadn't recognized her. His narrowed eyes blinked, and his face slackened, as if an invisible hand had reached over and plucked the muscle control from his brain.

Prince let out a low whistle. "Wow," he said, "you look . . . lovely."

Instead of curtsying, Beatrice dipped into an old stage man's bow, and everyone laughed. Except Benedick, who said, "You look great, too, Hero."

That went without saying, and Hero's smile said as much.

"As divine as your mother," said Uncle Leo.

"Thanks, Papa. Too bad for you boys"—Hero linked her

arm in Beatrice's—"I'm not sure we can be tempted to keep any male company tonight. Isn't that right, Bea?"

Keeping male company was not typically something that swayed Beatrice either way, but in the space of her silence, Prince made a little scoffing noise. Hero prickled, the arm around Beatrice's squeezing so hard she felt as if it might pop off.

"And neither of us is very impressed by the present offerings," Hero added, pulling Beatrice away. Now Benedick frowned, too, and Beatrice thought maybe for a minute she might sneak away. One of the offerings didn't seem so bad.

Beatrice didn't recognize most of the faces in their journey across the room. Vanilla beer served at the bar and champagne passed around in crystal flutes. Everything smelled of perfume and gossip.

Hero went into it like a lioness.

Nothing soothed a battered ego like a nice salt bath of admiration after all. "You know, this will be more fun without some tiresome date hanging on my arm," she said, gaining steam. "I can do as I please—"

Claude appeared in the center of the room, flute in one hand, the other extended, as though he were onstage about to begin his act. Hero's arrival was his cue. He looked distinguished and breathtakingly handsome in his suit. He raised a hand and instantly had the room's attention. In that moment it was easy to picture him as a future politician. "Ladies and gentleman, our guest of honor has arrived. Welcome again to Miss Hero Stahr's eighteenth birthday soiree. I'm your host and Miss Stahr's latest devotee."

The word *latest* carried an edge. He was smiling, but something about his congeniality felt wrong to Beatrice.

As the crowd clapped and cheered, Claude held out a hand to Hero. "You are going to dance with me, aren't you, love?"

"I don't know what to say." And it was clear she was talking about more than his offer to dance.

"As long as it isn't no, I don't care much what you say."

That fast she took his hand, and Beatrice moved out of the way. Men. Fickle as the weather . . . She craned her head around, looking for Benedick. He'd know what was going on.

"Any boys catch your fancy, Beatrice?"

She turned. Uncle Leo winked.

"My fancy is notoriously hard to catch," she said. "You look handsome, Uncle Leo."

"You flatter an old man. Looking for someone?" He caught her eyes wandering past him. She blushed, especially when he made a show of coughing and tipped his head toward the far corner of the room, where Benedick and Prince stood together. "Anna and I tried not to play favorites with the boys, but it was no secret I had a soft spot for Prince, and Anna just adored Ben."

"Did she?"

"When she got sick, he spent hours at her bedside, telling her stories. Sometimes it was the only thing she'd listen to."

"He must have loved her, too."

"You can't tell at first glance," Uncle Leo said, "but he is one of the most tenderhearted boys I know." And then he wandered on without giving her a chance to respond. *What do I care for the softness of his heart?* she might have asked if Uncle Leo had let her. *What do I care for his heart at all?*

A thought that left her rather unbalanced, her presumably logical and scientific mind spluttering, and then, out of nowhere, came a blessed distraction in the form of Conrade Minsky helping himself to the peach-apple punch.

She strode over and tapped his shoulder. "You rat."

He turned. "Miss Clark. We meet again."

"You underhanded rapscallion."

"Yes, that's what I thought you called me."

"I'm positive we didn't invite you."

"I never received my gold-embossed card, no," he said. Like Benedick, he looked perfectly at ease in his snazzy clothes. "But I happened to run into Mr. Blaine earlier today at the train station, on his way to Rhode Island. I thought it was a shame to let a few hurt feelings ruin a good birthday party."

He paused. Beatrice waited nonchalantly, as if she knew exactly whose feelings had been hurt and over what. "And you convinced him to return, your good deed done for the day?

I suppose it doesn't hurt that you were able to weasel in here under Claude's arm."

"You continue to wound. All I want is a dance with you. Or maybe two, if you enjoy it the first time."

"You seem very confident that I will."

"Think however you like." His teeth flashed in a brief grin.

"I always do."

He lifted the small dance card from her wrist and looked over his choices. "The two-step," he mused, "by 'That Mysterious Rag.' That sounds like a dance for us, doesn't it?"

"Careful how you throw around that pronoun."

"I'll also put us down for a waltz, as I am confident by that point you'll be close to falling in love with me." He signed his name twice with a flourish. "Enjoy the champagne, Miss Clark." He kissed her hand and disappeared back into the crowd.

"Applesauce," Beatrice muttered, and hurried to find Benedick.

CHAPTER 28
DONE TO DEATH BY SLANDEROUS TONGUES

Benedick finally managed to snatch one of the flutes off a passing waiter. One sip confirmed that not only was it *not* ginger ale, it had possibly arrived straight from Paris. "Prince, the drinks—" Benedick turned.

But Prince was slumped against the wall, like a wounded gazelle in a herd of wealthy lions. Most of these people had been invited by Claude, and it showed. He kept his eyes on Hero from across the vast hall, as she mingled like a hummingbird; the only sign of any distress on her part was an occasionally sagging smile, which she immediately pulled upright again.

"I don't belong here," Prince murmured.

"No, you don't want to be here," said Benedick. "There's a

difference. Why don't you just talk to her? Tell her the business with John bothers you, and she'll put a stop to it."

"I'm not jealous, Ben," Prince growled. "Do you know what he said to me? In the hall? He said: 'Don't worry about the speakeasy.' He knew exactly what we'd seen, even without our saying anything. And it's just—that's my *point*, Ben. Money. It's always money. Claude's or John's, it doesn't matter."

"But you've never cared before," Benedick pointed out. "Only when it was John."

"You don't get it. You've never taken the silver spoon out of your mouth." Prince sighed. "You can just go home if everything falls apart."

The champagne blurred the retort; Benedick nearly heard his father's voice saying it and had to work not to look like it hadn't been a cool slap in the face.

"Having a good time?" Claude approached them, his balance ever so slightly off center, a swallow of liquor left in the lowball glass he held. His accent was heavier, the words slurred. "You look like you could use a drink, both of you."

"You look like you've drunk enough for all three of us," Benedick said. Poor sentimental Claude. Forget the spoon. He was made of silver.

Claude laughed away Benedick's comment, though it sounded more like a sob. He turned, his unfocused eyes quickly locating Hero. "She is remarkable, isn't she?" He smiled at Prince. "She never broke any of your hearts. What is your secret to remain so immune? You—" He poked a finger into Benedick's chest. "I hate you, I think. You're the reason I got dragged into Hey Nonny Nonny, and you don't love your own mother. Hero's little trick with Beatrice didn't work. I said, 'There's an effort in futility, my dear,' not that she listened. Or ever listens."

"You're talking utter nonsense," said Benedick. "And more than a little sauced, I'd wager." *Wait*, what trick? What didn't work?

"True," Claude said. "And you could be, too."

"Don't tell Hero I'm crossing enemy lines." Beatrice appeared, looking, as she so often did, like a girl on a mission. Seeing her, Benedick recalled her apology in the orchard, the timing of it just after he'd overheard that she loved him, every smile since, that kiss on the porch—all on the basis of *her* affection—and wanted to sink into the floor. Claude could be wrong; Claude was also drunk.

Beatrice pointed at Prince. "You, mister. You've got a lot of nerve, leaving me alone with all these dandies. You're going to dance with me right now." Surprised, Prince relinquished his spot against the wall to follow her.

Benedick's shoulders slumped. He turned back to Claude. "I see you changed your mind about Rhode Island."

"I did. I was at the train station, and I met that fellow Minsky, you know, the one at Roosevelt Field. I told him what had happened, and he said—rightly so, at that—'Old sport, you can't run off like a dog with its tail between its legs! You must confront her. Gain back the dignity you lost. At the very least,' he said, 'a man deserves a nice stiff drink after being bludgeoned by a girl,' to which I told him, naturally, that I'd better go someplace else then since this party would be dry as a cactus."

Benedick stared at him. "What did you say?"

Claude snapped. Or tried to; his fingers fumbled. "Yes! That was just how he looked. *Very* interested in that. Felt so sorry for me he offered to bring what God intended every man to have after a girl tosses out what's left of him."

"Conrade Minsky brought the champagne?"

"I see that telltale woe on your face, but there's no reason to get uppity over it. His family bought it—didn't they?—and packed it over." He paused, as if he were rallying to meanness but couldn't quite get there. "What do I care anyhow about Hey Nonny Nonny?"

Indeed. Benedick looked over the dance crowd and found Prince and Beatrice. Beatrice caught his eye so quickly it was like she'd been waiting for him to look over. She jabbed a finger in Hero's direction.

He grasped her meaning immediately. Whether she loved him or not, he always could. He sighed, then clapped Claude farewell on the shoulder. "Stay here, and try not to do any more damage."

He sauntered up to Hero and tugged on a piece of her hair. "How about a dance, birthday girl?"

"Took you long enough," she said with a relieved grin. She abandoned the girls she'd been talking to without so much as a good-bye and took his hand.

"So is this a pity dance?" Hero asked.

"Give me a break; I love you like the sister I never had."

She bit her lip. "Ben, do you think I'm self-centered?"

"Sometimes, I guess."

"But do you hate me for it?"

"Don't be ridiculous."

"I'm not so sure it's ridiculous." She glanced over to Beatrice and Prince swirling around. They were on beat only every other step but seemed unconcerned about their ineptitude. "So what's the trouble? I know you didn't come over here just to get a taste of my fancy feet."

"The champagne," Benedick said.

"Yes, that was a surprise." She knew. Of course she did. She hadn't stopped paying attention for a moment, and she certainly still gave a damn about the speakeasy. "Is that why you're worried? Oh, don't be, sweetie. Nobody's paying for the drinks, and Claude said he got it as a gift, so they probably came out of someone's family vault."

"I suppose."

But the Minsky vault? Benedick had trouble believing Conrade felt so sympathetic to Claude's plight that he was willing to shell out a truckload of champagne for nothing. He looked again, and Beatrice caught his eye. She mouthed: *Switch*. Resigned, he turned Hero on point, their hands connecting again seamlessly, and guided them in a collision course with Prince and Beatrice. For Beatrice's part, Prince was too much of a gentleman to stop her rather forceful takeover as she led him toward Hero and Benedick.

"Ben," Hero said, "careful, or we're going to—"

Benedick twirled her away from him, hard enough that she spun on one foot, her arms flailing. Beatrice was less discreet. She shoved Prince with both hands, and he stumbled directly into Hero.

Prince caught Hero before she fell, as Benedick knew he would. Benedick was already leading Beatrice away, one hand on her waist. He turned them around so they could watch. Hero's cheeks flushed bright pink, and indecision tightened Prince's face. Beatrice tensed beneath his hold. *Come on, idiot*, Benedick thought.

Prince didn't turn her away. Everyone was looking at them after all. However hurt he might feel, he still couldn't bring himself to humiliate her in front of so many people. He took her hand, drew her in, and they started to dance without so much as a glance at Benedick or Beatrice. In fact, since they'd touched, they hadn't looked at anything but each other.

"They don't exactly look pleased, but he's the problem, not Claude." She sighed and looked at Benedick.

He was suddenly very aware of the places they were in contact: their loosely bound hands; his palm settled in the curve of her waist, his fingertips barely against her back, her other hand perched on his shoulder.

"Forgot about where you'd end up, Clark?" he asked, paving the way for her to denounce their closeness and in the process remind him the past few days had been a product of his own skewed perspective.

"Don't be ridiculous," she said. "I'm exactly where I wanted to be." And then she got closer, of all things. Her voice dropped. "Do you know Conrade is here?"

His mouth pursed. "Claude might have mentioned it."

"Yes! He saw Claude when he was leaving. He's the one who convinced Claude to come back. Why would he do that?"

"To get through the doors, for one."

"Ah. Then the real question is why he wanted into the party? This doesn't have to do with the fuss this morning at breakfast, does it?"

"Conrade can't have known about that. Whatever he's up to, it's not planned."

"What *is* the fuss? Why did Claude leave?"

Benedick sighed. "We might have happened upon Hero and John in a rather compromising position last night."

"You mean?" The dominoes tipped, and Beatrice adopted a look of proper indignation in an instant. "Hero wouldn't do that!"

"Don't be so righteous," said Benedick. "People make their own bargains, and Hero's no saint."

Her cheeks puffed. Her eyes narrowed; then she let out the breath in a defeated, unself-conscious raspberry. "But *John*. I don't believe it. And didn't he seem a little attached to Maggie when he was here?"

"I guess so, but he's the one who got Maggie her wiggle into the Cotton Club."

"So maybe *she* was putting *him* on?" Beatrice's eyes widened in amazement. "Doesn't anyone like anyone else honestly in this house?"

That was an excellent question.

Perhaps she thought the same thing because she suddenly got a bit pink around the ears. "What? Why are you looking at me like that?"

"I wonder, would you tell someone so honestly if you liked him?"

The blush deepened; that could mean anything, and Benedick wasn't sure which outcome he preferred at this point.

Eventually she said, "I would. If someone thought I didn't like him, and there was no hope, he would only need to ask me to be sure."

Wait a minute, who was the object of affection in this scenario? He wasn't worried about *her* rejecting *him*; he'd only meant to suggest an excuse for her not being honest about her own secret pining.

Unless, of course, Claude had been right and she wasn't pining.

And had never pined and was probably this minute assuming he was the one in love with her. Benedick laughed; he couldn't help it. Oh, he was such a fool. They'd nearly had him, the bastards. "I really thought—" Knowing there was no risk of attraction made it easier to tug her in close, so she was nestled against him. "Oh, thank God. That could have ended very ugly for us, sweetheart."

She tensed in his arms, pulling back to re-create the distance between them. Perhaps it was the angle, but her eyes, with that special blend of ferocious question, seemed larger than ever. The unexpected wave of attraction hit him so hard he nearly fell right into them.

"What are you talking about?" she asked.

He searched her face and pinpointed the source of her misunderstanding. "Uh-oh. Looks like they got to you, too. Nobody's convinced you recently that I might love you, has anyone?"

Her eyes dropped.

"Don't look like that." He touched her warm cheek. "I didn't mean it how it sounds, that it's laughable you would even consider I might love you. I only mean that I heard the same thing."

"What?"

"That day in the orchard. I overheard that you were hopelessly in love with me. I'm guessing that didn't come from you?"

"No." Her shoulders sagged. With relief? "Oh—*oh*." Finally she smiled, too. "I can't believe I didn't guess. They sure have a skewed sense of a joke." She eyed him, as if to double-check that it was indeed a joke.

"Not a very funny one. I even started to fall in love with you, too," he added with a soft laugh, "against my will. It was awful." The only trouble, the only teeny-tiny hiccup, was he was still fighting the urge to kiss her. Temporary, he was sure, and certainly not an indication of love, just the natural desire of any man to be congenial with his species.

"Do me a favor?" It was easier to speak into her ear than lean back.

"What?"

He glanced down, studying the slope of her bare neck as it met her equally bare shoulder. "Tell me you don't love me."

She was quiet for a moment; then she began to speak, with dramatic fashion: "Benedick Scott—" She halted. He pulled back so he could see her face. She looked horrified. "I don't," she said shortly.

"You don't?"

"Love you," she whispered.

That didn't work as well as he'd hoped. He might actually want to kiss her more.

A loud shout carried across the dance floor. "How dare you!"

Benedick turned and saw Prince and Hero at the refreshment table. "Don't touch me," Prince snapped, jerking his arm back. He seemed unaware of anything but the girl in front of him. "I saw you."

Guests had arranged in sporadic fashion around them. The music faded as the band strained their necks to see what the commotion was.

"Hero," Beatrice murmured, breaking away to get closer.

Benedick followed her. Through the crowd, he saw Hero's fists clench. "You've got some nerve acting like you have any right to be angry in the first place when you've made no claim—"

"What gossip, Hero?" Claude broke in, his drunkenness blurring him like a poorly taken photo. Prince startled out of the bubble he and Hero created, finally realizing they had an audience.

"That you're a liar?" Claude asked. His voice was quiet but piercing. "That everyone around you is no more than a pawn to give you what you need?"

Hero's face went red. Even boiled as an owl, Claude caught her wrist before her hand connected with his cheek. She tugged back, but he tightened his grip. His voice rose. "John's always been there, hasn't he, a distributor you keep on a leash? Give a tug when the speakeasy's in trouble?"

"Let go of me, you unbelievable ass," she said. "That's what this is about? You're jealous because you think someone else manhandled what's yours?"

Prince moved. "Claude, let her go."

"Go ahead and have her." Claude didn't push her, but he threw her arm back so violently Hero stumbled. She knocked into the table, tripped over the hem of her dress, and fell to the ground, spilled punch dripping down onto her cream dress.

Without preamble, Claude plopped onto the polished wood floor like a child exhausted after throwing a fit. His chin trembled, and he whispered, "I loved you," and started to cry.

Hero fought her own tears, flushed, her chin wobbling as she attempted to stand up. Beatrice was at her side in a moment, helping her. The crowd came to life, murmuring, forming snow-balls of gossip that would soon careen out of control. "How could you?" Hero asked. She didn't spare Claude another glance; her eyes were for Prince, full of betrayal. "You didn't even ask me—"

"You didn't ask *me*," Prince shot back, with a small gasp, as if surfacing from some deep ocean. "You just assumed I'd fail, that I wouldn't be able to save it. And then you went to *John*, of all people, instead of—"

"That's enough!" Leo's voice boomed out. The burnished look of his cheeks meant he wasn't as stone cold as he ought to be, but he spoke with only the slightest tremor, with devastating effect. Prince shrank. "This is *my* speakeasy," Leo continued.

"And that is my little girl. It's clear that one of them means much more to you than the other. Get out of my house, young man."

Leo could not have struck Prince harder than if he'd swung the blade of an ax into his chest. Prince staggered back a step.

The party reeked of ruin, Prince pushing his way out of the crowd, Hero at last unable to pinch back the first few tears.

Benedick grabbed Claude under the armpits and hauled him to his feet. Beatrice gathered Hero against her and managed to tug Leo into helping after he slugged back the rest of his champagne. They made their way toward the bar, the wide-eyed crowd parting to let them through. Slowly, awkwardly the music started up again. "I think I may be sick," Claude groaned, arm around his stomach.

"Serve you right," said Benedick, but he guided Claude to one of the flower-crested tables and eased him into a chair.

Benedick looked for Prince, but his tall, messy head had disappeared in the sea of coiffed bobs and slick pomade. Benedick strode forward. He wasn't sure what he was going to do. Maybe find Conrade and strangle him with his own bow tie—who knew?—but if there was a time to harvest one's murderous tendencies, now seemed like a prime opportunity—

He stopped.

A scrambling, weightless fear swept through him; as if he'd been pushed off a cliff and there was nothing to do now but fall and hope to brace his landing.

Dogberry and Verges were sitting at the bar. Disguised to the teeth in vibrant purple and green suits, bright daisies in their lapels, bowler hats stuck with feathers. Thick blond mustaches. Prince had given Francis their pictures, just in case, but it appeared Francis had been fooled. Benedick only recognized them for the contrast: crane and pigeon. That, and their somber expressions, so different from the aghast tittering of the rest of the guests.

Benedick approached them slowly.

Dogberry glanced over. "There's sad news here, Mr. Scott."

"How?" Benedick asked. "We didn't sell any liquor. We don't have a still. You have no proof that any of the beverages weren't privately owned—"

"You know the law pretty well, Mr. Scott. I suppose you also know that the *transport* of alcohol is illegal as well as the sale and production." He reached into his jacket and pulled out a bottle of champagne. His finger tapped the label, the tiny gold words *Produce of France*.

"That's not our champagne," Benedick whispered.

"Well, it was brought into your speakeasy, and it's your name on the delivery receipt."

"That's impossible."

Dogberry shrugged; the daisy bobbed up and down. "Then I guess you've got nothing to worry about."

Conrade Minsky. Son of a bitch.

It was too late, far too late for it to matter, but Benedick still stepped away from them. "Raid," he said, voice cracking a little. His eyes closed briefly. Then he yelled: *"Raid!"* The music ground to a halt. "Up and at 'em, ladies and gents; we're on the lam. Move it right now, or we're blaming you."

A ripple of confused laughter, and then finally people shuffled toward the exit, looking around for the gun-toting bureau. Dogberry, decidedly gunless, shook his head.

CHAPTER 29
I WOULD EAT HIS HEART IN THE MARKET-PLACE

S*tairs.*

Beatrice hated stairs. Among other things. They'd trudged up the first set into the pantry, and now they faced the main stairs descending into the pantry. Hero had turned into a sniffling weight on her hip and now decided this was as far as she wanted to go and wilted onto the first step without further ado.

Beyond the front door, voices swelled, car doors opened and closed, engines started.

Perhaps without the main attraction, the party was over. Good, she thought.

"Uncle Leo," she said, turning, but she'd lost him in the journey from pantry to foyer. He'd managed to give Prince the boot with something suggesting sobriety, but he was not sober. He had soaked up the unfiltered champagne like a thirsty sponge. He'd blubbered worse than Hero up the stairs, mourning the speakeasy, Hero's childhood, or maybe Prince. *Prince*, who was God knew where like a coward instead of looking the damage he caused in the eye. Claude might be in a gutter, for all she knew.

Beatrice was itching to hate the male race in general, but then Benedick appeared, Uncle Leo draped on his shoulders. "Here we go," Benedick muttered. *Hold on*, he mouthed to Beatrice, then helped Uncle Leo to the drawing room couch. Beatrice, who never held on for any boy, waited for him and was more than a little glad when he returned.

He knelt next to Hero. "Here, sweetheart, let me help you."

Hero resisted for a moment, but his touch was gentle, his voice so caring Beatrice hardly believed it belonged to him. With a tiny nod, Hero allowed him to tuck one arm under her knees and the other against her back. He hoisted her up. "Thatta girl."

Beatrice let go, but Hero lunged for her wrist. "Beatrice!"

"I'm here," Beatrice said, weaving her fingers into Hero's. She'd never seen her cousin like this. Her cries faded to shuddery breaths and the occasional soft moan. Beatrice went ahead and opened the door, so Benedick could set Hero on her bed. Bent over, Benedick lifted his eyes to meet Beatrice's, but before either could say anything, Hero clutched Beatrice again. "Get this dress off me," she croaked. Yanking at the fabric, she attempted to sit up. "Get it off!"

She twisted and dug at her collar. Beatrice's jaw set, and she moved decisively behind her and worked at the zipper. Benedick joined her without a word, and together they undid every button, unclipped every piece of jewelry.

"You should go," said Beatrice, not looking at Benedick.

Briefly touching her shoulder, he left.

No thanks to Hero's panicked flailing, Beatrice managed to tear the dress off her. Her underclothes were just as stained, and Beatrice stripped her of those, too. "Good riddance," Beatrice said, gathering the entire bundle in her arms and tossing it out the window, before coming to tuck her cousin—naked, pale, and shivering—into the sheets.

Beatrice lay next to her. Hero stank like cigarette smoke and booze. "It's okay," said Beatrice, running fingers over her hair, past her shoulder.

"I know what everyone says about me, lock up your husbands, but I only flirt." Her eyes squeezed closed.

"Oh, Hero." Beatrice kept stroking her hair. Poor Hero, longing for true love with all her tough little heart. Beatrice stayed until Hero's breathing evened out. Then she crept downstairs to the drawing room, where Benedick was tugging one of Uncle Leo's shoes off, making him comfortable.

"My girl was always a brat of a biddy," Leo said to himself. "Never listened to her betters. Can't clean a rug without ruining it and don't even know how to make tomato soup, but she can out-curse any sailor. Perfect. Just perfect."

Beatrice sank onto the love seat. In moments Uncle Leo was snoring. Crying wouldn't help, so she didn't, or at least she told herself very strictly not to. She assumed Benedick would leave but was surprised when his weight settled beside her, perfectly; the moment he did she felt more centered. He touched the corner of her eye.

"I don't think I've ever seen you cry. I don't care for it."

Embarrassed, she wiped at her eyes.

"Don't do that," he said, drawing her against his chest. She resisted for a moment, then crumpled against his chest. She cried right into his tender heart. "I'm not sad"—she sniffed—"so you know. I'm very angry."

"The devil you aren't." He responded by pulling a handkerchief from his breast pocket to give to her: pristine white, with a satin silver border around the edge, the initials BJS embroidered in the corner, probably worth more than her entire outfit. Of course he didn't love her. Not this boy—who belonged to the world of the brilliant, beautiful, and rich, and himself a hazardous package of all three—but who only seemed to want, of all the silly things, to be happy.

"Why are you here?" she asked.

"Where else would I be?"

"On Park Avenue! Drinking fine wine and blowing your nose with dollar bills! Examining how the world looks laid at your feet instead of dangling out of reach! Not—not writing some stupid novel and sitting on a ratty couch while some lunatic girl yells at you!"

She leaned over and buried her face in her hands. Then she told herself to stop her nonsense. That argument didn't even make sense. With a deep breath, she opened her mouth to apologize—tiredly, dejectedly, with no idea why she'd lashed out in the first place—but he laughed. *Laughed.*

God, he was unrelenting. There was something deliberately pigheaded in the way he continued to miss the gist. "Some boys never learn," she said.

"I prefer you in snapping form," he said, "like a turtle."

She laughed and thought, *I love you.*

That was when she fell, tumbled right off the branch, with no bottom in sight.

She poked at the feeling the way one might a rabid animal and discovered it was not only there but alive. Of course she loved him.

She blushed to her hairline.

He gave her an odd look. "Now what?"

Now what indeed? A fine time to fall in love with a fellow, after he tells you he only just managed to endure your presence because he thought you loved him, and thank God he didn't fall in love back. *Hypothetically*, she might say, *I love you after all. Quite seriously.* He'd be so disappointed.

And wasn't she relieved, too? She'd never *wanted* this; the whole thing was a damned nuisance and a distraction, and she was glad to be done with it.

She shifted away. "What happened with the party?"

"Broke up."

"I hope Conrade is pleased with himself."

"We can at least satisfy ourselves that he's saddled with a zozzled and weeping Claude Blaine the rest of the evening." He breathed slowly, sounding as weary as she felt. "Go to sleep, Beatrice. Trouble keeps overnight. We'll tackle it fresh in the morning."

There was something else, something he wasn't telling her. But then they weren't partners. Weren't in love. So why should he want her comfort or support? She nodded, added something about her head feeling terrible, and went back upstairs to Hero's room.

The next morning Hero was gone. Beatrice reached for her, but her hand met with depressed sheets. The clock said ten minutes past nine o'clock. She hurried to get dressed. "Hero?" Beatrice checked the washroom first, but it was empty.

In the drawing room she found Benedick where she'd left him, sprawled on the love seat. Uncle Leo was possibly dead. Benedick's jacket was draped on a nearby chair, but otherwise he was still done up in his dress clothes. She hesitated, not sure if it was fair to wake him up, but he roused as she came in, sitting up and rubbing his face. He looked entirely put together in less than a second, as if the world couldn't give him enough problems to stop him from functioning at top form. If Beatrice hadn't been so worried about Hero, she'd have been annoyed.

"Hero isn't in her room," she said.

"Try downstairs in the speakeasy."

Beatrice turned to go, then paused. "Did you sleep here all night?"

"I . . . was waiting for Prince."

"He didn't come back," she guessed.

"No." His face stayed placid, but his eyes were pinched.

She nearly mentioned that Prince deserved a night in the cold after what he had put Hero through, but Benedick's expression stopped her. "He'll turn up," she said instead. "This is his home."

Hey Nonny Nonny was ransacked. Overturned tables, shattered glass. The air was ripe with spilled champagne and wilting gardenias. The only light was from the chandelier hanging from the ceiling like an upside-down bouquet. The leftover mess looked eerie beneath the rain of glittery light. The corners of the basement remained invisible. It was like looking at a dream or a bad memory.

Hero was sitting in the far corner of the stage, where the old piano had been shoved, plunking out round after dreary round of "Chopsticks." She wore a gray dress, tight buttons at the wrist and a high collar with a small lace border. A white wrap held back her hair and made her look like a poor milkmaid. There was not a touch of rouge to her cheeks, and her eyelashes were so bare and pale they were nearly invisible.

All this was nothing compared with her eyes. Hollow; windows into an empty room. Her hands stilled as Beatrice climbed onto the stage and sat beside her. "Hero."

Hero inhaled slowly, mouth forming a small smile. The expression was only a positioning of muscle; it gave no light to her eyes. "Good morning, Beatrice."

Beatrice tried to smile back. "Are you all right?"

"I feel better, yes."

Beatrice waited, and Hero went back to staring off the empty stage.

"What are you doing here?" Beatrice asked.

"Saying good-bye. Saying I'm sorry."

Beatrice swallowed and set her hands on her cousin's, as if she could massage life back into them. "It was only one bad night, Hero, and none of it was your fault."

For a long time Hero gave no indication she heard her. Then she blinked. That tiny action was enough to startle Beatrice.

"I didn't kiss John," Hero said in a flat tone, and Beatrice's stomach twisted. "But I may as well have, for how easily they accepted it. *Of course she did it*, that's what they were thinking. *She's just the kind of girl who would.*"

A fresh wave of anger crept over Beatrice. She imagined viciously puncturing every one of the bloated faces that dared judge Hero last night.

Tears leaked down Hero's cheeks. Watching the slow, salty tracks trail from such deadened eyes was an eerie sight. "I miss my mother so much," she whispered.

"I know," said Beatrice, leaning in.

"No one would have believed a rumor like that about her." Hero closed her eyes. The girl Beatrice had admired only days ago was so absent from the one in front of her that it was as if she'd died. Where was that minxlike wit? The impression of something about to explode out of her, something you wanted? This girl was flattened, buried under glacial guilt.

"Hero," Beatrice begged, clinging to her, "please come back upstairs with me."

"Not yet," said Hero. "He's gone."

"Who? Claude? Good riddance, I say—"

"Prince. You didn't see how he looked at me. Like I was trash."

"Prince was wrong. Not you. He ought to be the one groveling and moping. Not you."

"Don't you see? Even if he was wrong this time, I've done a hundred other things to make him leave, given him a hundred other reasons. I pushed him too far."

"Enough! I can't take this miserable wallowing when this isn't your fault!"

For the first time life blazed into Hero's face. She glared at Beatrice. "Oh, now you're going to judge me, too? Because I'm not acting feminist enough for your tastes? What do you know, Beatrice Clark? You've never loved anyone in your life."

"I love *you*, you dumb girl." Beatrice sighed, rubbed a hand on her forehead. "And I love you no matter how many boys you kiss."

"I'm tired, Beatrice. Kissing and drinking and dancing haven't done anything for me, and I'm fed up. Go away now, please. Find someone else to bully."

"Fine." Beatrice pulled away. Over her shoulder she said, "For the record, *I* like you just as you are. I'd rather see you drunk or with a new boy every night than like this."

CHAPTER 30

I DO LOVE NOTHING IN THE WORLD SO WELL AS YOU; IS NOT THAT STRANGE?

Benedick dragged himself up to his room. He plugged the rickety sink in the corner and let the water run, taking solace in the idea of clean clothes, a fresh shave, a little something he had control over and could make better.

Once dressed and no longer smelling of spent booze, he'd find Beatrice. Irritated, he thought, Why? Not only had she apparently decided to take priority in his mind over Prince, but now she'd also pushed out breakfast.

Look here, he told himself, *we've decided as a unified body not to be in love with her, so stop it.* When he got downstairs, he heard a hammer pounding rhythmically outside. His first thought was Prince. But—

Having hurried around the side of the house to the source of the sound, Benedick froze. Prince wasn't there. Dogberry and Verges stood by Hey Nonny Nonny's outside entrance. Dogberry finished nailing a notice sign to the wood-planked cellar door and stepped back.

CLOSED

For Violation of the National Prohibition

By Order of the United States District Court

All persons are forbidden to enter the premises without

orders from the United States Marshal.

Benedick stared at it. There was a secured padlock around the doors. "Why?" he asked finally. "Why us?"

Dogberry scoffed. "Why not you? You're breaking the law same as anyone."

"It was a birthday party," Benedick snapped.

"Verges, how many speakeasies do you reckon are in New York City alone?" asked Dogberry.

Verges stretched his bobbing neck. "Why, it'd have to be fifty thousand at the minimum. Probably closer to a hundred thousand, if you counted the smaller joints, too."

"I reckon you're right," said Dogberry. "So why would we spend our time bothering with a has-been speakeasy in Flower Hill that only opens by special invitation anyway?"

"I guess if we got an offer we couldn't refuse."

"I guess so."

Benedick didn't want to understand what they were talking about, but it was hard not to. "I thought you didn't take bribes," he said.

"We don't take bribes to disobey the law," Dogberry said, correcting him. The hints of intelligence that had crept up in small doses now fully dominated the agent's face. Still, he seemed sorry, affected with the kindness he'd lauded earlier. "We don't take bribes to turn the other way or hurt nobody, but we'll take an extra nice paycheck to do what we're sworn in to do either way. We had a client express interest in seeing one speakeasy in particular shut down and, well, who were we to turn down good work?"

"My father," Benedick said. It was just the sort of thing he would do, big balled and not to be outbid by a third party, even his own son. Benedick stepped forward, his feet heavy, and touched the freshly posted sign. Closed. This was his fault. He'd brought the agents right to Hey Nonny Nonny's door.

He considered all the questions he ought to ask, the indignation he had every right to feel, and instead he was simply tired. He felt pity, not for himself but for the entire world, the whole rotten state of human affairs. Why even try? "I thought—"

"Now, don't take it so hard, son," said Dogberry, watching him. "We already knew there was a speakeasy here, and we would've pheasant hunted straight into winter until we had proof. If we didn't get you last night, it would've been another night. Know what your pop said to us before we came? He said, 'My son is no slouch. He's smart as a devil. He'll figure out you're Prohibition agents, and then he'll try to talk you into leaving, and he's a really fine talker, so don't fall for it.' "

That his father thought he was anything other than a lazy, useless dreamer was surprising. The knowledge wormed its way into Benedick's fury and made a mess of it, softening edges he wanted to stay pointed.

"And you know, he was right," said Dogberry.

Benedick tried to put his anger on Claude but couldn't do it. He couldn't even fully blame Conrade. The bottom line had his own privileged, delusional signature all over it. He sighed. "What's going to happen?"

Dogberry handed him a folded receipt. "We got our proof last night," he said. "But then with what happened with Miss Stahr and it being her birthday, well, we decided to wait. Still, the law's the law." From his other pocket, Dogberry retrieved a crisp court summons. "There'll be jail or a hefty fine."

Leo was already on a downward slope; this would bury him. Hero would be left alone with no way to support herself. Prince could be anywhere. Even Beatrice, applying for college, would have this family shame hanging over her head.

On the receipt, the sloppy signature at the bottom read:

"care of Hey Nonny Nonny, LLC." No name. Of course Leo's name was on Hey Nonny Nonny's ticket, but who would ask, if a fellow was willing to take the blame?

"I own this establishment," said Benedick.

Dogberry gave him a doubtful look.

Benedick crossed his arms over his chest. He summoned every inch of the Ambrose Scott in him and tilted his chin in an imperious manner. "I'm eighteen. I have every right to own property. Why do you think my father was so concerned with shutting the place down? I bought it off the original owner and have been managing it through the back door for a year." He snatched the court summons right out of Dogberry's hand. "I'll see you before a judge, sir. And I'll thank you to give me an honest man's business day to get my affairs in order."

That was taking the bluff perhaps a tiny bit too far, but Dogberry didn't argue. He smiled, as if he understood. "All right," he said. "I reckon a summons could get misplaced for a day or two—"

"In the post," Verges suggested.

"Or under a coffee mug." Dogberry leaned in and winked. "You'll have until next week, but if you don't take care of it . . ."

"Don't worry," Benedick said grimly. "My father hates tardiness." He didn't think he'd go to jail. His father would pay whatever fine was needed; but that meant Benedick would be in his debt, and he'd have to go home. College or Wall Street. No more Hey Nonny Nonny.

Dogberry tipped his hat. "Pleasure doing business with you, Mr. Scott."

Benedick waited until the agents were gone, then went back to the entrance to pry the sign off. He'd deal with the court summons, and no one would ever know the speakeasy went under. Those agents wouldn't be back again.

He shook his head and wiped sweat off his temple with his shoulder. He wrestled the end of the crowbar under the sign and tugged, grunting, but the plywood sign only bowed.

"You need a hammer, for the nails."

Benedick jumped.

Hammer already in hand, Beatrice came beside him. Dungarees on, like the first day they'd met. Her hair was positively demonic, coming out of her pins ten different ways. The difference was that today she seemed considerably less full of bean and buck than so many weeks ago. But the standard of gloom for the day was such that compared with Leo and Hero, stewing in gin and waiting for the end, she looked almost indecently cheerful.

She pried each nail out one by one. When she was finished, Benedick silently lifted the sign and turned it around. "Wait one moment," she said, and pulled another tool from her pocket. This one she used to pick the padlock and tugged the chains loose.

"This is a federal crime," he told her.

"So's murder," she muttered, with enough dark promise he wondered if she had a list already prepared. She looped the chain over her shoulder.

"How is our girl?" Benedick asked, following her back to the porch.

"Not good. Not anything. Her spirit's been squashed like a bug. I'd like to tear Claude's heart out and eat it. Then Prince's for dessert. Conrade Minsky's I'll wrap for Monday. When they strap me in the chair, please let them know the killing was just." She stopped and frowned, getting a good look at him. "Are you all right? You seem—"

"Just tired. Long night."

They trekked their way up to his room. He kept the sign inward, and every few seconds he'd catch it sticking its tongue out at him. Beatrice dropped the chain on his floor without further ado, *tack-tack-tack*. Benedick stuffed the sign behind the sofa, which he sank onto, propping his arm up on the back.

Beatrice looked at the arm, then at the chest to which it was attached. She pulled on one of her freed curls, then at last sat and edged in his direction. After a minute of silence, except for slightly labored breathing after the upstairs trek, he concluded that the kissing problem was still at emergency level.

The dungarees in fact had made it worse.

Go figure.

He cleared his throat. "Naturally I'm relieved to once again take up the position of your mortal enemy with no fear of breaking your heart. If you in fact have one."

She turned and smiled at him. Like a swinging baseball bat. "Sure. We remain unscathed from this whole mess precisely because we were wise enough to stay away from love."

"Exactly."

"What will happen? Does Leo have to go to jail?"

"Of course not," he said brusquely. "In fact those chains are just a formality. Speakeasies reopen all the time. You check the office, you get a slap on the wrist, and off you go."

She frowned. "Even without—"

"Trust me," he interjected. He took her hand and squeezed once. "Trust me; this will be taken care of."

She slid her fingers free, rubbing them. "All right." She tipped her head back; all at once she deflated, as if shedding a top layer that had made her taller. Her eyes fluttered with exhaustion. "I wonder if I ought to stay, just for a year, and help out."

"Absolutely not. You're going to pass your regents' exams, study at some fancy college, become a surgeon or whatever—"

"And win the Nobel Prize, don't forget."

"And win the Nobel Prize. The rest of us are counting on your coattails to carry us along, so I'm afraid there's no other choice."

For a minute she said nothing. Then, half asleep, she mumbled, "And you'll be here at least. I won't worry if you're here."

He hesitated. "Beatrice . . ."

"Hmm?" She blinked at him.

He lost his nerve. "Are you hungry?"

"Gosh, yes. Enough to eat you alive."

Later Benedick sat on Hey Nonny Nonny's porch as the sun went down, twirling a pen (at this point purely decoration) between his fingers, around and around. The chairs along the porch were weatherworn and haphazardly placed. Cigarette butts had blown off ashtrays to join smeared sparrow droppings. From here the speakeasy's entrance wasn't visible, and there was only an expanse of shadowy trees before him.

After a phone call from Maggie, Beatrice had taken the car to pick up their favorite jazz singer from the station (and promised to ask around for Prince while she was there). Benedick was on the porch now, he admitted to himself, to wait for her return. He was partway through a terrible love sonnet when the front door opened and Hero stepped through, taking a lot of care to shut the door behind her quietly.

"Good evening, St. Helen," said Benedick.

She turned around and gave him a displeased look. Her dress came with sleeves and a collar; Benedick was unaccustomed to seeing so much fabric on her at once. With a small sigh of defeat she perched on the chair beside him. She propped one heel up and reached to a lace garter, where a silver flask was lodged. She removed it and set it on Benedick's knee, then dug a cigarette case from her brassiere. "Got a light?"

Benedick got up and found Prince's stash of matches, hidden under one of the heavier ashtrays. She looked away as he lit the first cigarette but didn't refuse it when he passed it to her. Flask in hand, she said, "Should I make a toast?"

"I was just thinking the scene could do with a bit more dialogue."

"Here's to never again putting on shoes that hurt my feet and undergarments that pinch, and never giggling at boys who aren't funny, and especially never being a good sport about it."

"Here's to that noble experiment the Eighteenth Amendment," he said, "which makes a toast so thrilling and this wonderful, mad time in history in which we live."

"Show-off." Her grin was a pale imitation of the original, but at least it was there. She glanced at his papers. "How's the great American novel coming? Ready to deliver your inspiring message to mankind?"

"Alas, it's beginning to look like unless I hit my stride some time in middle age, mankind will remain a message short. I did finish a poem that you're welcome to read and then use to light your next drag."

Hero looked at him, the smoke from her cigarette casting a hazy screen around her face. "Give it here."

He passed her the scrawled-upon piece of paper.

"'The god of love, who sits above, and knows me, and knows me, how pitiful I deserve—'"

"Oh, God. It's even worse out loud."

"Well, it's not Shakespeare." Hero lowered the paper and touched her knuckles to her chin. "What is it, some kind of love poem?"

"Your doubt speaks volumes. Perhaps it will serve better as a torture device for future blackmail. . . ."

"Love poems aren't your usual style, that's all."

"Maybe I'm in love."

"*Are* you?"

He closed his eyes. "I hope not," he said. He opened his eyes to glare at her. "Which reminds me, I think you owe me an apology for that particularly ill-thought-of joke."

Hero's eye rolling was not of the apologetic sort. "Well, pardon me, but no one's holding a gun to your head, making you write sonnets. It's Beatrice, isn't it? I knew it. You're good at seeing people, Ben; you're good at seeing what they truly are and not making a fuss about the gap in between." She cupped her face in both hands, cigarette pointed away from her ear, and, blowing out smoke, leaned her elbows on her knees. "That's one good piece of news anyway."

"Good news! Is that what you'd call it? I'd like to hear your name for reciprocated love."

"Why, she turn you down?"

"Like a bedspread. No. I don't know. Not exactly. I didn't ask, but I didn't have to ask to know the answer was no, you know?"

"You're a mouthful," Hero said affectionately. She straightened. "And I guess I do know, don't I?" She paused. "We're both here on the porch waiting after all."

"You love Prince?"

"I hope not. But probably." Hero scowled. "I didn't even know you could love a person like this without ever kissing him."

Benedick had to force his brain not to imagine kissing Beatrice.

"Or maybe I don't after all," said Hero. "I'm so mad at him for leaving. He's got a lot of nerve abandoning us because his feelings got hurt. You know whose feelings are hurt? Mine."

"Right. Who needs the big lug?"

"Maybe we just expected too much once and for all." The cigarette burned between her fingers, resting on her knee, the smoke curling up like a question mark. Her voice dropped to a whisper. "I got used to him protecting me."

"So what's it going to take, darling? For you to forgive him?"

"Nothing," she said shortly. "Haven't I asked the world already? Let him go. Join the mob and live off showgirls." She set her chin and paid no mind to Benedick's plaintive look.

"Are you going to rally the speakeasy?"

"I don't know," she whispered. "Never done it without him."

"He can't stay away forever. I'm sure of it."

Hero sighed, just as the car roared up the drive. Beatrice waved to them with her whole arm as they got closer. Not glamorous but tremendously capable. The kind of girl who drove a six-stroke automobile with one knee while loading her rifle with her free hand.

"Well," said Benedick.

"Goodness," Hero murmured. "I see it all right. You poor boy."

The car parked, and Beatrice climbed out from the driver's seat, Maggie from the passenger side. Kohl was smudged at the corners of Maggie's eyes; fatigue hung off her clothes, but her face was lit up with a big smile.

"I did it!" she announced, hands spread. "I got the spot!"

"Oh, Maggie," Hero said, "that's so wonderful!"

And then she burst into tears.

Maggie's smile fell. "Hey now, it's not like I'll never be back."

"I know, I know." Hero hiccuped, scrubbing the corners of her eyes. Benedick handed her a handkerchief (he was going through them quickly), and she blew her nose in it. "I mean it. I'm happy for you. But just on top of everything else—"

"Beatrice told me about Claude ruining your party," Maggie said.

"Hero. Why didn't you tell them it was me?" She glanced at Benedick, then Beatrice. "*I* kissed John. In Hero's room. Claude must have seen it."

Benedick's stomach dropped. Never mind Claude. If Prince didn't feel awful already, this revelation would put him through the wringer.

"I said *I* didn't, never mind who actually did." Hero sniffed. "Everything happened so fast, and when it was all over, what did it matter anyway?"

"But in the hall," Benedick said, "you acted like—"

Hero glowered at him. "I was keeping Maggie's secret! I thought John was walking out on her, and no girl wants an audience for that if she can help it."

"Unless John planned for him to see it all along." Maggie's fist clenched; if John's face had been nearby, Benedick thought that was where her fist would have been headed. Maggie strode up the porch. "I think I know how to find Prince, and if I have to drag him home by the ear myself, we'll get him back."

CHAPTER 31
AS THE GREYHOUND'S MOUTH, IT CATCHES

Maggie went the next morning. The pocket of Mulberry Street where she found John's apartment was rough, but today it was just the kind of place to fit Maggie's mood. The shop signs were in Italian, as were the gruff conversations out on the street. And if that large man on the corner kept looking at her like that, she'd knock his block off.

She stopped near a café. A woman swept the stoop. Past a striped overhang was the tenement building matching the address John had written down for her so many days ago. The only way to get up there was by a rickety set of iron stairs bolted into the building's brick side.

"Hey, honey." The man on the corner had his hands tucked

under his armpits, elbows sticking out, feet spread. "What you looking for?"

Hurrying to the rusted staircase, Maggie ignored him.

"Talking to you, princess. What kind of business you got up there?"

Her lips pressed together. She might have been asking the same question if this had been her street and a stranger was nosing around, but she was itching for a fight. She turned.

"I've got business with John Morello," she said. "If he's not home, I'll wait till he is."

"Say"—the man mused—"you're not—"

If he said "that jazz singer," she might scream. That gal John got into the Cotton Club. That sucker he'd kissed to dupe one of her dearest friends. That's her all right, what do you know?

"—Margaret?"

She whipped back around. Her fury somehow spiked and vanished at the same time. Up on the top landing, John had emerged. She'd never seen him so underdressed, a thin undershirt bunched around his elbows, suspenders loose against his thighs. Set in front of the afternoon sun, his hair looked almost soft. All the things she wanted to say welled up like a river.

You should've heard me on that stage. I lit the place up.

She'd expected him to be at the club, and he hadn't been. But standing on that stage in front of Duke Ellington and his cigarette and focused eyes, she hadn't needed John, or Hey Nonny

Nonny, or anybody else. She knew who she was, up there.

It was only after—when she was done celebrating with Tommy, Jez, and some of the other new chorus girls, when she was watching Hero's eyes fill with tears—that she realized it hadn't been entirely true that she didn't need anyone. She'd been able to sing in front of Duke Ellington with everything she had because she'd known Hey Nonny Nonny would catch her if she wasn't good enough. Somehow, it would be there; *they* would be there.

And John, whose kiss filled her with the best music, who already thought she was good enough for the Cotton Club?

You kissed me. You kissed me and it was like heaven and you used me, you bastard, you bastard, you bastard.

John cut his eyes down and across the street at the man who'd called her honey.

The man held up his hands. He said something in Italian that she couldn't understand, but it sounded like an apology, a please-don't-cut-off-my-head-sire kind of apology. John answered brusquely, and lo and behold, the street cleared like magic, people off to mind their own business.

John jumped down the stairs so fast they rattled. "What are you doing here?" he asked when he got to the bottom. His thumb almost brushed her cheek, but he caught himself and drew back. His collarbone peeked out of his collarless shirt, and for half a second she was transfixed by this part of him she'd never seen before.

And damn it, still wanting to touch him was the last straw. Her hand bunched into a fist. His eyes widened. Fighter that he was, he knew it was coming; but he didn't stop her from swinging into his rib cage, his shoulder, anywhere she could reach. She bet it hurt her more than it did him, but she didn't care.

Eventually she gave out, her body listing toward the chest she'd just abused. "I'd keep at it," she said, panting, bracing on her knees, "if I'd had any breakfast."

"I guess I deserve that." He rubbed a spot on his upper arm where she'd belted him good.

"You better believe you do."

"I'm sorry." He looked away.

"I know why you did it." Maggie bit off each word, straightening. She brushed her curls out of her eyes. "To break Hero and Claude up, make Claude think she wasn't faithful. Not that it means I forgive you, but I understand you. I always have, top to bottom."

"What are you talking about—"

"You kissed me. You brought me close to the window. You could have told me. Then at least when you did, I would have already known it was a lie."

He closed his eyes. "Margaret—"

"I'm glad I got to say it"—she interrupted—"but it's not why I'm here. I'm looking for Prince. Do you know where he is?"

"John?" A tall, dark-haired woman stepped out onto the

landing above them. "I can't find Pedro." She disappeared.

John pressed his lips together, then motioned Maggie to follow him.

The hall leading to his apartment had carpeting, but it was thin as paper, and the air smelled of yeast and sauce and cigar smoke. He led her through an unmarked door between number 7 and 9.

Inside, the woman sat in an old armchair, her hands clasped in her lap. She was wearing a red velvet dress, a large silver clasp around her high waist, matching her starkly pale skin. The stitching was barely holding the dress together, it was so worn. Like her, it looked as though it might have been beautiful a decade ago. "Who is that Negro girl?"

"I'm a friend of your son's," Maggie said, ignoring John's flinch.

"Pedro will be along shortly; he's playing in the street. Come in, come in."

John wilted, as if somehow his mother had sucked life out of him with her words, but he set his jaw and motioned Maggie in. The apartment was on the small side, but was immaculate, for all its plainness. A small library of leather-bound books, mostly poetry. The glass in the windows looked recently replaced.

John muttered for Maggie to wait, gesturing gruffly to an old wooden rocking chair; then he shepherded Mrs. Morello into her bedroom. Maggie heard her say, "I said never to touch me again,

Don Morello!" and then: "Where is Pedro? Where is Pedro?"

"Let me." A familiar voice. Maggie inched toward the hall-way and glanced around the corner toward the bedroom. There was Prince, back at home in spite of everything John had done to keep him away. Prince was a head taller than his mother and took her by the elbow. She softened at his touch, but John stopped him. He murmured something to his brother, and Prince said, "Our Maggie?"

Maggie stepped back.

A few seconds later Prince appeared, looking as if he'd been somersaulting through hell, his hair more disoriented than usual, his eyes bruised underneath.

"Hello, soldier. You look beat."

"Look who's talking." Wary as a wounded animal, he low-ered himself into the chair his mother had vacated.

"I was planning on getting some rest today; only I found out a friend of mine needed to have his dear self dragged back home."

From down the hall, a low piteous sob rose out of the bed-room. Prince turned, as if he could see his mother through the walls. Neither he nor Maggie said anything for nearly a minute; then Prince ran a hand over his mouth. "I used to think—I always thought that if I ever got a family, I wouldn't do to them what they did to me. And this whole time . . ." He looked down. "I didn't know she was like that. I didn't know John was taking care of her, while I did what I wanted. John refuses to take her to an asylum. He never told me. Not once."

"John does what he thinks is best without asking for anybody's opinion first."

Prince studied his knuckles. "He told me he didn't kiss Hero. Said I should go back."

"You should," said Maggie. "With me."

"What's the use? The speakeasy isn't going to last. I treated her like I—like I swore I never would, and I can't leave Mama like this, not now that I know."

"The speakeasy's closed," Maggie said. "Hero's taking it real bad. Beatrice says she hasn't even left her bed; she got sick." Not strictly true, either one, but Maggie had promised Hero she'd get Prince back if she had to drag him by his hair.

Prince frowned. "Sick with what?"

"I don't know." Maggie sighed. "But . . ."

But that was how it had started with Anna, too. One rough night, and she'd been in bed the next morning—and then never gotten up. Prince looked stricken.

"Go, Pedro." John's voice slipped between them like the crack of a whip. "You can always come back," he added, braced against the corner with his hands in his pockets. He looked like a frayed old rug that had been picked apart by fate's ruthless tread.

Prince's mouth pinched together, but Maggie thought she recognized the set to his eyes. Hope died hard in him. "All right.

All right. God dammit." He stood, then faced John. "Let me talk to Mama first," he said to John. "You can't keep protecting me from everything. I'm going to help."

When he strode out of the room, John let him go.

Left alone, neither John nor Maggie spoke. He'd apologized once and he wouldn't do it again. That wasn't his way.

"I didn't know," he said finally. His expression was strange. At first she thought he was angry. But the tight lines in his face were nerves; she just didn't recognize it in him, he was so rarely nervous. "I didn't know they saw us kiss. I only talked to Claude about the speakeasy."

"Then why did you leave?" Maggie whispered. "Why did you say it was nothing?"

John's hand errantly brushed over his chest, but there was nothing there but his own shirt. No gun holster, his usual way out of an unpleasant situation. "You know why," he said finally.

"I got the part," Maggie said. "I'm in the chorus."

He swallowed. "I'm not surprised."

"I sang 'His Eye Is on the Sparrow.' Tommy said I shouldn't, said it was too slow and sweet for a dance club. But my voice is suited for slow and sweet singing." She stood, stepped closer. He backed up to accommodate her and bumped into the wall. "When I hit the last note, I knew I had them. I knew it in my bones before anybody said a word. Tommy didn't understand, John, because he hadn't heard me sing it yet."

His eyes squeezed shut. He looked as if he'd rather be shot. "This isn't the same."

"I think you love me, John Morello."

His eyes opened: dark and unreadable as night. Her voice faltered. "In case you're wondering," she said, "I love you, too. I know what you are and what you are not, so—"

"Stop. Christ," he said, voice breaking. "What do you want from me? What about—"

"The laws? Kind of like the ones against bootlegging, extortion, gambling? That's never stopped you before. Who's asking for a proposal anyway?" She put a hand on his icy cheek, half laughing. He cringed like a yard dog. "I just want to be near you."

"*I'm* asking," he said, slicing her mirth to ribbons. "If I had you, I wouldn't let you go. It only makes it harder to have you in reach but not actually in reach."

"I know what I want," she said. "Life's already hard, John. And it's not going to be fair, not to either of us. I'm tougher than I look, and I look damn tough."

His shoulders sagged. He stared down at her without seeming to breathe. His lips parted a crack. "God in heaven," he whispered.

"Do you love me or not?" she asked.

He took her hand from his face and held it between his own, so they were left standing there linked at the hands, staring absurdly at each other; like a couple at the altar. "Yes." He considered her hand, then brought it up to kiss her palm; his lips lingered there a moment. She leaned forward in a more straight-forward attack and kissed him on his hard mouth, which only remained hard a moment. He melted soft as butter when she knew how to do it. She pulled back enough to catch her breath, and he drew his thumbs over her cheeks and mouth and chin. He kissed her again, and swore.

"Should I apologize?" she asked.

"Yes," he said.

"Too bad." She tucked her arms into him and he fit his neatly around her back. His embrace felt safe; he, too, was tougher than he looked (and he looked terrifying). "And just in case this whole booze enterprise doesn't work out," she said, "I'm also on the lookout for a manager."

CHAPTER 32
SILENCE IS THE PERFECTEST HERALD OF JOY

Beatrice had woken with that particular restless itch in her middle that always led to trouble, and she hadn't gotten rid of it, even though she'd spent all morning putting to work the only thing that never failed her: her mind.

So what if she was lousy at comfort? That wouldn't matter if she found a way to save Hey Nonny Nonny. The one thing they had going for them was the estate. Leo and Hero owned the land and the house outright, and Flower Hill had a lovely climate for farming. If they sold a few things—maybe the Lambda, maybe the speakeasy's piano—they could get started on crops. They could reopen a speakeasy known for fruit-based ciders, not to mention feed themselves and get some produce revenue in the meantime.

Of course that might take over a year to truly gain traction, but it was possible. They would keep a small farm, obviously, until they could hire some real hands, but there were other jobs, too: cleaning on the weekends; Hero could take on seamstress work maybe.

And surely Uncle Leo . . .

He hadn't answered Beatrice's knock on his door that morning or much of anything since Hero's party; she'd let him be.

Beatrice's head ached. The pounding sounded like *doctor, doctor, doctor.*

She went in search of Hero, a written-out plan clutched in her hand. Hero wasn't in her room, but when she passed the open door of Prince's, Hero was kneeling on the floor, her arms around a wrapped box on her lap. She looked up as Beatrice came in. "Can we skip to the part where we love each other again?" she asked softly.

"Oh, Hero." Beatrice knelt next to her, and for the moment, the plan was forgotten, their arms around each other, the box sliding to the floor.

"What is that?" Beatrice asked, pulling back.

"They got me a birthday present," Hero said, sniffing. She turned the tag around so Beatrice could see:

"Happy Birthday, Helena Rose. With love, your boys."

"Aren't you going to open it?" Beatrice asked.

"Should I?"

"Of course you should. It's yours, isn't it?"

Hero smiled, then ripped off the paper without hesitation. She unearthed a brand-new sewing machine and several swaths of cut fabric. "Oh." She hushed.

"It's beautiful," Beatrice said.

For several minutes Hero just looked at the box. She didn't even open it. "I wish . . ."

Whatever she wished, it was with decidedly suspicious timing that a car engine rumbled up the drive. Hero glanced at Beatrice—what were the odds?—then hurried to the window to look out. The car was a mustard yellow tourer, not any vehicle Beatrice recognized, but she did recognize the mop of messy dark hair and long body striding across the lawn like a robust panther. Hero gripped Beatrice's wrist so tightly it hurt, and objectively speaking, Beatrice understood.

"What do I do?" Hero hissed.

"Hero?" Maggie's voice shouted down the hall.

"In here!" Beatrice called, and Maggie skidded in a moment later out of breath.

"I told him you were sick," she gasped. "Get in bed—quick! Act bedridden."

"What?" Hero asked. "Sick how?"

"For God's sake, you've gone the color of a cherry," said Beatrice. "That's the opposite of what we want."

"I'll stall him," Maggie said, and ran out as fast as she'd come.

"Quick, quick! I'll just pull the sheets up over my face!" Hero sprinted down the hall toward her own bedroom—below them, the front door closed—and dived onto her bed in record time. Never mind that she was now further flushed and out of breath. "Look doctorly!" Hero whispered.

"I always look doctorly," Beatrice muttered. "Listen, why don't I leave and then—"

"No!" Hero protested. "You can't leave me in the same room with him alone, or I'll crumble like the last muffin and kiss him on his big, stupid mouth."

"What? Hero!"

Hero wiggled under the covers, shimmying out of her dress, which she tossed over the side of the bed. "I wouldn't wear a dress to bed if I were sick, would I?"

"I doubt he'd notice."

"He'll notice *now* all right."

A soft knock came at the door. "Hero?" Prince's low voice, a little muffled by the door. Too late it occurred to Beatrice to wonder where Benedick was. He might have saved them a lot of time intercepting Prince.

Beatrice opened the door. "Hello, Prince."

Hero dragged the sheet up and let out a piteous groan. Beatrice managed to keep her face straight, eyebrow twitching. He *was* rather sad looking, hunched as if afraid Beatrice might draw a sword and slice and dice him. "Can I come in?" he asked, glancing past her shoulder to the bed. "How is she?"

"Difficult to say at this point." Beatrice stepped back to let him inside the room.

He walked around to the side of Hero's bed, his movements stiff and guarded. He lowered himself to the very edge of her bed. Hero stayed twisted up under her sheets, only her red hair visible on the pillow. "Hero . . ." Prince extended a hand to her curved form.

The sheets whipped away, along with Hero's restraint, and she sprang up and slapped him clean across the face, her whole arm behind it. "Ow!" He reeled back, touching his reddening cheek. He stared at her: first in shock, then in blatant relief, then in annoyance. "You're not sick at all."

"Oh, yes, I am." She moved for him again, but he caught her chin between his fingers.

"Don't kiss me, Stahr." His voice was husky.

She blushed. In lieu of kissing, she shoved him with both hands, with her feet, trying to send him off the bed. "You son of a bitch! I didn't kiss John! I never asked you to do anything but be here! Do you hear? Do you?" She pulled his hair for good measure. Her cheeks were wet. She stopped, worn out.

Prince took her hands and kissed each little fist. "I know."

Hero pushed Prince off and gathered the sheets up to her chin. "Well, I do not forgive you."

"I've got plans to set things right, so just listen, okay?"

"Fine."

"I'm coming home," said Prince. "I'm bringing my mother into one of the empty rooms, and I'll watch after her and this place. Don't I owe Leo at least that? I have two hands to work. I can get a job, or two or three. I'll—"

"Come closer," Hero broke in.

He leaned in.

"Clooooser."

He got so close their noses almost touched. Hero drew down the sheet and fluttered her lashes. Prince didn't take the bait, but he frowned in a peculiar way that put a line up his fore-head and made a tic jump in his jaw.

Hero got a tell-tale look in her eye. "Would you mind terribly tasting my lips for any death germs?" she whispered.

"Now why would I do a silly thing like that? Suppose there are death germs and I die, too?"

"Oh, you." Hero pushed against his chest with both hands, but this time he didn't budge. He grabbed her wrists.

"I'm sorry. I was always yours, no matter how you looked at me, but I forgot, is all. I got jealous, and I acted like an ass, and Claude's a fool if he doesn't court you all summer and give you diamonds and tell you you're the prettiest girl he's ever seen."

"Shut up and kiss me right now, Pedro Morello, or I swear I'll never forgive you for as long as I live."

The restraint, the frown fluttered away like a loosed bird. He looked back at her with unguarded desire, and kiss her he did.

Beatrice was almost excited to tell Benedick, to see his face warm with relief, for his silly tender heart to convince her not to be so mad at Prince; she wanted to show him her plans and get his opinion about them. She took the attic stairs two at a time and opened his door with a single knock as warning. "Ben, I hope that you're—"

She stopped. His room was transformed. Everything was packed up. All that remained was the ugly couch, his bare desk, and a small cot that existed after all on the other side of the room.

When had he done this? She ransacked the past few days for any mention of his departure and came up empty. Two folded letters waited on his desk, her name scrawled on top. She tore open the first; the words barely entered her psyche.

"By now I'll be on the 2:17 train . . .

". . . home to Manhattan with my father . . .

"I'll start university in September . . .

". . . second letter is a copy of the one I sent to Payne Chutney, but I thought you'd like to read it . . .

". . . *terrible* at good-byes, but you'll tell the others . . ."

How dare he, how dare he!

Then finally:

"Give 'em hell, Clark.

"—B

"P. S. It seems I fell in love with you after all, on my own, in spite of that trick. Isn't that strange?"

She bounded down the stairs, his useless letters clutched tight in one hand. He had a lot of nerve, prattling on about his plans willy-nilly, telling her he loved her as if it didn't matter. Oh, by the way.

"Home to Manhattan"!

This is your home, idiot.

Wasn't it? How could he act as if it weren't?

She stared at the tall grandfather clock in the drawing room. Hours. He'd been gone for hours; she was too late. Somewhere her name was being called, but she didn't move until Hero and Prince found her still standing in front of the clock.

Hero had a broom in one hand, Prince a bucket and rags draped over his shoulder. "I can't find the good soap. . . ." Maggie said, trailing behind them.

"We're going down to whip the speakeasy back into shape," Hero said. "Coming?"

"Yes," Beatrice said. "I—yes."

"You seen Ben?" Prince asked.

"He just—he left to do this thing, but he'll be back." Wouldn't he? *You'll tell the others.* Like hell she would. He could tell them himself if he were so inclined.

She followed them down the secret entrance and through the door.

But the lights were already on, and the speakeasy was clean.

"Papa?" Hero asked, clutching the broom handle.

Uncle Leo set a chair right side up, his steps slow and heavy, as if he'd aged twenty years in one night. The tables were bare and returned to their normal positions. The bar counter gleamed with fresh polish, and not a speck of shattered glassware was left on the floor. The only evidence from the party was the sprinkling of forgotten gardenia petals, wilted and curled, like a dusting of white tears.

He must have worked all night to do this.

Without acknowledging them, he moved to the stage and grunted with effort, getting the piano back in place. Prince jumped up beside him to help. When they were done, Uncle Leo stood in the middle of the stage. Hero came to his side and wrapped her arms around his torso.

"What do we do, kiddo?" Uncle Leo whispered.

"I've got just the thing," Hero said. She extracted herself from her father's side and hunted beneath the stage, past the partition, and came up a few moments later with an old gramophone and a box of records. She flipped through until she found the one she wanted and blew off any dust.

Beatrice turned to Maggie. "What are those?"

"Recordings from the speakeasy," Maggie murmured.

Hero shooed her father and Prince off the stage. Once the gramophone was in place, she dropped the needle with a wistful sigh and stepped back. Static echoed in the empty space, and then a little, fuzzy voice called, "Hello, suckers! Ain't it a grand, grand night? Welcome to Hey Nonny Nonny's first ever Masquerade Ball!"

Anna's voice. Beatrice knew it by more than a faraway memory; she sounded like Hero. Hero stood on the stage and mimed each word perfectly as a spotlight glowed over her. Barefoot in a plain summer dress, she nevertheless appeared to Beatrice to be drenched in pearls as she winked and mimed along with Anna, saying, "You may be all the world to your mama, but you're just a cover charge to me," and the audience laughed because they didn't believe it. She led the way right into a song, "And it goes like this!"

The band played, tinny and true, through the gramophone. Hero sang along theatrically, without making a sound herself, clapping silently on beat. The illusion was flawless. Beatrice imagined a young girl practicing hundreds of times in her bedroom. Then it bled into a blues song. Hero danced. It was the Charleston, but she moved so slowly, in time with the slow tune, it looked like ballet. She swung out her arms like petals unfurling, kicked out her leg like an arch of sunlight over a mountaintop.

The song finished, and Anna said, "Give the little girl a great big hand!" Hero held up her arms, and applause surrounded her. "Okay, folks," Anna continued. This time Hero didn't mime with her. "That's all from me for now. Enjoy the party!"

Hero bowed deeply, and the recording clicked off into static.

Uncle Leo hadn't moved, but tears tracked down his cheeks.

He reached over to Prince and fisted a hand in his shirt to tug him closer. "My sweet girl."

Hero's arms hung to her sides. "I'm tired, Papa," she said, voice cracking. "And Mama isn't here anymore." Uncle Leo walked to the stage and held out his arms to his daughter. She put her hands on his shoulders and fell into the embrace, her own arms latched tight around his neck, her feet dangling.

"I think I'm going to have to move to Harlem," Maggie whispered. "The show is five nights a week, and it's such a long trip."

Everything would change. Yet it wasn't all bad.

Beatrice unfolded Benedick's letter again. University, away from them, from Hey Nonny Nonny. She opened the second letter. In it, Benedick had written to Payne Chutney—about her and her desire to become one of the city's finest doctors. He talked about her schooling, her setbacks. . . .

With a whump, she realized the source of that restless feeling. One minute she was strolling about and the next landing in a hole, all her breath gone. Today was the day of her exams. She'd missed them. With everything that had happened, she'd let herself forget. She'd done it to herself.

And she decided, heart pounding, that she would not go after Benedick after all.

CHAPTER 33
I DO SUFFER LOVE INDEED

The Cotton Club was lit up on Broadway with a neon sign and flashing advertisements. Duke Ellington! Dinner $1.50! 50 Copper-Colored Gals! It was July, a late Manhattan Fourth of July party, all done up, the sweat melting off glasses into your palm. Frankly the first cocktail sent such a zing to Benedick's head his constitution had soared up like a helium balloon into the evening sky and was not quite down yet.

He resisted the urge to turn his chair toward the cheap seats. He sat with his father at a front table that was decidedly uncheap, but Maggie would have invited the rest of Hey Nonny Nonny, found a way to get them tickets. *Suppose*, he thought, *suppose I'd just invited Beatrice as my date, just to see.* If he needed her, he felt certain he could write or telephone; but that was based on her definition of the word *need*, and he doubted there was room for loneliness in her standard of necessary. *The emergency*, he'd say when she arrived, *is that I'm desperate for you to sit with me and talk with me. That's all.*

Claude Blaine was here, too. "What kids we were," he'd said, as though it hadn't been merely a few weeks ago. Helped by the lectures of relatives and his hosts, he'd come to the opinion that his adventure—and by consequence, Benedick's as well—was but the rebellion of a recently graduated boy. Everyone did *something* that first summer after school. And why not? They were going out in the world to begin the lives that they would live until they died, to change from boys to men. "I mean," Claude said, "you were never going to really give up your inheritance to live in some Village closet and write books. Not realistically."

Hero told Benedick that Claude had called. *Somebody* had let him know that she'd never been unfaithful. That it was all to do with a sordid plot of the Mafia. Claude was rich and self-centered; it wasn't hard for him to believe he'd be a target for virtually no other reason than who he was. He'd sent Hero a generous care package with swaths of silk and chiffon and gingham and a seamstress workbox, the nicest set his converted pounds could buy. He included a note in his elegant, educated script: "J'espère te voir bientôt à Paris. Je serais ton guide et nous irons boire du bon vin."

I hope to see you soon in Paris. I'll be your guide, and we'll drink fine wine.

Flirtatious, while not a direct invitation. A show of faith toward her aspirations without further commitment. An apology of the grandest nature.

The music, loose and unpredictable, played by a full stage band, surrounded them. There was no way to hum along. The mere act of listening, holding on by your fingertips, was a dance in and of itself. A line of chorus girls danced on the middle bar, their bodies shimmying in their sequined dresses like restless trout. Maggie sang with two other girls near the piano, their microphones lined up side by side.

When the number finished, Ambrose Scott leaned over to Benedick. "I got an interesting letter from Payne Chutney last week."

Benedick looked up from his glass, which, in spite of his best intentions, he was having trouble getting down. His father's face was poker blank, meaning he was going somewhere with this, and it probably wasn't good. "Payne Chutney . . . who died a few weeks ago?"

"Yes, written from the grave. Apparently a good chunk of his fortune went to setting up a medical scholarship fund at Cornell. After his will was read, his solicitor sent along a short note addressed to me, with the request that I pass it along to my son."

Benedick forced a hard sip. "And?"

"Well, I'll find it for you later. You ought to have it. But the short of it was that you told the old man, and this is a quote, the most moving story he'd ever heard, about a young orphan girl who'd overcome all sorts of hardships in her dream of becoming a doctor, with only her wit and will to aid her."

Benedick said, "I talked with him at Lucky Lindy's launch about it. Only later I wrote him about her because I thought he'd be interested or maybe he'd give her a recommendation. I told the truth; I didn't know about the scholarship fund."

Mr. Scott held up a hand. "Never sound like you're apologizing for something you did, whether it was right or wrong. Secondly, how is Miss Clark doing?"

"How do you know the girl was Miss Clark?"

"He set up the scholarship in her name. Well?"

Benedick shrugged. "I wouldn't know. We were never that close to begin with."

"That's a shame. She's a real asset to lose."

"Whose asset?"

"Yours! Do you think you would have done what you did with those agents a year ago? Not a chance. And it's also a shame because she rang up the apartment yesterday."

Benedick's head snapped up. "What? Why didn't you tell me?"

Mr. Scott's eyes widened. "Why, because you were never that close to begin with."

Benedick rolled his eyes and turned back to the stage. "Why don't you go ask city hall if they'll let you be a lawyer in your free time? Then you'll have an outlet for all your urges to be right and spare those of us who have to live with you."

"Since you mention it," Mr. Scott said, undeterred, "I think *you'd* be a fine lawyer. Cornell has a strong comparative literature program. Perhaps even English. Get a foundation in humanities, then on to law school."

Benedick narrowed his eyes. His father didn't look at him; he was taking an unconcerned drink of champagne. Who could tell, but it sounded suspiciously like a concession. Benedick had only promised his father an undergraduate degree. Perhaps by then his father assumed he'd grow out of novel writing and make the choice on his own, but either way it was a gesture of trust.

"Comparative literature definitely," said Benedick. "Not English. Broader discipline, farther range of culture and practical implementation."

His father glanced up, the hint of an approving smirk coming along. "Well, it's a shame you weren't closer with Miss Clark. There she is now." Mr. Scott pointed his cigar across the room, where Leo, Hero, Prince, and Beatrice were weaving their way to a table.

Hero arched up when she saw him and waved. Baffled, he lifted a hand in reply. She tugged on Prince's jacket sleeve and pointed. They sat, but Beatrice moved past them—straight for Benedick's table.

"Why is she coming over here?" he asked.

"Because I invited her. Close your mouth, son; it makes you look stupid." Mr. Scott stood as Beatrice approached, and

Benedick mimicked him. Beatrice wore a dark dress and an uncommon pair of heels that made her nearly the same height as Benedick. She took Mr. Scott's offered hand without hesitation. "Thank you for inviting me. This is a swell spot."

The band, loud and raucous, started up again.

"Perhaps join us in one of the back rooms a moment?" Mr. Scott asked.

The back rooms were for card games and gambling and smoking men. For making deals. Beatrice agreed, glancing briefly at Benedick, but he said nothing to her, even as they walked away from their table to the back of the club. He tried not to stare at her pert profile, admirably collected, not a single stray nerve out of place, if she had any; she kept her eyes ahead.

The room was vast and impressive, full of leather and smelling of cigars. Beyond the couch set was a dealer's desk with a lamp and telephone.

Beatrice spoke first. "Yesterday I mentioned a letter Ben wrote about me—"

"Yes, yes. Please sit first, Miss Clark. Do you like scotch?"

"I . . . Sure."

Mr. Scott smiled. "I wanted to thank you in person, Miss Clark. You were dead right about that allergy. I felt like a new man after I switched cleaners. Sit *down*, Ben."

"I'm glad I could help," said Beatrice, taking a seat kitty-corner from Benedick's father.

"May I see the letter?" Mr. Scott asked.

"Dad," Benedick warned.

"If you like." Beatrice passed the folded paper to Mr. Scott's waiting hand. She gave Benedick an apologetic look.

Mr. Scott read quickly, then slower. His face became something it almost never was: soft. "Is all of this true, Miss Clark?"

She wrung her hands. "In a way. But not really. It's not a lie. He just, well, it's the way Benedick talks. You know what I mean, don't you, Mr. Scott? I sound very noble and all in the letter, but I don't feel like I was, in truth."

Mr. Scott folded the letter again and rested it on his knee. "What college were you hoping to attend?"

Her face developed a certain run-over look that pained Benedick to see. "The Woman's Medical College of the New York Infirmary, sir."

"Could you be persuaded to change institutions?"

"I can be persuaded to nothing this year. I never finished high school, and I missed the entrance exams this summer. I have to wait until winter to take them again, and I'll miss enrollment."

"Nonsense," Mr. Scott said briskly. "We'll arrange for you to take them privately. Henry Brown is on the Board of Regents, and he owes me a favor. And three hundred dollars, lest I forget. After that we'll get you a meeting with the dean at Cornell. You're a bit late, and the medical scholarship isn't properly set in place yet, but given that you're the gal who inspired it, I'll bet we can get them to make an exception so you won't get behind. You'll have to get nothing but *A*'s to keep them off your back, but I think you're up to the task."

Beatrice's eyes grew big as plates. She glanced at Benedick in frightened question. "I'm not—I don't understand."

"Do you want to go to school?"

"More than anything. But I don't want any favors I can't pay back, and I don't want to sneak my way in, I want to earn it."

"But you have earned it!" Mr. Scott declared. "The scholarship I'm talking about came about in great part because of your story, and you said yourself it isn't a lie. And I don't help anyone if it won't help me, too. I expect you to be my personal physician till the day I die, Miss Clark, and the sooner I get you trained, the better."

Her smiled wavered. "You're healthy as a horse, Mr. Scott. That will be a long time yet."

"What do you say? I'll set up the appointments myself."

"I can't think of a thing to say. This is the kindest thing anyone's ever done for me."

"That sounds like a yes to me." He patted her knee. He was, to Benedick's growing astonishment, quite parental. A bossy cad still, of course, but . . . Beatrice was infecting them all. Mr. Scott stood. "I'll set up a more proper appointment for us next week, Miss Clark. My secretary will ring you."

"Won't you call me Beatrice?"

"Beatrice, then." Mr. Scott smiled. "You kids can catch up while I'm gone."

Left alone, Beatrice stared at Benedick. She didn't smile; she looked half-terrified, her cheeks bright pink. She was very pretty.

"What's the matter?" Benedick asked. "I thought you'd be ecstatic."

"I *am* ecstatic," she said, with a big old frown. She twisted her hands. "Oh! He took my letter with him."

"You can get it when he comes back. Are you sure—"

"Did you know he was going to do that?"

"Are you kidding? I didn't even know you were coming until after you were inside. If I could predict his shenanigans, I'd be using the ability to get rich selling to his enemies."

"Hush. He's practically saving my life."

"Maybe you need a glass of water."

"No," she snapped when he started to stand. "You stay where you are, Benedick Scott."

He sank back down, eyes wide. She stood and knelt in front of him. He flushed. "Hey, don't—" He tried again to get up, but she yanked him back to his seat, one-handed. He looked at her warily.

"I'm happy about going to college," she said, and leaned up so her ribs pressed against his knees. "I'm so happy I'm this close to crying, and you'll think I'm saying this because of that, but it's not true. I would say it anyway. I came here in the first place to say it."

"What are you rambling about, you nonsensical contradiction?"

"I know what you did. You went to court instead of Uncle Leo. You let your father bail you out, and that means you gave up what was most important to you. Don't try to deny it."

"Well, then I won't," said Benedick. "But it's like you said. My father bailed me out. Who would have bailed out Leo?"

"But your writing—"

"No one cares about what I write."

"I do," she said. "I do because I love you, and that's my job. I want it to be my job, rather. I promise to be the person who cares to read everything you write, even the rotten stuff, even your grocery lists. You have a forever audience."

"I'm going to Cornell, too," he said, almost bewildered. His father had pushed for that school, and only now did Benedick understand why: That's where his asset was going. "It's okay. To be honest, I'd decided to go anyway. Mostly because of you. I figured maybe I'd try again later, if no premed student had swept you off your feet, and I'd have a better chance if I was educated."

"That's not why you're going."

"Not only why, at any rate."

"So, sometime, I suppose, you'll take me to get an ice-cream cone? Or something of that nature?" she asked carefully.

"I suppose. If that's what a girl like you is going for these days."

"Ben?" She was like a magnet, pulling him along some invisible primordial wire. He leaned in and kissed her as if it were the first and thousandth time. At first fervent and awkward—he was too tall, on his chair—and their mouths came apart, until he dumped himself off, right into her, and she caught him. Then it worked better because now they were so close, with nowhere to go but into each other, and she kissed him beautifully, slow and warm and the tiniest bit shy.

CHAPTER 34

FOR WHICH OF MY BAD PARTS DIDST THOU FIRST FALL IN LOVE WITH ME?

"**G**ood luck getting this to her dormitory by yourself," Prince grunted, heaving Beatrice's trunk the last of the way onto the train platform, where three hapless porters stared down at it with dismay.

"Did you know Cornell was one of the first universities to allow women students?" Beatrice asked. She lowered her campus brochure. "In 1870. I found an old newspaper article in the library that said in the very beginning the boys were almost unanimously opposed to coeducation, and vigorously protested the arrival of a group of sixteen women, who promptly formed a women's club with a broom for their standard, and '*In hoc signo vinces* as their motto. Do you know what that means, Ben?"

Benedick stretched out his back, wincing. "I passed the Latin exam same as you, sweetheart."

" 'In this, conquer!' " she said. "It's going to be my motto, too, so get used to it. *In hoc signo vinces! In hoc signo vinces!*"

He looked annoyed. "How long does it take to get to Ithaca anyway?"

"Five hours and twelve minutes, roughly," she answered.

Benedick wrapped his arms around her in a tight hug. "*Manus in mano,*" he said, and kissed her soundly on the mouth.

"People can see," she mumbled, blushing to her ears. "And stop showing off!"

"You two are worse than I ever was," Hero said. She'd overcome her most recent crying spell but was still a bit red around the eyes. "Here, I made this scarf for you, even though it's not quite cold enough yet. You wrap it around like this, see; it's how they do it in Europe."

"It's beautiful." Beatrice touched the embroidered fabric.

"I made it to match your eyes." Hero's bottom lip quivered again, but she held it back, mostly because Prince came up behind her and gently touched her shoulder. "You write every day. I mean it, every damn day or else. And a phone call each Sunday."

"Yes, ma'am."

"Oh, and I have one more present. Maggie sent one of her new records, and she signed it for you. So tell all your new doctor friends that you've got other friends back home, and one is a famous blues singer, and the other designs fashion scarves."

Only after Hero moved on to say good-bye to Benedick did Uncle Leo come forward. He was thinner, his mustache grayer. He'd been trying hard to drink less. His hands trembled like train tracks as he held out a small case to Beatrice, but his eyes had the warmth of two suns.

"I'm not sure if you know, but some of your father's things were sent to us after his death. Little things. Not much, but I thought maybe you could use that."

Her father's name was engraved on the side of the slender case. ANTHONY STAHR. Inside was a dark green fountain pen.

"Not the newest model the kids are using, but it was his."

"Thank you, Uncle Leo." She hugged him and kissed his cheek.

They stumbled through more teary good-byes until finally Benedick said, "Criminy, who are all you people anyway? Get out of here." Hero pinched his cheek.

Beatrice and Benedick boarded the train together and waved out the window the entire way until the train was out of sight. Only then did Benedick give her another wrapped present. "I don't know if I can handle any more," said Beatrice.

"Just open it."

She removed the wrapping slowly; it was nice and red, and she wanted to save it. Underneath was a brand-new copy of *Gray's Anatomy: Descriptive and Applied.* That and a curt note: "Don't expect anything at Christmas."

"I picked it out," said Benedick, "but Dad paid for it."

"Neither of you had to get me a gift at all," she said.

"I only did it for the kiss."

"Who says you're getting one?"

"I knew we should have gotten the stethoscope."

"Ben, I've never had this much help before."

"You've never been to college before either." He kissed her temple. Touched the parting of her hair. Added, quietly, "I love you."

She closed her eyes and tucked his fingers close, right where they belonged. "Against your will."

"With so much of my heart, none of it is left to protest."

AUTHOR'S NOTE

The real challenge in writing about the 1920s is narrowing down what to include. Sandwiched between two world wars, it was a decade of breakneck, glamorous, hold-onto-your-hat-kid changes. Even its nicknames were exciting: the "Jazz Age" and the "Roaring Twenties." But a full cast of characters allowed me to explore a number of aspects of the era. Through Maggie, I touched on jazz music and the blues; through John, I brushed up against the advent of organized crime and the Italian Mafia; through Hero and Beatrice, I showed the surge of new feminism after women won the vote in 1920, and the rise of the "flapper"; through Benedick, the influx of literary genius that emerged after World War I. And, of course, the speakeasy itself is rooted in that great noble experiment of the Eighteenth Amendment, otherwise known as Prohibition. I could set ten more books in this era and still not cover every interesting piece of history.

Yet, for the sake of aligning history with the heart of Shakespeare's play *Much Ado About Nothing,* I also had to take some liberties with history.

HEY NONNY NONNY:

As far as I know, there was no speakeasy operating in an estate mansion's basement in the heart of Flower Hill. Long Island was by no means a dry area during Prohibition, but generally speaking, its parties rarely *charged* people for the booze. (The most famous rendering of this culture appears, of course, in F. Scott Fitzgerald's *The Great Gatsby.)* Most speakeasies were in Manhattan and Brooklyn. However, Long Island saw a lot of bootlegging action because of its coastline. Long Island's South Shore was the initial hot spot for rum-runners, but activity shifted to the North Shore in the early 1920s because there were only two Coast Guard boats patrolling the entire North Shore, and the coves and terrain made it difficult to be detected. This is essentially the business proposition Prince gives to John, though technically, this shift had already taken place by 1927.

THE COTTON CLUB AND DUKE ELLINGTON:

The Cotton Club was a real New York City nightclub located first in Harlem and then briefly in the Theater District. It closed for good in 1940. Like a lot of nightclubs at the time, it was managed by an underworld gangster named Owney Madden ("the Killer"); John's world and Maggie's world rubbed elbows more often than not.

In September 1927, King Oliver, a jazz bandleader of the time, turned down a booking contract as the house band, and so the offer passed to Duke Ellington. As John tells Maggie, Ellington had to increase from a six- to an eleven-piece group to meet the requirements of the Cotton Club's management. I moved these events up several months in order to accommodate the novel's timeline.

Even though some of the most popular and most talented black entertainers of the 1920s graced the Cotton Club's stage, its patrons were exclusively white, and its shows often reproduced racist imagery of the time. Still, I imagine Maggie using it as a launching pad to an unapologetic, brilliant career of pushing down barriers, á la Bessie Smith, Billie Holiday, and Adelaide Hall.

Here are the songs Maggie talks about or sings in the book:

"My Blue Heaven" (pages 101–102) was composed by Walter Donaldson, with lyrics by George A. Whiting, in 1923. My favorite cover, and there are many, is by Norah Jones.

"After You've Gone" (page 131) was composed by Turner Layton, with lyrics by Henry Creamer, in 1918. My favorite cover is by Nina Simone, but you've got your choice between Bessie Smith, Ella Fitzgerald, and Frank Sinatra, among others.

"St. Louis Blues" (page 130) was composed by W. C. Handy in 1914. The jazzman's *Hamlet*. I'm not telling you what to do, but the 1925 version sung by Bessie Smith, with Louis Armstrong on cornet, was inducted into the Grammy Hall of Fame.

"Crazy Blues" (also page 131) was composed by Perry Bradford in 1920. The recording of this song by Mamie Smith and her Jazz Hounds is often considered the first blues record.

"Always" (page 192) was written by Irving Berlin in 1925, as a wedding gift for his wife Ellin Mackay. Go for the Billie Holiday cover.

"Downhearted Blues" (page 314) was composed by Alberta Hunter and Lovie Austin in 1922, and made famous by Bessie Smith in 1923.

"I Wish I Could Shimmy Like My Sister Kate," often simply "Sister Kate" (pages 314–15), was written by Clarence Williams and Armand Piron in 1919. This is the song Maggie uses to tease John in Hero's room. The song I originally wanted to use was "Come On In (Ain't Nobody Here But Me)," which contains the delightful lyric "I'm drunk and disorderly, I don't care / If you want to you can pull off your underwear," but it was written in 1931.

THE MORELLO GANG AND GENOVESE FAMILY:

One of the biggest questions I've always had about *Much Ado About Nothing*, second only to why in God's name Hero would take Claudio back, was why Don John was such a jerk to everyone. This guy basically tries to ruin everybody's life, and his excuse is (and I quote): "I am a plain-dealing villain." He's like a test run for

Shakespeare's later villain Iago, in *Othello.* He's just a rotten person.

For me, Don John needed a little more motivation for sticking his nose in things. Because *Much Ado About Nothing* is set in Italy, it only seemed fitting to tip my hat to the Italian presence during Prohibition.

In history, the Genovese family is the oldest of the Five Families, with roots going back to the Morello gang. With the onset of Prohibition in 1919, the Morello family built a lucrative bootlegging operation in Manhattan and eventually gained dominance in the Italian underworld by defeating the rival Neapolitan Camorra of Brooklyn.

In 1920, Giuseppe Morello was released from prison and Brooklyn Mafia boss Salvatore D'Aquila ordered his murder. A lot of blood and death later, a man named Joe "the Boss" Masseria came out on top and essentially took over the Morello family; Giuseppe Morello (who had escaped the murder contract) became his underboss. Masseria continued to expand his bootlegging, extortion, loan-sharking, and gambling rackets throughout New York. He recruited a lot of ambitious young mobsters, including Vito Genovese. In *Speak Easy, Speak Love,* Vito Genovese is the man John reports to. *However,* the Genovese family would not be officially established until a few years later.

In 1928, the Castellammarese War gets under way, a bloody power struggle between Joe "The Boss" Masseria and Salvatore Maranzano. By 1931, Maranzano's gang had won, and he declared himself *capo di tutti capi* ("boss of all bosses"), but was promptly murdered by a group of young upstarts led by Lucky Luciano, who then established a power-sharing arrangement called "The Commission," a group of five Mafia families of equal stature.

To my mind, John is among these "young upstarts." But holding my story directly up to history, the lines get a little blurry.

There's no factual evidence that Vito Genovese commanded a bootlegging unit in Nassau County, though it's certainly *plausible* that any Mafia racket had at least a finger on the pulse of rum-running. If the timelines were kept in perfect historical alignment, there would probably be no kerfuffles in Flower Hill over some stolen crates, because they had bigger fish to fry. They were on the verge of war. But it does help illuminate why John is so desperate to keep his brother away from what's right on the horizon.

Izzy Einstein and Moe Smith:

When I was originally drafting *Speak Easy, Speak Love,* I wasn't sure I'd be able to fit Dogberry and Verges in. Like many of Shakespeare's comedic acts, they exist nearly on their own (probably to give stage actors time to set up new scenes and change costumes), except for one crucial illuminating contribution.

And then, I stumbled upon the true-life figures of Izzy Einstein and Moe Smith. History could not have crafted a more perfect Dogberry and Verges. In the play, Dogberry is a man of the law, but he's kind of an idiot. In life, Izzy Einstein was a man of the law, and he pretended to be an idiot so people wouldn't take him seriously, which was actually *genius.*

Dogberry and his men are the ones to discover Don John's plot, the *only* ones, and Borachio and Conrade more or less confess just to get him to shut up. Actually genius?

The real Izzy and Moe were Prohibition agents who achieved more arrests than anyone else in the first half of the decade, rarely used guns, never accepted bribes, and were, naturally, fired before Prohibition ended. Izzy and Moe relied mainly on disguises, and Izzy called his methods "Einstein's Theory of Rum Snooping."

The scene in the novel where Dogberry argues with the bartender did happen—at least according to an account in *Articulating Biographical Sketches of Diminutive Luminaries.* Izzy told the bartender he was Izzy Epstein, the famous Prohibition agent, and when the bartender argued that it was Izzy *Einstein,* Izzy bet him double the price for two drinks, and that was that.

The jar of pickles is true, too. In Izzy's own words, "Who'd ever think a fat man with pickles was an agent?"

OTHER RELATED FACTS:

Scofflaw, as a word, really was invented during Prohibition as part of a contest sponsored by banker Delcevare King in 1923. Two separate entrants, Henry Irving Dale and Kate L. Butler, submitted the word and split the $200 prize.

The character of Payne Chutney was based on a real historical figure, Payne Whitney, a wealthy businessman who died on May 25, 1927, in Manhasset—five days after Charles Lindbergh's flight. (I gave my version of his character slightly longer to live, so he'd have time to set up a scholarship fund.) His will bequeathed more than $20 million to hospitals and other educational and medical institutions. His estate funds contributed hugely to the medical school at Cornell University, which was indeed the first coeducational institution among the Ivy Leagues, even though it took them a while longer to treat their female students equally.

I was lucky (pun intended) that Lucky Lindy's flight across the Atlantic Ocean lined up with the timeline I set for my characters. When I learned that he took off from Long Island, it seemed like a shame not to include him. Lindbergh was a young airmail pilot when he ordered a small monoplane built to his own design. He christened it the *Spirit of St. Louis* and then, taking off from a rainy airstrip on Roosevelt Field, Long Island, on the early morning of Friday, May 20, 1927, he flew it nonstop to Paris in thirty-three and a half hours. It was a feat that electrified the world and changed commercial aviation.

Minsky's Ragland was based loosely on Minsky's Burlesque, a vaudeville performance venue that thrived during Prohibition, after showing respectable films at their theater failed to take off.

SOURCES

Alfasa, Josef. *Articulating Biographical Sketches of Diminutive Luminaries.* Pittsburgh: Rose Dog Books, 2012.

Blumenthal, Karen. *Bootleg: Murder, Moonshine, and the Lawless Years of Prohibition.* New York: Roaring Brook Press, 2011.

Burns, Ken & Lynn Novick, directors. *Prohibition.* 3-part miniseries; 5 ½ hours. http://www.pbs.org/kenburns/prohibition/.

Critchley, David. *The Origin of Organized Crime in America: The New York City Mafia, 1891–1931* (Routledge Advances in American History). London: Taylor & Francis, 2008.

Dash, Mike. *The First Family: Terror, Extortion and the Birth of the American Mafia* . New York: Simon & Schuster, 2009.

Davis, Angela Y. *Blues Legacies and Black Feminism: Gertrude "Ma" Rainey, Bessie Smith, and Billie Holiday.* New York: Pantheon, 1998.

Fass, Paula S. *The Damned and the Beautiful: American Youth in the 1920s.* New York: Oxford University Press, 1977.

Kobler, John. *Ardent Spirits: The Rise and Fall of Prohibition.* New York: Putnam, 1973.

Lawson, Ellen NicKenzie. *Smugglers, Bootleggers, and Scofflaws: Prohibition and New York City.* Albany, NY: State University of New York Press, 2013.

Okrent, Daniel. *Last Call: The Rise and Fall of Prohibition*. New York: Scribner (Simon & Schuster), 2010.

Steinke, Gord. *Mobsters & Rumrunners of Canada: Crossing the Line.* Edmonton, Alberta: Folklore Publishing, 2004.

Waters, Ethel (with Charles Samuel). *His Eye Is on the Sparrow: An Autobiography*. New York: Doubleday, 1951.

Williams, Iain Cameron. *Underneath a Harlem Moon: The Harlem to Paris Years of Adelaide Hall* (Bayou Jazz Lives). New York: Bloomsbury Academic, 2002.

Zeitz, Joshua. *Flapper: A Madcap Story of Sex, Style, Celebrity, and the Women Who Made America Modern*. New York: Broadway Books, 2007.

And, of course, William Shakespeare's *Much Ado About Nothing*. The chapter titles and the speakeasy's name (and its password and rally song, taken from a song in the play called "Sigh no more") are all from Shakespeare's most romantic comedy.

ACKNOWLEDGMENTS

Writing acknowledgments for your first book feels like trying to thank the entire universe for helping you become a writer.

Thank you, first, to my tireless agent, Katie Grimm, for carrying this book even when I was done with it, and for making me laugh (even though most of the time I don't think you're trying to). And a huge thank you to the whole team at Don Congdon Associates, especially Annie Nichol and Cara Bellucci, for all your work, and for being the ones to read my first drafts (sorry).

Speak Easy, Speak Love couldn't have found a better home than Greenwillow. Thank you to my wonderful editor, Martha Mihalick, for getting my book right from the start and for taking a chance on Hey Nonny Nonny. Huge thanks also to Katie Heit and the rest of the team at Greenwillow and HarperCollins, including but not limited to: Lois Adams, Sylvie Le Floc'h, Gina Rizzo, and the Epic Reads and marketing teams.

To early readers and support: Ryan Brown and Daniel Friend, for editing help; and to Victoria Candland, for your suggestions and for your confidence and sanity during our internship. Mackenzi Lee, thank you for reading an early version of this book, and being a support as I navigated

Authorland. Ashley Finley, for keeping an eye on my white girl mistakes and being a badass. Patrice Caldwell, thank you for your incisive feedback and sharp eye; the book is so much better for your help.

To my teachers: Jeff Carney, for not telling a brand-new writer how far she still had to go—thank you; Cheri Pray Earl, for being hilarious and telling me I had that something extra; Lance Larsen, for letting me work on this book in your class instead of writing short fiction; Pat Madden, for unexpected wisdom; and finally, Lara Burton, who said things that will never leave me and I don't think you even know.

To my friends: Molly Cluff and Sara Butler, the best writing crew a girl could ask for. You guys are my people. Thank you for cheering me on, for reading countless pages and countless reiterations of this book. I love you. Julia Barclay, for always being there, and for making me feel brilliant even when I'm not. To all my other friends who have supported me, thank you. I remember you, even if you're too numerous to name here.

To my family: my sisters, Lauren and Kelcie, best friends and confidantes, thanks for being my heart, and the heart of Beatrice and Hero's relationship; my knight-in-law, Blair, I'm so glad you're part of our family and I'm sorry you're always fixing my problems; my brother, Deven, whose face is loved by my face, and Kaela, sister-in-training; my dad, for never telling me this was a waste of time; my mom, for her love; and my stepdad, Bill, thanks for making me hot-dog grilled cheese sandwiches while I wrote the first draft and for always asking how it was coming along; my cousin, Ben, unanticipated book buddy and support; and finally, my grandma. You have believed in me more than I believe in myself. Thank you, and I love you. And to my nephews, Kayson and Kai, who are too young to read this yet, you are the stars in my sky—and look! Your names are in a book!

To my library family at the Day-Riverside branch, you are book warriors, and I love you guys, truly. Thanks for everything.

Last but not least, thank you to the misfit crew at Hey Nonny Nonny. I know you're not real, but when I look back at this book, I see my heart splintered into six characters, chasing after a dream that matters more than anything. Thanks for seeing me through to the end.